Sault Ste.Marie   Three Rivers   Québec
                   Montreal   Champlain
        Fort
        Frontenac

Fort
Detroit

ATLANTIC

OCEAN

FLORIDA

CUBA

Fort de Paix   ST.
                DOMINIQUE

CARIBBEAN SEA

RIDE THE RED EARTH

BY *Paul I. Wellman*

Novels

BRONCHO APACHE · JUBAL TROOP · ANGEL WITH SPURS
THE BOWL OF BRASS · THE WALLS OF JERICHO · THE CHAIN
THE IRON MISTRESS · THE COMANCHEROS · THE FEMALE
JERICHO'S DAUGHTERS · RIDE THE RED EARTH

History

DEATH ON THE PRAIRIE · DEATH IN THE DESERT
Republished together as The Indian Wars of the West
THE TRAMPLING HERD · GLORY, GOD AND GOLD

Reminiscence

PORTAGE BAY

BY *Paul I. Wellman*

Ride the Red Earth A NOVEL

1958

DOUBLEDAY & COMPANY, INC., GARDEN CITY, NEW YORK

With the exception of actual historical personages, the characters are entirely the product of the author's imagination and have no relation to any person in real life.

To LAURA

who has shared the ups and downs with me these many years: not only with affection, loyalty, and patience—which, traditionally, a man is told he may expect of a wife—but also with a sense of humor, which is not in the contract, but which, since it enables a woman sometimes to view her husband's vagaries with mirth, may in the end be worth as much as any of the rest.

Contents

BOOK THREE   THE HELL OF HOLINESS

BOOK ONE *La Demoiselle*

1.   From the Depths

It is night again. I know this because the opaqueness of the chill dark is absolute now, so that I can see nothing at all, however I strain my eyes. Even in the daytime, when the sun shines in God's great world above, only a faint grayness filters down into these lower tiers of the dungeon: yet this alone, I believe, keeps us in our cells from going entirely blind, like those fishes of which I have heard that spend all their lives in the eternal blackness of waters in vast caverns underground.

I lie alone, and quietly, for silence is enjoined on us, with punishment too terrible to brook, if we make any noise. Behind the pallet where, from weakness, I now spend most of my time, I can feel the stone wall, dank and slimy, of this prison of the Inquisition in which I am buried. Sometimes I lift myself, to shift my position. When I do so my arms, which once swelled with splendid muscular strength—the arms of an adventurer, a soldier, a wooer of women, a commander of men—can scarce support my weight, so shrunken and feeble have they become.

My face, I know, is shockingly changed also. The cheeks are sunken, and the haggard hollow eyes stare out from the tangle of matted hair and unkempt beard which have grown, uncombed and untrimmed, in these long months. The face and body are those of an old man, an old sick man, and yet I am still young—in years, at least.

As nearly as I can compute, for long ago I ceased trying to keep track of the days by scratching them on the wall, this is the year of grace, 1715. That would make my age thirty-two. It is the prime of a man's life: the prime, that is, of men who live and breathe and move about, free in the world above. But it is the end of life for me. For I am doomed, and I know it.

Sometimes I have longed for a glimpse once more of the purity of the sunlight—the sunlight I knew all my life, and took for granted without realizing what a boon it was until it was taken away from me. And then I have shuddered back, cowering at the very thought. For the day when I see the light again will be the day when they come for me to take me to the Audience of Torment, the last prelude before the iron stake and the agony of the flames.

I am not a man who has been given to cowering. Yet to such a state have I, Louis Juchereau de St. Denis, chevalier of France, been reduced by long loneliness, and weakness, and by the pitiless judges and familiars of the Inquisition, in this city of Mexico, capital of New Spain.

The dreadful irony of it is that they punish me for that of which I am innocent. Thinking back on my life I must confess that I have been guilty of some sins, God knows, as are all of us poor mortals—perhaps even more than my share of sins. But I will deny to my last breath, even when the flames themselves sear my lungs and seal my lips, that I am what they say: a traitor to the Holy Catholic Church—a heretic.

Sometimes I groan; yes, in my weakness I have wept like a child, beating my head against the wet stones of this cell wall. And why? I am not mad. Better for me, perhaps, if I were. I groan because I wish to die and cannot. If I could give up my ghost, here in the darkness, alone and even unshriven, I would thank the merciful Mother of God for answering my prayers to her and thus intervening for me. But death does not come.

Many men have died in this prison since I have been here: of prison fever, and from punishments inflicted, and of sheer heartbreak. But death passes me by. Too stubborn and deep-running is the current of life within me.

This is one of my terrors. I do not know what fate is reserved for me. The Inquisition does not tell its victims what will be done to them, and when. That is one of its subtle and devilish ways of torturing the mind before the body, in order to break down the will. But I know that when at last they bring me to the Audience of Torment, with its various horrid engines, and put me to the "Question"—that euphemistic and hypocritical word meaning the extortion of any admission they desire through agonies inflicted—I will last a long time, be too good a subject for the fiendish arts of the torturers.

In my mind's eye I have often imagined the scene: the sworn tormentors, masked and ready to begin their work on me, as I lie stripped and bound helpless to the machine; the notary with his quills and papers, to make a scrupulous record of the proceedings; the inquisitors in their seats, asking questions, urging me to tell the "truth," leaning forward to note the effect of the anguish given, and to catch any answers, even if they be no more than the outcries of my extremity, that they can twist into that "confession" they seek, for which they can pronounce my doom.

But to dwell on this is horror. And horror leads to madness. And in spite of all, my being recoils from the thought of the raving, or the equally terrible, dull, mindless imbecility, to which some of the wretches in this prison have come. Better it is to turn my mind backward and think upon the past. For not always have I been thus miserable, sick, and unhappy. I have known my great days: days of triumphs, loves, and joys. And days of discouragement and sorrow, too, which are a part of life, and on which I look back now almost as good.

It is a long road that lies behind me. And always, from the beginning, it seems to me, I have been a puppet in the hands of fate, my destiny forecast.

I think of my childhood in my father's home in Canada, on the banks of the mighty St. Lawrence, where I played and wrestled and hunted with the Abenaki Indian boys and spoke in their own Algonquin tongue as readily as my own: and Cootee, the Iroquois woman, a slave captured from our inveterate enemies, but kind and tractable in her servitude so that she lived and died almost as a member of our family, and from her I learned the harsh Iroquois language also, for I was quick and gifted in this respect.

Then, as a youth, my life's path led elsewhere: across the great sea to France, for my family, though poor, was of the *petite noblesse,* and my father obtained for me an appointment to the royal military school in Paris.

The cities of Europe! Once more I seem to see the teeming streets of Paris; the great buildings of the ministries and the King's palaces; the cathedrals and churches; the slate roofs of the École Militaire, where the wild youths, of whom I was one, studied mathematics, military history, the practice of arms, and tactics, made love to the little *mignonettes* of the Théâtre de Bourgogne, drank and gambled, and dreamed fiery dreams of fame and favor won by deed in battle for the lilies of France.

They are scattered now, those youths, many of them dead; and all of those who live, perhaps, are as cynical and bereft of ideals and illusions as am I.

I think of gay Bayonne, where, proud as a pouter pigeon, I was assigned when I gained my new commission; and of Madrid, where as an ensign I soon found I was a nonentity in the train of Philip of Anjou, placed on the Spanish throne by Louis XIV of France, whereby the whole world was plunged into war.

In Spain I liked the people, and there I came to know the supreme friend of my boyish heart, young Don Beltrán de Córdoba, a junior officer in the Spanish horse, of my own age and temperament, with whom I sported and gamed and laughed, and with whom I learned the charm a fine uniform possesses in a woman's eyes.

Beltrán! More than friend; to this minute I love him still, like a brother, for I can think of no unkindness he ever did toward me, and his loyal acts were many.

I have said that a good figure in a brilliant uniform pleases women. Although I was no more than a stripling in the gaudy palace guard at the Escorial where the King sat, I was pleasing to a charmingly wayward little Madrilena, and this was decisive in my life. For because of her—and two duels—I was sent back to France in disgrace, and said farewell to Beltrán, never expecting to see him again.

From France I was ordered overseas to Canada and there began the long campaigns against the English and the Iroquois—the extension in America of the bloody War of the Spanish Succession in Europe—in which I fought under the great Iberville. In that war I gained some little reputation as a soldier: for, in all honesty, I do not think I lack either courage or the knack of leadership.

I also, however, gained some detractors, who said of me that my temperament is so impetuous as to lack proper judgment at times, and my quarrels too numerous; for if my character is sometimes erratic, it is at least positive. There are those also who have said of me that self-interest is superior in me to any other emotion; but to this I can answer that it is a failing common enough in men. And if it is true, I am at least capable of loyalties and possess a code of honor peculiar to myself.

Looking back, it seems to me now that from the allurement of women has stemmed most of my misfortune. I might have taken a lesson from the episode in Madrid, but I learned from it nothing—I shame to confess it—being at the age of youth and recklessness when one considers himself a man of the world only if he is something of a rake.

If men have found in me sometimes that which arouses their antagonism, women on the whole have been kind to me; some, perhaps, too kind for their own good and mine. I have found them charming, and tempting always, each in herself a challenge to me. And it has ever been my instinct to make myself agreeable, whether in the salon of a French Countess, or an Indian camp; going to the one in brocaded coat, with sword and plumed hat, and to the other, like as not, in breechclout and blanket, with an eagle feather fluttering from my braided hair.

Since women found it easy to smile on me, and I, on my side, discovered in the game of intrigue a special kind of adventure—with perhaps an extra fillip of danger if the lady happened to have a husband —I managed, between the long, hard campaigns of our war, to erect for myself something of a reputation in the boudoirs of Quebec and elsewhere. This I say without pride, for it is not the sort of thing of which a man should boast.

Nevertheless, because of it, I gained also a different kind of reputation, no better than the first. For my *affaires d'amour* were the frequent causes of the quarrels already mentioned, and though I have never killed a husband, I have had to defend myself from some, and dealt them hurt; and my duels did not escape the notice of officialdom, to my detriment.

Ah, if I had some of Bienville's icy blood! But I do not, and even now, in this black cell, the faces of women to whom I have made love come back to torment me with longing: tall or petite, fair or dark, titled lady or peasant girl, yet all at one moment the same—for every woman is beautiful when kissed. . . .

This thing I know: woman is a subtler element than gold, more closely guarded, more dangerously sought. And each in her being carries the fateful seeds of mighty good or ill; in my case, it seems, always ill.

From the wayward little lady of Madrid to the last three with whom my life has been entangled—La Demoiselle, Doña Joya, and Dolores— the tale has been the same. Each, whether by good will or bad, has helped me toward this doom.

Those three: my mind goes back to them. As if it were yesterday I remember now the day when I first saw the new French town called Mobile, and took up the thread that led me to the Pit in which I now lie, that day when the last chapter of my life began.

2. *The Lady in the* Calèche

The path led from the shaggy forest out upon a sedgy coastal plain, revealing a prospect of sullen levels, varied by salt-grass swamps and dark mottes of live oak, with lighter hued fringes of tall reeds on the shore, and the great gray sea standing up beyond.

In the hazy distance lofted raw wooden towers above a palisade, and I drew rein. Behind me, my two Canadians jolted their rough ponies and the pack mules to a halt also, for even in the wilderness I kept discipline, and it was my rule that on the march my men rode to my rear, save when some military necessity intervened.

Now I eased myself on my horse's back, half standing, with one foot in the stirrup, the other long, leather-clad leg slung across the saddle, shading my eyes with a flat hand against the sun glare while I studied the far structures. A wild, almost barbaric group, the three of us must have made; leather-garbed and weather-beaten, the leader dressed like his men, with musket slung across back and knife in sheath at thigh, save in this respect: out of pride I kept a clean-shaved face, while they were villainously bearded to the eyes.

On that afternoon late in May, in the year of grace 1713, late in the reign of the old King, Louis XIV of France, I was just past my thirtieth year, tall and lean from much hard wilderness living, and very swarthy from exposure. In truth, I might almost have been taken for an Indian, had it not been for the eyes of gray color with which nature has gifted me, for I wore my black hair long and bound at the nape by a leather thong, my brows are too heavy and thick for fashion, and my nose is something high-bridged and prominent, so that it may be thought too aggressive by some, although it always was Iberville's saying that no man was born to lead who did not have a bone in his face.

Pierre Le Moyne, Sieur d'Iberville! Even then, though the needless and untimely death of that great soldier and statesman, my patron and hero, was seven years past, I could not think of it without a clutch of sorrow. To be the aide and intimate companion of Iberville, most notable of Canadians, had been my privilege before I was twenty.

I am not unwilling to risk my life if occasion warrants it, and I have an ability with languages, which I have mentioned—for after being schooled in France and serving in Spain I spoke Spanish almost as well as French, could converse besides in English, and knew both the Iroquois and Algonquin savage dialects—and these qualities won for me the regard of Iberville.

That was the best thing my life had known. I was with him in the brilliant campaigns when Newfoundland, Acadia, and the Hudson Bay area were wrested from the English by the valor of French arms; sometimes beside him, sometimes as a commander of *partisans* on separate assignments.

From Iberville I gained something: during nights in forest bivouacs, and on long marches and in hot battles, I caught from him the vision of one who thought in terms of continents. Those northern conflicts of ours, however brilliant, Iberville made me understand, were unimportant compared to the momentous question of who should be master of the vast central part of the American continent—whether England, Spain, or France.

Not from the court of Versailles but from Canadian soil sprang the grand French scheme of territorial expansion: from the minds of Iberville, and Frontenac, and La Salle, who alone at first saw the possibilities and necessities of the world situation. All this I imbibed from Iberville until it was a tenet of my thinking, a part of my very self.

So long as Iberville was my leader, that vision was uppermost in my mind and heart. But now the great commander was dead of the yellow fever, while on a needless voyage ending in the harbor of Havana; and I, who had come with him to the lower Mississippi and the Gulf of Mexico, was seeking with indifferent success to make a new career for myself, the mighty dream of the great man I had followed all but lost in the eddies of personal concerns that beset me.

2.

These thoughts, or some of them, were in my mind as I completed my survey of the distant coast. But we could not remain here. I called.

"Marbot! Jaccard!"

My Canadians booted their ponies forward.

Marbot was shockheaded and wizen-faced above his bush of beard, undersized, in stained buckskins, a rascal with a jackdaw grin and the morals of a tomcat. Jaccard was taller, lank and saturnine, equally bearded, equally devoid of saintly qualities, and never smiling. Both were expert foresters and devoted to me, and though they bickered continually with one another, they were boon companions.

"Do you take that for the fort?" I asked.

"It must be, Monsieur," said Marbot.

"But where is the settlement?"

Jaccard had been studying the distant view. "Aren't those the masts of ships rising above that copse of trees near the shore?" he said. "Surely the harbor must be there—and by it the town."

Though we three were veterans of the lower French colonial country, we had never seen the new settlement named Mobile. It had been established on the bay only two years before, although there was previously a village a few miles up the river that emptied here into the Gulf. In that interim, we three had been north, in Canada, on a certain business concerning which I entertained some great hopes.

From the distance came the dull report of a musket shot.

"An alarm," I said. "They see us."

My men assented.

"Remain here," I told them. "I will go forward and speak to the fort alone. In these wilds, with English ships prowling the seas, the Spanish threat in Florida, and the Indians restless, garrisons are inclined to be nervous, and three men, approaching unidentified, might have a volley of musket balls about their ears as the first challenge."

I spurred my horse and cantered away, leaving them at the edge of the forest.

The weather was the weather of May on the Gulf, all gleams and glooms; now sunshine, now great billowing clouds. No rain was in the air, but there was a smell of brine from the sea, and of sour marsh water from the fens, and an infinity of mist shifted and altered over the horizons. As I rode toward the fort, my thoughts ranged like those mists afar.

Yonder, in that new settlement, was the residency of Iberville's brother, Jean Baptiste Le Moyne, Sieur de Bienville, Governor of Louisiana. I was glad to see the fort and the French flag fluttering in the light breeze, for my men and I had been a weary three months coming down the wild and dangerous Mississippi in a clumsy bateau, thence with horses obtained at Biloxi through the forest to here, and this was to be the end of our journey. I knew the Governor, although I did not have for him the same regard that I had for Iberville, since the former lacked the latter's warmth and kindness, being cold and recessive by temperament. Nevertheless I hoped that my services to the family might be remembered, and within my leather shirt I carried, in an oiled packet, letters which might bear weight in my favor.

Now I was in musket shot of the fort and saw the armed sentries in red coats and white pantaloons eying me from the palisades; now an officer in blue and red appeared on the platform above the great beamed gate, accompanied by two soldiers and a gray-robed friar; now a challenge was shouted, the musketeers brought their weapons to their shoulders, and I drew up my horse a stone's throw from the closed gate.

The officer lounged over and gazed down: a middle-aged, red-faced man, with the look of the dram bottle about him, attired in the extravagant fashion of Paris. His blue coat with red facings was exaggeratedly wide-skirted, those skirts stiffened with wire or crinoline to make them more bouffant; his long, curled peruke, dead black in hue, fell down over his shoulders; his black hat with wide curling brim had a sweeping ostrich plume of white; a white-gloved hand rested affectedly on the gilded hilt of his sword. To me he was a stranger; and it was obvious that he was newly arrived from France, and equally obvious that he regarded my wilderness garb as a badge of inferiority.

"Who in the devil are you?" he asked, pulling at one of his coarse, upturned mustachios.

"I am Louis Juchereau de St. Denis, by your leave, a loyal subject and servant of France and the King."

"*Vraiment?* His Majesty, the King, would appear to have a surfeit of servants of scant worth in this accursed wilderness."

I held my temper, which is inclined to be incandescent, carefully in check.

"I am just arrived, with two men, from Canada," I explained. "And I bear letters for His Excellency, the Governor."

A stir of interest at this. "Letters from whom?" asked the dram-bottle officer, after a brief pause.

"From the royal Governor of Canada, the Intendant, and others."

"To whom did you say these messages are addressed, Monsieur—what was it?"

My patience was becoming a little frayed.

"St. Denis," I said shortly. "A chevalier of France. And the messages are for Governor Bienville."

"Ah, for Bienville." It was as if some doubt had been cleared in his mind.

He turned to the priest, with whom he held a brief low-spoken conversation. At once the latter descended from the platform and a moment later the gate opened for him to issue forth.

Very bony and sallow of visage, with the tonsure and hood of the Recollet friars, he approached and fixed on my face his eyes, which were somber and made the more so by heavy dark circles under them.

"I am Abbé La Vente, chaplain and secretary to the Governor," he said in a voice which was a surprising rumbling bass. "You are to give me such papers as you may be carrying."

I hesitated, then opened a wallet at my side.

"My commission, as Captain, in the provincial army; and my passport," I said, tendering the documents.

He made no move to accept them. "You said you had correspondence for the Sieur de Bienville."

There seemed something odd in this whole manner of dealing, and now I made up my mind.

"I regret, Monsieur l'Abbé," I said, "but these letters I was instructed to place in the Governor's own hands."

The priest's gaunt, dark face stiffened. "Perhaps a word of advice will be of benefit to you, Monsieur. The officer who addressed you above is Captain Edmond de Noirel, of His Majesty's *regular*, not provincial, army. He is brother to the Marquis du Tyrac, who as you know is nephew of the Minister of State; and he also is commandant of this post, Fort Conde de Mobile. Even if you see fit to refuse me, the Governor's secretary, it would be most advisable for you to do as Captain Noirel directs, since he is a person of consequence and possesses authority."

I looked him directly in the eye. "I am a Frenchman, bearing proper credentials. If Captain Noirel wishes to inspect them, he is at liberty to do so. But the correspondence for the Governor I deliver in person."

"Be warned! Captain Noirel can order your arrest if you refuse."

I gave him the glint of a smile. "I think Captain Noirel will hardly take it upon himself to arrest a bearer of direct messages to the Sieur de Bienville."

A faint and unfathomable change flitted over the priest's gaunt features. He hesitated and glanced back at Noirel, on the platform; but the captain turned away as if he washed his hands of the whole affair.

"You personally know Bienville?" La Vente asked, directing his attention once more to me.

"I have the honor of his acquaintance."

It was as if he was about to say something, then changed his mind. Instead he bowed coldly.

"You create for yourself unnecessary difficulties, Monsieur," was all he said.

"You wish to inspect my credentials?"

"No. You may keep them—as also those letters. But you may not thank yourself for refusing them to us."

Abruptly the friar's gray-robed figure turned away and the gate of the fort closed behind it.

For some minutes I sat my horse before the gate, a prey to puzzled speculations. Why did the dram-bottle captain demand the letters addressed to the Governor? And why did the friar appear to be angered, to the extent of a veiled threat, when the letters were refused?

Noirel had disappeared from the platform above the gate, and only the common soldiers remained, looking down with derisive grins. They were typical Paris gutter-sweepings, forced into the army by press gangs; who yet, because they were from the Continent, were contemptuous of all things provincial.

Presently one of these shouted, "Hola—you! Get along!"

"To the town?" I asked.

"Where else?"

"The Commandant has no further business with me?"

"He has more important affairs than talking with a woods runner."

The "woods runner" was an impertinence. Yet nothing could be gained by parleying with this jackanapes in uniform, and nobody superior to him in rank was visible. I knew the embarrassment had been put upon me deliberately. Nevertheless, in a nameless uneasiness which had for some reason taken possession of me, I was hardly angry.

It was clear that I had gained the ill will of the Commandant of the fort. This did not particularly concern me. But there was something else—an undercurrent which I could not grasp, more in fleeting expressions of features and inflections of voices than anything else.

I shrugged. When I saw Governor Bienville it might all be explained and I felt reasonably sure of my position with the Governor when I should see him. I turned in my saddle and made a wide sweeping motion with my arm, signaling my men to come on.

3.

The settlement called Mobile, as we came in full view of it, was a frontier village infinitely cruder, because newer, than the established Canadian towns of the day. No stone or kiln brick was here; the buildings were of the material readiest to hand. Sun-dried mud brick, such as the Spanish call adobe, was the composition of most of the huts, with a few structures more substantially built of logs or hand-sawn planking. It was notable that every house possessed heavy shutters and doors, which could be strongly barred for defense. Beyond the roofs of the squalid buildings which straggled along either side of a single muddy street, the masts of two merchant ships and a man-of-war rocked lazily in the tidal wash, with the spars of lesser craft about them.

Dogs raised a canine tumult about us as we spattered into the town, the hoofs of our horses sucking in the muck of the undrained street, and an unclean smell of slops and offal assailing our nostrils. *Habitants,* many of them in peasant smocks and *sabots,* with here and there an occasional tarry sailor or sober-dressed merchant, stared with unsmiling and almost hostile curiosity.

Then, from an upper window, feminine laughter trilled; and farther along, across the roadway, fluttered a kirtle and cap.

"Women, ha!" said Marbot with a grin.

"Dramshops also," I said dryly. Marbot looked virtuous.

Pulling up my horse, I swung out of the saddle, handing my gun and the reins to Marbot.

"I will try that inn yonder for lodgings," I said.

Before, however, I could take a step on the slippery street, shouts came from the direction whence we had just ridden. The two Canadians, still in their saddles, craned their necks to see.

Toward us, along the road from the fort, a hooded *calèche* was whirling at a gallop of the team of horses that drew it. Before it rode two soldiers and behind it two more, all four of them slashing with whips at pedestrians who did not skip nimbly enough out of the way.

"Hi! Hi! Off the road there!"

Obediently, Marbot and Jaccard sought to crowd their horses and the baggage mules over to one side of the narrow street. They had trouble, however, and Marbot, finding difficulty with my mount which he was holding by the reins, did not move over as quickly as Jaccard.

Spattering mud, the horsemen careered down upon us. One of them wheeled over toward Marbot, and his whip left a stinging weal across the little man's face.

"Learn to clear the way when you're told!" He scowled.

But the scowl changed as his horse reared back, jerked almost on its haunches by my angry grip on its bridle. An instant later, as the man tried to right himself in the saddle, my furious leap pulled him to the ground, where he rolled back and forth in the mire, while with his own whip I lashed him again and again.

The *calèche* came to a sudden stop, its liveried driver rigid on the front seat. The three other outriders moved to the rescue of their comrade, who was howling under the blows of the whip, but hesitated when Marbot and Jaccard turned snarling, unslinging their muskets from their backs.

"Get up, you cur!" I cried, throwing the whip down in the mud. "And hereafter keep your lash for your own kennel mates!"

Already the inevitable crowd was gathering, people running from every direction, to push and crane and gawk and elbow at the spectacle in the street. Muddy, disheveled, his coat torn, the outrider scrambled to his feet and stood glaring about as if undecided what to do.

Then a voice came from the *calèche*, cool, scornful, and with a brittle quality of anger in it.

"Get back on your horse, Jacques," it said. "You may become a soldier when hens shall have teeth—but no sooner."

The voice and the biting slur brought my eyes to the *calèche*, and I could not help my stare.

Sitting alone under the low hood of the vehicle was a woman. Physically, she was beautiful or not, according to whether one accepted conventional criterions. Her dress, rich in satins and ribboned rosebuds, clad a fine feminine figure of slender curves. Thus far she measured up to a high, though customary, standard.

Her face, however, set her apart. It was a face not easily to be forgotten, the cheekbones wide and the cheeks slightly hollowed, the eyes
large and burningly bright in deep sockets, the nose short and straight,
the sharp chin lifted arrogantly. Her skin was almost colorlessly white
and made to appear the more so by the jet-black hair of her haughty
head, curled after the fashion of the day, untrammeled by a bonnet,
and with the usual "love lock" on one shoulder—although assuredly
there was no love in her expression.

Rather, her nostrils expanded angrily, and for half a minute she returned my stare, her eyes seeming to darken to greater depths.

"You dare chastise one of my men?" she cried out at last.

"Madame, you need to teach your men manners," I replied.

"You have some authority for saying that?" It was a sneer.

"I know soldiers. And I know soldiers must be disciplined."

"*You* know soldiers?" Her contempt was open now. "A woods
runner?"

"One dresses for one's work, Madame. I am a *partisan* ranger, but also
I am a gentleman, and a Captain in the army of France."

She looked me up and down as if she thought I lied. Then she said,
"And you believe this gives you the right to teach me my business?"

"You have not informed me what your business is."

For the flash of an instant our glances crossed like rapiers.

"You call yourself a gentleman," she said, her lip curling. "A gentleman is never impertinent."

"If I have been impertinent, I crave your pardon. It was the last
thing I intended."

"It was impertinent to flog my rider!" she flared.

I gazed at her directly and calmly, almost impersonally. "You do not
realize, Madame, that I saved his life for him."

"Why do you say that?"

"Had I not flogged him—immediately, and publicly, before all these
people—Marbot or Jaccard would certainly have killed him. My men
are no peasants—or *canaille* of the streets—such as you may be accustomed to in France. They are free foresters and hunters. Whipping your
outrider wiped out the insult, or you would have seen real tragedy."

"Your men would have been hanged!"

"Perhaps. But they derive their ideas of honor from the Indians, and
they would have died with that honor unsullied."

"You are exasperating, Monsieur!"

"I am your servant, Madame. If I have done that which offended you, I deplore its necessity, and most humbly beg that you forgive it."

I spoke as winningly as I knew how. Now, as I stood with my hat held over my heart, half bowing, half smiling, and trying to look contrite, a subtle change seemed to come over her.

"Monsieur, I begin half to believe you," she said.

"Even for that half, I thank your graciousness."

"Tell me, what is your name?"

"I am the Chevalier de St. Denis."

"St. Denis?" she repeated. "Then you must be the man who refused to submit letters of some kind to Captain Noirel at the fort a little time ago!"

"I was unfortunately compelled to do so. The correspondence is for the Governor, to be delivered into his hands."

"You intend to visit the Governor?"

"As soon as possible."

Another change came into her eyes, so slight as to be almost indiscernible, but I wondered if it contained amusement of some kind.

"Monsieur," she said, "I was within Fort Conde, visiting one of the ladies of the officers' establishments, at the time you were there. I must tell you that you have bitterly offended Captain Noirel. And I should inform you further that Captain Noirel is a dangerous man when offended. He has a reputation in Paris. With the rapier—not the whip!"

The discomfited outrider had now stumbled to his horse and mounted it. Seeing the staring crowd about, the haughty beauty signaled her driver to proceed.

"One more word," she said over her shoulder. "I hope that your visit to the Governor—will not too greatly disappoint you!"

The *calèche*, with its liveried driver, its four outriders somewhat chastened, and its remarkable feminine passenger, sped on in the direction of the docks beyond the town.

4.

For a moment I stared after it.

"A disappointment?" I said aloud, though to myself. "Now who is she? She warns me against Noirel; who has a reputation with the rapier

—not the whip." I grinned at the gibe. "*Touché*, there. Ha! It may be worth while to know something more of this one!"

Then I looked toward the inn. Above the door hung the painted likeness of a gilded rooster, and a lettered sign: Le Coq d'Or. Pushing my way through the crowd, I went up the hewn-log steps.

A moment later a fat innkeeper, aproned, stood before me, massaging his hands and shaking his head.

"No rooms, Monsieur," he said.

I glanced past him into the taproom. It was evident that I had happened on the chosen resort of the younger officers—the cadets—of the garrison, who disliked the intrusion of any stranger in their domain. The place was filled with them. Strangely, I did not know one of them, although I had been well enough acquainted with the military staff at the former post up the river, before I left Louisiana three years before.

Yet, though I knew none of these young men individually, I was well acquainted with the type: younger sons of old aristocratic families of France; spoiled, indolent, arrogant; sent abroad to mend their fortunes and despising the provinces and all provincials; fencers, fighters, roisterers, braggarts, libertines, and fops. To a man they wore silks, plumed hats, and long curled wigs. To a man they carried swords at their sides. Most of them were more than a little drunk; and it was evident that in the idleness of garrison life their chief occupations were the gaming tables, dueling perhaps, and such other mischief as they could contrive. With them were half a dozen young women, tolerably pretty, costumed extravagantly and provocatively, some sitting on knees, some being embraced, accepting caresses and liberties with careless laughter, unsequestered and daring, their occupation evident.

My brief words with the innkeeper had drawn the attention of these people, and every face was turned toward me, with scorn and dislike on all. I returned their collective stare coldly.

"These persons all lodge here?" I asked.

"No," said the innkeeper. "The young sieurs are quartered at the fort, or on Dauphin Island, where is situated the Governor's residency."

"Then assuredly you can find me and my men rooms of some kind——"

"I regret, Monsieur. I said no rooms."

"And I demand to know why!"

I allowed my voice to rise angrily, and some of the young dandies rose from their tables with a scraping of chairs and thudding of feet, while the girls squealed with excitement.

All at once, behind my back, the door of the inn opened and slammed, and boots tramped forward. A hand grasped me roughly by the shoulder and spun me around.

Scowling face, upturned mustache, black peruke and white-plumed hat—it was my acquaintance of the fort, Captain Noirel.

"So I find you here!" he exclaimed harshly.

"It appears you do," I replied.

"You hear what Mine Host Tiernay tells you? He has no rooms!"

"Your pardon. I have reason to think he has."

A stir among the cadets, and a girl's nervous titter. Noirel's face flushed darkly.

"This tavern, Monsieur Leather-breeches, is reserved for *gentlemen*," he rasped. "We dislike the smell of your company. Now begone!"

A ruffler and a bully, obviously; to me it appeared there could be but one way to handle such a man.

"You perhaps consider yourself a gentleman?" I asked.

"No man will deny it!"

"*I* think you are a pig!"

Noirel almost gasped. Then, his face suddenly contorting with fury, he leaped backward into the taproom to gain space, overturning a chair and whipping his sword from its scabbard with a vicious whine.

But as he leaped, I leaped with him.

I had no sword. Instead, I seized from a table a heavy brass candlestick. Just as Noirel cleared his point for the thrust, the candlestick, hurled with all my might, struck him full on the forehead. Without a cry, the man went down, his rapier slithering across the floor.

From the others in the tavern came a roar of amazement and anger, and a dozen blades flashed out.

Quickly I stooped, picked up Noirel's sword, and faced them: with a weapon now, but knowing how long were the odds against me, opposed by so many fencers, almost effeminate in their laces and silks, perhaps, but without any question deadly dangerous.

Then, for a second time, a voice spoke behind me. "Messieurs! What is this?"

Faces of the young fops changed, and rapier points were lowered as the newcomer came forward. Still on guard, I glanced at him: a slen-

der man of medium height, not more than two or three years older
than I, attired in a coat of pink watered satin belted tightly at the waist
to display a graceful figure, lace at wrists and throat extremely long
and delicate, knee-length tight breeches, white silk stockings, silver-
buckled shoes with high red heels, and the plumed hat and curled
peruke of the mode.

A coxcomb—and yet no coxcomb at all, when one looked at his face.
The eyes were wide-set and cold gray, the nose long, the mouth small
but without softening curve. It was a face of ice, a frozen countenance
with all expression chained beneath the surface. Whatever his garb,
here was a man of force and distinction, to be respected and never
taken lightly.

"Seigneur Bienville!" I cried in amazement. "Your Excellency!"

"So it's you, St. Denis?" said Bienville without a change in his face.
"You have been long in returning from Canada."

"It is a journey hardly to be skipped over lightly or quickly, Your
Excellency."

Bienville gave a slight nod, as if he understood that as well as anyone.
As for myself, I made my best bow, in which was a certain modicum of
gratitude: for I saw that, with his arrival, danger of immediate conflict
with these hotspurs was over. Even a courageous man may own to a
sensation of relief when the prospect of facing alone a dozen swords
is averted: especially when that man is perhaps a little rusty at fencing, due to long disuse of the weapon and lack of practice, since the
sword assuredly is not an arm to carry in the wilderness.

Somewhat grudgingly blades were being sheathed. The prostrate figure on the floor uttered a moan.

"Who is that?" Bienville asked.

"Captain Noirel," said one of the cadets. "This man struck him down."

"He is bleeding. Assist him, some of you, and send for a physician."

Still half stunned, with blood running from an ugly cut on his forehead, the Captain was lifted and seated on a chair. Bienville looked
at him.

"His injury is not serious," he said, as if dismissing the incident.
"Take care of him. And you, St. Denis, be good enough to follow me."

He led the way out of the inn. When we were in the street, Bienville
said, in his singularly cold manner, "Quarreling as usual, I see."

"A quarrel forced upon me," I retorted.

"I have never heard that it required very much 'force,' as you call it, to stir up a quarrel where you are concerned. How long will it be before you gain sense? Had not someone brought me word of an altercation on the street, so that I came, arriving at the inn just when I did, you would have been skewered by those hotheads."

"I would have endeavored to defend myself," said I stiffly.

"You might have found it difficult. Some clever swordsmen are in that crowd. And you would have deserved your fate—you know that, do you not?"

I half nodded, feeling my face flush.

"As for Noirel," Bienville went on, "he is a Gascon and a brawler. Perhaps he received his deserts. Nevertheless, I do not think you have heard the last of this, my friend." He glanced over toward Marbot and Jaccard, still sitting their horses in the street. "Your men?"

"Yes, Excellency."

"Foresters, with the camp grease black on their buckskins—and you sought quarters for *these* at the Coq d'Or?"

"Yes."

"You chose the wrong inn. This one is affected by our Paris gallants, newly arrived from France. Yonder, near the docks, is a better place— La Dive Bouteille, where sailormen and suchlike go."

"I understand."

"Lodge your men there. As for yourself, I will be pleased if you will come to my house. I have somewhat to say to you."

"Your house? But—is not the residency across the bay on Dauphin Island?"

"I do not reside on Dauphin. There is my house." Bienville pointed to the farther limit of the town, where, overlooking the bay, stood an edifice somewhat better than the average in the settlement, but still far from pretentious.

With astonishment I gazed first at the house, then at my companion.

"But I thought—Your Excellency——" I paused.

Bienville frowned slightly. "I am too far out of sympathy with the present regime. I prefer an abode here."

"The—*present*—regime? Are you not the regime itself?"

He gave me a quick, sharp glance. "I forgot that you have been on wilderness trails where news might not reach you. Do you see the three tall ships in the harbor?"

"Yes, Excellency. One is a ship of war."

"That is the *Maréchal d'Estrées,* of thirty-six guns. She arrived here three days ago, convoying the other two vessels. They are heavily laden with goods, but she herself carried the most important cargo."

"Of what did it consist?"

"For one thing, women. For another, a royal order supplanting me as governor of this province. For a third, my successor—who now occupies the residency on Dauphin Island."

I gave a gasp. "But if you are not the Governor—then in God's name —who——?"

"Antoine de la Mothe, Sieur de Cadillac, is the new ruler of this colony."

"He who commanded at Fort Detroit on the Great Lakes?"

"The same." At the astonished expression on my face, Bienville almost broke his iceberg composure with a smile. But instead, after a moment, he continued, "Mine has been a thankless task here, but I see no good in this change. By a special order I still retain the rank of Lieutenant Governor, which does not please some of my enemies. Nevertheless it gives me yet some standing."

"I am stunned—I cannot express myself."

"Never mind. I will explain to you fully. Meantime, I will give your men instructions as to where to take your baggage and where to dispose of themselves. I count on you, St. Denis"—Bienville paused and gave me a sidewise look—"as one of my brother's officers, to be of service here in what may be a situation demanding a certain amount of courage, decision, and loyalty. Let us proceed to my house, where we can discuss at leisure that which evidently amazes you."

3. *"Heard Anyone Ever a Thing So Fantastic?"*

To see the Sieur de Bienville picking his way along the muddy street, now and again taking snuff, and shaking out the white laces at his wrists, it would have been hard for one not knowing him to imagine that here not only was a bold soldier whose deeds had earned for him the Cross of St. Louis, and a member of the noblest and most famous family of Canada, but also an able administrator, who, whatever his faults, had held together this far colony of Louisiana almost single-handed since his elder brother Iberville, who founded it, met his death.

His habitual chill manner repelled any effort at conversation, which was perhaps fortunate, since I had little to say. I suited myself to his book, and strode along beside him, a good three inches taller than he, and carrying my head especially high because of the contrast his silks must have made with my thrummed buckskins, worn and black from weather, camp smoke, and grease.

Meantime my mind wrestled with a new and knotty problem. Bienville no longer governor? It was enough for the moment to strangle speculation in any other line.

Presently my companion halted before his house, which was built of logs, with a high-pitched roof of hand-riven shakes—an adaptation from the Canadian style, though unnecessary here in a land where it was never known to snow.

"Enter," he said, and added with a touch of feeling unusual in him, "It is not often I can open my house to a fellow Canadian. How I long at times for the cold winds, the snows, and the dark pine forests of my native land!"

Still somewhat dazed, I allowed him to conduct me to a room within, dim because it had only one small window, on the walls of which maps were tacked haphazardly, while some few chairs and a couple of iron-bound chests were scattered in confusion about a table covered with papers and books.

"We moved in hurriedly, bag and baggage, only two days ago, and have had as yet little time for housekeeping," Bienville said in apology, for he was precise and delicate in his tastes and could not bear slovenly surroundings. "But at least we can talk here and have a glass of wine," he added. "Let us sit."

He rang a small silver hand bell, at which a servant entered with lighted candles to dispel the gloom; and after that brought a tray with wineglasses and a bottle.

The man was attired in white wool stockings, black shoes, and a long-tailed coat and breeches of blue color—Bienville's livery—but the coarseness of his black hair, which was cut short at the level of the jaw, the darkness of his face and eyes, and his grim mouth, revealed the full-blooded Indian. I knew him: Solta, Bienville's Shawnee servant, a hunter from the shores of the Great Lakes, who had followed his master to this place out of loyalty. Having drawn the cork and poured the wine, Solta withdrew.

Absently I tasted the wine, and found it so fine that though my mind still was in a whirl, I could not forbear complimenting it.

"Having in this wilderness few of the softer joys of life," said Bienville, "our zest is sharpened for those that remain. The best wine in the world comes from France, and the best wine in France from Burgundy. This which you praise is from a celebrated vineyard near Macon, and I flatter myself that it would not be despised even in Versailles."

It was as near as he had ever come to boasting, or indeed to unbending on any subject, to me.

After a moment he added, "Solta, my servant, is another who longs for Canada, like myself. Did you observe that he brought the best wine, without my order? For an ordinary guest in his estimation—that is, one not a Canadian—he would have brought a vintage far less worthy."

"Under these unhappy circumstances," said I somberly, "I would that I, also, were back in Canada."

"This sudden change has perhaps complicated matters for you?" As usual, Bienville avoided the direct question which was in his mind—the exact nature of my business.

When I did not respond to the opening, he urbanely took a different course in his conversation.

"You will find matters much altered," he said. "Your arrival, with your Canadians, is pleasing to me, as it is to my good Solta. It should be a welcome event for all here."

"*Should* be? Then it is not?"

"The new regime, I fear, does not look with much favor on Canadians: and this in spite of the fact that Cadillac himself served in Canada. They are too vigorous and independent for his taste, yet I consider them the most valuable part of our population, which consists otherwise chiefly of lazy offscourings and rogues from France, half-mutinous and ill-disciplined soldiers, and women who are worse in some cases than the men."

I gave a nod. "Some of those women were in evidence at the inn."

"Are you aware how came such doxies to this far settlement?"

"No. I have been much away—twice up the Red River, and once up the Mississippi and back. Though I knew women were being brought in, this species had not occurred to me."

"It was inevitable," Bienville said. "The scheme itself was strange in its conception. Some time ago the French ministry hit on the idea of shipping contingents of women here as wives for the colonists. Inasmuch as each is provided with a casket containing a wardrobe, besides a small dowry in money, furnished by the King, they are called *cassette* girls. A new bevy of these, by the way—thirty of them—has just arrived aboard the *Maréchal d'Estrées*, direct from France, and will be landed tomorrow. If you are curious you can witness the event."

"They are recruited from the Paris stews?"

"Not entirely. The first shipment was not bad, consisting of peasant girls, strong and accustomed to work. They were married off quickly enough. But the quality declined after that. Because it was almost impossible to induce women of virtue to come to this remote and savage region, the government began sending over inmates from the Hôpital Général of Paris, where, as you know, prostitutes, vagrants, and thieves of the female sex are held. These, coming largely against their will, are offered to the colonists as wives."

"How are they received?"

"You know the old saw: 'The devil requires ten hours to deceive a man, a woman only one hour to deceive ten men.' This is the more so when women are scarce, whereby the commodity of sex becomes more precious. Many *cassette* girls have found husbands. On the other hand, not a few have established themselves in the profession they practiced in Paris: and so have come the first houses of vice in Louisiana."

"But not all women here, I take it, are *cassette* girls?" I was thinking of the lady of the *calèche*.

"By no means. Some colonists brought families from France. There are also the wives and daughters of officials of the civil and military governments. And now we have a whole new society, the feminine category of Governor Cadillac's entourage, just arrived."

"Cadillac—do you know him well?"

"Not well, but well enough," Bienville answered in his coldly bitter manner. "You will find him amply gifted with the kind of intelligence that consists in quick observation, sharpened by an inveterate spirit of sarcasm, a grasping disposition, and no complete trustworthiness."

I nodded.

"He has a reputation for cruelty also," Bienville went on. "And to complete matters, he rules here for that huckster Crozat, rather than for the King. Which means for the fattening of Crozat's moneybags, rather than for the glory of France."

I blinked. "You speak in riddles, Seigneur. Who is this Crozat?"

"Your pardon. I had forgot again that you are not informed on this most amazing turn of affairs."

"My head—I confess it—feels somewhat dizzy."

"It will be more so, when you hear the whole story," Bienville said. "First, as to Antoine Crozat. I have never seen him, but I have heard somewhat concerning his career. Crozat was born on the estate of one of the great feudal noblemen of France." He gave a little sidewise glance. "I will not name this noble, but he was very close to the royal family itself."

I comprehended. It could have been any of several great aristocratic figures of France, and the names of the great are dangerous to bandy about.

"Presumably," continued Bienville, "Crozat was the son of a peasant on that estate. At least it is certain he was the son of the peasant's extremely comely young *wife*——" He paused significantly.

"There is, then, a cloud on his ancestry?" I suggested.

"If there is," he said with his sleety smile, "it has been at least a rosy one."

"Ah?"

"Consider this, St. Denis: early in his youth Crozat was named *foster brother* of the only son—legitimate, that is—of this nobleman. Why, I ask you, would the child of a simple peasant be so honored?"

I shook my head.

"Then," Bienville went on, "he was sent to school by his noble patron, again a matter of unusual circumstance. Furthermore, from his very childhood he was marked by acuteness of intellect that seems very strange in one sprung only from crude peasant forebears. And, having received an education, he was placed as a clerk in an important commercial house in Paris, through the influence, once again, of the noble patron—who appears never to have lost interest in the remarkable and precocious youth."

Bienville paused to take snuff, and flicked a few grains of it from his lace jabot.

"By his natural ability," he resumed, "but also, it is whispered, by the investment of sums of money coming from *some source*—above and beyond his salary as a mere clerk—he rose in twenty years to become a full partner in the business, married the daughter of his former employer, and, shortly after that happy event, found himself, at the death of his father-in-law, head of the firm and one of the richest merchants in Europe."

I smiled at my wineglass. "Strange events," I observed, "sometimes arise out of the—friendly interest, let us say—of a grand seigneur in the pretty wife of one of his tenants."

"I perceive that you are not entirely unsophisticated," remarked Bienville. "But Crozat's good fortune did not end there. He was able to lend the government large sums of money in periods of emergency —in return for most profitable monopolies—and even after the death of his noble patron he managed, through his finances, to keep strong friends at court. By the combination of these influences he has lately been made one of the *noblesse*, with the title of Marquis du Châtel." There was a sneer in Bienville's voice at this mention.

"A notable rise indeed for a peasant woman's son," I said noncommittally.

"But now," he continued, "the strangest elevation of all has come to him, and it is to this that I have been leading. Versailles is in one of its recurring periods of economy; and the King, weary of the expense of maintaining this colony, and to put an end to requisitions on the royal exchequer, has given to Crozat a gigantic concession—*with complete powers*—to all of Louisiana!"

I simply stared, trying to grasp all the implications.

"You realize what this means?" Bienville asked. "It means that all this great territory, far larger than France itself, richer than the whole of Canada, with all its rivers, forests, lands, minerals, and peoples, extending from the English colonies on the Atlantic coast to the great mountains of the West, and from Canada to New Spain, is a royal province no longer! It is a farm—a *farm*, St. Denis! Neither more nor less. A farm, held and operated for this pawnbroker Crozat's financial advantage. Heard anyone ever a thing so fantastic?"

2.

For some moments I sat silent, trying to digest this astounding news, and finding it most difficult to do so. Then I rose, making some sort of a stumbling excuse that I wished to step out for a few minutes to see how my men were faring at their inn.

Bienville nodded. "Dinner will be served in an hour, at which time we can resume this discussion. And, until you find accommodations which better suit you, a room in this house is at your disposal."

So absorbed had I been in my conversation with him that I had not marked the passage of time. But as I stepped outdoors, night was falling. The sun had dropped below the horizon and, although the western sky still flamed with glories of gold and scarlet, the town lay in darkness, the oblongs of brightness from windows and doors of the cabins along the straggling, muddy street only accenting the gloom of early night. In the bay I could see the riding lights of the ships at anchor, those on the towering masts of the *Maréchal d'Estrées* being easy to identify.

Sounds of the evening had begun in the village. From one house came the squeak of fiddles and the bray of mouth organs, with the stamping of feet and frequent laughter telling of dancing in progress. From another I heard the clink of mugs and rattle of dice. It was evident that the French love of gaiety and pleasure was not diminished by this exile from the motherland.

Down by the docks I heard a voice uplifted, singing a gay and very amorous little French *chanson* with a tra-li-ra chorus, which was greeted with shouts of applause and laughter. I recognized the voice: it was Marbot, and revelry must be in progress at the inn called La Dive Bouteille.

Making the best of the slippery underfooting, the hazards of which were increased rather than diminished by the scanty illumination from cabin doors or windows, I turned my steps in that direction; and as I walked, my mind beat a dreary refrain of gloomy thought.

For these three months I had toiled toward Louisiana as to a goal of hope, only to find that overnight fate had changed everything for me. No longer was this province a King's colony, with laws and government dependable, and linked with other provinces through the interlocking colonial system. It had become, in effect, a sort of foreign land, independent of every other French possession, a law to itself, to all intents and purposes the personal property of that shadowy, grasping, somehow menacing figure, Antoine Crozat.

All at once I remembered the letters I carried, so carefully wrapped in oilskins within my leathern shirt. I had depended on those letters as an entering wedge into preferment and opportunity in Louisiana; now they seemed worthless. A sickish sense of disappointment overwhelmed me.

Another line of thinking: at least this gave an explanation for something that had puzzled me—that eagerness of Captain Noirel and the Abbé La Vente to gain possession of those letters. Without knowing the change—for not a whisper of this sudden shift had been in the wind when I left Canada—I had informed that pair that the documents were for Bienville. This was not strictly true, since the packet was addressed simply and formally to *"His Excellency, the Royal Governor of Louisiana."* At the time I supposed Bienville was Governor—which, it appeared, he was not.

Nevertheless, Bienville still was Governor when I left Canada, and the messages most probably were written to him directly. Perhaps Cadillac, for whom Bienville evidently felt no love, might like to see those letters to the man he had succeeded. It was possible that they contained intimate and unguarded observations and references, written when nobody had an inkling of the change that was to take place. Intrigues were ever-present in governmental circles, secret matters between officials, sometimes schemes they hardly wished to have known by possible enemies, certainly not by Versailles.

I had no way of knowing that the letters I carried contained such information, but it struck me that there was evidence of some sort of weakness in Cadillac's position, in that his orders did not invest the Commandant of the fort with authority to arrest a messenger such as myself, and take the papers by force, if need be. Perhaps Bienville still wielded some power in this colony after all . . .

Bienville—youngest of the great Le Moyne family* and Iberville's brother—but how different from the glorious Iberville! In his lifetime Iberville had been all warmth, inspiration, farsighted vision, daring, and generosity to friends—sometimes even to defeated enemies. On the other hand Bienville was cold, secretive, brave enough, and, I believed, honest, but giving no inspiration to those who served under him.

The coldness of his nature was exemplified by the fact that he shunned the society of women, save when the necessities of his position forced him to attend some function at which women were present. And then he was all aloof politeness, his courtesy a polished glitter of ice: for above all things he desired to form no relationship which would break his distant reserve, or cause him to share his thoughts, let alone his fortunes.

A strange man, Bienville. Though I had known him more than a decade, I could not call him friend. This evening, indeed, was the first time Bienville had so far unbent as to invite me as a guest to dinner, let alone offer me a bed. Some reason lay behind this, it occurred to me, for Bienville never did anything without reason; and if his hos-

---

* No Canadian family was so illustrious as the Le Moynes. Starting with the father, Charles Le Moyne, of Montreal, who was a member of Frontenac's council and a military commander, every one of the ten sons did distinguished service militarily and administratively for colonial France. The sons, known by their land estate titles, were Iberville, Longueuil, Sérigny, Assigny, Maricourt, Sainte-Hélène, Châteauguay (the elder), Châteauguay (the younger), Bienville (the elder) and Bienville (the younger). The younger Châteauguay inherited the estate from his elder brother at the latter's death. The Bienville who was governor and then lieutenant governor at Mobile inherited from his brother Charles, who was killed in a battle with the Iroquois. None, including the father, equaled the military achievements of the eldest son, Iberville.

pitality was somewhat chill, it was also in some sort an honor, so the reason must be important.

A new kind of weight seemed suddenly to attach itself to those letters in the oiled packet, of a sort I could not yet quite appraise. Written to Bienville they were, perhaps: but addressed to the *Governor*, and presumably on official business. That left a question, *pardieu*––

My thoughts were interrupted by a shout, followed by the rough snarling growl of voices uplifted, and then a high, wild cry:

"À moi! À moi! In the name of God, help me, friends!"

So evident was the distress in the voice that without hesitation I began running toward it. Here and there people came out of their homes to stand and listen to the outcries, and through these I jostled my way, trying to make speed, and leaving behind complaints and curses.

Then, suddenly, a small figure bounded through the dark directly toward me, gasping and terrified. I caught it in my arms.

For a moment I had to put forth all my strength to hold the struggling little man. Then my captive relaxed.

"Release me, good Monsieur!" said a pleading voice. "By all the blessed saints, by my own mother, by my life, it would not be worth your trouble to take me! I am very weak, unable to do any work! And I am afflicted with innumerable diseases, stupid in the bargain, and have a large family of starving children to support! I could not possibly be of any use to you aboard your ship, but only in the way—and another mouth to feed, too, for I have a voracious appetite——"

"Marbot!" I exclaimed.

"Is—is it you, Monsieur?" he gasped, peering through the darkness. "Who else?"

"Now God, His Mother, be praised! At the next feast of Saint Lawrence, to whom I particularly look for heavenly intervention in my behalf, I vow to light twelve wax candles——"

"What is all this about?" I interrupted. "You are strong as a horse, have no diseases, and as for starving children, if you have left a few here and there behind you in the Indian villages where squaws bedded with you, this is the first time I have known you to concern yourself about them."

"I—I thought you were one of the pirates——"

"Pirates?"

"*Certainement!* They have taken Jaccard and all the others at the inn!"

"What happened? Tell me exactly and instantly, Marbot!"

"It was quick as the winking of a light, Monsieur. We were supping, with perhaps a few bottles of wine, and a girl for each when we showed them the color of money—for you had just paid us—and also a half dozen or more good fellows, peasants and fishermen and the like, who for our company and our wine were good friends with us, and I was singing a *chanson* to great applause——"

"To the point, to the point!"

"I am coming to it, Monsieur. Jaccard and most of the others had perhaps drunk too much, and I might also have been in their case, had it not been for my *chanson*, which was somewhat long, and the girl also, around whom I had my arm, and to whom I must pay attention, so that I was behind the others a bottle or two, but with every intention of catching up——"

"Yes, yes! What happened?"

"A big man, seafaring by his clothes and look, with a red cap and a yellow beard, came into the inn, followed by a score or more—pirates, every one, for never were seen men so ugly, some having sword slashes across their faces, one with an eye and ear entirely gone, and none but showed signs of vice and knavery, tarred and brown as so many Iroquois——"

"A curse on your long-windedness! Tell what occurred!"

"That is what I *am* doing. The big man with the red cap gave a shout, whereat from each side two of his fellows seized upon each of us men and began to bind us."

"You also?"

"I was lucky, for I was not so drunk as they expected. I know the trick of the foot called *la savate*, and having kicked one under the jaw, and the other in the groin, I twisted away from them, and won free, coming with all haste to warn you——"

"To warn *me?*"

"Well, perhaps a little to save myself."

I swore heartily. "These are not pirates, Marbot. It was a press gang, no doubt from the *Maréchal d'Estrées*, sent to seize men for the crew. We must hurry!"

"Where?"

"To head them off."

"But—they might seize *us*——"

"I should like to see them try," I said grimly, setting off at a run. Marbot, after a moment's hesitation, followed.

When we reached the docks, however, we could see some distance out across the dark waters a pair of longboats, with coxswains exhorting the oarsmen to give way. So shrouded by night were the boats that nothing could be made out of the prisoners, who probably now were gagged and bound, or perhaps too drunk to realize what was happening to them.

"Too late—they're gone!" I exclaimed with intense disappointment. "And they have Jaccard—a forester! He will die on that ship!"

"What shall we do, Monsieur?" asked Marbot.

"I must consider. For the present you will come with me to Bienville's house, where I will arrange to have you stay the night."

One thing at least was settled for me. I had made up my mind concerning the packet of letters I carried within my shirt.

3.

"*Mon Dieu*, what's happened?" cried Bienville, springing to his feet when he saw my face.

"A press gang has carried off one of my men," I replied.

"Ah?" Bienville relaxed. "And this is the other?" He glanced at Marbot, standing behind me, and shrugged. "These King's ships are always prowling for recruits."

"I want my man back."

"One man? I would not concern myself. You can find another."

"But I do concern myself!"

Bienville gazed at me as if faintly amused. "You are given to overmuch emotion, my friend. What is one follower, more or less? Resign yourself, for the *Maréchal d'Estrées* is hardly likely to give him up."

Emotion! Bienville did not understand such a thing. But I did, and Jaccard had been with me for eight years.

"Is there no one in authority?" I demanded. "Cannot the Governor order him freed?"

"I suppose so," he said negligently. "Yes, if he wished to do so, he has the authority."

"Then I go to Cadillac tomorrow."

"Easier said than done. The Governor is seen by appointment only, and the appointments are made through La Vente, his secretary."

"Nevertheless, I will make the effort."

Marbot stood listening, mouth agape. Observing this, and learning that I wished him quartered where he would be safe for the night, Bienville summoned Solta with a bell, and gave orders to provide food and a sleeping place for my retainer.

When Marbot and the servant were gone, he considered me almost curiously, as if wondering what could impel a man to go to such trouble and encounter such difficulties for a mere follower. At last he said, "You have, I take it, some errand here of perhaps personal interest?"

"Assuredly. I did not make this long journey for amusement."

"Perhaps you will indicate to me its nature?"

For a moment I thought, frowning. "I hardly know—since this turn in affairs," I said. "But I will tell you what I had hoped. I have seen much of this continent, and fought against both the English and Indian enemies of France since my youth. It appears to me that I have reached the age and experience to hold a position of authority, of service to the King, and perhaps of profit to myself."

"A trading monopoly, for example?" he asked shrewdly.

"It is possible."

"Has it occurred to you that you may jeopardize this ambition if you annoy the new Governor with petitions for the release of a man impressed by a ship of war?"

"It has. Nevertheless, I cannot leave this man Jaccard, who has shared many dangers and privations with me, without an effort to save him from what to him would be worse than slavery."

Bienville spread his hands in the manner of one who is helpless in the face of insanity and illogic.

"I will speak frankly to you," he said. "In his letters to me, my brother, the Chevalier d'Iberville, more than once mentioned you, and I myself have had some opportunity of observing you. I know more about you than you perhaps think."

"And what is your conclusion from this knowledge?"

"That you have a record somewhat erratic."

"Erratic?" I cried. "Is it then erratic to fight for the King of France from the snows of the Arctics to the tropical forests of the Gulf? Erratic to risk my life, run the peril of death by torture, times without number

against the bloody Iroquois and their allies, the English? Ha! Is it erratic
to toil with my handful of men for the first time civilized beings have
been up the Red River, as I did five years ago, as far as the man-eating
Attacapa savages and the Natchitoches tribesmen? Is it erratic to spend
my young manhood in leather and on hard fare, carrying weapons on
the frontiers, when I might have enjoyed silks, good wines, and pretty
women, in the court of the Governor at Quebec?"

Bienville heard me out, his glacier face never changing.

"You have enterprise," he said. "You have courage, even audacity—
this is conceded. But there are whispers"—he glanced cunningly up
under his eyebrows—"of certain smuggling operations, whereby furs
passed down the Great Lakes without paying the King's levy—ah, do
not take time to deny it, I make no direct accusations—and there are,
furthermore, tales of a more romantic nature—and of quarrels——"

"I admit," said I stiffly, "that I have had my little difficulties. A gentleman must protect his honor."

"Even from husbands?"

It was a shrewd thrust, and I felt my face redden. "As to that, perhaps I did exchange shots or cross swords——"

"Tut, tut! Name me no names. I merely wished to show that I am
not entirely ignorant of your doings." Bienville paused. "Nevertheless,
if I were now Governor, I would grant you the trading field you seek,
for I believe in your hardihood and daring—though meantime I might
perhaps take what precautions were needful to protect the interest of
the government."

"I—I thank you," said I, making a stiff little bow, for I was uncertain
as to how I should take this rather ambiguous compliment.

Bienville returned the bow with irony.

"However," he went on, "I am not Governor. I would only be a hin-
drance to you in any plan you have, for Cadillac holds me in no affection. In point of fact, I may have done you a disservice already—
without intending it—merely by inviting you into this house. Those
who have dealings with Bienville these days are suspect on Dauphin
Island."

"Seigneur," I said at this, "I do not ask your help with the Governor.
And if your hospitality has been of disadvantage to me, I nevertheless
am grateful for it."

It seemed somewhat to please him, and he motioned me to a seat.

"Since you are determined to undertake the uncertain quicksands of Cadillac's court," he said, "and since I may have slightly prejudiced your cause, it is only fair that I give you some information that may be of help to you."

"I shall be your debtor."

"If Cadillac has little love for me," Bienville said, "his wife and daughter have less."

"He has only one daughter?"

"He has three, but two are in convent school in France."

"Of what sort is his wife?"

"Madame is, I believe, a woman of considerable determination."

I smiled. "A somewhat tepid compliment, I should say, in describing a lady. What of the daughter?"

"The daughter is more remarkable. She is commonly spoken of as La Demoiselle, as if she were the only demoiselle in the colony." Bienville gave one of his rare, cold smiles. "Not only has she her mother's determination, but she possesses other qualities."

"Such as?"

"Everything that can make a woman formidable. Wit, intelligence, beauty——"

"I should call these qualities exemplary."

"But also vanity, selfishness, and that peculiar feminine lack of scruple which sometimes makes women disastrous."

"These things can be expected, almost forgiven, in a beauty."

"To me," Bienville said, "her beauty is like the beauty of death."

"Death?" I could not help being struck by the simile.

"Death can be attractive under certain circumstances," he said seriously.

All at once I thought of the woman of the *calèche*, and her pale, almost eerie beauty.

"Does this daughter ride in a *calèche* driven like the chariot of Jehu, with four outriders?" I asked.

"That could only be La Demoiselle," said Bienville.

"Then I have spoken to her."

"When?"

"This afternoon. One of her men struck Marbot with a whip. I dragged him off his horse and gave him a lashing."

"What did she do?"

"She seemed furious at first. Then she calmed. And finally, when she left me, she said she hoped I would not be disappointed when I visited the Governor. I wondered at the time, but now I understand that saying."

"Since you conversed with her, tell me your opinion of her," he said.

"I think she would be passionate, impulsive, furious both in love and hate—in a word, intriguing."

"True," nodded Bienville. "In fact, an understatement—if you enjoy the intrigue of danger."

"You speak of her as La Demoiselle," I said, "but I addressed her as Madame. She seemed of an age to be wed."

"That is one of the odd things about her. She is, I understand, near her thirtieth year, and she has both beauty and position, yet she has never taken a husband." Bienville twisted his eyebrows. "I have heard, however, that though she is unwed, La Demoiselle is hardly a virgin."

"Truly?" I pursed my lips. This is always an interesting matter to discover about a woman, particularly a pretty one.

"Do not let it lead you into misconceptions," he warned. "Her whim is Cadillac's law."

"The Governor dotes on her?"

"More, much more. He *depends* on her."

"For what reason?"

But at that moment Solta entered to announce dinner. Bienville rose.

"Let us go in," he said. "Since I am under a cloud, I live alone these days. Whereas I never sat down with less than twenty at table when I was Governor, I now usually break bread by myself. Your company is therefore welcome, and I trust you will not find our fare too bad."

Nor could I, during the excellent meal that followed, bring him back to the subject we had been discussing. Instead, Bienville avoided it in such a way that out of politeness I felt impelled to drop it.

4. "You Are a Barbarian, Monsieur"

"The coat, Marbot."

"Yes, Monsieur."

It was the morning following my long conversation with Bienville, and I was dressing, somewhat grimly, for my effort to obtain an interview with the new Governor. From the apparel which had been unpacked from my baggage and which now littered the room, Marbot, whom I had impressed into service as a valet, held up the garment for which I asked, with an expression somewhat rueful.

"*Peste!*" I exclaimed.

The coat, for which I had paid more good livres than I could well afford, was of soft mouse-colored leather, the hue, cut, and material very much in the mode in Quebec, and it had been my especial pride. But in our long journey south, during which we frequently encountered the elements, it had become stained, even though it was carefully packed. A large discolored blotch ran down the middle of the back and another up the right sleeve almost to the elbow.

For a moment I stared at it, then shrugged. "It is the best I have, and there is no time to get another. Help me into it."

"*Mon Dieu!*" exclaimed Marbot, as he obeyed. "It fits most tightly!"

"It is supposed to have a snug fit."

"But—like a corset, Monsieur?"

"Corset? What is this about corsets?" I spoke a little sharply, for truth to tell the garment did seem to have shrunk somewhat when its back was wetted and stained. "A gentleman's coat is supposed to conform to his figure," I added with more dignity.

"But—how can you breathe, Monsieur?"

"I breathe well enough!" I snapped. "No, the bottom six buttons are left open, for the elegant flaring of the coat skirts——"

"Pardon, Monsieur, but when left open in that manner it appears more than ever like a corset——"

This was past bearing.

"Marbot!" I almost shouted. "Give me credit for knowing how to wear my clothes, without comments from a—a woods runner!"

Marbot's face took on a sullen expression, and with some reason, for if he was a woods runner, then so was I.

"Now give me the baldric for my sword," I commanded. "No, not the sash first, you fool! Did you never see a gentleman dressed for polite society? The sash goes on last, to bind the baldric to the body."

Then, seeing how crestfallen he looked, I added, more kindly, "I fear me that trying to make a valet out of a free hunter like you, is akin to asking a wolf to fetch game like a dog."

At this approach to an apology, Marbot recovered his spirits. I examined myself in the wall mirror. The mouse-colored coat fitted me well—almost too well, as some of the tightly pulled buttons suggested—and the pantaloons were of the same material and color. High, soft boots reached my thighs, with the tops turned down to reveal cinnamon-brown linings. Silver spurs jingled on my heels, and at my throat was a white lace jabot. Over my right shoulder hung the wide baldric, embroidered and richly fringed, and I hoped that its breadth across my back would cover at least some of the stain on the coat. From the baldric at my left hip hung my cut-and-thrust sword of good French make, and the scarlet sash about my waist gave a fine flare of color, which was matched by the curling scarlet plume—perhaps a little crushed in transit—of my wide hat. Lastly, I pulled on my hands tight gauntlets of doeskin, reaching almost to my elbows and trimmed with lace.

When partly concealed by the baldric across the back and the gauntlets on the sleeves, the weather stains on the coat did not appear nearly so glaring and I gazed at myself with more confidence. One of my small weaknesses was a fondness for fine feathers, and I hoped that I did not look too badly.

"What is your opinion, Marbot?" I asked. "Do I present an appearance sufficiently good for an audience with the Governor?"

"Yes, Monsieur, except——"

"Except what? Always, it appears, you have some reservation!"

"If Monsieur had a wig—a beautiful, curled peruke——"

"A thousand thunders! Why a wig, Marbot? One might suppose you a member of the Académie des Perruquiers! After all, what is a wig? A mere fad of fashion!"

"A fad established, so I have heard, by the King's own majesty, Monsieur."

"And suppose it is! Kings are but human and sometimes forestall their own plans. Our Louis, growing bald in his old age, began to wear a wig to give him the appearance of youth among his ancient courtiers. *Allons,* everyone came out with a wig in imitation of the King, and Louis was no better off than before."

Nevertheless, I again contemplated my head in the mirror. My hair, which was very black and thick, was well combed, tied at the back with a scarlet ribbon, and hung to my shoulders. My complacency left me.

"Vraiment," I admitted, "to wear one's own hair these days is something of a confession." Again I glanced at the mirror and gave a little sigh. "Perhaps I might borrow a peruke from Bienville."

Marbot brightened, but then I shook my head. "No, that would require cutting short my hair. And you know how the Indians regard a close-cropped head. They believe that a warrior worthy of respect leaves his hair long so that a foe, if victorious, may more easily take his scalp."

"True, Monsieur." Marbot knew he had lost his point.

"A savage notion of a chivalrous practice." I shrugged. "After all, we cannot afford to lose face with the people upon whom, if we are lucky, we may shortly be trying to make a good impression, can we?"

"No, Monsieur." Marbot spoke almost sadly.

"At least I cut a better figure than I did in buckskins, you agree?"

"Yes, Monsieur."

"The boatman is ready?"

"He has been waiting this hour," said Marbot.

"In my absence, what will you do? Sit in a dramshop?"

"Not I, Monsieur! I received my lesson last night. Today I shall stay sober. The *cassette* girls are to be landed this morning." He grinned at the thought. "Perhaps I shall watch."

"Take care that none of the *cassette* girls catches you."

"The greatest of care, Monsieur."

"You might wish the press gang had caught you instead."

"True, most true, Monsieur." The rascal looked so demure that I almost laughed.

"*Bien.*" I cocked my hat a little farther over one eye and strode out of the room.

2.

The day was fine; the sun, three quarters toward the zenith, touched the little wavelets of the bay with ten thousand sapphire jewel flashes. Sturdily the boatman, an old fisherman with a face like seamed leather, pulled at his oars, sending the skiff toward Dauphin Island, which lay athwart the entrance to the bay.

Sitting in the stern of the little boat, I scowled across the water at the *Maréchal d'Estrées,* with her towering masts, her gun ports, and the rich carving of wood on her stern and quarter galleries. Somewhere below decks on that ship was Jaccard.

All at once I became aware of a strange confused babble, and saw that about the ship of war clustered a number of small boats.

"*Nom de Dieu,* what is that racket?" I asked.

The boatman grinned. "The *cassette* girls. They're taking them ashore. Poor creatures, they've been cooped up too long aboard the ship. Listen to that clack!"

Thirty female voices, all raised at once, scolding, complaining, laughing, screeching and chattering, made a cacophony far-carrying and unmistakable.

Already one of the boats was headed toward the docks, its course such that it passed our skiff at a distance of perhaps thirty fathoms. I gazed at it curiously. Two seamen were rowing, and an underofficer sat at the tiller. There were in it six women, all moderately young, all dressed in finery somewhat tawdry, their luggage heaped in the middle. Four of them waved and called shrill greetings across the water, to which the old boatman grinned and shouted back. Two remained silent, one looking intently toward the shore, the other apparently weeping. In each of the six was evident a different form of excitement, almost hysteria.

"Many are at the wharf to greet them," the boatman said. "It is always a great curiosity to see the women come in."

I glanced back. The docks seemed to be black with people. Marbot, I reflected, probably was in that crowd.

"Some of the women do not seem to relish their future," I commented.

"They shouldn't feel too badly," said the boatman. "Women, on the whole, do well enough in this colony. My own wife, Clothilde, was a *cassette* girl, and, though she has a husband somewhat old, and now a baby somewhat young, she has nothing else to complain about."

"What will happen to these?"

"They will be housed in the dormitory we call the 'Nunnery,' with Madame Didrot, who is nicknamed the 'Abbess,' to regulate them until they get their bearings and make some sort of an alliance."

"With men?"

"With men of course, Monsieur. What other alliance would women make?" The boatman paused to light a short clay pipe before he resumed his oars. "Any that are comely always go fast. Unfortunately, they are few." He made a grimace. "Crows—cats—cows—these are what we chiefly get. Paris keeps what is worth while in the female line and sends us the castoffs."

The women in the passing boat were of an inferior class, I acknowledged to myself; quite evidently, as Bienville said, from the Hôpital Général, that asylum of feminine flotsam, and probably here against their will. Hard-eyed and calculating, some of them. Broken-spirited and hopeless, others. Pathetic all. I hoped the poor creatures who already, certes, had experienced enough of life's evil, might find better fortune in this new world to which they had come.

Then I turned my face again toward Dauphin Island, and my mind occupied itself with my own problems. Cadillac, by reputation, was arrogant, and Bienville had indicated that it was difficult to gain audience with him, still harder to obtain from him any favor. Furthermore there was an added obstacle to surmount—the new Governor was said to detest Canadians.

But then I thought of poor Jaccard, in irons below decks on that grim ship, where the system of brutal discipline would break his spirit or kill him once the *Maréchal d'Estrées* left port and the routine of her voyage began. Jaccard had been with me in Canada, and on my various expeditions in Louisiana. At times he, and Marbot also, had been in the thick of battle with me, when the arrows flew and muskets thudded among the forest trees, and the howling of the Iroquois was like the hunting cry of wild beasts who have the smell of blood in their nostrils. They had stood by me manfully then; I could not do less for one of them now.

I had with me the package of letters from Canada, and it had given me more than a little thought, trying to reason out the rights of the matter. It was not as easy as fighting, for I was pulled two ways.

The messages probably were written to Bienville, though they were addressed to the *Governor*. In his cold way, Bienville had been most kind and hospitable to me. Never, in fact, had I experienced such condescension from the least likable of the Le Moyne brothers. Why did Bienville take this sudden interest in me, even to the extent of speaking quite frankly his mind about the new regime, when never before, in all the years I had known him, had he so much as warmed that chilling reserve which so characterized him?

One possible reason suggested itself: Bienville, man of ice that he was, had the vision of all the Le Moynes, the continental scope of the great chess game between France, England, and Spain. Ambitious for himself he no doubt was; but still he was loyal also to his King.

Since he deemed Cadillac unfit to govern Louisiana, especially under the sordid conditions of the Crozat concession, he would not hesitate to undermine that official in all possible ways, hoping, at Cadillac's failure, to recover the chief power himself: for reasons perhaps selfish, and yet not entirely selfish, either. It would be natural for him to estimate all factors, and I, who had been Iberville's close follower and friend, might fit well in his plans. A hope to win me to his cause, once he had sounded me out and found that our views were somewhat similar, could account for his sudden change in attitude.

All in all, I was not entirely unsympathetic with Bienville's position. But there were other considerations, to me more immediate. I must save poor Jaccard's hide first, and in any test of loyalties my follower came ahead of the cold former Governor.

I had, furthermore, my own destiny to think about: and I added to myself, as if to convince myself of the rectitude of what I contemplated, Bienville himself had said that by his very hospitality he might have injured my cause with Cadillac. It was, I argued, the more reason that the letters I carried should be used to further that cause, after they had served what purpose I could find for them in the interest of Jaccard.

And yet, after all these arguments with myself, I still felt an uneasy sense, almost of guilt, as our boat neared Dauphin Island.

3.

When I landed I put these doubts aside and even managed something of a swagger, gauntleted hand on sword hilt, wide skirts of my coat ruffling in the breeze, and plumed hat cocked aggressively on the side of my head, as my long booted legs strode toward the gate of the wooden stockade surrounding the residency of the Governor.

Two sentries at the gate came to an ominous *porte* with their bayoneted muskets, and I halted.

"Your business?" demanded one of them.

"I seek audience with the Governor," I replied.

"You have an appointment?"

"No."

"His Excellency sees nobody without appointment."

"He will see *me*." I spoke with perhaps more assurance than I really felt.

It seemed, however, to have its effect. "You have a *carte d'identité?*" the sentry asked.

"I bear dispatches," I told him.

"From whom?"

"The royal Governor of Canada."

With an air of dubiety, coupled with heightened respect, the two soldiers regarded me as if puzzled as to their duty under these exceptional circumstances. Then they spoke together in low tones and presently one went to the residency while the other held me at the gate.

Minutes passed. I had opportunity to observe my surroundings. Rambling and awkward, built of rough stone held together by mason's mortar and a framework of heavy timbers, the residency was of a single story, except for its central part where it rose to two, with a steep roof of shakes, and dormers of Norman style, and an iron-clamped door pierced for musket fire.

Surrounding it was a square log palisade, from the corners of which brass cannon peered through embrasures. The whole array was inexpressibly crude, raw and new, as were the few other structures I could see on the island—cabins, small houses, and what evidently was a barracks building of logs, for the soldiers. On a high platform overlooking the sea a lookout was posted; and a squad of recruits, evidently fresh from France, drilled awkwardly at the bellowing of a sergeant.

All of this advertised the constant threat of an attack by cruising hostile ships; yet it took no very experienced eye to see that if an enemy man-of-war chose to heave to off the island and let fly a broadside or so, not much would be left of these feeble fortifications.

I thought of the Château St. Louis at Quebec, with its lofty walls of dressed stone, its towers and steep slated roofs; and of the convents and monasteries, the bishop's palace, the residences of nobles and rich factors, the fortifications standing about it, and the cathedral raising its spires beyond. That—even that—was but poor and squalid compared to the great royal edifices of France, but it was dignity and magnificence compared to this. As a loyal Frenchman it seemed to me shameful that a King's governor should have to dwell in such surroundings.

But now the door of the residency opened and a slim, sprig youth, very bouffant as to coat skirts, very mincing as to pace, very supercilious as to manner, advanced down the path toward the gate, followed at a respectful distance by the sentry who had summoned him.

"Monsieur?" he said to me, with a stare that made me feel uncomfortably conscious of the stains on my coat, and my wigless head.

The stripling had a very small, almost invisible silky mustache, a yellow peruke, and a face as fair as a girl's; but I did not doubt that he fenced, wenched, and gambled like all the other cockerels of hell, his fellows of the garrison.

Hauteur, however, can be met with hauteur, and it has never been easy to face me down merely with a look.

"Whom do I have the honor of addressing?" I said harshly.

With exaggerated and satiric courtesy, he replied, "Ensign Étienne de la Crevillon, officer of the guard this day."

"Ensign?" I barked at him. "Since when have ensigns of the line achieved a rank to parley with a personal courier of a royal Governor?"

The startled youngster drew himself erect, almost saluted. But the weather stains on my coat restored his confidence somewhat.

"I was informed that you bear dispatches," he said.

"I do."

"Display those dispatches."

I thrust my head and jaw forward with a glare. "The dispatches I carry are not to be opened save by His Excellency's own hand!"

The ensign was visibly shaken by my manner, but he rallied.

"I fear that will hardly do," he said, "we are under orders."

I spurned that, and scorned the speaker. "The Abbé La Vente is here?" I demanded.

"*Certainement.*"

"Go at once and tell him that the Chevalier Louis Juchereau de St. Denis awaits with the correspondence *of which he knows!*"

It was evident that the name of the Governor's secretary-chaplain, and the emphasis on the last four words, carried weight. Young Crevillon hesitated, moistened his lips nervously with his tongue, and finally turned toward the residency.

"Be so good as to follow me, Monsieur," he said.

4.

Without another word he led the way, entered the door into a hall, down which he proceeded, and ushered me into a large waiting room, evidently leading to the audience chamber.

"You will wait here," he said, passing through a door before which, at rigid attention, stood two armed soldiers.

I gazed about me. In the anteroom were at least a dozen persons, all seated. Some of those thus cooling their heels were elegantly attired, others in military uniform, two or three wore the sober garb of merchants, and one, in the white silks of an officer of the French navy, obviously was from the *Maréchal d'Estrées*, lying out there in the harbor.

Since every chair and bench was occupied, I was left standing. Without pretense of politeness my predecessors turned their stares on me, so that for perhaps the dozenth time that day I was reminded of my hair and my stains, and the inevitable mental observations they must arouse in these gentlemen. I therefore deliberately turned my back on them, flaunting, as it were, my very dilapidation, with a sort of angered defiance. Behind me I heard whispers, and a snigger, not loud enough to be understood, but assuredly concerning me, and derisive.

Then the door to the audience chamber opened, and I turned to see Abbé La Vente step forth, followed by Ensign Crevillon. At the priest's appearance every man of the waiting crowd leaped to his feet and began showering him with questions and demands.

"How long, Monsieur l'Abbé, must I be kept waiting?"

"Have you presented my name and message to His Excellency?"

"These two hours have I sat here without an answer!"

"Surely, by this time, my business, which is pressing, must have come to the Governor's attention!"

"Softly, softly, Messieurs," replied La Vente to these queries and ejaculations, and it was evident that he relished his position as arbiter of the order of precedence before the Governor. "You will be informed in good time when His Excellency can see you. He has much business to attend, and you are all required to display patience."

Then he came directly over to me.

"Monsieur," he said in his bullfrog voice, "be pleased to step with me for a moment to the outer terrace."

Giving no heed to the looks of surprise and annoyance with which the others saw me thus singled out for especial attention, he led the way through a side door out into an enclosed garden.

This small area was surrounded on three sides by wings of the building and screened on the fourth from vulgar eyes by a thick hedge of flowering shrubs. It was graveled, with flower beds, shrubbery trimmed in formal shapes, and provided here and there with a few benches and seats of wrought iron. The prospect, which was rather charming, was Bienville's doing, while he occupied the residency. Obviously it was a private pleasance, to which the present Governor's family could gain access from the two-story residential wing on the far side, through an entrance screened from my sight by a large clump of decorative shrubs occupying the center of the area, at a place where normally a fountain would have been situated.

Closing the door carefully behind him, La Vente drew me a few paces down one of the walks, shot a cautious glance about him, and when he was sure he was not overheard, said in a lowered voice, "You have with you the dispatches?"

"I have," said I.

"Did you not inform me yesterday that they were addressed to Bienville?"

"I thought, at the time, that Bienville was Governor."

"And so?" A cunning side glance from the lean, saturnine visage.

"I have since learned that Bienville is no longer Governor. It is for that reason I am here."

"Ah? But Bienville—he has, of course, seen the messages?"

"He is not aware that they exist. I did not think it necessary to mention them to him."

"And yet you are a friend of his, and accepted his hospitality?"

"I should not presume to say friend. Rather an acquaintance. It is true that last night I slept under his roof."

A long, slow, appraising glance from La Vente. "It is in my mind, Monsieur St. Denis," he said, "that you are capable of some things I had not suspected of you."

"I am capable, Monsieur l'Abbé, of following my orders as I understand them, and of guarding my own destiny."

La Vente favored me with a sly grin. "Of the last, at least, I am assured. And it induces me to believe that an understanding can be reached between the two of us which may be of mutual advantage."

"Make yourself clear."

"You have some petition to lay before His Excellency? I will facilitate it, and I think I can promise you at least careful consideration, which is as much as anyone can count on these days. Perhaps it may even receive a favorable decision." Again that appraising grin. "Meantime, since the routine of procedure, and my office as secretary to the Governor both require that I sift all correspondence—otherwise His Excellency would be burdened with excessive numbers of useless communications—you will entrust the letters to me, so that I may in due course bring them to his attention——"

I shook my head. "As I told you, I deliver them in person."

He hesitated, then said coldly, "If you refuse to conform to the rules of the Governor's court, Monsieur, you may find it difficult to obtain the audience you seem to desire."

"Why are you so eager to read this correspondence?" I asked bluntly.

The priest was silent.

"You know what it concerns, perhaps?" I persisted.

La Vente turned on his heel. "Whatever it concerns, my motives at least do not concern you," he said in a voice that rumbled with irritation. "I appear to have wasted my time, when I but sought to befriend you. You may wait in the anteroom. Perhaps the Governor may eventually get around to you. I cannot promise."

Abruptly he walked toward the door from which we had come into the garden.

As, more slowly, I followed his gaunt gowned figure, with the coarse robe swishing about its sandaled feet and its tonsured head bent, I confessed to myself that I was unable to feel for myself any deeper respect than La Vente evidently felt. And yet, somehow, I thought I was doing as right a thing as I knew how in this sea of complications that had arisen.

5.

The Abbé already had passed into the residency, and I, following, was within a few paces of the door, when I heard a woman's laugh. I halted. A moment later, to my surprise, a large ball of India rubber, gaily painted with alternating lozenges of red and white, such as children play with, came bounding from behind the clump of bushes across the garden toward me. It rolled to my feet, and, hardly thinking, I stooped and picked it up.

Immediately a fantastic figure came leaping after it—a little Negro boy, perhaps ten years old, clad in Moorish pantaloons and slippers of scarlet silk, a blue jacket with a working of scarlet and yellow beads, and a very tall yellow turban. Such a costume is sometimes seen on the trained monkeys which street troubadours in Paris carry about with them to attract crowds with their antics at the playing of the fiddle, and to collect small coins in a cup from spectators.

The child stumbled over a shrub in his haste, and halted, staring openmouthed at me.

"Give me the ball, Monsieur!" he begged. "Please give it——"

"Did you throw it, little man?" I asked. "See, you have broken that shrub with your galloping."

"No, I did not throw it—but I must fetch it——"

From behind the clump that screened the door of the opposite wing a woman called, "Pepi, hurry! The ball! Bring the ball!"

I recognized the voice. Acting on an impulse which even then my better judgment told me was unwise, I walked across the garden toward the island of foliage. Then I stopped stock still.

From around the shrubbery stepped the lady of the *calèche*—La Demoiselle, the Governor's daughter. With her was Captain Noirel, the dram-bottle look quite evident this morning, and his toplofty manner hardly diminished by a bandage across his forehead.

She was the first to speak. "Monsieur—St. Denis—I believe?" Her voice was cold and devoid of expression.

I bowed as deeply and humbly as I could. "Mademoiselle, your servant."

"Ah," she said bitingly, "he has a tongue. And he does us the honor of proving that besides being a whip wielder, he is also a mighty wrester from children of their toys."

"The ball came to me. I but thought——"

"It now appears that he also thinks," she said in the same icy voice. "Perhaps he will explain this intrusion into the Governor's private garden."

"This man is trespassing!" broke in Noirel. "I will call the guard and have him seized!"

I had begun to collect my wits, and to realize that I was perhaps guilty of a serious offense in blundering across the private garden of the Governor, without invitation or permission, instead of following La Vente quietly and quickly to the anteroom. If I were to avert the consequences of this folly, I must in some manner avert the anger of La Demoiselle. I therefore deliberately turned my attention and my tongue on Noirel.

"Make certain, Monsieur le Capitaine," I said, "that *this* time you have a strong guard of men to do your work for you. Today you behold me again, but this time with a sword, instead of the candlestick which was the only weapon I had to oppose your rapier yesterday." I allowed my eyes to rest on the bandage across his forehead.

Noirel's face flushed scarlet as he took a menacing step forward, his hand falling on his hilt.

"No vagabond brush captain of Canadian scum dare so speak to me——"

"I am neither vagabond, brush captain, nor scum. And I proclaim such a statement as a slur and slander, as well as a falsehood!"

"By the gullet of God! You give me the lie?"

"A matter of interpretation, Captain. I said the *statement* was a lie. You, perhaps, repeated it out of misapprehension and will retract it?"

I must have made a somewhat paradoxical figure there in the Governor's garden, in stained coat and hat with broken plume, yet sneering at the bullyragging captain. In La Demoiselle's eyes glimmered amusement.

But no amusement was in Noirel's face. "For that I would kill you," he cried in a choked voice, "if one of the blood of Du Tyrac could stoop to cross swords with a woods runner!"

"You speak of woods runners," I said, deliberately baiting my man. "Permit me to suggest that my family was already old in the time of Henry of Navarre. The title of the first Marquis du Tyrac, if memory does not play me false, was created in the present reign—a couch consideration, was it not, during the ministry of the Italian Cardinal?* I believe that any pursuivant would say that a St. Denis of the direct line is at least the equal of a *cadet* of the Du Tyracs."

There was a moment of stunned silence. I had uttered the deadliest of gibes, for it was an open secret that the complaisance of the first Marquis du Tyrac, who was able to blind himself to the gay abandon of his wife, who yielded herself first to the bed of the Minister of State, and then of the youthful King himself, had secured for him the title and patent of nobility. More than one aristocratic family of France owed its rise to the charming promiscuity of its women; but to be reminded of it was not palatable to Noirel for all that.

"This is too much!" he roared, whipping out his blade.

I drew also, but I was reluctant, in spite of my badgering words, to cross with him. The Captain was by repute a skillful and deadly fencer, and I probably was no match for him in swordsmanship at my best, while at present I was very much out of practice and rusty. Almost I could already feel the point pricking my ribs.

Then La Demoiselle laughed out loud: a silver tinkle, almost cruel. "Desist, desist, Messieurs!" she cried. "I will not have you quarrel here!"

"Here—anywhere—I do not care!" said Noirel furiously. "This impertinent woods cock needs his comb clipped!"

"I forbid it!" La Demoiselle's voice was sharp and imperious. "What, trample my rosebushes like a pair of buffaloes with your brawling? On my honor, you will answer for it—both of you—if you do not cease this unseemly disturbance instantly!"

---

* The reference is to Giulio, Cardinal Mazarin, born in Italy, but a naturalized Frenchman, who succeeded Cardinal Richelieu as minister of state and served in that capacity in the latter years of the life of Louis XIII, and through the youth of Louis XIV, until his death in 1661, when the young King was twenty-three years old.

Noirel hesitated, and seemed to control himself by a mighty effort. Sheathing his sword, he turned toward her where she stood with up-lifted chin, commanding obedience.

"Mademoiselle," he said, his voice still thick with rage, "your lightest wish is my law." His eye hardened as he turned again on me. "As for you—you will answer to me—soon, and at a more suitable time and place!"

I do not think I can be accused of timorousness, yet I owned to a feeling of relief when the other's sword went into its scabbard. Satisfied now that I had erected a quarrel so personal that the Captain was hardly likely to call the guard, I also sheathed my weapon, and turned my attention to the woman.

"Mademoiselle," I said, doffing my hat and sweeping the ground with it, in my bow.

"What have you to say in explanation?" she demanded.

"Only this: heaven itself would forgive a poor cavalier who, hearing your voice, did not aspire to behold its author."

"You knew my voice?"

"Among ten thousand!"

"Continue." She did not seem displeased, but I gained from her an odd impression, as of a cat playing with a mouse.

"When I saw the ball," I said, "rolling to my feet, it came over me that, greatly presuming, I might use it as an excuse—however lame—to gaze once more on beauty I had seen all too briefly."

But I laid it on very broadly, too broadly even for a woman who loved flattery.

"You did indeed presume," she said, so coldly that my heart sank. "Did it occur to you that for this act you may face prison and the whip-ping post?"

"Mademoiselle must know that for a great privilege a man will some-times take great risks."

It was bold, and perhaps I had been too bold before: but boldness, I have found, is sometimes esteemed by women as a tribute to them, provided it is clothed in seeming respect.

For moments that ticked slowly she studied me silently, with the veiled scrutiny of a woman of the world, who can look over and estimate a man in a manner very similar to that with which a man looks over a passing girl. Every detail her eyes took in: my breadth of shoulder, my face heavily tanned in contrast to the simpering pallor of the elegants of her father's court, my black hair worn without a wig, even the weather stains on my costume. I must have seemed a novelty to her; a variation from that to which she was accustomed. And novelty was pleasing to one of her capricious and self-indulgent nature.

"You are a barbarian, Monsieur," she said at last.

Again I bowed. "I cannot deny it. Yet even a barbarian knows the brilliance of a star in the heavens when he sees it."

She seemed inwardly to smile at that, less in pleased vanity than in that it perhaps touched some chord of shrewd perception. Then she said, "It is in my mind that you may not be as great a barbarian as I thought."

"Mademoiselle is kind," I murmured.

But immediately she hardened again. "The less excuse for bursting into my garden! There is little kindness in me, Monsieur. Only a disposition to do what pleases me. You do not please me!"

"Mademoiselle!" I fell back a step in consternation, for her face had gone suddenly cold and I was reminded of Bienville's phrase that her beauty was the beauty of death. At the same time I saw a secret triumph in Noirel's eyes.

But she was full of surprises. "If, for the second time, I choose to overlook your acts, what would you say?"

"That Mademoiselle is a fount of mercy—even though she denies her own kindness."

"Then explain your presence in this garden."

Noirel cleared his throat harshly. "Surely, Mademoiselle, you will not permit this impertinence to be given an excuse——"

So fiercely did she turn on him that for all his self-assurance he seemed to shrink.

"Impertinence, Captain?" she cried. "It appears to me that the greatest impertinence is to tell me how I am to act! On my honor, I am fully capable of conducting my own affairs!"

"I only sought——"

"I am weary of your importunities, Captain! It will please me if you leave at once!"

For a moment rage, humiliation, and something else struggled in the man's face, as he stood silent before the cold beauty. Then, as he saw that she waited for his obedience with no thought of relenting, he bowed and tramped away, unable to speak because of his choked feelings, leaving us alone in the garden.

Hardly knowing what to say after this tempest, I waited, hat in hand.

"Come," she said, "your explanation!"

"I was brought into the garden by Abbé La Vente," I began.

"For what reason?"

"He wished to speak with me alone."

"So the Abbé is interested in you? A very reynard is our Abbé. And what did he desire to discuss so intimately with you?"

For some reason—a caprice, an inspiration, a sudden pride, I know not what—I withheld the true reason for La Vente's interest.

"I have a grievance to place before the Governor," I said.

"The nature of this grievance?"

"A man of mine, named Jaccard, was last night seized by a press gang from the *Maréchal d'Estrées*."

"A close friend?"

"Say rather a follower. A *coureur de bois*, but he has been faithful——"

"You seek my father's intercession for a woods runner?"

"This man, Mademoiselle, has on occasion saved my life!"

My face must have shown my feeling, and again she studied me.

"You have curious eyes, Monsieur," she said unexpectedly. "They are strangely pale in your dark skin. I am interested in eyes, for I regard them as the true mirrors of character. When Captain Noirel drew on you just now, your eyebrows became one straight black line and the pupils of your eyes seemed to contract to the size of icy rapier points. It strikes me that you are a dangerous man. I like dangerous men."

All this she said in a manner so impersonal, as if she were discussing the points of some horse of which she approved, that it left me somewhat confused and wondering.

"But you have not told me everything," she added.

"What do you mean, Mademoiselle?"

"I know La Vente. Passing well do I know Monsieur l'Abbé La Vente! He would not do a favor for his own mother unless there was in it some benefit for himself. Now what does he want from you?"

I hesitated, not knowing how to answer her.

"You may as well tell me," she went on. "I am disposed to be interested in you. I am bored, and you have given me an unexpected moment of diversion. Have you any conception of the dreariness of this place, after Paris—even after Quebec? If I do not soon end this exile—but, happily, it *must* soon be over!"

Her eyes lit with inward joy. Then they became intent again as she continued. "I think Noirel would have killed you had I not interfered. He is death with the rapier. In three years he had sixteen duels. That is one reason he was gazetted to this outpost in the colonies." She paused as if to let that sink in. "But at least you did not appear to fear him. And it gave me an opportunity I have been awaiting. Captain Noirel is too assiduous. It was time I taught him a lesson."

This extraordinary statement left me more speechless than before. If I read her implication correctly, Noirel was a suitor of hers, and that meant I had incurred an enmity more mortal than I thought. Yet for the moment I was more interested in the strange, pale beauty before me than I was in considering my difficulties with the captain.

"What happened at Fort Conde yesterday?" she demanded, suddenly changing her manner. "Do not forget I was there at the time. I advise you to discover it to me, for I will find it out."

It was true. I was in a cul-de-sac from which there was no escape.

"Mademoiselle," I said desperately, "you have placed your finger on the trouble of an unhappy gentleman."

"And it is?"

"A question of honor that touches me closely."

"Be explicit."

"I came to Mobile bearing letters from certain high personages in Canada. They are written, I suspect, to the Sieur de Bienville. But they are addressed to the royal Governor of Louisiana."

"Ah?"

"You see my dilemma? Bienville and the Governor are two different persons, although this was not known when the messages were given me to deliver. What is my duty?"

"A nice point," she said slowly. "Now I understand La Vente's interest—even Noirel's. To bring this correspondence, if it contains valuable information, first to my father's attention, might gain favor for him who did so. Further, to be privy to such knowledge, if the letters were opened and read, would place the holder in a position of new influence. Our two friends neglect no steps to advance themselves."

With the toe of her slipper she made little marks in the gravel, as if pondering. Then she looked up at me again.

"It amuses me to aid you," she said. "Partly this is because I dislike La Vente, who has grown too officious for my taste. Partly because Noirel needs further disciplining. But chiefly because of a certain curiosity which has grown in me. One does not often encounter, these days, a person concerned over questions of honor, and I am intrigued as to the outcome of your debate with yourself. Therefore, let us for the present say nothing of this to my father. Meantime, perhaps we can circumvent La Vente in the matter of seeing His Excellency."

In complete astonishment I gazed at her.

"I will impart to you a little secret," she went on. "Though the excellent Abbé tells those waiting for audience that my father is busy with the affairs of government so they must wait, the truth is that he overslept this morning. Probably he awoke in ill humor, an emotion—alas! —he often experiences after fitful slumber which is all too frequently his lot of late, what with the disappointments he has suffered, and the heavy duties he must bear."

All this was said with a peculiar inflection and odd emphasis, so that while the words sounded respectful and even seemed to show concern, I had the unavoidable impression that she was speaking with irony, like a spoiled young woman who is contemptuous of her elders, or perhaps too clearly sees their weaknesses.

"It is always well to allow him time for his breakfast," she added, "but I happen to know that he has finished eating and is now taking his chocolate. His temper should be mended. Come with me."

5. *The Sieur de Cadillac*

As she paced slowly beside me across the garden plot, her head hardly reaching to my shoulder, La Demoiselle was all smiles and charm; the change in her from the creature I had seen a few minutes before, menacing and imperious, so great that it would have been unbelievable had she not been a woman.

And even among women, to whom these shifts of mood and appearance seem to come with bewildering ease, she was remarkable, I reflected. The power of beauty was hers, in a graceful light figure, and a face strangely though unquestionably handsome, whether in anger or determination, or as now, in playful conversation such as any young, pretty, and empty-minded member of her sex might carry on. Yet about this one, as I well knew, there was nothing empty-minded.

Keeping up my end of the conversation was difficult, for I was the prey of bewildered and confused thoughts. Decidedly my position was anomalous. For better or worse I was at the disposition of the whims of this woman, a status new and not particularly pleasant to me. Evidently she was willing to take sides against Abbé La Vente, merely to spite him. Evidently, also, she enjoyed watching me squirm on the horns of my dilemma, for though she did not refer again to my dispatches, she must have had them in mind and she was not unaware of their possible importance. Bienville had said she ruled her father. It was believable.

"I must apologize," she said as we entered the wing of the residency devoted to the living quarters of the official family and servants. "This is still a camp rather than a civilized dwelling." She pointed to some men carrying in furniture from outside, and to women cleaning and polishing woodwork in the hall. "We are not yet fully moved in, and some of our effects have just been brought over from the ship. It takes time to settle into a house, and *this* one——" She broke off and gave a little shrug of distaste.

The workmen took care to stand respectfully out of her way as she conducted me down the hall to a small room where, looking out through a window upon the sea, sat a man alone at a round table, attended by two liveried servants. I knew instantly it was the Governor himself.

The first impression of Cadillac was hardly prepossessing. In his middle fifties, he was what is termed "well preserved," but showed the effects of petulance, nervous disability, and perhaps dissipation. His visage was an exaggerated likeness of that "Knight of the Rueful Countenance," immortalized by the Spanish writer Cervantes: and if he did not possess Don Quixote's unthinking foolhardiness, he did possess the cadaverous form and features that made the tilter at windmills a figure of satire. His many-curled peruke, with its long brown locks falling upon his shoulders, concealed his almost complete baldness, but his cheeks were fallen in, there were dark hollows under his deep-socketed eyes, and his nose, long and curving, with wide flaring nostrils, added a lugubrious touch to his whole appearance.

At the moment we entered, Cadillac, who was still finishing his chocolate, took up from the table a hand mirror to study his face; surveying it with apparent deep distaste, for it displayed indubitable evidences of approaching age. When he looked up and saw his daughter he thrust the mirror into the hands of a lackey, with an irritable exclamation.

"*Crevettes!*"* he said. "The shellfish of this coast are poison, as is everything else here! Those blotches on my cheeks and my coated tongue are the result of eating shrimp brought in yesterday from the Gulf, a sign that the humors of my body are again in a state of fermentation. You"—he indicated one of the servants—"bring me a dose of the physic which Gaspard, the physician, prescribed for me, and tell the chef that henceforth he is to serve me no more shellfish. Those *crevettes!* Bah!"

While one servant departed for the required medicine and the other began to take away the dishes, the Governor turned to us.

"Ah, *chérie!*" he said to his daughter. Then, more coldly, "Who is this person who accompanies you to my private breakfasting room?"

"A gentleman just arrived from Quebec, papa," replied La Demoiselle.

Cadillac's eyebrows shot up, then came down in a frown. "A Cana-

---

* *Crevettes*—prawns or shrimp

dian? I am sorry, Monsieur, if I do not seem cordial at the introduction. We have Canadians enough and too many in this colony—refuse who have thus far only cheated the gibbet of its due!"

So violently was this said that even though I had been warned of the Governor's contempt for Canadians, I was astonished in a most unpleasant way by it.

But at once Cadillac's voice became milder, as he added, "*Bien entendu*, Monsieur, I do not for one moment lump you with the baseborn muskeg jumpers who afflict us. Your quality is evident, and you will not take it that I meant anything I said as a personal affront."

I remained silent, reflecting that this apology was further evidence of the influence of the Governor's daughter.

"I do not believe I caught your name," he continued.

"Louis Juchereau de St. Denis, Chevalier of France, Your Excellency."

"Ah! A good name. I am acquainted with some of the continental members of your family. You can wear your quarterings, I take it?"

"Yes. We of Canada are of the direct line."

Cadillac nodded. "A gentleman is a gentleman, wherever he chances to be. Now that I think of it, there are a number of excellent families in Canada. Frontenac, of course, was of the *noblesse*. As also La Chesnaey, Dufresneau, and others of whom I can think, even including the Le Moynes, detestable as I have found them. It is the roistering, lazy, unruly commonality of Canada to which I object."

"Your Excellency," I said, "it is for one of that objectionable commonality that I come to ask justice of you."

Again the Governor's rather impressive eyebrows went up. "Justice from me? What justice?"

"This: I arrived in Mobile just yesterday with two men who are attached to my person. Last night one of them was seized against his will and carried aboard the *Maréchal d'Estrées*. I beg Your Excellency to order him freed."

"What?" rasped Cadillac. "Why should I intervene for such a fellow?"

"This man, Excellency, has a record of good service for his King."

"Then set your mind at rest," said the Governor with bitter cynicism. "He will continue in the service of his King."

"But—on a ship of war? This man knows nothing of the sea, and has no desire for it."

"He will be taught his duties fast enough, I am led to believe!"

With such choler did Cadillac say this, and with such an air of dismissing the subject and me with it, that I felt with a sinking heart that my intervention for poor Jaccard was unavailing. Yet there is in me a stubborn streak, and I made one more effort.

"This man, Jaccard, can do far more for the King, and also for you, Excellency, here on land than at sea," I said.

At this, which he may have considered an impertinence, Cadillac gave a snort, and was about to reply, perhaps devastatingly, but at the moment his servant returned with a wineglass filled with thick brown liquor. It evidently was the physic the doctor had ordered. Cadillac swallowed the dose, made a truly dreadful face, and hastened to drink a glass of sweet wine which the servant held ready, to take the taste from his mouth.

"Ugh!" he said. "What I suffer for my duty!"

Then, as if the bitter medicine had further heated his ire, he turned on me again.

"Your man would do more for *me,* you say? More for himself, rather! In this entire colony there is nobody of high or low degree who does not devote his entire thought to getting something from me! Is there one person willing to do something for the colony? If so, I have failed to find him. Decidedly, this place is inhabited by profligates steeped in vice, and vagabonds without subordination to the laws, without respect for religion, or for government! And miracles are expected of me! The cause of it? Fictions of the fabulists! Has it been asserted that there are mines in the Mississippi country and elsewhere? It is a deliberate error. Has a set of writers of romance published that this country is a paradise? Its beauty and utility are phantoms of the mind. I protest that I have never seen anything so worthless! I know how to govern as well as anybody, but poverty and shiftlessness are twin morasses through which progress can be made by no administrator, however able!"

Throughout this tirade I stood silent. But when the Governor stopped for breath, I spoke.

"May it please Your Excellency, if you are seeking a man who is willing to do something for the colony—I can suggest such a one."

Cadillac bent on me a look none too friendly. "Who is this man?"

"Myself."

The Governor's face was even more wrathful and his lip curled as he looked me up and down, taking in my shabbiness and stains.

"And what might *you* propose for this colony, Monsieur Oldclothes?"
he sneered.

The gibe stung, but I showed nothing of it in my face. I saw the
Governor's daughter, standing beside the table, her eyes on me as if
to see what answer I could give.

"You have spoken of mines and agriculture," I said. "I venture to
suggest a third means of profit to the colony—French trade."

From Bienville I understood that commerce had become a paramount
consideration because of Crozat's interest in Louisiana. Cadillac's sudden calculating look confirmed it.

"French trade, you say? In what manner?" he asked.

"I would set up relations of friendly exchange with the Natchez
Indians of the Mississippi country."

"Ah! You know these Indians, I presume?"

"I have visited them. They live in eight populous towns, worship the
sun, cultivate crops, weave cloth, and have some wealth in goods and
fur. Trade with them would be profitable for the colony."

"And for the trader, too, I suppose?" He gave me a cunning glance.

"It should work both ways."

"It is reported that the Natchez are dangerous. You know their
reputation?"

"I would erect a fort and take my chances."

Still more cunning grew the Governor's look. "And I suppose you
would ask a monopoly for this trade?"

"How else could I be certain of making a success of it?"

"Where would you get the goods?"

"Furnished me by your order. On a commission basis."

"I thought so!" Cadillac's voice was triumphant. Then he scowled
again. "Always there is an eel under the rock! A fine proposal—merely
to get something for nothing! You are like all the others, promising
mountains and miracles, yet waiting for roasted skylarks to drop into
your mouth!"

He was working himself into another rage, and I thought my chances
were gone. But I still had much to learn of La Demoiselle, who had
stood silent through this entire exchange. One thing I was to discover
was that her self-will extended even to her caprices.

"Keep in mind, papa, those humors of your body," she now cut in,

chidingly as one might speak to a child. "Rage increases their fermentation."

To my astonishment Cadillac sat back in his chair, and the change
in his face as he looked at his daughter was almost ludicrous. He was
a confirmed hypochondriac, and I later learned that any suggestion that
he was in ill health often had a surprising effect on him, as if he enjoyed being told the worst. But there also was something deeper here.
It was as if La Demoiselle suddenly had reminded him that not I alone,
but she also, had brought to him this proposal.

"Yes, that's so," he said in a voice that had lost its strenuous quality.
"I must watch my temper."

She gazed at him steadily and unsmilingly, as he pondered, his bony
hand on his chin.

"At least, Monsieur St. Denis, you're not bashful in your asking," he
said presently. "Do you realize what a great thing a monopoly of the
Natchez trade would be?"

"It would be as great only as the man who conducted it," I answered.

"And you consider that you have this greatness?" Again the sneer.

I chanced to glance at La Demoiselle. She was watching me almost
with amusement in her eyes. The letters! Obviously this was the time
to mention them, and she was interested to see what I would do concerning them. I knew she was diverted by my inward confusion, and I
also knew, in that moment, that whatever course I took would be derided by her. It angered me.

I turned my attention to Cadillac and spoke with a different tone.
"Your Excellency is the chief magistrate and representative of the
King's majesty in this colony. You are also a gentleman of honor and
good judgment. I ask your advice on a question of propriety."

I saw in La Demoiselle's look a sudden inward questioning thought.
The Governor appeared surprised at my sudden shift of ground.

"Propriety?" said he, puzzled.

"I bear correspondence from high personages in Canada," I went on.
"I have reason to think it may furnish satisfactory identification of myself and certify my capacity to accomplish what I propose to do, if
given permission. But I do not know to whom I should deliver it."

"To whom is it addressed?"

"To the Governor of Louisiana."

"I am the Governor."

THE SIEUR DE CADILLAC 73

"But you were not when I left Canada. The Sieur de Bienville was. And that is exactly my problem. Should they go to him, to whom presumably they were written—or to you, who have so recently succeeded him?"

In La Demoiselle's eyes was something almost hinting approval. I had placed the responsibility of the decision on the Governor himself, and it was a subtlety she appraised with the appreciation of a woman who herself constantly dealt in subtleties.

For a moment Cadillac thought, stroking his lank cheek with his forefinger. Then, in a voice almost mild, he said, "Where are these letters?"

"I have them here. I was instructed to deliver them in person to the hands of him to whom they are consigned."

For the first time a grin came into the Governor's face—a gargoyle twisting of the features, less mirthful than spiteful.

"I approve your discretion in this matter, Monsieur. The letters are official?"

"So I believe."

"And sealed?"

"Yes."

"Then their very nature solves your problem. Since they are sealed official documents, they must be given to me."

"I bow to your judgment, Excellency."

Taking the oiled packet from my pocket, I rather ceremoniously presented them.

La Demoiselle watched silently, her face devoid of expression, and I wondered what she was thinking. At the moment a servant approached the Governor and murmured in his ear.

"Eh?" said Cadillac. "La Vente? Yes, let him enter."

Lean and dour, the priest appeared. Only momentarily evident was his surprise at seeing me, but his eyes took in the oiled packet of letters and fixed themselves there.

"Well, Monsieur l'Abbé?" said Cadillac.

La Vente raised his glance to the Governor's face. "I desired only to remind Your Excellency——"

"You have quite a menagerie out there?"

"About a score await audience at present."

"I have told you to keep the number down! They wear me out with their importunities!"

"All save the most important have been eliminated." La Vente shot a glance at me, however, which clearly said that he did not include me among the important ones; and I gathered that I had gained nothing in friendship when I by-passed the secretary-chaplain in gaining this audience.

"And who are these 'most important'?" asked Cadillac testily.

"The Sieur de Cocteau——"

"That dolt again? He was worth a fortune but played ducks and drakes with it at the gaming table. Now the very hairs of his head are mortgaged. Am I to be responsible for every fool who lets the sharpers of the garrison cheat him at cards or dice?"

La Vente stood silent, his lean face impassive, as if accustomed to such displays of spleen.

"Cocteau is a nephew of the Minister of Finance," he said when the outburst ended.

"Yes, that is true." The Governor spoke more quietly, as if reminded of something he had forgotten. "Well, I suppose we must consider what can be done for him. Who else?"

"Le Page du Pratz, concerning an allotment of land——"

"Bah!"

"A delegation of merchants, petitioning that the goods of Monsieur Crozat be sold only at wholesale, since if they do not retain the retail business their trade will be ruined——"

"Bah!"

"Duclos, the commissary——"

"Bah!"

"La Loire des Ursins, agent of Crozat."

"Ah! Is there further news concerning Monsieur Crozat?"

"I do not know."

"Perhaps we should see La Loire first."

"There is also the Chevalier de Jenningros, captain of the *Maréchal d'Estrées*, waiting to report and pay his respects——"

"He can continue to wait until I have talked with La Loire."

But now, for the second time, La Demoiselle intervened. "Perhaps we should see Captain Jenningros first," she said.

I noticed that she used the word "we," but it seemed to surprise neither Cadillac nor La Vente.

"La Loire may have important business——" the Governor began, a note of peevish protest in his voice.

"I am sure Captain Jenningros is a very busy man," she said calmly, hardly paying heed to the protest. "He must be anxious to get back to his ship. Transacting our business with him here and now would save you the time and energy of writing and dispatching formal orders."

Such insistence would have angered most men; and Cadillac was highly irascible. But he gazed at her, then at La Vente, and finally said in a voice oddly contemplative, "Perhaps so. Yes, ask Jenningros to come in. I will greet him here in the breakfast room before I begin the formal sitting in the audience chamber."

With a baffled expression, as if he did not understand what was at the bottom of this, La Vente bowed and departed.

2.

While we waited, Cadillac opened the oiled package and began to examine its contents. And quite freely his daughter leaned over his shoulder, reading the letters also, or now and then taking one up which she found especially interesting, to give it closer perusal.

I found myself wondering about her. No woman I had ever known could be more determined in having her way than she. As witness this present event: having made herself sponsor for my petition in behalf of Jaccard, she was set on carrying out her wish, even though the matter could be of little importance to her.

Or was it of importance? If so, why?

A sudden thought: could it be that, stained coat and all, I had found more than passing favor in her eyes? This opened new and interesting possibilities, and mine was not a nature to discount them. After all, was I not taller than most men? And wide of shoulder? Women liked that. Was my face deformed or scarred? No. My tongue lacking in grace? No, she had shown pleasure at my bold compliments.

As for La Demoiselle, she was choice—besides being the Governor's daughter. I began to think that this affair might have a happy augury.

As they continued reading, however, my thoughts changed to wonder what, if anything, of importance was in the letters, and my conscience assailed me somewhat for not having at least warned Bienville about them, as my impulse had suggested.

But then I reflected that La Vente and Noirel both knew of the correspondence, and if I failed to show it to Cadillac, they would be certain to make capital of it to my disadvantage. Then, La Demoiselle had induced me to confess possession of the letters, and her knowledge was dangerous if I withheld them from her father. Lastly, Cadillac still had made no decision concerning Jaccard's fate, and when all was said and done, I was here this morning primarily in behalf of my faithful forester.

Conscience ceased to gnaw so sharply. After all, I told myself, Bienville was an icicle of a man, only looking for some way to hitch me to his political chariot. In any case, the decision was made, and I, who am inclined "to pull the devil by the tail," as the saying goes—in a word, to make decisions quickly—felt a certain relief that matters were out of my hands.

Both Cadillac and La Demoiselle now glanced up at me.

"You know the contents of these letters?" asked the Governor.

"No, Excellency."

"You are well commended by the Governor and Intendant of Canada."

"I am gratified."

"I learn that your military record is excellent."

I bowed. Then I ventured, "May I ask—if this is all?"

"All that concerns you. Whatever else is contained here concerns the colony and my predecessor, Bienville."

Cadillac said this without any undue emphasis or apparent feeling. But in La Demoiselle's face was an enigmatic something. I did not know exactly what.

3.

At this moment the naval officer I had seen in the anteroom was ushered in by La Vente, who announced him as the Chevalier de Jenningros. The priest lingered near the door while the captain of the *Maréchal d'Estrées* advanced and bowed first to La Demoiselle, then to Cadillac.

I thus had a good opportunity to study this figure in the white silks of the royal navy. Jenningros was of middle age, with delicate hands and features which seemed hardly appropriate for the commander of a ship of war. He was attired in all respects in the mode, his manners were exquisite, and it was evident that he was a courtier who had won advancement perhaps more by his graces than by his maritime abilities.

After acknowledging his complimentary greetings, Cadillac waved a hand toward La Vente, who hovered near the door, perhaps hoping to hear the ensuing conversation.

"You may return to your duties, Monsieur l'Abbé," he said. And when the secretary somewhat reluctantly departed, he turned to Jenningros.

"I wish to report, Excellency, that all the *cassette* women have been landed," the captain began. "And it is a relief, for no ship ever carried a cargo more likely to set the gunpowder afire."

"I did not notice any difficulties with the women on the voyage over," said Cadillac.

"Difficulties! Pardon, Excellency, but you and your family took the air from the stern gallery, and so had less opportunity to observe——"

"Not always," interrupted La Demoiselle, twinkling. "I sometimes went on the quarter-deck. And I saw the hussies, and have some inkling of your trouble, Captain."

"Thank you, Mademoiselle. Trouble it was, as you say. Thirty females in the large cabin and three hundred ruttish hellions in the forecastle! And every one of those women using every device she knew or could imagine to stir up the men—flirting, calling, making eyes, when they took exercise on the deck, which was necessary when the weather was fine. My crew was beside itself with lust, and the girls ready and willing to go to any lengths with the men. The crew of the *Maréchal d'Estrées* is not composed of innocent spring lambs, Excellency. Rather it is a herd of abandoned he-goats, where women are concerned. And I was under orders to deliver those women in the condition they were shipped!"

Jenningros paused, as if mentally to wipe his brow; and I saw that La Demoiselle's eyes were dancing with mirth.

"My crew was at the verge of mutiny," the captain went on. "I ordered any man who so much as whistled at one of the baggages to be flogged, and there were floggings daily, but it did not abate the danger. I placed an armed guard over the women, day and night, but I could not be sure of the guards themselves. *Ma foi!* We have no eunuchs on my ship, and if some of your slightly soiled doves turn up pregnant, do not blame me! As for the women, when they were below decks it was like Babel itself, or an alleyful of fighting cats, frizzing each other's hair buns and calling each other names that would make a hardened sea dog blush. One more voyage like that would put the spiders in my ceiling for all time."

La Demoiselle laughed out loud.

"Pardon my mirth," she said, "but the picture you paint is irresistible. And none of us in the after cabin really knew what a volcano we were sitting over!" She tried to compose her features.

Jenningros looked as if he did not quite know how to take this, standing very erect and somewhat red-faced.

"Please do not be offended," she went on. "I sympathize with you, and I'm sure my father does also." But she could not restrain another giggle.

He bowed stiffly and Cadillac sought to put him more at ease.

"I did not realize, as my daughter says, what was going on during the voyage," he said. "But you have finished creditably an annoying duty. I will write a commendation of you to the ministry of the navy."

"I profoundly thank Your Excellency."

"What next?"

"My orders are to resupply my ship, for which I have given requisition to Monsieur Duclos, the commissary. And then sail for St. Dominique."

"Duclos will provide what you need. There is, however, one small matter——"

"Yes, Excellency?"

"You had a press gang ashore last night?"

"It was necessary to fill deficiencies in the crew. We did pick up a few scavenging vagrants. Nobody, I assure you, of any consequence."

"I understand the necessity and do not criticize," said Cadillac, "even though this colony is scanty enough in population already. But there is one man I must ask you to release."

"Excellency?" Clearly this was unpalatable to Jenningros.

"His name is——" Cadillac hesitated. Then, impatiently, "What the devil is the fellow's name?"

La Demoiselle looked at me, and I answered, "Jaccard. A forester."

"Yes, that's it—Jaccard," repeated the Governor. "Being a forester he would be of little use to you, I think, Captain, without training——"

"As to that," said Jenningros grimly, "we would undertake to teach him smartness quickly enough. It's surprising how a rope's end inspires the most stupid to learn." He hesitated, then appealed to the Governor.

"There are in this awkward considerations, Excellency, which you will appreciate out of your knowledge of handling men. To release one of a gang such as was taken aboard last night may have a bad effect on the others, even on the crew as a whole."

"Nevertheless, I must repeat my request," said Cadillac, after a glance at his daughter.

"I have a personal interest in this poor man, Captain," added La Demoiselle with her most brilliant smile.

At that Jenningros was all the courtier, bowing to her. "I would, of course, accede to His Excellency's request out of my devotion and respect for him. But when a lady so charming interests herself in the matter, it makes it doubly pleasing to be of service."

"Then do me the favor of setting him ashore at once," she said. "And, Captain—be our guest this evening—at dinner."

He bowed his thanks, and if he was displeased with his necessity, he concealed his feelings as he departed, his hat under his arm.

"Well, *chérie*, does that satisfy you?" Cadillac asked when he was gone.

She nodded. "Thank you, papa."

He rose. "I must go to my duties and that accursed audience."

I bowed to him as he departed. Then La Demoiselle tucked her hand into the crook of my arm, and with me passed down the hall through which we had come and once more out into the garden.

"My deepest thanks," I said, when we were alone.

She did not answer me directly. "I think you will not spend a second night with Bienville," she said.

I returned her gaze squarely and frankly. "You consider that I committed a treachery to him in the matter of the letters?"

"Do you not so consider it?" she asked.

"No, for my loyalties belong not to him, but to someone else."

"Who else?"

I had meant Jaccard, but she put the question with such a hint of coquetry, and a sidelong glance under her lashes, that it sent me on a different tack.

"Can't you guess, Mademoiselle?" I asked, lowering my voice.

"How could I?" she parried. "I cannot read your mind."

"Oh, but I think you must. Beauty never loses a battle, and your beauty, since the first moment I saw you, has caused me only to desire to serve you." I made my voice soft and persuasive.

She gave me that odd appraising look of hers.

"Words come easily to you, I think," she said, but I did not believe she was displeased.

"Words come easily when they come from the heart," I assured her.

She smiled, and her eyelashes drooped, and though I was sure she put it down as flattery, she accepted it; for she was not one to dismiss praise of her beauty or words of warmth toward herself. In her, the coquette was ever uppermost.

All at once her voice changed from intimacy to raillery. "Upon my soul, Monsieur, you have made a fat morning of it! You've put me to endless trouble, infuriated Noirel, discommoded the Governor my father, outmaneuvered La Vente, and forced the Chevalier de Jenning-ros to swallow what was most unappetizing to him!"

"Without your gracious favor, none of this would have taken place."

She laughed a little, light, brittle laugh. "Those letters you brought—they were filled with extravagant praises of you. Do you know the question that is in my mind?"

"No, Mademoiselle."

"I have not been acquainted with governmental ways for these years without knowing that a man who is truly valuable is kept jealously by administrators of colonies, rather than lavished on other administrators," she said shrewdly. "Now why is Canada so eager for Louisiana to have you?"

"If that is so, I know not why." I was abashed by her question.

"Perhaps I have a theory," she said. "Does it have to do with the ladies? I said a while ago I thought you were a dangerous man. I meant dangerous to other men—in conflict. But are you also perhaps a danger to a woman—in love?"

Again her voice had fallen low, intimate, almost to a whisper.

"Never a danger," I said softly, "unless devotion is a danger."

She seemed to linger in the garden, holding me there with her, as if to prolong our little tête-à-tête.

"You will be returning to the residency?" she asked.

"I must. His Excellency has not answered my Natchez proposal."

"You think his answer will be favorable?"

"If I had a friend in court, I think it might."

"Perhaps you have," she said, with a faint shadow of a smile.

"Most fervently I pray it is so."

"It depends on yourself entirely."

"What must I do?" I asked.

"Prove that you are my father's friend—and mine."

I raised one of her hands to my lips.

"I am more than your friend—I am your slave," I swore.

"If you mean that, I might find it difficult to refuse you"—she hesitated—"*anything*," she finished.

I raised my eyes to hers and for a moment our gaze met, naked and open. Then her eyes veiled.

Almost humbly I said, "Command me."

"Come when I summon you," she said.

With that strange farewell she dismissed me, and I went wondering what was her full meaning and how far I might hope.

And not a word had been said concerning whether the references of those letters to Bienville were good or ill.

6. *A Shot at Six Paces, Scant*

Once more back on the mainland, I went from the dock directly to Bienville's house, and found my host seated at his writing table, with ink-stained fingers and a sheaf of written pages at his elbow.

"Seigneur," I said, "I am come to give my thanks to you, and transfer my effects to the Coq d'Or."

"You are leaving me? Why?" he asked.

"Your hospitality is wonderful, but I bear in mind the saying: A guest and a fish begin to stink on the third day."

Bienville chewed on the feather end of his quill pen.

"I suppose you have a better reason than that," he said, "but I will not press you. If you wish to go, by all means you are free to do so. Tell me, did you see the Governor?"

"Yes."

"And what of your petition?"

"It is my understanding that Jaccard is to be released."

"But this is extraordinary! Pray sit down and tell me by what miracle you brought this about."

Briefly, I recounted the meeting with La Demoiselle and Noirel, and the circumvention of Abbé La Vente, omitting, however, any mention of the letters from Canada, for my feeling of guilt seized me again, and I could not bring myself to confess this act which he might construe as faithlessness, since he had a right to feel that I was under some obligations to him.

"The daughter of the Governor," said Bienville, slowly and with a peculiar significance. "This explains much. Did anything else come up in your conversation with Cadillac?"

"I proposed that I be granted a trade concession with the Natchez."

He made a gesture of strong distaste. "I do not like the Natchez Indians. When one of their chiefs dies, the calumet smoke may rise to their devil gods, but the servants of the deceased are killed and burned with him, and all his relatives, save one designated as heir, are strangled. A horrible people. Yet, for savages, they are rich. If you should receive this license it might make your fortune—if it did not mean your death."

"I confess that I see little chance of receiving the concession," I said.

"You appear to have taken La Demoiselle's fancy." In Bienville's voice was a strong edge of sarcasm, in which I felt a criticism, as if he implied that I used a woman to further my ends.

"At least she exerted herself in my behalf," was all I could reply. For a moment he was silent, drawing idle designs with his pen on a paper. At last he said, "I had hoped I might count on you as a friend."

"I trust, Seigneur, that I am your friend."

"But you are not my ally. A lone wolf, as the Indians in Canada used to say. Your own affairs are paramount to you."

"Can you blame me for this?"

"No." Bienville spoke in his singularly cold, judgmatical way. "I do not blame you, knowing men to be what they are. So you do not become my enemy, I ask nothing else of you."

"An enemy to you I will never be."

"I feel constrained to advise you," said Bienville after a moment. "La Demoiselle is very much to be reckoned with in this colony, and since by some means you have interested her in your affairs, you ought to know somewhat more about her, for there are perils in such interest on her part."

"I am eager to learn more of her, Seigneur."

"Before I tell you this, I want you to understand that I cannot vouch for its entire truth. Yet knowledge of common rumor can do a man no harm in adjudging his conduct."

"True." I nodded.

"Yesterday we spoke of the interesting fact that La Demoiselle, though at an age which would be spinsterhood in an ordinary woman, has never been a wife."

"It is indeed odd for one with her beauty and situation."

"What I am about to tell you may explain it."

"A vow?"

"Hardly." Bienville smiled thinly. "At least not the kind you mean. You remember my recital of the career of Crozat?"

"Most vividly."

"That peasant, turned noble, is in his middle fifties and a widower. But he by no means lacks virility or interest in the opposite sex. Though he is not prepossessing in appearance, his wealth, so I am told, has made it easy to gratify his fondness for women."

"Wealth often does."

"Crozat has a daughter, moderately young and moderately homely," Bienville continued. "And *she* has a friend, who, though somewhat older than she is, is far from homely, but on the other hand very charming." He paused. "So charming, indeed, that Crozat—so it is whispered—becoming acquainted with her through his daughter, has extended his own friendship to this delightful feminine friend with such warmth that his benevolence has reached even to her father."

I stared. "La Demoiselle?"

He nodded.

"So it is to his daughter," I mused, "that Cadillac owes his appointment as Governor."

"Thus runs the gossip."

"But," I objected, "is not an elderly libertine, interested in a young woman, usually more jealous, more insistent in his infatuation, than a man much his junior in years? Why would Crozat send his mistress—if such she is—across the ocean where he cannot see her?"

"For one thing, Crozat is no ordinary aging lover," replied Bienville. "He is, first of all, a man of affairs, intensely practical, and thinking of his finances above everything. One never knows what pressures are exerted in the royal court. Perhaps Crozat, who is a widower, has plans for another marriage—of convenience. Or perhaps the King had need for a hostage, so to speak, and stipulated that the young woman be sent to the colony, as a guarantee of Crozat's loyal duty in this new great power. Perhaps, again, she was getting out of hand, as they say, and Crozat banished her for a time, to teach her a lesson. Or perhaps it was the other way around—they quarreled, and lovers' spats between young women and elderly lovers are not infrequent—and she came to America, with a high head, to teach *him* a lesson. The possible explanations are infinite in number."

"But La Demoiselle holds the real power on Dauphin Island?" said I.

"You saw yourself that her father humors her in everything."

"That can have only one meaning." I spoke positively. "She has *not* broken with Crozat—if he is the source of her influence."

For a moment Bienville studied me. "You feel yourself capable of dealing with La Demoiselle?" he suggested.

"I would not say so."

"But I see she is a challenge to you." He knit his brow, as if thinking. "And I will pay you the compliment of saying that I believe you can hold your own with most members of her sex—indeed your record, what I have heard of it, proves it. You have a certain animal magnetism that women find attractive. Yes, I think women find it quite easy to become very fond of you." He paused. "Unfortunately for yourself, I fear you are as addicted to women as they are to you. Too greatly addicted, perhaps, for the kind of game this is."

"How can you say this? I spend many months at a time in the wilderness, far from any save savage females—who do not interest a man of taste."

"But when opportunity returns," said Bienville, unperturbed, "you make up for this deprivation—or am I misinformed?"

Before his cold gray eyes I again felt discomfited.

"A man cannot live like an anchorite forever," I muttered. "I confess that I find women entrancing, and perhaps have received my share of their favors, ever since I was a youth."

"You find them much alike?"

"Now heaven forbid!" I cried warmly. "Each woman is a different womankind. This is their great attraction—the variety, the exploration, the unexpected revelation. Women are the poetry, men the prose, of life."

"You are a romantic, my friend." Bienville gave his chill smile. "Yet learn this: in one respect all are the same. Women and men are natural enemies, held together by the necessity of sex. Were it not for that they would invariably hate, not love, each other. And in woman even love is suspect, because it is her nature to be fickle. Loyalty in a woman is contingent on her dependence. Give her power and she is invariably a tyrant. Give her freedom of fancy and she is a traitor."

"If I am a romantic, Seigneur, I fear you are a cynic."

"I am a realist." His brief smile faded. "And I say these things to you for a reason. The particular woman we are discussing is more perilous than most of her sisterhood. Against her I warn you most gravely, St. Denis. Me she hates: partly because she believes that I am still a

danger to her father's position and hence possibly her own; and partly
—perhaps more importantly—because she knows I see through her."

"It is always dangerous," I observed, "to allow any woman to believe
that you understand her fully."

Bienville did not relax his sober mien. "I know not what adverse reports concerning me have gone, or will go, to Versailles because of her.
But this I do know: I would not be surprised, on the arrival of any
given ship from France, to find myself under arrest and facing trial on
some charge contrived by that pair—Cadillac and his daughter."

Once more those accursed letters I had given to the Governor leaped
into my mind. What information did they contain? Should I even now
inform Bienville of their existence?

But I restrained myself from doing so. For the present my own
future was so clouded that it gave me profound concern; and inasmuch
as I could say that I delivered the letters as a matter of official obliga-
tion, I need not mention them. Nevertheless, for all this rationalizing,
I could not look upon my actions with much pride.

2.

Not long after, Jaccard presented himself at Bienville's, where I had
remained awaiting his arrival. He was filthy and bruised, for he had
been roughly handled aboard the *Maréchal d'Estrées*, but he was so
devoutly grateful for his deliverance, and so sheepish and crestfallen
withal, that I could not be very severe with him. I scolded him mildly
for forgetting all his woods cunning and allowing himself to be taken
by a press gang, and then sent him to find Marbot, the two of them to
carry my luggage to the Coq d'Or, whither, having made my acknowledgments to Bienville, I now betook myself.

At this time of day the taproom of the inn was empty, and Tiernay,
the portly landlord, knowing now the quality of his visitor, was happy
to furnish a good room looking out toward the bay. There I sat alone,
having had a small luncheon sent up, and thought long thoughts.

Wherever my mind turned, it seemed to encounter a forbidding wall
of discouragement. The Natchez project, on which hung my hopes, had
been received so coldly by Cadillac that I made sure it was doomed to
failure.

It is an ill thing to ask favors of those in power; but when a favor
in spite of this is asked, it should be great enough to be worth while;

for a small favor uses up as much patience and credit as a large one. In the present instance, I felt, I had used up what small change in consideration the Governor might have for one like myself in asking him to exert his authority for the release from a ship of war of a man so obscure and unimportant as Jaccard.

And even this much I had not achieved for myself. With some little humiliation, I reflected that it had been accomplished through the whim of a willful woman. La Demoiselle! Whatever Bienville's opinion of the sex, I thought to myself, it is certain that women sometimes are capable of surprising expenditures of themselves for the men they favor.

Most bitterly had Bienville spoken of Crozat and Cadillac and especially of La Demoiselle. But was she really what he said of her?

In my lifetime I had experienced women of many kinds, and I was far from naïve. My viewpoint, indeed, was perhaps as cynical as Bienville's, with this difference: far from shunning the sex, I found in women a stimulus, a duel of wits and wills which was an attraction in itself, apart from all sensuality. I regarded them as all free-living men regard women—fair game if opportunity and inclination matched. Feminine virtue I hardly believed in.

An old Spanish saying, learned when I was a youth in Madrid, came to mind: "*La mujer y el vídrio siempre estan en peligro*—a woman and a glass are always in danger."

3.

Spain—ah, Spain! The thought of it brought me back to my life there, and my first friend, and my first love affair, and my first duels. The Spaniards were proud, brave, often handsome, and warmhearted. And all of these adjectives fitted Don Beltrán de Córdoba, fearless, pleasure-bent, laughing and loyal, with whom I found a comradeship such as young men sometimes have, and which little else equals in this world.

It was Don Beltrán who introduced me to pretty Doña Lorena de Yeregui, my own age but already married two years, with whom I studied the language of the country, and also the language of love. She taught me both of them well: the liquid Spanish tongue so that I had facile use of it forever; and the furious way of a Spanish woman's love, unthinking and heedless of consequences, once it is set aflame. Too unthinking and too heedless was her love, for we were most unfortunately caught in a compromising position.

I remembered again that gray morning on the outskirts of Madrid, when I fought Don Benito Esteban de Yeregui, my mistress' husband. I used a sword passably well in those days, and wounded him: no great feat, for Don Benito was a weak fencer, who fought halfheartedly, since he was pushed into the affair by another, and really cared little about his wife for all her good looks, since he had another love of whom he was more enamored.

Then, at dusk of the same day, I fought again, this time with Captain Julio de Vanegas, who nursed his hate for me when I succeeded with Doña Lorena, whose lover he had been before me. It was his sneer that forced Don Benito to challenge me, and when the husband failed, the captain took up the gage himself. In that second duel of a single day I was lucky, for I crossed rapiers with a better swordsman. But a momentary slip on the damp turf by Vanegas, and my blade was between his ribs. He was carried away more dead than alive, though he did survive.

In both those duels Beltrán stood with me as my second: as clean-grained evidence of love and loyalty as could be given, since Spanish sentiment generally was against the foreigner, and he himself later was forced to face down slurs, once going to the field for a bloodletting of his own with a friend of Vanegas. For this I could never be sufficiently grateful to him; and when, after the circumstances of the duels were known and I was gazetted back to France in disgrace—for the husband was of the grandee class, and the lover of some moment also, and the new King was very chary of offending his half-won Spanish subjects by upholding a junior French officer against them in a scandalous affair—Beltrán embraced me like a brother, and wept that we should part.

Beltrán . . . Beltrán! I wondered where that warmhearted friend of my youth had gone, and what was his fate. Perhaps he was dead, killed fighting in the Spanish-French armies against Marlborough of England or Prince Eugene of Savoy, at Blenheim or Ramillies or some other great battle of the War of the Spanish Succession, brought about when Louis XIV made that primping youth, Philip of Anjou, King of Spain.

Perhaps, on the other hand, he had risen to high station in Madrid, or in one of the Spanish colonies—Peru, for a venture, or Cuba, or even New Spain—for his father was a *conde* and a grandee and his family noble, and Beltrán had the qualities of mind and person to commend him for advancement and the colonies offered greatest opportunities to

young men. Perhaps—but why speculate on it? Even if he still lived I
would never, in any probability, see Beltrán again. And if I did, the
long years intervening would have so changed us both that even if we
recognized one another in meeting, we would most likely go our separate ways, strangers now, unable to recapture ever again that strong
devotion we once had.

4.

Well, enough of that. I turned my mind to a consideration of my life
since the Spanish days; and considering it, I felt that I was able to
judge the rumors about Cadillac's daughter realistically. Much of what
Bienville said, I reflected, might come from the natural resentments of
a man who had been supplanted in office, and this should be taken into
account in appraising it.

Was La Demoiselle as baneful as he had suggested, or was she perhaps much maligned? The whole story of her relationship with Crozat
might be no more than spiteful such as continually ran through official
and aristocratic circles. Hardly any lady of prominence, either in France
or the colonies, but had some such calumnies whispered about her. It
was an evil of the times—of an age typified by Voltaire, already famous
as a wit in Paris, and Molière, the cynical dramatist, and the free-living
Louis XIV himself—the wittiest, most luxurious, and most abandoned
age in European history, since Roman times at least.

On the other hand, I said to myself, such gossip was often justified.
Women of the French court were little concerned with conventions or
preachments. They were governed by their hearts and their vanities,
rather than by responsibilities and the moral code. Their ideal was the
ideal of beauty, and their virtue—if it could be called a virtue—was the
virtue of love.

In France, a courtier who possessed no mistress was almost a nobody
at the royal court; and the King himself set a notable example of
libertinism—although he was superannuated now, to be sure, and devoting himself to the Mass. On the reverse of the medal, a lady of quality who had a more or less openly acknowledged lover, or even a half
dozen of them, outside of her marital sphere, seemed to lose nothing,
but perhaps rather to enhance her standing in sophisticated society by
that fact.

Names of some of the aristocratic heroines of boudoir adventure in

France, in the present reign, came easily to mind: the beautiful Marie
Mancini, the charming and delicate Adrienne Lecouvreur, the scheming yet entrancing Henriette d'Orléans, the lovely and almost innocently amorous Louise La Vallière, the exquisite Françoise de Mon-
tespan, the gay and precocious Marie de la Veauville—every one of
them dispensers of their favors freely, unashamedly, and quite without
secrecy to Kings, Dukes, and Cardinals, yet courted, admired, and
flattered by all. And this was to name only a beginning.

Considering everything, I thought that regardless of Bienville's rancor, his opinions ought to be taken into account. If La Demoiselle was
the key to Cadillac's favor, La Demoiselle must be treated as such; and
the approach a man makes to a woman who "though unmarried is
hardly a virgin," as Bienville put it, obviously is different from that to
a timid girl who is innocent and inexperienced in life. The one desires
spice; the other only fears it.

I remembered the appraising look the Governor's daughter gave me
in the garden, the look of a sophisticated woman of the world, deliberately measuring a man's qualities as a connoisseur might. That look
removed whatever scruples I might have felt concerning her. She was
quite able to think for herself, and to act of her own volition: and she
had deliberately challenged me.

I thought back on her manner, at first cold, then warm, then biting,
then encouraging, but always baffling: and my experience was that no
woman practices such inconsistencies toward one to whom she is completely indifferent. Uncertainty and delay are the weapons of women
and statesmen, and neither waste them on issues that lack importance.

My imagination leaped forward. To be sure, I was below La Demoiselle in station. Yet I myself had on occasion wooed a cottage maid as
fervently as I wooed her mistress, a titled lady; and perhaps, in the last
case, I brushed a rival in some servitor of base descent. In affairs of the
heart prerogative has never been everything, and history tells of pages
who held queens in fee.

La Demoiselle had told me I must come when she summoned me.
When she summoned me! When would it be?

I came to my feet. I would at least see how far this went, even though
the path might be perilous to tread. At that thought, feeling that I must
make a better appearance when next she beheld me, I counted
the gold pieces in my wallet—they were not as heavy as I would have

liked, since I paid my men out of my own pocket—and went out to seek a new wardrobe.

5.

I was fortunate. I found a tailor's shop, owned by a little shrimp of a man from Rouen; who, as soon as he learned of my wants, displayed a good coat of green velvet, with breeches and waistcoat of the same material but gray, which fit me passably well.

"You can have them at a bargain, Monsieur," the tailor said, "since the clothes were left on my hands."

"Left in what manner?" I asked.

"A duel, to be sure. You have no conception what a trial duels are to a tailor. One morning a young Sieur comes in and orders a fine outfit, but before he can come for it and pay you, some other young Sieur spits him like a roast partridge, over a chance remark, or a lady's glance, or the color of his complexion, or any excuse. Duels—duels! It is the boredom of this place that brings so many of them about—and they are the ruin of us who try to make a living, however meager, and have to deal with the hotspurs of the garrison."

The little tailor's words reminded me forcibly of Noirel. A duel with the dram-bottle captain seemed an inevitability, and after La Demoiselle's remark that he was death with a rapier, the prospect seemed highly unpleasant.

But I have never been one to live an event before it happens. So I shrugged, and bethought myself that though the recent *affaire d'honneur* had been most unfortunate for the unnamed young Sieur, it was fortunate for me, since the new suit did me very well. So, making my bargain with the tailor, I directed him to send the garments to the inn, and took my own way thither.

It was growing dark, and the night lights were being lit by the time I returned to the Coq d'Or. Already a number of younger officers were in the taproom when I entered, and I received some stares so significant that I could not but be reminded that Noirel had sworn to kill me.

There was, however, no sign of the Captain, so I went up to my room. For a little time I thought deeply. I did not wish to cross swords with that deadly victor in sixteen duels, rusty as I was in practice. At the moment I had much to live for, and I knew very well that, barring some unlikely chance, a meeting with rapiers would end badly for myself. If I fought, it must be with weapons other than swords, but how could I arrange for that?

Too clearly I pictured the probable sequence of events: Noirel, the ruffler, deliberately placing some insult or affront upon me; my necessity of challenging; Noirel's naming of the place and weapons; the clash of the thin blades and the pang of death.

But now an idea occurred to me. I took from my baggage a pair of pistols, which I carefully loaded and primed, saw that the flints were in good order, then placed them in the capacious side pockets of my stained leather coat. Having done so, I went down to the taproom, took a table in an inconspicuous corner, and ordered my supper.

As I expected, the door of the inn was presently thrown open, and with loud talk and much tramping and laughter, three or four officers of the garrison came in. One of them was Noirel. I recognized also Crevillon, the young Ensign I had put in his place that morning at the residency. The others were strangers, but all were quite evidently under the influence of brandy.

When his eyes fell on me, Noirel gave a hard stare, and half moved as if to come over to my table. But then he halted, and instead of approaching, he went to another table across the room with his friends, where they sat eying me, talking together with an occasional ugly laugh.

I made sure they were discussing me, but affected to ignore them. After several minutes a waiter laid a covered dish on the table before me.

I looked at it. "This is not what I ordered for supper," I said. "To whom am I indebted for it?"

"It was sent with the compliments of Captain Noirel," said the waiter.

"Lift the lid," I ordered.

He did so. The dish contained a greasy mess of boiled cabbage—the accustomed fare of the lowest class of French peasants. Both the implication and the insult were evident.

I did not, however, alter my expression in the slightest.

"I must return the courtesy," I said to the waiter. "Listen carefully."

Thereupon I gave him some brief instructions and dismissed him. When he was gone I began quietly to sup off the cabbage as if nothing had happened, though I found it rather nauseating, since it was cooked crudely in pork grease.

Noirel and his friends seemed greatly amused, growing open in their laughter, and calling the attention of others in the room to the byplay. Still I continued to eat of the cabbage as if it were the most acceptable of dishes. Presently the waiter appeared again from the kitchen, and this time he bore a covered dish to Noirel's table.

His surprise was evident. It was more so when the lid was lifted, and the dish disclosed one of my loaded pistols, which I had given the waiter to serve up in this manner.

All in the room saw it.

"Pistols, *pardieu!*" exclaimed one of Noirel's companions, with a roar of laughter in which every man in the room joined, save the Captain and I.

The novelty of the trick had caught the fancy of the young cockerels of the fort. All knew Noirel's intention to provoke a quarrel to be settled with rapiers. None had any doubt of the outcome of such a combat. But this manner of answering the insult of the cabbage with the presentation of a pistol left him no alternative, if he were to keep countenance, but to accept the challenge as offered.

Scowling, Noirel lifted the pistol from the dish, and for a moment fingered it. He had anticipated a certainty; now he faced a gamble, for he knew that I, his adversary, must be well versed in arms.

I rose at my table and bowed. Suddenly the room became still.

"The pistol is loaded, Captain," I said. "We are at a very pleasant distance for a shot. I propose that we settle the matter between us here and now."

With an oath Noirel sprang to his feet, cocking the pistol. At the same time there was a rush by the other diners, chairs overturning and feet clattering, to get out of the direct path of the bullets.

For a moment he and I glared at each other across the room. Silence had fallen again, and one could have heard a whisper had one been uttered.

Then Noirel brought his pistol up.

"Die, damn you!" he shouted, and fired.

A glass wine decanter on my table was shattered by the leaden ball, splashing wine over the cloth and my leather coat. For a moment the room seemed filled with pungent powder smoke which made it impossible to see across. When it cleared, Noirel and I stood exactly as we had been before the shot, I with my weapon still cocked and unfired.

"You are precipitate, Captain Noirel," I said. "See, you have further stained this poor coat of mine by spattering wine over it."

With the color draining from his face, Noirel stood, the empty pistol in his hand, a little thread of smoke still rising from the muzzle.

"Messieurs," I went on, addressing the others present, "I think you will agree that I am entitled to my shot?"

Around the room there were reluctant nods. Not even Noirel's companions could dissent from a rule of the code so indisputable. Nor, for that matter, did Noirel himself. He stood erect, pallid where he usually was flushed, but unflinching, waiting for the fatal bullet.

For a moment I extended my arm, pistol cocked, aiming steadily at his heart.

"Messieurs," I said again, "I estimate the distance to be six paces. Will one of you oblige us by verifying the guess?"

"Don't prolong the affair!" cried a voice.

Another said, "Monsieur, he is at your mercy!"

But I fixed my eyes on Crevillon, the youthful Ensign. "If you please, Monsieur, favor me," I said.

As if he hated every move he made, he paced off the distance from where I stood to the spot on which Noirel seemed fixed.

"Six paces, scant," said Crevillon, frowning.

"At such a distance it would be impossible for me to miss," I said so all heard. I paused. "But I choose to defer my shot," I finished.

Every face bore a question, a speculation as to what hidden meaning was in the words. Noirel stared grimly, not moving.

"I call you all to witness," I went on, "that I still have my shot, to which I am entitled, at six paces, scant. Messieurs, I do not want Captain Noirel's life. I give it to him. But if ever the question of a duel between us arises again, I shall demand, whatever the terms, my right to my shot—*first*—at this exact distance."

A long, heavy silence.

"Since we appear to be all agreed, Messieurs," I continued, lowering the hammer on my pistol and laying it on the table, "I invite you all to join me in a toast." I lifted a glass of wine. "I drink to this gentleman present, Captain Edmond de Noirel. Whatever may be our differences, I do hereby freely assert that I have never seen any man look death in the eye more bravely than he."

From the crowd came almost a sigh, showing its relief. Glasses were raised to the toast. Noirel sat down heavily, as if dazed.

Servants removed the smashed decanter and stained cloth from my table, and I took my seat, ordering up the dinner I had previously commanded. As I began imperturbably to eat, while the others in the tavern talked eagerly among themselves, I saw Noirel rise and come to me. I rose to meet the Captain.

"Monsieur," said Noirel stiffly, "my compliments."

"And mine to you, Captain," I replied.

"I care not for my life."

"Of that I am certain."

"I conceive that I have lost no honor if I say that I greatly admire your deportment."

"I have expressed my esteem for your conduct already."

We bowed.

"Monsieur."

"Captain."

Noirel tramped out of the inn.

7.   *A Beauty in Her Boudoir*

Yet that evening, before I retired, the note came. It was formal, written evidently by some secretary, saying that Mademoiselle de Cadillac would be pleased to see the Chevalier de St. Denis the next morning, at eleven of the clock. A *carte d'identité* was enclosed.

That night I found it difficult to sleep. I had settled, at least for the moment, my most pressing problem, the quarrel with Noirel, who hardly would pursue an encounter in which he must, as the first act, stand at six paces, scant, and receive my pistol shot. There was, of course, no way of knowing whether Noirel's friends might press the matter and cause new trouble.

Other questions, however, twisted in my head bewilderingly, as I tossed in my bed.

I was thirty, my youth gone, though my prime was before me: and I was beginning to think I had spent all that glorious youth chasing will-o'-the-wisps. I had gone on great, distance-consuming expeditions to places unknown, had fought not only British and Indian foes, but also arctic cold, desert heat, starvation, exhaustion, and sickness. And all this in pursuit of a dream, Iberville's dream, the dream of the greatness of France.

The dream had seemed well worth the devotion of my life at the time, especially when my leader and idol, Iberville, with his keen aquiline face glowing, discoursed on honor, and the King, and the nobility of suffering and perhaps dying for *la patrie*. I believed it, then.

But now Iberville was gone, and with him his dream, and it seemed to me that I had wasted myself in those years when I sought nothing for myself, and gained nothing. All I had to show for my labors and perils was the little gold left in my wallet, and what reputation I might have gained: and that reputation, certes, could not be converted into bread or lodging.

In my bitterness I conceived that I had come to the critical moment of my life, when I would either make or break. And I sought to sum up what was before me, and what I could do now that I had assayed my resources and knew my objective.

Nothing was as I had anticipated in Louisiana. Crozat, through Cadillac, now ruled the province. The enormous power of the great merchant, of whom I had only just heard, awed me. Moneybags, I thought, outweighed anything else in the scales of a man's destiny.

Because of his moneybags, Crozat, the son of a peasant woman, spoke on familiar terms with King's ministers, even the King himself, made or unmade royal Governors, commanded all the revenues of this vast part of the New World, and dictated its laws and policies. More strongly than ever, it was borne in on me that to be important one must be rich. I said to myself that nothing would stop me now; neither man, nor the devil, nor fate itself, from one day gaining a fortune that would put silks on my back, fine houses over my head, coaches and blooded horses at my beck, servants at my call, rich foods and wines for my table, charming women to my pleasure, and the pride and precedence that only wealth could give. The dream and fantasy were over: the reality had begun for my life.

It seemed to me that my way led through La Demoiselle, that soft and feminine creature, all silks and laces and ruffles and perfumes, frivolous and trivial, spoiled and indulged, a woman like myriads of other women, neither greater nor less than they, save for one thing: she held, through his infatuation, rule over the will of the powerful merchant-courtier, Crozat, her lover. How often had I seen it before—the girl, light, pretty, frail, perhaps not very wise or witty, but with the wondrous gift of the enticement of her sex, winding about her dainty finger a mighty man, and thereby holding fateful sway through him over the lives and fortunes of countless others.

In my mood of disillusionment I said to myself that such a mistress would be a gay and pleasant thing to possess. Never before had I considered anything so permanent as such an alliance, my life being too busy with far adventure, and all my love affairs being stop-and-go seductions, the conquests quick and gleeful if I was successful, more important for themselves than for the women who yielded the triumphs. Women might have loved me; but I could not truly say that I had ever been in love with any woman.

Nevertheless, one does not have to love in order to make love, for all women, I thought, seemed to delight in being wooed, whether subtly or openly, the supreme adventure of their nature to be pursued and besieged. Now I decided that if in Louisiana the hidden power was held by La Demoiselle, so long as she seemed willing—and she seemed more than willing—to La Demoiselle I must pay court.

With that resolve at last I found sleep.

2.

Midmorning next day I awoke. Marbot was not available, so I dressed myself in my new velvet green and gray, with buckled shoes and silk stockings. I rather fancied myself in knee breeches, for I showed a good calf, to which an active life had given that muscular grace that is attractive to feminine eyes. Donning at last my baldric and sword, and snatching a quick breakfast, I had myself rowed to Dauphin Island.

The *carte* I now carried gave me instant admission to the residency. A footman in powdered wig bowed before me and conducted me up a stair to a door, behind which I heard a trilling laugh I knew. A moment later I was announced and entered La Demoiselle's boudoir.

A dainty chamber it was, filled with flowers and their perfume, with delicate china and rich silver on the small tables which stood here and there, a French clock under a glass dome on the mantel, some Watteau paintings of a pastoral nature on the walls, and windows, set off with the fluffiest of curtains, commanding a view of the sea.

Far more entrancing than all of this, however, was the mistress of the chamber herself, lying still abed in charming dishabille. She wore a peignoir of light peach-colored silk, with blue cornflowers embroidered on it, very décolleté, so that the hidden beauties of her bosom were almost fully revealed. Propped up among her pillows she sat, a flowered coverlet drawn up to her waist, her bare arms gleaming with a lucent light, as if she had been surprised in this state by her callers. Yet the perfect array of her hair, the penciling of her brows, the tinting of her lips, even a beauty spot on one cheek, suggested most clearly that the attitude and situation were by no means impromptu.

I knew the custom of the *lever*, as practiced by the *haut monde* of Canada, but never had seen it in this continental perfection. A beautiful woman, thus displayed, is devastating; for the intimacy of the bed is suggested, and the imagination stimulated to all manner of pulse-stirring fancies. And this was the object of it all, for already in the boudoir when I arrived were four gallants, chatting, laughing, sitting, posturing, sipping cups of chocolate, nibbling of cakes or fruits which were carried about by two waiting women and the little Moorish-clad Negro boy, while all attention was engrossed on the beauty among the pillows.

"So it is you!" exclaimed La Demoiselle at my entrance. "You are late, Monsieur St. Denis. Is it possible you forgot our little invitation?"

"Heaven forbid!" I said fervently. "It has been uppermost in my mind and heart since the moment I received it last evening."

"At least you are a diplomat. Abbé La Vente is a kitten beside you."

"If this be mere diplomacy, may I perish where I stand!"

"Perhaps I should keep you standing there," she said gaily, "to see if the fate you have invited will overtake you and prove you untruthful. But I will relent, for you must meet these gentlemen."

Quite prettily she made the introductions. Two of those present I already knew—Captain Noirel and Ensign Crevillon. The others were a Lieutenant le Maynadrat and a Monsieur Philippe Hequet. To each in turn I bowed, and Noirel gave me a look and twisted his mustache. I observed that Monsieur Hequet must be deep of pocket, for he wore a suit of silver brocade that must have cost many a gold louis.

"Will you sit, and have a chocolate?" she said to me, still in a tone of light raillery. "Ah, Messieurs, I perceive that the mode of our friend, in wearing his own hair instead of a peruke, attracts your interest. Tell me, is this a custom of the Iroquois savages?"

"No, Mademoiselle," said I. "The Iroquois shave their heads—like our French gentry—leaving only a scalp lock as a handle for their enemies."

She gave her silvery laugh. "Not only a diplomat, but quick of tongue! What say you to that, Messieurs of the shaved polls and wigs?"

The question and its manner of asking did not appear to please the Messieurs, and she laughed again at them, then turned once more to me.

"Come, give an account of yourself," she commanded.

"I have but little to tell, Mademoiselle."

"You spent a quiet evening at the Coq d'Or, I suppose?" In her eyes was a sparkle of malicious amusement.

"In the main, yes."

"But not entirely?"

I felt most uncomfortable, with Noirel there in the room. "Perhaps there was one small contretemps," I said, trying to pass it off.

"Come, Monsieur! You are as ponderous as an Archbishop! What was this contretemps, and what came of it?"

Goaded, I hardly knew what to say. Noirel was looking at me fixedly.

"Nothing came of it," I managed at last. "I introduced a suggestion which seemed to dissolve the argument——"

"Such as a loaded pistol in a covered dish?"

I sprang to my feet and looked at her astounded, seeing the trick she had played on me.

"You have heard?" I asked.

"By an unimpeachable witness." With a smile neither fastidious nor disdainful, but rather sly and vicious, she glanced across the room.

"Captain Noirel?" I exclaimed.

"Yes," she said. "And made a most entertaining story of it, did you not, Edmond?"

The man was uncomfortable, and showed it. "I trust you were entertained, Mademoiselle," he said gruffly.

"I was entranced, I confess it," she laughed. "Especially did we all admire Monsieur St. Denis' *volte coupe*, whereby he turned the tables on you, Edmond, leaving your fangs drawn, as it were." Again the silvery cruel little laugh.

I sensed malice here. It was evident that a report of the proceedings of the evening before had reached her, and that she had taken advantage of her *lever* this morning to torment Noirel. I felt that I could not participate in the mortification of a man whom I considered brave, so I bowed to the Captain.

"I perceive that Captain Noirel has told the tale all in my favor," I said.

La Demoiselle shrugged an admirable bare shoulder. "Edmond loves a good story, even when he is the butt of it, do you not, Edmond?"

"A rare quality these days," I persisted.

"We must seek what amusement life affords, do you not think?" She gave me a sidewise glance from her narrowed eyes.

"In any case," said I, "Captain Noirel is most generous, for I assure you the matter was not at all one sided. It is my pleasure to say that I never knew a man more gallant in the face of death than he."

In Noirel's eyes came a look almost of gratitude. The speech had the effect of drawing the smart from his wound, and diverting from him the embarrassing center of attention.

For a moment La Demoiselle's face was petulant, as if she were deprived of her prey. Then she spoke to her waiting women.

"I am ready," she said.

The process, almost the rite, of dressing was about to begin. They came to her bedside, one a formidable elderly female with a bustling manner, the other evidently a peasant girl, rather pretty, with a shy, effacing manner. The older woman signed to her assistant and the latter wheeled forward the toilette table, covered with perfumes, tints, unguents, and other essentials for preparing a lady for the day.

Thereafter, one by one, the two of them brought forth not fewer than a score of different gowns, displaying each before the critical eyes of their mistress, who waved them aside without a word, until at last she nodded when one was presented that pleased her. Thereat they began working over her swiftly, dressing her as if we men did not exist in the room; while for La Demoiselle's part, she devoted all her attention and her conversation to us, her male visitors, as if it were her women who did not exist.

In the next half hour I had the not unpleasant experience of watching a beautiful woman attired from head to foot, with the momentary revelations of intimate charms which not only were inevitable, but part of the ceremony—for such it was—of a lady of fashion dressing in her boudoir before gentlemen. When her stockings were drawn on, we were permitted glimpses of slender legs of rare feminine beauty; her neck, shoulders, breast were in turn bared; and once, when she stood up in a diaphanous undergarment to have her gown placed upon her, her figure was outlined for one breathless moment as clearly as a Greek bas-relief.

Of all this the charming center of attention seemed unaware, or at least indifferent, as she chatted gaily with us. When she was fully dressed she dismissed her tirewomen. Her next words were:

"Messieurs, thank you all for attending me this morning." And then, "Monsieur St. Denis, do stay after the others have gone to their no doubt important affairs."

Whatever importance there was to the affairs of the gentlemen, I saw disappointment in their faces when they knew they were to leave.

But leave they did, with bows and many compliments, while she placed her small hand on my arm, and together we descended the stairs.

"I should scold you," she said archly to me, "for spoiling my fun with Edmond."

"If I did so, I am most contrite."

"Well, I forgive you. Perhaps the sport had progressed far enough. Poor Edmond, I gave him a rather sharp time of it. He was squirming."

I was silent, thinking that women have a special heartlessness.

We passed out into the garden, where for a time she amused herself by tossing the painted ball for Pepi, the little page, to fetch; a pointless sort of sport, but fashionable, since one of the King's mistresses had set the example some years before.

Tiring of this, she turned to me. "So you left Bienville's house after all—I thought you would," she said.

"I prefer not to be beholden," I replied.

For a few paces we stepped along the garden path, Pepi following behind with the ball. Then I ventured a question.

"Since you have mentioned Bienville, is it proper to ask if there was anything in the correspondence I carried that might affect him?"

She did not at once answer, but presently she looked up at me.

"I know not why I give you this satisfaction, if satisfaction it be," she said. "But I will tell you that the letters were only official communications. There was nothing prejudicial to Bienville. But does that alter the fact that it *might* have been otherwise?"

It was evident that she wished to make me feel guilty, but I only smiled. "I am relieved, for I owe Bienville no ill will. Nevertheless, it would have made no difference to me, since between his cold face and the beautiful eyes in which I now find myself lost, there could be no question of where lies my fealty."

She gave a little purring laugh. "Upon my soul, pretty speeches are the more piquant coming from a face as fierce and brown as a wild Indian's."

I felt she was well disposed toward me: perhaps more than that. But I wanted proof, and here was a matter of nicety.

I had two theories concerning the pursuit of women. They might be wooed with lies and madness, poetry and protestations, yet a man must take care against being too headlong, for it is the sudden motion that

scares the bird away. On the other hand, sufficient boldness is needed also, for love often blows cold when slow. To strike the exact balance between these two apparent contradictions is the essence of the art.

We had reached the arbor of bushes and for a moment paused in its shade. A silence fell between us. As if on idle impulse La Demoiselle took the ball from the little Negro and sent it flying away to the farthest corner of the garden, with his scarlet slippers twinkling after it.

For a moment the two of us were thus alone, and I could not believe it was accident, entirely. She was looking at me with a small smile, and I read a question in her eyes.

"Mademoiselle——" I whispered. "If I could only dream——"

I took her hand. She did not withhold herself, but came to me.

"Dream of what?" she breathed.

Very close we stood, our bodies touching, her face upturned to mine, her lips half parted.

On a wild impulse I drew her closer, and laid my lips on hers. For a moment she did not resist, her kiss seeming to fuse with mine.

But for a moment only. She pushed me away with a sudden motion.

In consternation at my own rashness I stepped back. "I—I most humbly beg your forgiveness—your beauty so intoxicated me——"

Her expression was impossible to read: whether it was surprise, perplexity, displeasure, or something else. The moment was critical.

Then she smiled almost inwardly.

"You are different," she said. "So different from the others that I must judge you on a different basis. If another had your temerity, it would be an insult, and I would punish it. But in you—it is instinct—rather than presumption—isn't it? You follow your emotion directly, as you would follow the track of a deer in a forest."

When a woman takes the trouble thus to reason away a man's boldness, it is significant. But I knew enough to continue to play the penitent.

"You are not angry?" I put entreaty into my voice.

"I should be. But I am not." It was the final, feminine justification, and I inwardly relaxed. Still she contemplated me with that little smile. Then, impulsive, she held forth her hand. "My regard you have already —Louis," she said. "How strong it will become depends on the future —and yourself."

Wordlessly I kissed her perfumed fingers in gratitude.

3.

Throughout the boat trip back to the mainland, I had the heady
feeling that I had succeeded better than I hoped; and this by utilizing
the very traits which were not fashionable, yet emphasized my own
qualities.

I had, it appeared, read La Demoiselle correctly. Always capricious,
she was pleased by my weather-darkened face and vigorous manner,
as a relief from the languid gentlemen whose poses and compliments
had become tiresome to her.

Evidently she was suffering from ennui, seeking novelties, as if to
while away the time while waiting for something long delayed. I con-
jectured that this had to do with her lover in faraway France, and
some occurrence, or decision that was to be made. Meantime, while she
marked time, she was not unwilling to divert herself—to perhaps "fish
in strange waters" as the saying went—or so I thought from the looks
she had given me, and her intimate manner including the use of my
given name, and the pressure of her fingers on my arm, and her lack
of anger at my momentary hot embrace. In short, I believed I detected
a score of little evidences women employ to hint to men of their favor.

An even more important mark of that favor had occurred before I
left her, when after the episode in the arbor, instead of dismissing me,
she conveyed me to her mother's presence in the salon of the residency.
I was received there coldly by Madame Cadillac, and from this I judged
that she disapproved of her daughter's interest in me. She seemed to be
of the termagant order: with a dictatorial manner toward everyone save
La Demoiselle herself, who clearly held the whip hand in this household. Yet this good dame had the virtues of her faults, and was afraid
of nothing, having accompanied her husband, Cadillac, in their
younger days, when he established Fort Detroit, among the ferocious
and intractable savages in the wilderness, without a tremor at the perils
she encountered.

During the interview La Demoiselle and I jested a little, and I told a
few tales of my soldier's life. After a time Madame Cadillac relaxed
sufficiently to ask me some questions about persons in Canada whom
she knew. And her daughter quizzed me shrewdly, with feminine probing of a smiling nature, as to any attachments of a tender kind I might

have. In this I answered her lightly, though in all truth honestly enough, that none existed.

When I left, the mother invited me to come to worship with the family in the chapel of the residency the following Sunday.

The daughter had a proposal warmer and more immediate. "Come tomorrow—for late supper," she said, as she lingered for a moment alone with me in the hall, saying farewell. "There is a tiresome official dinner tonight, and too many always attend my *lever*. But tomorrow evening —late—are you at liberty?"

"Always I am at liberty—for you," I murmured.

"Then it shall be tête-à-tête. You will tell me more of your adventures —for me alone. And I play not too badly on the harp, so I am told. And sometimes sing."

"I will be ravished to hear you."

"I know we can be—such good friends," she breathed.

Once more she was very close to me, her face turned up, lips parted. I was shaken with temptation, but bent my head, took her hand, and kissed her fingers.

Thus we parted, and to me it was as if a window had suddenly opened, revealing great vistas. The Natchez concession! That Cadillac would do as his daughter wished in that matter was rather apparent. And if, meantime, there were to be a pleasant interlude with the daughter herself, why there was nothing in *that* to be unhappy about!

In this, of course, there could be serious danger. Always there is peril in love affairs conducted outside the conventions. When a woman grows too fond, she usually shows it. And if she is married, there is the husband. Even if she be unmarried, there remain assorted men with whom one may have to deal—jealous rival suitors, perhaps, or male relatives who feel their honor touched. In the case of La Demoiselle, Cadillac might prove difficult. Noirel was only one of many who sought her favor. And always there was the shadowy figure of mystery and power looming over the horizon—Antoine Crozat, Marquis du Châtel.

Yet, considering everything, I thought that though perhaps I had chosen a chancy path to tread, the risk itself was not without some appeal. And given a little luck I might through it achieve ambition, while along that path I might also take some drops of honey from the thorns that seemed to beset me.

4.

So pleased was I with myself that when we landed at the town wharf I paid the boatman twice what he deserved, and walked with quite a lilt up the street.

But at the door of the Coq d'Or my thoughts took a different direction, for there my rogues awaited me: Jaccard, saturninely silent as usual, and Marbot bubbling with some new enthusiasm. With them was a woman, whom Marbot pulled forward by the hand.

"Monsieur"—he grinned—"this is Babette."

I looked her over. She was plump and sly, with a pair of eyes that knew no rules or bounds. Even as she bobbed me a curtsy, she gave me a look that I had no difficulty in interpreting, and a smile anything but coy. Bold, that one. She would flirt with an archangel or the devil, so long as he was male. No mistaking her, she could only be one of the newly arrived *cassette* girls; and about her entire lack of virtue there was not much question.

"Good day," I said to her somewhat coldly.

"Good day to *you,* Monsieur." She smirked.

"Babette and I are affianced," announced Marbot with a deplorably fatuous grin. "We are to be married."

"Married?" I exclaimed.

"As soon as the banns are said," Babette put in, with that peculiar half-defiant proprietary manner of women who are sure of their hold on a man against any other authority. And certes, from the way Marbot made calf's eyes at her and massaged her plump arm with both his hands as if he feared she might fly away from him, he seemed very deeply in.

It was disturbing. Though I made it a rule not to interfere in the private affairs of my men, even finding some amusement in watching Marbot, who, to use Bienville's phrase, was notoriously "addicted to women," the question of so permanent and burdening a relationship as marriage had never arisen in his case before. In some manner this Babette, who probably never dreamed of getting an honest husband before coming to America, had her hooks all too well sunk in my susceptible forester. I had counted on Marbot in the adventures I planned ahead. But it seemed that matters already had progressed too far for me to attempt any intervention now.

I shrugged. After all, it would require some few days for the banns to be said, and I could only hope that in that time Marbot might come to his senses. Otherwise I must leave him behind when once again I entered the wilderness.

So I dismissed the three of them, with some noncommittal word, and entered the inn, none too happy over the episode.

The first persons I saw in the taproom were Noirel and Crevillon, drinking brandy together. Noirel gave me a nod, and a waiter hurried over.

"Captain Noirel presents his compliments," the man said, "and begs you to have a glass with him and his companion."

For a moment I hesitated, then walked over. The two rose to bow as I approached.

"Please to sit with us," said Noirel bluffly, "and this brandy is by no means bad."

"Thank you." I accepted a glass.

For a few moments we drank silently. Noirel was the first to speak.

"La Demoiselle was having rare sport at my expense," he said, "until you arrived this morning."

"And nothing Edmond could do about it," added the Ensign, "for none care to thwart her."

"I offer my thanks for coming to my rescue," Noirel said.

"It is nothing," I assured him. "I cannot abide to see a man derided when his bearing has been unassailable."

"With her it is difficult for one to know which foot to dance on," observed Crevillon.

"Nevertheless," Noirel said to me, "you seem to know the trick. Not only did you get me off the hook, but in a manner that did not offend her."

"Rather," put in Crevillon, "it appeared to arouse her interest in you."

I was mystified by their manner.

"You are just back from Dauphin Island?" Noirel inquired.

"Yes."

"And had audience with the Governor?"

"Not today, but La Demoiselle was kind enough to present me to her mother."

Noirel gave a low whistle. "A rare condescension on her part."

"Then perhaps I should be the more grateful to her." I wondered if they guessed at any of what had taken place at the residency.

All at once Noirel blurted out, "St. Denis, do you hold a fast quarrel against me?"

"Not I," said I, my mystification growing.

"Nor have I one with you," the Captain said. "If I uttered any word you have cause to remember with displeasure, I gladly retract it."

"What men say in the heat of misunderstanding is easily forgotten. As for what I said to you——"

"Tut!" said the Captain hastily. "It has passed from my mind already."

Another silence as we sipped. To what was this leading? Why this sudden offer of peace, almost friendship, from Noirel, who only a few hours ago had sworn my death?

"La Demoiselle extends her friendship to very few," ventured the young Ensign, Crevillon, presently.

"It may, or may not, be fortunate for him to whom it is extended," remarked Noirel, "depending on the way the cat jumps."

"And speaking of the cat," added the Ensign, "it has made a most surprising jump."

"In what way?" I asked.

"Within the hour the ketch *Rosanna* arrived in harbor from Fort de Paix, St. Dominique. She brings word that the *Sieur de Seignelay,* a King's ship of seventy-one guns, direct from France, was in port there, taking on fresh water, and would be sailing in a few days for Mobile."

"With a most important passenger," put in Noirel.

"None other," said Crevillon, "than the worshipful lord of this entire province of Louisiana—the King's *Concessionaire,* Antoine Crozat, Marquis du Châtel."

A dead silence. I cleared my throat. "The Governor knows of this?"

"By now, assuredly," said Noirel. "As soon as the ketch's longboat came ashore and I heard the news, I sent word to Dauphin Island. The information should be in His Excellency's hands at this moment."

"It had not arrived there when I left the residency, of that I am sure." I was thinking of La Demoiselle's farewell and her invitation. She had given it in the manner of a woman quite free in mind as to her liberty to follow whatever bent she chose; not that of a woman who anticipates, or even dreams, of an early check on her caprice.

"Hardly," Noirel answered my remark. "I dispatched the boat with the message only a short time ago. It probably passed you in the bay, as you were returning."

"This is interesting," I said. "I am most curious to see the King's *Concessionaire*. By every report he is a remarkable personage." I rose. "My thanks for the brandy. If you will excuse me, Messieurs?"

I bowed to them, and went up to my room.

5.

So Crozat was coming in person to inspect his colony! It put a different face on many things.

Among the first questions to be considered was that of La Demoiselle. I was sure I had been on the verge of a most interesting experience with her. Almost from the beginning, the rakehell in my nature had recognized the wanton in hers. We had arrived at a quite natural, quite unspoken, quite mutual understanding. I was as sure of her thoughts as I was of my own, almost. When next we met and opportunity presented itself, I did not think much time would be lost in finding what we both desired. . . .

The opportunity, in fact, already had been planned—and by *her*. A supper, and music, late in the evening and alone . . . the hour of intrigues, whispers, and kisses, when a woman grows willing in a man's arms.

I felt a sensation of acute disappointment: but it was not solely connected with the conquest I had anticipated, and which it seemed now would be denied me. La Demoiselle was two things to me: an emotional adventure in herself, and the key to her father's favor.

As to the first of these two aspects of her, I could shrug. I had played and lost in the intimate game. Well, I was a good gambler in that respect, and there were other women in the world who would make me forget her.

But I could not shrug off the loss of the second hope. Through her I was to gain my Natchez trading monopoly, and I had spent some little time reckoning the prospective profits of that commerce. Based on my expert knowledge of the fur trade, it was a modest estimate that one thousand Natchez hunters would bring in bales of furs worth two hundred thousand livres a year. And that was not considering what other neighboring tribes, such as the Choctaw and Quapaw, might add to the total.

Even with only a one-fourth commission, in five years I could have a fortune that would allow me to retire to Quebec, or even France, and live well the rest of my life. And it would be strange if I took only a modest fourth from the trade. I had no loyalty to the Crozat-Cadillac regime, and the ways of smuggling are inherent in the fur business; might almost be said to be inherent in the very blood of a Frenchman. I saw no harm in slipping a few contraband boatloads of furs past the royal customs now and then; I knew the tricks, and a river as broad, as crooked, as forested, and as untenanted as the Mississippi seemed designed as if by Providence for such personal ventures.

Now I almost groaned aloud at the thought that these entrancing possibilities had ended. La Demoiselle had her own chestnuts to think about now. I had lost both the livres and the lady.

Then I remembered that I had her invitation. If she sent no message canceling the engagement, what should I do? I could hardly ignore it.

All at once it occurred to me that while there might be danger in the situation, there might also be advantages in it. In a certain way Crozat's expected arrival removed a possible complication.

Women—that is, unmarried women—have a disconcerting tendency to expect matrimony of a lover. It was this in the past that had caused me, who had no desire to encumber myself with a wife, rather to devote myself to women who already had husbands. I would rather have faced a pistol than a priest at the altar.

Far removed from France and lonely in Louisiana, La Demoiselle might conceivably have some notion of becoming an honest woman through me. With her lover just over the horizon, however, she would hardly have such thoughts. It was almost as if she were married, and I felt free to approach her in that manner.

The game began to gain zest. I decided to make myself as agreeable to her as I could, perhaps even continue to pay secret suit to her. And she? I did not know Crozat, had never seen him, but from what I was told the merchant-noble was old enough to be La Demoiselle's father, and none too prepossessing in appearance. Between such a man and myself, it would be for another to make the comparison . . . and that other would be no less a one than La Demoiselle.

Hope that had faded began to return. I must tread most carefully, but I would use judgment, and perhaps a little audacity, and trust to luck.

At the moment I was far from despairing.

8. *The King's* Concessionaire

And yet how quickly can the plans and destinies of men and even nations change!

No later than noon the following day, while I was having a salad and a bottle of wine in the taproom of the tavern, the hollow boom of a cannon rolled across the bay.

Tiernay, the fat innkeeper, who was crossing the floor, turned so quickly at the sound that the apron strapped about his gross belly swirled like the skirt of a dancing girl in a pirouette.

"An attack!" he cried, his face gone mottled gray, his mouth flapping like that of a fish.

Another boom, and another, followed by a continual thunder of mighty guns, seemed to shake the timbers of the building.

The two or three guests in the taproom rushed for the street outside, to see better; and I heard shouts and cries of consternation through the open door. In Mobile the fear of an incursion by enemy ships, with looting and massacre, was uppermost in every mind, and a panic was beginning.

Yet I did not rise from my table. After listening a moment I said, "Calm yourself, Tiernay. It is not an attack. It is a salute."

I had marked the regular, spaced intervals at which the great rolling reports of the cannon were coming.

The innkeeper relaxed, color coming back into his face, but now a sudden thought brought me to my feet.

"It can only be the *Sieur de Seignelay!*" I exclaimed. "Here before she is expected!"

With that I also ran out into the street and hurried down to the wharf, where a crowd had gathered. As I neared it, I heard cries:

"There she is!"

"A tall ship, *ma foi!*"

"She flies the lilies of France—she's one of ours!"

A cheer of joy and relief went up from the dock.

I watched her: a tall ship, as someone had said, her white cloud of canvas grandly filled by a strong breeze from the sea so that she rapidly narrowed her distance from the town. She was a new ship without question, with three gun decks; her bow and stern magnificently carved and painted in gold and red; her gun-port levels outlined by white stripes against which the lifted port lids shone vividly, their red linings edged with gilt and with gilt fleurs-de-lis in the centers. The *Seignelay* she was, and it was her salute to the French flag at the residency that had alarmed the town. Already men were in her tops, furling the sails. Presently her anchors went out and she came to rest not far from the *Maréchal d'Estrées*, which she fairly dwarfed in size.

Antoine Crozat, the King's great *Concessionaire* had arrived! And days ahead of the earliest expectation. The ship must have left St. Dominique very shortly after the departure of the ketch that brought news of her.

I could imagine the turmoil that must be going on at the residency with this surprise. But the immediate effect on myself was more important to me. My calculations of the previous day were all out of reckoning. The supper with La Demoiselle, for example. However uncertain it might have been before, there was one fixed fact about it now: it would never take place. With Crozat at the residency, the Governor's daughter would devote her arts to him, and him alone.

It was the end to any hope of the Natchez trade also, probably. I felt a sort of resentment that the matter should thus be resolved, and suddenly, also, a new sensation took possession of me: I was ashamed.

By so narrow a margin, it came over me, had I, who had never in my whole life used a woman for any advantage, been saved from that dishonor now. A revulsion went over me. I remembered Bienville's little ironies, and my face reddened. Yet he had, in spite of his opinion of my actions, given me some sound advice. A strange man, Bienville.

All at once a distaste for everything, not fully formed before, took possession of me. The thought of this province, ruled by a Governor who was a tool of an ignoble money magnate, and for the whims of a woman who was unvirtuous, cruel, and selfish, disgusted me. This had not been Iberville's way. I said to myself that I would forswear the Natchez concession—unless I could obtain it by some honorable means, which seemed now impossible.

Yet at the same time I was mightily curious to see this Crozat, and behold what manner of man it was who had risen from the antecedents he possessed to the power, almost royal, he now enjoyed.

2.

There was nothing further to keep me at the wharf, so I turned my steps back to the Coq d'Or and my unfinished luncheon.

As I approached the inn I saw Marbot, squatting by the steps like an Indian, and wearing a most disconsolate expression.

"Hola, Marbot!" I said. "Why do I see you here, instead of down at the dock watching the new ship come in? And where is that woman you are to marry?"

Marbot rose to his feet with a funeral face.

"Where is she?" he said. "I do not know. I do not care. Forever I am through with women, for I have had such experience of their treachery as to cure me of them for all time. I am ready, Monsieur, to go with you wherever you lead, so long as it is soon, and not in the vicinity of their accursed sex!"

"*Mon Dieu*, you sing a different tune today! When last I saw you, I thought you most enamored and eager to be a bridegroom."

"You touch me in a raw spot, Monsieur," he said, with a face of tragedy. "To think that I allowed myself to sink so deeply into the pool of deception, only to discover the creature Babette was without any honor or scruple whatever!"

I forbore from saying that this should have been apparent from the first, and encouraged him to proceed with his tale.

"It is Jaccard I blame as much as Babette," he said.

"Aha!"

"A traitorous friend is Jaccard, and I never want to set eyes on him again. I should have noticed his rolling eye and jackal grin from the time Babette and I made first our compact. But how could I expect such treason?"

Marbot cast his eyes skyward and spread his hands in so ludicrous a gesture of hopelessness that I could hardly refrain from smiling.

"Tell me what occurred," I urged, instead.

"It was after we left you yesterday, Monsieur," said Marbot. "We went to La Dive Bouteille, knowing no other place to spend the night. There we had some drinks, and dinner, and then some more drinks, and after that still more drinks. When it came time for bed we be-thought ourselves that we had but the one room between us, Jaccard and I. This was a cause for concern, but Babette herself solved it in the most sensible manner. She suggested that we all three share the room, and inasmuch as she and I already were as good as married, why not anticipate on time a little, and she would sleep with me, leaving the other bed for Jaccard?"

Again he rolled his eyes skyward and gave a profound sigh.

"I must say that the arrangement suited me," he resumed, "so I took still a few more drinks to cement it. Why, oh, why did I do so? I should have kept my wits about me. Even then that hellhound, Jaccard, was busy ogling my Babette—and she him—but I was too greatly occupied in celebrating the occasion to have anything but good will for all."

"None of us are exactly prophets where the petticoats are concerned," I observed dryly.

"They waited," Marbot continued, "until the wine made me drowsy, then all three of us went to our room and to bed, Babette snuggling up beside me like a very wife indeed, and I with my arms lovingly about her. But the wine—curse the treacherous cup!—took from me my amorousness, so that before I knew it I was snoring, my arms relaxing from about my companion in my sleep."

"A capital mistake to commit with any woman," I commented.

"Mistake? Well may you say so, Monsieur! No sooner had I fallen into slumber than Jaccard—the dog, the wolf, the pig—came in the dark-ness and whispered to her, then took her by the hand. And she—treach-erous trollop—very willingly stole out of my bed, and off to his. And there Babette, without an outcry or murmur or even a shrug of defense, blithely yielded herself to another man than her affianced husband-to-be, to whom she had sworn eternal fidelity!"

"It has happened before, Marbot, and to wiser men than you."

"But the ignominy of it! I slept on, not dreaming that my friend and my fiancée were betraying me, until I chanced to turn over and felt an emptiness where a soft form had been in my bed."

Marbot paused, as if to strengthen himself to endure the recollection.

"It brought me wide awake at once, you may believe me! I sat up and listened. They were asleep, the betrayers! I could hear them breathing in slumber, having exhausted themselves by their guilty pleasures. Ah, Monsieur! How I groaned to myself at the realization that there is no honesty in woman's love! For a time I debated whether I should use my knife on the two of them, making a sleep of death out of their adulterous slumber. But then, instead of slitting their throats, I slapped Babette across her bottom so loudly that you could have heard the clap of it throughout the inn."

Marbot made a gesture, with the open palm, showing the manner of administering his admonishment to the faithless *cassette* girl.

"She gave a yelp," he went on with a certain grim satisfaction, "and sat up whining, knuckling her eyes and rubbing the spot where, I warrant you, the print of my hand was still red. I lit a candle. Jaccard also sat up and I gave him a murderous glare.

"'Traitor! False friend! Judas!' I shouted at him. 'You have destroyed our friendship forever!'

"If you will believe it, Monsieur, the scabby magpie had not a word to say in his own defense. He rose, pulled on his clothes, and then said, with a kind of villainous smirk, 'Who gets the girl?'"

Once again Marbot stopped, as if conjuring up this unpalatable picture to refresh his indignation.

"Until that moment," he went on, "I had excused Babette in my mind, thinking that she was perhaps too drunk and drowsy to realize what she had done. When Jaccard asked that question, I considered it beneath my dignity to answer it, for was she not affianced to me, and was I not ready to forgive her?"

"What did Babette say?" I asked.

"Nothing just then," answered Marbot. "It was Jaccard who spoke. Drawing his hunting knife he said, 'Do you believe I'll leave her to you without a fight? Think again, friend! The girl is mine, and I'll take her if I have to carve out your liver to do it!'

"At that, Monsieur, I out with my own blade, and was about to throw myself on the scoundrel, when Babette began to implore us not to fight, that nothing could be gained by shedding blood, and she alone was to blame. 'If you must have blood, let me die,' she sobbed. 'I was the unfaithful one, upsetting your friendship! Cut my throat, both of you!'"

All this Marbot recited with woe in his face that was comical.

"Such self-accusation is remarkable in a woman," I said.

"Ah, but it was only more treachery on her part!" exclaimed Marbot. "When she pleaded thus, after a moment both Jaccard and I

sheathed our knives, since neither of us desired especially to kill her—
quite the contrary, in her shift, with her bare arms and round form,
she looked most tempting in the candlelight. Then Jaccard made a
proposal.

" 'Let us settle the argument peaceably,' he said. 'The girl herself
must choose. It is only fair, after all, that she should have the right to
select her own lover. Let her go to the man she prefers.'

"To me, Monsieur, it sounded like a very judgment of Solomon. Had
not Babette and I made vows so binding that it was almost as if we
were married already? So sure was I of her decision that I agreed with
all my heart: indeed, I jumped at the idea, and made haste to have
the question put to the test before Jaccard backed out of it."

"And what took place?" I prompted, as Marbot paused again woe-
fully.

"As one man, Jaccard and I turned to Babette," he said. "Ah, ah!
Imagine my astonishment, my rage, my chagrin, when without any
hesitation, or even pretense of giving thought to a matter that should
have been so important to her, she sprang up and seized Jaccard's
vile paw! Ah, the infamy of it! Ah, the falsehearted deceiver I had
taken to my bosom!"

Marbot clutched at his bristling beard to illustrate his despair, then
went on.

"So stunned was I, Monsieur, that I staggered back against the wall
and fell down on my bed. In my bitterness and misery I could have
slit my own throat and thus ended my anguish. But the thought that
this would only be the final triumph for my enemy caused me to give
up the idea. As for Jaccard, that contaminated, irredeemable scoundrel,
he went out swaggering, with the woman clinging fulsomely to his arm
and simpering up into his face with odious sheep's eyes, leaving me
abandoned and brokenhearted in an empty room!"

With so lugubrious a moan did Marbot end his tale that once more
I had much to do to keep from bursting into a laugh. Yet I knew it
would never do to wound the little man any farther. Moreover, the
situation had its serious side, for Marbot and Jaccard were the men
on whom I had depended, and to have them at dirk points with each
other was an evil thing.

So I kept a straight face, wondering what I could do to reconcile
them, and after a moment said, "Comfort yourself, Marbot. You are

well out of this. From the moment I set eyes on her, I knew the baggage was sly and faithless. Had you married her, she would have made you regret it every day of your life—it is that one's gift to sprain the truth with every word she speaks, even when she does not outright break it. Mark my words, Jaccard will rue it that he attached her to himself, and come crawling back to us begging to be taken into our good graces again."

At this Marbot brightened somewhat; and grew still brighter when I gave him a coin and told him to go comfort himself with a bottle. He even displayed a slight hint of his old swagger as he went off, his spirits rising as he imagined Jaccard's possible undoing. I went into the Coq d'Or.

3.

More than ordinarily sprig and flounced in his silks and laces, with yellow peruke and white-plumed hat, young Ensign Étienne de Crevillon brought the message toward evening, preening his silky little mustache and obviously considering his errand one of importance.

"I have the honor," he said to me, "to conduct you to the residency. The official pinnace awaits your pleasure."

The official pinnace! I was a little startled. This had an impressive sound, portending something more momentous than a private supper with the Governor's daughter.

"What's the meaning of this?" I asked.

"I don't know, Monsieur." But the Ensign's heightened respect showed that he, too, regarded it as placing me in a new and more important light in the affairs of the colonial government.

"What's afoot on Dauphin Island?" I next inquired.

"I only know that there's a hell's hullabaloo since Monsieur Crozat, the Marquis du Châtel, arrived this afternoon."

"It was a surprise?"

"Apparently an entire surprise." Crevillon smoothed his light mustache with one finger. "I gather that in spite of word of his coming, that he would arrive so soon was the last thing expected."

"They are disturbed, I take it."

"As busy as a hill of ants. Officials and servants rushing about as if their bottoms were afire, and Cadillac—between ourselves, of course—looking as uneasy as the devil in holy water."

"I will make myself presentable and be with you."

To go to my room, shave my chin, comb my hair, tie it with a new ribbon, and don my best attire took no very long time. But in that short while my mind was busy with conjectures.

The official pinnace meant that the summons was from the Governor himself. Did it have something to do perhaps with La Demoiselle?

I wondered if, with the arrival of Crozat, some crisis might have arisen over a whisper—perhaps by La Vente—that an upstart Canadian was in her favor. What did La Vente actually know? Nothing, I told myself. Had someone seen that kiss under the arbor? The more I speculated on this, the more uneasy I became.

On the way to the wharf, with Crevillon mincing at my side, I felt not a little like a prisoner under guard, and though I bore no visible chains, I could almost feel them invisibly clanking on my wrists and ankles. The situation appeared most menacing.

Six sturdy oarsmen were in the pinnace, but since the wind had turned favorable and the sail took the little ship across the bay easily, it was not necessary for them to row. On the way across I continued to rack my mind for reasons why I was summoned—other than those having to do with La Demoiselle—and to my disquiet found nothing that satisfactorily answered my questions.

When we landed on the island, Crevillon conducted me through the palisade gate, where the sentries saluted us, and to the anteroom of the audience chamber in the residency. There, in the dim shadows of evening, for the lamps had not yet been lit, lurked a lean figure. It came forward to meet us.

"Abbé La Vente!" I exclaimed.

The priest responded with a slight bow.

For a moment we gazed searchingly at each other, I contemplating La Vente's gaunt countenance, while the priest gave me a curious studying scrutiny in return, as if seeking to determine what my thoughts were and what manner of man I was, by outward examination.

"Can you tell me why I was sent for?" I asked presently.

"It has graciously pleased His Excellency, the Sieur de Cadillac, to have you to dinner this evening, with a musicale to follow," he replied.

"*Vraiment?*" My voice reflected wonder. I had an invitation, from La Demoiselle—but it was for supper, a late collation, and tête-à-tête. *This* invitation was from the Governor himself, for an earlier, more formal repast, presumably with the family. Was there some connection between the two?

"Allow me," said La Vente, "to conduct you to the domiciliary wing."

Leaving Crevillon to go to his duties, the two of us passed into the garden. But instead of going directly across it, the priest paced slowly along the path with me, evidently in no hurry.

"Before we go in to His Excellency's presence, there is something I would say to you," he began presently.

"What is it?"

We halted.

"Monsieur," said La Vente, "I wish to be your friend."

"This is to laugh!" I retorted.

"Perhaps we were not in full agreement at first," he replied. "But, *omnia mutantur et nos mutamur.* You have Latin?"

"Very little."

"The phrase broadly signifies that one is capable of changing his opinion."

"If yours has changed concerning me, why?"

"That is neither here nor there. But I would do you a favor."

"Well?" I did not trust this man.

"This is a matter of delicacy. *Vigilantibus, non dormientibus, Deus subvenat.*"

He waited while I tried to puzzle that out in my head, finally arriving at the rough meaning that God helps those who are awake rather than asleep.

"Very well," I said at last. "What is this matter of delicacy?"

"What would you say if I told you that His Excellency, the Governor, looks with favor upon you as a member of his own family?"

For once, I was stunned.

"But this is incredible!" I exclaimed.

"I can see how it would be almost impossible for you to believe, Monsieur. Nevertheless, I am empowered to inform you of this beforehand, so that you will not be entirely overwhelmed with gratitude and joy when it is announced to you, and may be prepared to make the proper expressions of happiness."

I was beginning to recover. "Explain!" I demanded.

"The Sieur de Cadillac desires his daughter to take unto herself a husband," said La Vente with the utmost gravity.

"And so?"

"Mademoiselle, out of her good will and affection for her father, has agreed. Her choice has fallen on you."

Once more I was struck speechless.

La Vente gazed at me with impatience. "Monsieur, you do not give very good evidence of the transports which this remarkable good fortune should create in you. Do you realize the meaning of this?"

"I—I am too confused to think."

"As the Governor's son-in-law, you will become one of the great men in the colony. Perhaps even Lieutenant Governor, when we rid ourselves of that serpent, Bienville."

It was becoming abundantly apparent why La Vente was displaying this sudden friendship.

But I could only stammer. "I—I have—not asked such preferment——"

"Furthermore," went on the priest in his curious deep rumble, as if I had not spoken, "you will be certain to receive the license for the Natchez trade which you desire, and perhaps that for other Indian nations as well. It will make you rich, Monsieur! And under these circumstances you will not even be under the necessity of yourself going to those places, but can appoint agents who will do all the work and take all the risks for you, while you reap the rich profits and live in ease and splendor!"

It was my dream answered! Answered beyond its fairest expectations: wealth, power, ease, security, and honor, all were within my grasp!

And yet something within me misliked the whole thing.

"In exchange for this I must have a wife to order my comings and goings?" I said.

La Vente's face grew more cunning in the deepening dusk.

"That is the very meat of the nut!" he said. "Knowing you for a man who above all else prizes his freedom, the whole plan of this should be infinitely pleasing to you. For not only will you not be ordered by a wife—you will not even see her after you are wed!"

"Not *see* her? How is this?"

"The marriage is one of convenience. I need not inform you of the expedients of the sophisticated world. Suffice it to say that Mademoiselle de Cadillac has reason to wish to return to France, and in so doing she prefers to go as Madame de St. Denis."

All at once the whole thing became startlingly clear to me.

Crozat desired to take his mistress back with him to Paris. But under the curious conventions of the time, an unmarried woman could not maintain her own establishment, must have at least a pretense of chaperonage, was handicapped in many ways in the exercise of her volition and conduct—ways that a married woman was not.

The King himself had made it a practice to marry off his mistresses, as each came into the royal favor, to some figurehead of a husband, who never saw his wife, perhaps, after the spurious vows were said, but who gave her his name and in return received some tens of thousands of gold pieces from the royal treasury, or perhaps was placed in a sinecure position, or on a royal pension, while cynically shrugging at the knowledge everyone had of the "invisible horns"—the phrase of the day—that had been placed on his brow by his wife and her royal paramour.

What the King did, the great and rich men of his kingdom did also. Mistresses must be wedded, if in name only, since the estate of Madame was infinitely freer than the estate of Mademoiselle; and there was in addition the factor of protection for the libertine lover who arranged all this, should the lady in question get it into her head that she wished something more formal and legal than a mere bedroom alliance with him.

As this realization came over me, I drew a sharp breath.

"This is why I am invited to dine with the Governor tonight?" I asked.

"Yes, Monsieur." La Vente gave a smile that I thought odious. "And may I, in advance, offer my congratulations?"

I ignored the offer. "Who will be present?"

"The Governor, Madame, and Mademoiselle, of course. Monsieur Crozat, the Marquis du Châtel. Since this is an official dinner, the Sieur de Bienville, only because he is Lieutenant Governor. You, and my humble self."

A small and select group, certes, yet one containing every power. I considered.

"Very well," I said after a moment, "let us see where this leads."

4.

When the powder-wigged major-domo conducted us to the salon, the others already were there: Cadillac, his wife, La Demoiselle, Bienville, and a man I had never seen before, whom I knew must be Crozat.

The eye instinctively sought the King's *Concessionaire,* so overpowering was his personality. It was overpowering without being pleasing. He was a bulking man in a very splendid suit of dark maroon velvet, cut to show stripes of gold in it, yet failing to hide the shrunken legs in their silk stockings and also the potbelly, advertising approaching decrepitude. Under the heavy dark peruke, the expression of his eyes was lowering, yet with a glint of almost animal cunning, his brows drawn down habitually on the bridge of his nose, deep wrinkles in his forehead, his mouth broad, grim, and stubborn. In him the peasant was apparent: the peasant who had surmounted almost invincible obstacles, and in surmounting them had created in himself a habit of ruthless determination, an everlasting watchfulness for any advantage he might seize to further his still unbounded greed for yet greater wealth and higher station.

Beside him sat La Demoiselle on a demichair. In spite of everything I knew about her, I could not but compare her slender grace with the merchant-noble's grossness, as a gazelle beside a wild boar, with a sort of pity. And yet I was assured in my mind that she did not pity herself, but rather gloried in her hold over that man, so mighty through his riches.

At the far end of the room, beside the chair of Madame, stood Bienville, gazing at me with the usual coldness on his chiseled face.

Cadillac himself, in a tobacco-colored coat and waistcoat embroidered with metal thread and sparkling with paillettes, looked meager and sour in his clothes, which, however fine and carefully tailored, always had the appearance of being too large for his bony body. With a nod, he returned my bow, and then presented me to his guest.

"Monsieur St. Denis is the gentleman of whom we have been speaking," he said, after the introduction.

Crozat, who had not risen to answer my bow, swung his huge head around with a somewhat baleful stare. At the same time I saw in La Demoiselle's face the faint shadow of a smile of a most enigmatic nature.

I found myself trying to interpret that smile. Was it amusement? A glint of triumph? An appeal?

"Now that we are all here," said the Governor, "let us go into the *salle à manger.*"

Being last in precedence, I was last to enter the room. A table was spread quite splendidly with linen napery and gleaming crystal and silver, and lighted by many candles in chandeliers and in sconces on the walls. At the head Cadillac was seated, at the foot Madame. At the Governor's right was Crozat, with Bienville at Madame's left, and La Demoiselle between them. I was at Madame's right, with Abbé La Vente at His Excellency's left. The strangeness of this seating struck me, and I could only conclude that Crozat wished to sit beside La Demoiselle, and also that both of them desired to face me during the conversation.

At first nothing was said about the subject that must have been uppermost in every mind. During the soup course a few pleasantries were exchanged, but as the repast progressed, the talk grew weightier.

"You have, Monsieur St. Denis, traversed the region of the Red River?" Cadillac asked me presently.

"Yes, Your Excellency."

"And what is your opinion of it?"

Though puzzled by the nature of the question, I was relieved to speak on something so impersonal. "I consider it inhospitable, poor, a dreary wilderness," I replied with candor.

"What are the people?"

"Savages, who, if they are not cannibals like the Attacapas, are dwellers in miserable straw huts like the Natchitoches, without clothing save for aprons woven from grass or skins worn as capes over the shoulders."

The Governor's bony fingers toyed with his wineglass. "We have just received a message from that region," he said, "brought by an Indian to Biloxi, and forwarded here by official post."

"When I was up the Red River," said I in surprise, "no other white man had been so far. From whom was this message?"

"From a Spaniard."

For a moment there was dead silence as I tried to digest this news and the others waited for me to speak.

"This is a matter of gravity if true, Excellency," I said. "The Spaniards on the Red River? If so, they are on the threshold of Louisiana!"

He seemed to ponder that. "One Spaniard only, it appears," he said presently. "He writes that he is among the Neches. Know you this people?"

I frowned, perplexed. "I met no such tribe on the Red River," I answered. Then, "But let me think—I am reminded now that I heard that the survivors of the La Salle colony, twenty years or more ago, spoke of the Neches—also called Teches, whom in turn the Spaniards call Texas. But this people is far south of the Red River. Who wrote from among them?"

"A priest, signing himself Padre Francisco Hidalgo. He writes from what he calls San Francisco de los Neches, which seems to be a mission."

"A mission is ever the first outpost of Spanish rule!"

"A one-man mission could hardly be," said the Governor. "This Hidalgo represents himself as alone. His message, written in Latin, states that he has received no support from the authorities in New Spain; and wishing strongly to continue his work among the heathen, he asks us to send him supplies, pointing out—as a temporal inducement for our aid in his spiritual work—that trade relations with his Indians would be valuable for France."

For a moment I was silent. Then I said, "I believe Your Excellency would be disappointed in the results of trade with the Indians of that country. I have suggested already a far better outlet for French goods— the Natchez."

"You find nothing in this to interest you?"

"Most barren of interest, Your Excellency."

Again silence fell at the table. Then Crozat spoke, in his hoarse, rasping voice. "What did you say was the name of these people who would be good in trade?"

"The Natchez," I told him.

"They are friendly to us?"

"No, they are treacherously inclined to be hostile. Travel through their country is dangerous at all times unless in sufficient force to ensure successful resistance against attack."

"Yet you are willing to risk this danger?"

"Without risk there is no gain. I am accustomed to danger. And also I am accustomed to privation and the labor of life in the wilderness."

As I spoke Crozat gazed at me with a singular expression, as if in contempt. Like most parvenus, he was given to great pretensions, insufferably patronizing to all he considered beneath his station. I found myself cordially disliking the man.

I tried to read Bienville's look. Throughout the conversation he had been silent, and now I could make nothing of him. The usual aloof, recessive manner was all he displayed.

Cadillac gave his bloodless smile. "I think you may perhaps count yourself free of both danger and privation from this evening, Monsieur. You have been informed of the honor that is being accorded you?"

Thus, suddenly, was the matter thrown among us.

For a moment I was silent, then I glanced at La Demoiselle. "Monsieur l'Abbé has discussed the matter with me," I said.

She did not relax her position, and now upon her face came again the faint shadow of that enigmatic smile.

"You understand the—ah—conditions?" pursued Cadillac.

"I do."

Again the Governor grinned coldly. "In that case, since everything is understood, all that remains are the forms of marriage between my daughter and yourself, after which you will receive the *brevet* for the Natchez monopoly, and perhaps other privileges pleasing to you also."

"Mademoiselle agrees?" I asked.

"Perfectly."

I gazed about the table. They held my future in their hands: Crozat, Cadillac, Madame his wife, La Demoiselle, Bienville, even Abbé La Vente, the politico-priest. They could make or break me. And they were offering me a fortune undreamed of. Self-interest seemed to dictate that I accept, go through the forms, and reap the large rewards.

Yet at that moment I felt a sudden swift stiffening of pride. Perhaps it was the faint smile on La Demoiselle's face that goaded me.

It came over me that—as if I had no voice in the matter—they were assigning me to the living disgrace of a permanent role as complaisant cuckold to that coarse, ignoble vulgarian sitting across the table.

To be betrayed by one's wife is one thing; to be betrayed by her with one's willing consent, and for a bribe, is quite another. That the offer should be made to me was an insult: even worse, that they should all assume that I would accept it.

As if to strengthen this feeling there returned in me the sensation of contempt for the whole Crozat-Cadillac-La Demoiselle regime, and the shame of lending myself to venality and a woman's wanton whims.

Yet the situation, as the Abbé had said, was a delicate one. Now at last I fully understood that hint of a smile on La Demoiselle's face:

she had me where I must accept either humiliation or ruin, and she thought she knew which course I would take. Suddenly I longed to wipe that smile, so knowing and contemptuous, from her face.

Unconscious of the turmoil in my mind, Cadillac rose with his glass.

"The banns will be said at once, and the ceremony set for the earliest possible day, for my daughter wishes to return to France on the *Sieur de Seignelay*," he said. "And now, since a betrothal and approaching wedding should be occasions for rejoicing, let us drink to the health and happiness of the bride—and of the gentleman who is to be her consort."

All rose at the table. All raised glasses and drank to the toast.

All but I, who did not lift my glass.

"You did not drink!" exclaimed Cadillac.

"I cannot drink to that toast," I said.

Every face turned toward me: in Cadillac's was an expression of astonishment, in Crozat's unbelief, in Madame's incomprehension, in La Vente's a question, in La Demoiselle's sudden speculation. Only in Bienville's face was no change. It was as if the whole matter was of utmost indifference to him.

"You *cannot* drink? Explain!" demanded Cadillac.

His look had changed to anger, and I knew how deeply I had placed myself in jeopardy. To thus publicly refuse his daughter would be the deadliest affront: and that to a man who had supreme power, even over life and death. What should I say?

"The honor is too great for me—greater than I deserve——" I began.

Nobody spoke. As well as anyone present, I knew the excuse was too weak, the reason no reason at all. My throat felt suddenly dry and stiff. Yet I must speak again.

"Nevertheless," I went on, "that is not why I may not marry——"

Cadillac's face grew livid with fury. "*May* not? Why—*why?* Explain here and now, to this assemblage, what remarkable reason you have for refusing the daughter of the Governor of Louisiana!"

Later, I was to believe verily that I was as much surprised myself as was anyone there at the sudden answer which came unbidden to my lips, in a sort of desperate inspiration.

"I—I have *taken a vow of celibacy!*"

In the room stunned silence reigned. Every eye sought Abbé La

Vente, as if asking the Church's ruling in the matter; save only the eyes of La Demoiselle, which remained fixed on me. Of them all, she who had coquetted with me—she who had been in my arms and exchanged kisses with me, had heard my words of eagerness—she alone knew how little of a celibate in truth I was. In her eyes was no question: only complete comprehension and suppressed fury. Her vanity was terribly, mortally lacerated. The smile had been wiped from her face in good earnest.

"What of this, Monsieur l'Abbé?" Cadillac asked in a dry voice.

The priest replied with an odd note of bafflement. "If this man has taken such a vow, Excellency, he is by the rules of the Church ineligible for marriage."

Another long silence. Those about the table looked their hostility at me. They could not say I lied, yet they did not believe me. Only La Demoiselle could have offered evidence on this point, and that it was most inexpedient for her to do.

I bowed. "Under the circumstances, which are so regrettable, may I beg permission to withdraw?"

"Get out!" Cadillac shouted.

Bienville, still with his glass in his hand, took a sip of wine. And only I noticed that as he did so, he lifted it slightly, almost as if to me, in a pledge of some secret kind.

5.

Dismissed so peremptorily, I was rowed back to the mainland, knowing my ill fortune had begun again.

The inspiration that led me to plead a vow of celibacy was the only good thing that had occurred. Cadillac had supreme power in the colony, and Crozat had supreme power over Cadillac, and La Demoiselle, for that matter, had supreme power over Crozat. Yet my excuse was such that they could hardly take any direct action against me.

My bad luck lay in my having encountered La Demoiselle at all, and especially in catching her fancy so that she took it into her head to experiment with me.

My prospects for advancement in this colony were at an end, and I wondered where I should next turn. The following morning the decision was taken out of my hands. The message was brought by a common soldier while I was at breakfast in the tavern. I broke the *cachet* on the letter and read:

> To Louis Juchereau de St. Denis,
> Sometime Captain in the Irregular Troops of His Majesty,
> At the Inn Coq d'Or:
>
> On your peril! By the King's authority you are required to en-
> list a suitable company of men, take such goods as are assigned
> to you, and proceed at once to Fort d'Iberville, whence you will
> escort a tribe of Indians who have come to our province begging
> food, back to their homes on the Red River. There you will es-
> tablish a military post, which you will garrison and maintain
> until further orders, for the protection of the Indians aforesaid,
> and the frontier of this royal colony of Louisiana.
>
> > This at the command of,
> > Cadillac, Governor of Louisiana,
> > By La Vente, Secretary

Now I knew my fate. Unable to proceed against me directly, the
angry Governor, *Concessionaire*, and very likely La Demoiselle, had
taken council, and resolved to exile me. The nature of the order revealed its malice.

Not only was I banished, but banished to that exact savage and inhospitable region for which I had expressed my aversion: the poverty
of which was further advertised by the famine which had driven some
of its inhabitants to migrate and beg food of the French. And beyond
this, I was to establish and maintain, *until further orders*, a fort there,
which meant nothing less than perpetual expulsion.

For a time I sat with my head in my hands, at the breakfast table
in the taproom. There could be no question of refusing the order, for it
was peremptory, and Crozat was so close to the ear of the King that
disobedience would have the ugliest consequences: prison certainly,
perhaps execution for mutiny or treason.

While I sat thus disconsolate, I heard a step and glanced up. The
thin, elegant figure of Bienville stood beside me.

"May I join you?" he asked.

Gloomily I assented, adding, "That is, if you care to be seen in the
company of one in such bad odor as you know me to be."

He seated himself without replying, ordered chocolate, took a sip, and gazed about the tavern room, which at this hour was deserted, save for the tapster at the bar and a waiter lounging and gossiping beside him.

At length he said, "In ill odor, yes. And is it not deserved?"

"Why?" I asked.

"Has your behavior been entirely irreproachable?"

"Why do you ask that?"

"To begin with, was it just to me to say nothing to me of the letters from Canada which you knew were intended for my eye?"

I almost gasped. "You—knew?"

"From the first." Bienville nodded. "I am not entirely a fool, my friend. One like yourself, embarking on the long journey down the Mississippi, would most certainly be asked to carry dispatches. Since I was still Governor when you left Quebec, it follows that such communications would be for me." His coldly chiseled face turned directly on me. "I suspected it when I first saw you. I was sure when you returned from the residency and packed yourself off at once from my poor house. Last night it was confirmed by Cadillac himself, since the communications contained some business on which he needed my information."

"The letters," I began, "were addressed to the Governor, and I conceived that Cadillac was Governor and should receive them."

"This is to equivocate. You knew for whom they were *intended*."

From most men I would not have taken that, but now my feeling of guilt was too strong for heat. I remembered that I had not even used those letters to save Jaccard, but rather tendered them in my own interests.

At last I said, "If you knew this, why did you not speak of it until now?"

"I am interested in the behavior of men. It amused me to see what you would do."

"Those letters might have ruined you."

"Perhaps. But my conscience is clear in regard to my administration. I was not too apprehensive."

I drew a deep breath. "Seigneur, I am ashamed and I beg your forgiveness. You have all reason to despise me."

"I have few illusions about men. You did nothing I did not expect— until last night."

"That surprised you?"

"I confess I was interested to see you fling your refusal in the teeth of the Governor, braving his wrath and knowing it surely meant an end to your ambitions—rather than accept wealth and high place with dishonor. I have, after all, hopes of you, St. Denis."

"What manner of hopes?" I said bitterly.

"I believe you to be something more than a mere adventurer, and that you can be of use to France."

"Your conclusion comes belated. I am finished. Exiled to the most remote and desert spot in all the King's realms."

"I know," said Bienville calmly. "I arranged that."

"*What?*" I almost sprang up from my chair.

"Calm yourself. Your fate might be much worse. They were beside themselves with rage, and were casting about for some grave charge to trump up against you. Only because none had yet occurred to them, was my suggestion considered: that the most condign punishment would be to send you to the wilderness you so detest. It is better than an oar in the galleys."

"*Dieu!* Not so much better!"

"Ah yes. You have received the order?"

"Only a short time ago."

"Then you know you do not go without some authority and honor. That also I did for you. You go as an officer of France."

"An officer? Rather I go as a huckster. With 'such goods as are assigned to me.' Trade goods—I am to find some outlet for Crozat's merchandise, and without even a commission for myself!"

"It was only on this basis that I could obtain this much consideration for you."

"A huckster!" I exclaimed again. "This is to be my future!"

"Nay, look at it this way," said Bienville, with his imperturbable manner. "You are on the frontier. A frontier, no matter how remote and deserted, is never unimportant. It is the contact point between nations, the launching place for invasions and defenses. You will be a nerve end for France. What about this Spanish priest, Hidalgo, and his mission among the Neches? You yourself said that a mission is the first outpost of military rule. One of your most important duties will be to find that mission, seek to learn what it betides, and send word of the matter."

"Much good that would do! Cadillac and Crozat care not a fly for the frontier. They would sell all Louisiana for a few livres' profit."

"Perhaps. But there are those, too, who still think of France."

I stared. All at once the cold, thin face before me seemed to have a different meaning to me. In the corruption, inefficiency, sloth, and sycophancy of this place, here was one single thread of clear-sighted unselfishness.

I remembered suddenly that this man was a Le Moyne! And the Le Moyne family had expended itself from one end of the continent to the other, not for profit, but for a dream—the glory of France. I had thought that dream dead, but now it stirred within me again.

The man sitting before me did not possess the magnetism and warmth to make men love and die for him, which the great Iberville possessed. But I knew all at once that in Bienville was something of the same devotion which would allow no personal profit, convenience, or safety to stand in the way of his service to his King.

It seemed suddenly a welcome relief to be thinking again along the good, clean line of honor, as the only thing that counts.

Huskily I said, "I, too, think sometimes of France, Seigneur."

"Praise be to God!" exclaimed Bienville with a warmth rare and unexpected in him. "My brother, Iberville, loved you like a son, St. Denis. Yet he would have flung you ungrudgingly into hell itself, and me and all else he loved with you, and then followed himself after us, if by doing so he could serve the cause he held in trust."

"Seigneur," I said, "I thank you. You have given me back something I had all but lost."

But Bienville reverted to his old cold manner, as if such a burst of feeling discomforted him.

"Then let us understand each other," he said. "You have an opportunity. More than that, a duty. Below this colony lies the great stronghold of Spain in the Americas. Nominally, France and Spain still are friends and allies, but will this continue long? No, I anticipate it may cease on any day—perhaps with the death of our old King, who is now in his seventy-fifth year and seriously ailing. There are rumors—mere reports, but perhaps based on grim fact—that Spain contemplates making the long-delayed northward expansion from New Spain. If so, all of Louisiana, and in fact all the Mississippi territory of France might be threatened. This mission of Padre Hidalgo's makes the situation appear urgent. Will you undertake to discover, if possible, what are the Spanish plans?"

"I will try."

"You can perhaps do so by locating the mission, and questioning the priest."

"It is possible."

Bienville gave me his silent attention for a moment. "I can promise you no reward," he said at last.

"This is understood."

"But I will say to you this," he concluded, "I am in disfavor now, but the wind changes, and so do royal policies. The day may come when I will again be in the top of the basket, as the saying is. If that day comes, and you serve well this charge, on the word of a Le Moyne you may count me as a friend. For the present I ask only this: that you let me know how you fare and what goes forward in this new bourn of yours."

He rose, nodded, and went out with his odd, almost mincing gait.

For a time I sat where he left me, my head still bowed, my heart like a cobblestone in a pool. Bienville's chill offer of friendship did nothing to lift my spirits. What could his friendship avail? By his own saying, he was on the down wing now.

I knew my fate: perhaps forever, in a thankless cause, I was doomed to ride the red earth, smitten by the sun.

6.

About noon I left the inn to stretch my legs. At once I became conscious of a commotion in the direction of the docks. Shouts of anger and defiance, catcalls, cockcrows, jeers and laughter mingled in noisy clamor.

I turned in that direction to see the cause, quickening my pace as several curious persons hurried past me. When I came in view of the public square adjoining the docks, a singular sight met my eyes.

Two barrels, apparently provided with legs, hands, and heads, were reeling to and fro, and I was horrified to see that the head protruding from the top of one of the barrels wore the unhappy countenance of my good Marbot, while that of the other barrel displayed the equally sad visage of Jaccard.

They were wearing what the *habitants* called "drunkards' cloaks." A headless barrel was inverted, a hole made in the bottom—now the top—for the prisoner's head to go through, and openings cut in the sides for his hands, which were fastened there by gyves. It thus formed a kind of wooden garb of disgrace, extending down over the body from neck to mid-thigh. Each in his drunkard's cloak, helpless and at the same time looking for all the world like chickens half hatched from their eggs, my two rogues tottered about, their faces spattered with mud and rotten vegetables that had been thrown at them by the hooting mob which surrounded them, abusing them, spitting on them, pushing them this way and that.

But at the moment of my arrival the mob ceased pushing and hauling the two prisoners about. A small band of men, all leather-clad, suddenly appeared and gathered about the pair, warding off the crowd.

I saw what was happening. Other Canadians, arriving on the scene, were trying to protect Marbot and Jaccard from the brutal town rabble.

From the mob came cries of rage:

"À bas les Canadiens!"

"Spoilsports!"

"Louse-eaten woods runners!"

"Stand away before you, too, are rolled in the mire!"

And from the Canadians, who stood defying them:

"Vides poches!"*

"A handful of steel in the ribs of the first cochon who lays a finger on one of these men!"

But there were only fifteen of the Canadians, while the mob numbered more than a hundred, including not a few women, viragoes worse than any of the men. Stones began to sing through the air. It would go hard with the handful of foresters, and I was wondering desperately what I could do to help them, when there was a shout, and a troop of horsemen bore down upon the scene at a gallop.

At once the mob melted away, diving into the shacks and cabins from which it had come, so that when the horsemen arrived, only the Canadians, the two disconsolate rascals in the drunkards' cloaks, a portly man with a pike whom I took to be the huissier, or bailiff, and a few others, including myself, remained in view.

At the head of the troop rode Noirel. He wheeled his horse, glaring furiously about, while his men, with drawn swords, swirled their mounts in his rear.

---

* "Empty pockets," a sneer implying shiftlessness

"I thought so!" roared the Captain. "Canadians! When trouble rises, look for the scum of the North! I arrest all of you!"

The Canadians stood scowling, some with hands on knife hilts. But there were twenty mounted men, and the foresters would have stood little chance of escaping, much less combating, the swords of the horsemen.

A sudden idea occurred to me, and I stepped forward. "Captain Noirel!"

He swept his gaze about, upturned mustachios bristling, a frown knotting his visage. But when he saw me, his face changed.

"Ah—St. Denis!" he said, in a manner quite cordial.

"It was not these men who were causing the disturbance," I told him. "They were only trying to protect two of their comrades from abuse at the hands of the *canaille,* treatment that is no part of their just punishment."

Noirel glared at the two wearers of drunkards' cloaks.

"Why are you here?" he growled at them.

Marbot, with mud on his cheek and a broken egg in his beard, gave me a sheepish look, but I did not relax my face. So he addressed Noirel.

"We are here because of a woman, Captain," he said.

"Fighting over her?"

"No, Captain." It was difficult for the little forester to converse without gestures, but the confinement of his hands at the sides of his barrel made gesturing impossible, so he could only use his eyes and eyebrows to aid expression. "We were trying to forget her."

Noirel swore. "One of the new *cassettes,* I suppose?"

"Yes, Captain." Somehow, though one could not see his shoulders, Marbot managed to give the impression of a shrug of contempt for the woman. "She was mine, then she was Jaccard's, and then she went off with a whole gang of sailors, to go out to their ship with them, a strumpet with at least a dozen lovers at once, like a bitch in heat followed by a pack of dogs. What could we do, when she went with the stronger party? So Jaccard and I, who had been at enmity before, embraced as friends, and got perhaps a little drunk in celebration—and broke a little furniture and crockery in the inn—by accident, solely, I assure you—and so they called the watch, and we are here."

Noirel, to whom this recital seemed to sound more plausible than one would perhaps have thought, asked a question.

"What damage was committed?"

The portly man with the pike stepped forward. "I am Soircy, the keeper of the jail," he said. "The innkeeper of La Dive Bouteille gave me a full tale of the destruction by these two madmen. Chairs smashed, tables overturned, wine bottles broken and wine wasted, dishes thrown at the tapster and at the host himself, and other damage to the amount of not less than thirty livres, for which he holds them guilty."

"Ha, can you pay for it?" asked Noirel of Marbot and Jaccard. "No? You'll lie in prison long for that. As for you other Canadians, you will go to the fort guardhouse for this disturbance."

"By your leave, Captain," I said, "I have a suggestion to offer."

"Well?"

"I am under orders to raise a company for frontier duty. Release these men to me—on condition they enlist—and you'll be rid of them."

Noirel stared at me, then at the foresters, seeming to debate with himself. Then he said, "I agree. It would be worth much to get rid of that crew."

At that I walked toward the knot of Canadians, and gave them a searching scrutiny.

"You have the look of a Laurentian," I said to a black-bearded fellow among them.

"And what if I have?" he said sullenly.

"The St. Lawrence breeds men and hunters! What! I think I see before me men from Trois-Rivières, and Champlain, and Quebec, and Montreal, and Lachine, and Fort Frontenac, and even Sault Ste. Marie and Fort St. Louis on the Illinois!"

At the mention of these familiar northland names, faces brightened.

"Which of you wishes to stay here among the lazy *vides poches,* and in prison to boot, when he can have freedom and adventure? I am St. Denis, who fought with Iberville! I cannot promise you ease and soft living, but come with me and I can promise what men like you welcome more—new country to see and hunt in, excitement, adventure! Which is it? My company? *Or* the Captain's prison? Who will follow me west?"

I spoke to them as one Canadian to another, and the chord I struck was true. They looked at me, there was a moment's hesitation, and then, "Here's a St. Lawrence man for you!" said the blackbeard I had first addressed.

"And another!" shouted a shock-haired rascal with a great grin.

"And yet another!" cried a third.

The cries came quickly now:

"One from Quinte!"

"And from Quebec, two!"

"From Lachine!"

So the chorus ran, until every man had volunteered.

Noirel nodded to me. "You can have them, and I wish you luck with them."

"But I must have all," I said.

"What? Are there others?"

"Those two rogues in the barrels, too."

For a moment he stared, then roared with laughter.

"All or nothing?" he said. "By all means take them all! Unlock those two from the barrels, Monsieur Soircy. The innkeeper can whistle for his compensation and be glad he got off so light. I count Mobile most fortunate to be rid of the whole lot at once!"

He gave an order to his riders and the troop trotted off for the fort.

I ranged my men before me.

"You will be ready to march tomorrow," I said. "Be equipped with your arms. You will find me a commander who expects discipline without drill, obedience to orders, and the courage which Canadians all have. I will share with you whatever hardships there are, and you will not find me standing back from any dangers we may face. Before we are through with each other, I will make you into the finest *partisan* ranger company in the New World. *Vive le Roi!*"

They gave a cheer, and they were grinning and speaking cheerfully to each other when I dismissed them, to assemble the next day at early morning, in this same place.

Behind me a voice spoke. "Very well done, St. Denis."

I turned. It was Bienville.

"I saw the whole thing," he said, "the manner in which you took advantage of circumstances to recruit your company at one stroke, the way you appealed to the men and won their regard. You have the gift of leadership. Prove to me now that you have also the gift of loyalty."

7.

So I went; and it is of interest, perhaps, to reflect that my going pleased a score of persons at least. It pleased Cadillac, who was thus rid of my troublesome presence. It pleased Crozat, who, however she might hoodwink him, still nursed some lurking suspicions concerning his mistress. It pleased the scheming Abbé La Vente, who saw a check to his maneuvers removed. It pleased Bienville, with whom I had a last conversation the night before I left, and from whom I received a strict charge. It pleased the Canadians I took with me, most of all Marbot and Jaccard, for they were well weary of the settlement, its women, and particularly its jail.

One it did not please. Bienville told me that La Demoiselle, white and glooming, sat in her room and none dare come near her, not even her tiring women or the little Negro page, Pepi, who was her favorite. She hated me. She would neglect no opportunity that ever came near her to do me injury. And she and I only knew the real reason for this.

A flouted woman is a bitter woman, and this woman was doubly dangerous. But for the present I would be out of her reach. With my company I struck out at once for Fort d'Iberville and Lake Pontchartrain, to pick up the errant contingent of Natchitoches Indians and escort them to their home far up the Red River.

These things created in me a certain elation, so that I was lighthearted that day.

BOOK TWO

Daughter of the Dons

9. *The Land of Emptiness*

On the afternoon of a heated day near the beginning of September, I drew rein at the verge of some low bluffs and looked down at the river below me. It was the stream originally named the Seignelay by the explorer La Salle, but by common consent called now the Red, because of the unnatural ocherous russet of its waters, tinged with clay silt from the red lands through which it flowed.

Three months had passed since I left Mobile under something heavier than a cloud. Much had happened in that time, the events and mishaps of a long march, but little worth recalling. Later, however, I was to remember the moment when I drew rein on the bluffs of the Red River, for it was fraught with destiny.

At first, as I gazed down, it seemed to me that all I saw beneath me represented the end of hope and ambition. The stream itself was sullen, unnatural in hue, unsightly and treacherous, given to sudden floods and quicksands. Yet at this place some human life clung to it.

Among the scraggly trees on the crumbling banks of the nearer shore, at the foot of the bluffs from which I gazed, a faint fog of smoke arose. A closer look disclosed huts—thatched, haphazardly scattered, squalid, and so weather-beaten that they seemed to merge into the color of the soil itself. It was a miserable village of savages, the village I had been sent to find: and now that I had found it, it seemed fully to measure the ebb to which my fortunes had fallen.

Yet in that very moment, when I felt myself so bereft of all hope of glory, advancement, or profit that, as the saying is, I hardly knew which saint to dedicate myself to, since all seemed to have deserted me, my eye lifted and regarded the distant horizon. That way was south. Illimitably stretched the waste, sullen, barren and uninhabited, with nothing to draw the gaze or distract the mind, a void which seemed to imprison me as effectively in that direction as did the hatred of the Governor and his daughter in the other.

Then came a stirring of different thoughts, and the recollection of one who did not hate me: Bienville. I looked again at the horizon.

Emptiness? Ha! Not entire emptiness. In it savages, creatures desperate and hungry, ran wild. And somewhere among those savages in that vast waste was a mysterious white man, a Spanish priest, Padre Hidalgo. And he had come from the south. To me that was a reminder that beyond all the desolation—no man knew how many leagues beyond —lay New Spain.

Spain! And this river was the frontier. The very word frontier had a special meaning. I remembered Bienville's sayings, and at the same time the old lessons and the old concepts of the great, dead Iberville. In that moment, which was without hope, a new hope sprang into being. Instinct grew into thought, and thence into inspiration. Perhaps after all it was not my fate to live out my years here, grown old with roaming and gaunt with the everlasting struggle for existence, and finally to die unknown and forgotten. Perhaps I might still play a role on the stage of history!

Of a sudden that savage void across which I gazed seemed a challenge, as the sea is a challenge. If this Padre Hidalgo could make his long way north—a tonsured monk with sandaled feet and no weapon other than a crucifix—then, as God was great, I, a soldier, could ride south through that same waste!

Here stood France: Spain there. How far, and what doing? I suddenly conceived my plan: to probe, to discover if possible the secret schemes of the nation standing across the desert, to find if this advancement of a priest and a mission were truly the thrusting out of a tentacle, soon to be followed by greater force, to gulp more territory, perhaps Louisiana itself.

Spain laid claim, immemorially, to all the continent west of the Mississippi. If she chose to take it now, how could France resist her? I and my tiny handful were all that could be opposed to the might of the Spanish King, if it came. So heavy was this thought in me that I half expected to see the banner of red and yellow—symbols of blood and gold, the twin marks of the cloven hoof of Spain—fluttering on that horizon already.

Reason intervened. Spain was not here now; perhaps would not be for long to come. Yet the mission among the Neches must be a symptom of stirrings to the south.

I knew now the move that must be mine: a voyage of exploration, not on water but on land barren and stony, spiked with thorn and cactus, uncharted and filled with perils. To what bourn? No man could tell; yet at least it was not haggard slow extinction here. In that moment of moments, I said to myself that I would not end until I had tried that great unknown beyond this farthest frontier of France, and either learned the Spanish motive, or was subjugate in death.

2.

The thought meant action, and at action my spirits always rose.

"There is the town of the Natchitoches," I said to Marbot, who sat his horse beside me.

"*Mon Dieu*—a rat's nest!" he replied.

"Rat's nest, true. But perhaps not *our* nest."

"Monsieur?"

"The soles of the feet only know where a man is to die."

"Then we do not stop here?"

"Some of us stop here. We build a fort."

"And the others?"

"Will have a chase, perhaps a quarry, certainly an adventure."

From the huts below, human figures began to scurry, dusty and brown, swarming like ants in evident consternation.

"They believe we are enemies," I said.

Marbot nodded.

From the Indians beneath us shrill whoops arose. Women and children of the village were seen fleeing in ragged little groups up the river, but the men began ranging themselves, brandishing their crude bows and spears as if to give battle.

"Hasten back to Jaccard and bid him bring up the refugees with all possible speed," I commanded.

Marbot whirled his horse and galloped away on the back trail. I turned to the other men.

"Dismount and rest your animals," I said, "but under no consideration scatter, and keep an alert eye about for a possible attack."

The Canadians obeyed, most of them squatting and taking out Indian pipes of stone or clay, which they filled and began to smoke.

By this time the savages had spread out at the foot of the bluffs, still giving their shrill whoops and leaping about, brandishing their weapons up at us, as if they hoped to frighten us away with such display. I looked at them with contempt, for I knew these were not warriors in any accepted sense, and one volley of our muskets would scatter them in panic. Yet I wished to avoid any hostilities with them. It was my plan to send the refugees down to them first, as a token of our friendly character.

In an hour the ragged band of natives was herded up from the rear by Jaccard, Marbot, and the rest of the escort. Ever since we took them from among the Choctaws near Lake Pontchartrain, the refugees had complained of weariness and destitution, and our march had been slowed to the dreariest of crawls by them, since they possessed no horses and carried most of their possessions as well as their younger children on their backs.

Now, however, with some show of cheerfulness, they began to descend the bluffs by way of a gully that led downward at an angle, into the valley below, shouting and raising great ragged clouds of red dust in their going.

In the village, the inhabitants of which had not ventured to come near us in spite of their defiant gestures and continual yelling, the newcomers were recognized and received with joy, if the barbaric ululations coming up to us could be so interpreted. The sun was now nearing the western horizon.

During our wait, I had spent my time with a compass and small spyglass, making notes in my logbook and drawing sketch maps. My study had brought me a decision. Upstream from the Natchitoches village, a distance of perhaps a mile, was a low buttress of ground directly on the riverbank, surmounted by a level flat on which grew some scattering trees. It appeared to be an ideal site for a camp, and later a fort, well situated for defense, with natural escarpments and water available in case of siege.

To this, as soon as I was sure the savages below had received their friends and forgotten their hostile intentions, I marched my company and the pack train. The men were well trained in camp routine: small tents sprang up quickly, fires were lit, a mess gathered about each to cook supper and eat, the bales and packages of provisions and trade goods were unloaded from the pack animals and piled neatly together in the center of the encampment, night watches were told off, and the horses and mules were herded in the bottom to feed.

I went to my own tent. Within it Marbot already had laid out my blankets and opened my portmanteau.

"You desire a change, Monsieur?" he asked.

"No," I said.

"Will you shave this evening or in the morning?"

"The morning."

"Will you sit?"

I took a campstool beside one of the provision boxes that served as a table. There Marbot brought my supper: a stew of venison and a small heap of boiled rice, with chocolate in a pewter cup sweetened with honey.

I ate, hardly tasting the food in my abstraction, and presently pushed away my plate to write in my logbook what was necessary to record this encampment, before I slept.

3.

No need for going into details concerning the fort we built. I laid it out, a palisaded quadrangle, with a crude log barbican over the main gate, loopholes for gunfire, and log huts within for dwelling and storage. Before noon the men were busy felling trees, and since they knew their safety might depend on their work, they labored well and willingly.

Many times that day, and in the days following as the work went on, I gazed southward across the river and the vast country which stretched beyond my sight, and which white men knew not.

One thing I was assured of: the solitary priest, Padre Hidalgo, had not come this far north, for the Natchitoches had never heard of him. Those Indians, beggarly and dirty, after the first day of shyness, grew friendly: almost too friendly, so that we had to keep them out of the camp where they were prone to make small thefts. A few offers of trade proved what I knew from the first, that they possessed little of value and were not even good hunters, preferring to subsist on maize and squash, which they grew in little patches, and on such small game, including ground squirrels and lizards, as they could capture easily. There was no field here for enterprise or ambition.

At nights I went to bed with my thoughts, and thought is a restless partner. I had orders only to establish and maintain a post on the Red

River, but there was my secret understanding with Bienville, to learn more about the mysterious Spanish priest.

My destiny extended somehow out beyond that dusty, thorn-spiked land. But what dangers and possibilities lay there? Worth the risk? My life in pawn, perhaps? That did not greatly concern me. Habitually I left it out of reckoning if the stakes were worth it. But what stakes? Even now, my mind already made up to risk the great thrust into the unknown, I did not know if I found the Spanish mission, what I would do concerning it. Make friends with the priest? Imprison him? Drive him out? It depended on events, and events must rule my decision.

On the tenth day, when the palisade was finished sufficiently to leave it, I called Jaccard and Marbot to me.

"You, Jaccard, will be in command of this post. Complete the work I will lay out for you, and see to it that the goods left with you are not diminished when I return."

"Yes, Monsieur," said Jaccard, impressed with his responsibility.

"You, Marbot, choose five men to accompany me. We go on a hunt." I gave a list of baggage to be taken, trade goods, my portmanteau, and food.

Marbot nodded and departed.

Next morning, with Marbot and his five men all mounted, and two pack mules laden, I forded the Red River and set my face toward the vast enigma of the southward spaces.

I remember that journey as heated, dry, and without event. Never had I seen country more inhospitable. Sometimes we came upon stretches of open, covered with curly mesquite grass. Along the few water courses straggled cottonwoods, which the Spanish call *álamos*. But the lasting impression of the country, aside from the heat that beat down endlessly from a sun of molten brass in the sky, was of thorns.

"Never have I seen such thorns," Marbot said to me one day. "Every variety of vegetation, almost, seems to have been devised, not by the good God, but by the devil—for the torment of God's creatures, whereby the foul fiend invented for each a different kind of poisonous spike."

I thought his words rather apt. Always we encountered the mesquite, with its soft-looking leaves and treacherous claws, and the prickly pear, which grew to great size, bristling with barbs. But these were only the two most common.

Everywhere other varieties of thorned growth grew. Sometimes we came upon thick patches of evergreen coma with dirklike thorns; at others fierce thickets of retama, with adder-toothed spikes hidden under its deceiving green leaves. Worst of all were the all-thorn jungles, a growth entirely naked of leaves, but bristling with such a tangle of spears that the very birds avoided it. These were to name only a few, not including the many kinds of cacti, of which the cholla appeared to have more spines to a given amount of surface than any other plant known to man.

Continually we were forced, by these growths of deadly and bristling daggers, to halt our direct course and work around, seeking to find some way through the hostile interlocking mats of poniards. That meant delay and hardship, since the season was late and the watercourses few and often dry. Game there was. We killed deer and antelope when we had need for them, and saw the loping white lobo wolves, and a few small herds of the mighty bison, while coyotes bickered nightly about our camps.

Then at last one day the heat relented, heavy clouds gathered on the horizon, overspread the sky, and a drenching cold rain fell for days. Now our situation was reversed. Where before we suffered from thirst and blazing heat, we now suffered from cold and had too much water for comfort, finding it difficult even to make fire to cook with at nights in the wetness and icy winds brought from the north. Two of the men grew ill, and coughed, and the horses and pack mules were gaunt and weak.

Nevertheless I pressed on, until, one day early in November, I halted my men on the crest of a low height of land, and looked down into a wide, shallow river valley where by the stream there clustered what looked like a collection of huge beehives.

"I think that is a village of the Neches people, whom we seek," I said to Marbot. "I have heard their dwellings are of thatch, rounded like beehives. Dismount and let us prepare ourselves to meet these Indians."

Always the French have excelled in their art in dealing with savages; and I have been at pains in that direction, being as good or better, I was once told by Iberville himself, than most Frenchmen in understanding the minds of Indians and the importance of making a favorable impression on them. So now, from my portmanteau I took a new buckskin shirt with fringed sleeves and cape, bright with dyed porcupine quillwork, made by an Ojibwa squaw in far northern Canada, and preserved for just such an occasion. My hair I combed and braided in two thick plaits hanging on my shoulders, one tied with red, the other with a green ribbon. At the crown of my head, fluttering behind, I fastened by a string of sinew to my hair a single eagle plume, the base of which was decorated with a fluff of white down, its rib painted red, and at its tip a dashing tassel of red-dyed horsehair.

My men busied themselves to similar purpose, attiring themselves each after his fancy, some in fur caps, Marbot in a devilish headdress bearing the horns of a bison which he had traded from the Quapaws on the Mississippi. As savage as any Indians we looked, I must say: more savage, in truth, for, except for myself, we were bearded fearsomely.

Now, cases and portmanteaus packed and loaded once more, we mounted and rode down the long slope through groves of live oak and thickets of thorn, toward the river and the distant village.

"These people are rich in horses," remarked Marbot.

I nodded. Herds of the animals could be seen downstream from the village, watched over by mounted boys.

"Of this I am glad," I said. "We may be able to trade for horses to replace our own worn beasts."

As we neared the village, someone ran among the lodges with a long-drawn howl, during which his palm was continually struck across his mouth to produce an undulating sound—a shrill warning cry.

I called a halt within musket shot of the nearest lodges. Very soon we saw a procession issuing from the village and coming toward us.

"They come afoot," I said. "Dismount and greet them as they greet us."

In the advancing procession were at least thirty men. All wore garments of soft buckskin or woven grass cloth, and all had about their shoulders robes or mantles, woven and rather beautifully adorned with bright birds' feathers and other decorations.

We stood impassive, watching them, our muskets grounded butt downward, held upright in our hands. No gesture was made by us: it is important to refrain from peace signs, or the savages are prone to believe that you are afraid of them.

Nevertheless, as I stood motionless, I surveyed the oncoming Indians keenly, with deep interest. Almost without exception they were tall and dignified, tattooed on their faces, and wearing rings or bone ornaments in the septa of their noses. Their necklaces of bone, shell, animal claws, and even brightly colored stones such as turquoise, were numerous and rich, some wearing as many as ten separate adornments of this kind about their necks, falling upon their chests. These Neches, if such they were, appeared to be a superior people, with savage wealth and strength far above the wretched Natchitoches.

Now the leading man lifted his hand, palm forward. It was time for me to respond, and I did so with the same gesture. He then came superbly on, sweeping forward with considerable dignity, while his companions remained in a group standing still. At once I went to meet him, so that we encountered about halfway between our respective parties.

The chief was an old man, his hair shot with considerable gray, his face deeply lined, his expression one of utmost gravity.

"*Texias!*" he said.

From his manner and voice, I took this to mean "Friends." Later I learned this was true, and from this word the Spaniards named the tribe and the entire region Texas.

"*Amis,*" I replied in the same tone and manner.

For a moment the Indian regarded me searchingly, as if something were missing. Then he made a circular motion of his hand, the index finger pointing toward his breast.

"Bernardino," he said.

On his naked breast, among other ornaments, I now saw a small metal crucifix, the first indication of any manufacture of white men I had yet observed among these people.

Bernardino was the old chief's name—and *Spanish,* given him by a Spaniard! I hardly needed any other confirmation that I had come upon the very village of Padre Hidalgo. Perhaps the mission was close.

"*Yo soy amigo,*" I said, shifting from French to Spanish. Then I gave my own name, pointing to myself.

At the Spanish words the Indian's face lit up, and in the next few minutes I discovered that he had a smattering of the language, enough so we might get along to a degree in conversation.

He shook hands warmly, then turned and addressed his followers briefly in their own tongue. A chorus of exclamations of grave assent or approval greeted his words.

I had accomplished the first step in making friends of the Neches.

It was high time, too, for the rains, which had ceased temporarily, threatened again, and I welcomed the thought of shelter.

4.

I sat by the fire of old Bernardino. Rain pelted on the thatch and smoke filled the interior of the lodge, causing my lungs and eyes to smart; and the place was filled with savages, who crowded in one after the other, to see the white man and make whatever trades they could.

Their furs and skins were, on the average, poor: badger, wolf, coyote, deer, and a few buffalo robes, with here and there a fox or beaver more desirable. Trading was difficult. Without experience of these Indians to guide me, I must estimate each item as it came along and try to strike a balance between what I would give at the highest, and what the native might be willing to take at the lowest. It was essential that I must appear neither niggardly nor foolishly openhanded, and bear in mind continually the necessity of indicating that though few goods were here to speak for me, vastly more were to be reckoned where these came from. For this trading was diplomatic, rather than profit-making.

Bernardino, meanwhile, sat with eyes like coals of fire, speaking very little, and puffing at a pipe of black baked clay, the smoke of which made still more acridly unendurable the haze with which the rain-beaten hut already was filled. Once or twice, with disinterestedness quite remarkable, he interrupted the bargaining to say that this one or that was asking too much, and tossed over a bundle of furs for half what its owner was demanding, to the intense disgust of the Indian to whom it happened to belong. No one, however, disputed with the chief or refused to sell when he ordered, which was the highest proof of his authority.

At the end, I had a heap of furs of inferior quality, though cheaply enough gotten, which I set my men to baling for shipment, in the grass lodge that had been assigned to us.

Thereafter, as night fell, I sat with old Bernardino and his family: two aged squaws, his wives; a son of middle age, whose woman was much younger than he and rather pretty save for the disfiguring tattooing on her cheeks; and three bright-eyed little boys, the old chief's grandsons, of whom he was dotingly fond.

There was the usual Indian stew, tasteless from lack of salt and unsavory from much boiling, and into this we dipped while we talked, using the medium of the Indian's small Spanish, and such Neches words as my ear, quick for language, already was picking up.

I early brought up the subject of Padre Hidalgo, and saw that the name brought recognition to Bernardino's eyes. But when I asked if he was near, the old chief fell silent. I did not understand why, for though this Indian bore a Spanish name, perhaps given him in baptism, and I was certain he knew the man about whom I asked, he turned the subject so that I gave it up. I wondered if something had befallen the Spanish priest, or if these people for some reason disliked or mistrusted him. It was evident that I could get no information here, but I made up my mind to learn gradually what I could, although it seemed that it might take ten days or longer.

Thereafter, in politeness, I engaged with him in unimportant talk: generalities such as the weather, which was bad; some queries by the old man concerning the white people from whom I had come; mention of a scarcity of game in the country, which a day or so before had forced the village to send out a hunting party of young men to the west, looking for meat, a journey from which they had not yet returned.

Into this casual talk was dropped suddenly, like a stone into a placid pool, one word: *Comanche.*

The name appeared to carry fear, as if it described some deathly brooding menace looming beyond the horizon. I questioned, and Bernardino's answers gave me a sobering picture of a race lethal and abysmally savage, bestially bloody and fierce, raiders and killers without peers. A word applied to them in the Neches tongue meant "Horse People." They were said to be horsemen beside whom other Indians were nothing, a shadowy peril which had only just made itself manifest from the vast interior to the west, appearing and disappearing like snakes striking and gliding away, murdering with inhuman ferocity, plundering and stealing everything on which they could lay their clutching hands.

It was the first I had heard of the Comanches, and in Bernardino's voice as he spoke of them was a note that told me this people, newly come from somewhere afar, would in the future be a factor of enormous harm and peril on the plains. Bernardino mentioned villages of Lipans and Wichitas that had been destroyed by the Comanches. He feared the next blow might fall on the Neches themselves.

This danger, the old chief added, as if urbanely seeking to alleviate any apprehensions I might have, was not immediate. It was now late in the year, and war movements of Indians usually occurred in the spring, when grass was green and weather warming. Moreover, it was the season of heavy rains. Streams were up, and rain was a bothersome loosener of bowstrings and the lashings of arrow and lance heads. If and when they came, the Comanches probably would choose a fairer time. But, as a leader of his people, he must take all this into account and lay plans for it. Was there anything the white leader might suggest?

I considered. What of a confederation, I asked, of all the river tribes to resist this new menace?

Bernardino shook his gray head. There were enmities it would be hard to reconcile, the usual weakness of Indian peoples faced by any invasion.

I ended by suggesting a permanent scouting party, which should be kept out in the direction from which the Comanches might conceivably come, starting as soon as the grass began to green in the spring. With that I excused myself to go out into the night and to the lodge of my men. At the very minute I stepped out from old Bernardino's lodge, rain began pelting heavily again. Assuredly, I said to myself, this was the best warrant of safety. No war party willingly would travel in such weather.

It was no surprise to me, when I entered my men's lodge, to find that two or three of them had bedfellows, for the custom of the lend-wife existed here as among some other tribes I had encountered: a form of courteous hospitality extended to friendly strangers who were guests. My foresters were not of such character as to refuse the offer of an Indian woman for their stay. That satyr, Marbot, in particular, grinned through his beard as he lay in his blankets, and lifted the top to show the face of a girl no more than thirteen or fourteen years old, but quite willingly sharing his bed with him. Squaws were an old story with Marbot, and he was entirely lacking in scruples.

Since the matter was one of amicable agreement between the Indians and my men, and since it was a solution of at least one form of trouble, I said nothing, going to my own couch to sleep: but alone.

5.

In the night a shout arose, and I threw off my blankets, drawing on such garments as I had discarded for sleep, and went out of the lodge.

Other yells answered the first cry. The rain had ceased and the clouds were beginning to break, so that here and there a star briefly glittered. I hurried to Bernardino's lodge, and found the chief standing before it, with a look on his seamed face as of a man snake-bitten.

Nearby stood a horse, head hanging, sighing and heaving, its flanks and legs trembling with weariness. The rider who had flogged the animal to the limit of its endurance, a youth hardly more than a boy, was making a report to Bernardino.

The Comanches had come.

The bearer of the tidings said he was the only survivor of the hunting party of eight young men who had gone out from the village for meat two days before. They found game and were returning, with pack horses well loaded, when the wild foe swooped on them from an ambush in a copse of trees. He escaped only because the fastenings of the load on the horse he was leading had become loose, and he fell behind to make them secure again. By half a mile he thus avoided the general massacre, and, having under him a very fleet animal, managed to escape his murderous pursuers, riding hard for the village to warn his people.

Among the Neches panic was immediately evident. Women and children set up a wail, and looked wildly about as if they expected to see the bloodthirsty enemy in any direction. Some, even men, hurried away to catch horses and flee—somewhere, anywhere. Very deep was the brand of terror sunk by the Comanches here.

I reached Bernardino's side. "How far?" I asked.

"They slew our hunters a day's journey up the river," he said.

"Then they are nearer now. Perhaps just outside the village."

Bernardino nodded mutely.

"If so, they will attack at daybreak."

Again the chief nodded.

I saw that someone must take command here, and it appeared that I was the only one who could do so. "We must get ready for them!" I said.

"How?" half moaned the chief. "How can my people face those wolves of men? We are peaceful, unaccustomed to war——"

"Begin being warriors now! My men will fight for you—I promise the Comanches have not bargained for what they will receive!"

A resolute manner often instills courage in others. Bernardino brightened with faint hope. "Give me your counsel," he said.

"Have every warrior arm himself, and do what I tell you," I replied. "There is no time to lose."

In the stress of this crisis they turned to me. I spoke with confidence, taking care not to let them think that I was improvising plans hurriedly, on the spur of the moment—as indeed I was—but making every sentence have the measured surety of one who had prepared for an emergency just like this by mature consideration long in advance.

This was needful, for the unforeseen is the deadliest enemy to all Indians, the surest, most wide-spreading disruption. It was night, and no Indian is fully himself at night. To show calmness and speak as if I knew exactly how to meet the coming danger was the one thing that would halt the wild panic which could only mean disaster for the Neches, and for us, their white guests, as well.

The device was effective. My own men stood in a little knot, their muskets in their hands, as if awaiting orders. Now warriors, already poised for flight, stopped and came back to me, looking with anxious question into my face, as if to seek assurance there. If I had shown one trace of irresolution or confusion, they would have stampeded like a herd of frightened antelope.

But I returned their looks as if I had not a doubt, as if my confidence were supreme in my ability to do what I proposed. They gathered about me now, panic subsiding. Alone among them, they believed, the white leader was prepared, and the warriors and chiefs of the village, none more willingly than old Bernardino himself, listened and obeyed quickly my assignments to action.

Yet I, speaking with such confidence, was far from feeling it. I knew nothing of the Comanches, or their way of fighting. Even as I faced the Neches, I had only a bare hope that I might be able to stay the hostile barbarians when they came.

I turned to my six Canadians.

"How are your stomachs for battle?" I asked them.

They nodded grimly, and Marbot, laying back his head, gave a long howl like a wolf. These were all chosen men. They had smelled gunpowder before and knew Indian combat. They were not accustomed, it was true, to horseback Indians, and the peculiar *élan* of a cavalry charge such as the Comanches might be expected to give, since their wars had been fought on foot in the northern forests, against red foes who used every trick of concealment. Nevertheless, I regarded them as the hard core of my defense against the coming attack, their muskets to carry great weight in the battle.

It was still dark, but now the dawn was not far off, and what was to be done must be done quickly. I took stock of the situation: the terrain did not greatly favor defense, the site of the village not having been chosen for any strategic value. Nevertheless, it must do. I set about trying to use whatever advantages existed.

The Neches lodges stood beside the muddy flowing river, with trees scattered among them and forming about the outskirts of the village in small groves here and there. Of brushwood there was little in the near vicinity, it having long ago been cut away for firewood, and of this I was glad, since it would enable us to see our enemy when he came.

North of us, half a mile perhaps, there was a creek running into the larger stream, its crooked bed heavily wooded with live oak, cottonwood, pecan, and willows. If the Comanches were near, I reasoned, it was likely that they might even now be concealed among those trees, waiting for daylight.

My dispositions therefore were as follows: In one copse of live oaks, at the east of the village, I directed Marbot and three of the Canadians to conceal themselves. Their four guns would prevent the assailants from sweeping around the right flank of our little array. The river protected us on the west, which was our left. In the center, concealed in one of the outer huts, I placed the two remaining Canadians, and at once they began, with calm assurance, to poke holes through the thatch for their muskets.

"Don't fire until I give the order," I cautioned them.

I now had to account for the Neches warriors, who numbered perhaps one hundred and fifty men of all ages, including older boys. These I divided into two groups.

"Give me one of your trusty chiefs," I said to Bernardino. "I want a man who is very brave."

"Tokano!" he called at once.

A young chief stepped forward, his naked coppery torso a fine muscular display, in spite of the paint which daubed both it and his countenance.

"I want him to take fifty bows, and go forward to the small gully which lies two hundred paces north of the village," I said to Bernardino, who only could translate for me. "They are to lie there in hiding, and get in their arrows when the Comanches charge. Tell him this is the post of greatest honor."

When this was communicated to Tokano, his body became more erect, and his eyes gleamed with pride. Quickly he chose his fifty, and set off with them through the darkness, to take up the post assigned.

The rest of the Neches, about one hundred, I now scattered in the outward perimeter of the village itself, among the lodges, to fight there. Women and children and the useless aged already were streaming southward along the riverbank, to escape from the dreaded conflict.

By this time the first pale light of the coming dawn made objects near at hand more easily seen. Old Bernardino stood beside me, his bow and quiver on his back, a lance in his hand.

"Go to the left, by the river," I told him. "I count on you to keep your men fighting stoutly there. I remain here in the center."

The old warrior gave one grim nod, and departed. Presently I could hear him exhorting his warriors to fight like men and die bravely if it came to death, telling them this was a battle in which great renown was to be won by those who had courage.

Satisfied that I had done as much as could possibly be done, I went to the hut where my two Canadians were concealed. Of all in that village, at that moment, I, perhaps, was the least sure of the result of the coming fight. Yet I kept up my appearance of confidence as I stooped and entered the low door of the lodge.

My two men, one of them the black-bearded fellow who had been first to volunteer that day in the square at Mobile, whose name was Giron, were cool enough, seeing to their weapons, laying out powder horns and musket balls conveniently for quick loading, lying flat on the ground and peering out through their improvised loopholes, which they had made low in the thatch. They were jesting with each other, talking about what men usually talk about—women. The Indian lend-wives, it appeared, had been satisfactory, and they complained laughingly of having to leave their warm beds. Yet with ready Canadian adjustability, they were alert for the crisis impending.

"How goes it, Monsieur?" said Giron. "Do you think this is a false alarm? I would rather be cuddling my little squaw than lying here if the hostiles do not come."

"They will come," I said grimly. "See that you are ready for them."

"We are ready. I cut a cross with my knife on the ball in this gun, and it will find its billet, I promise you," he replied.

I nodded, and to make an opening through which I could see to fire, began tearing out a section of the thatch by handfuls. But instead of lying prostrate, I made my loophole high enough to shoot through it standing.

Dawn brightened.

All at once I saw the Comanches.

From the wooded creek bed issued a wild frieze of savage riders, feather headdresses fluttering, bows and quivers slung on their backs, carrying long lances. Though they rode without saddles, their naked legs hanging stirrupless, these people appeared to be welded to the backs of their horses, more beasts than men, every attitude and movement prowling and ferocious, suggesting wolves rather than human beings. I thought to myself that I did not wonder at the fear of the Neches. These were more terrifying than any Indians I had ever seen, even the terrible Iroquois of the northern lakes. I estimated more than two hundred of them in view, and a great qualm of misgiving came over me, not fear for myself, but a realization of the advantage in morale they possessed over my Neches.

"They'll be coming on horseback at the dead run. It will be tricky shooting," said Giron.

"Then we must wait until they are close enough so that we are sure," I answered.

The Comanches were fully aware that our village was ready for them, although they had no thought that they were dealing with any but native warriors. With confidence bred from continual victories, they advanced, slowly at first, giving the peculiar bloodcurdling Comanche war scream, which once heard is never forgotten, and is unlike anything except the cry of a panther making his kill. Forward they rode in a wide extended line, a superb barbaric spectacle, as if they expected to sweep back any resistance by the mere terror of their appearance.

It had that effect, too. Many of the advance party of Neches in the gully ahead lost heart at these fierce yells, and sprang from their concealment without shooting an arrow, fleeing for life toward the village.

With that the Comanches charged.

In a swirling swoop, at incredible speed, they came. Over the gully where the brave Tokano still held his few remaining warriors, they leaped, spearing some of those who fought there where they stood. Then the Comanches were among the fleeing fugitives, lances at work.

A wail of horror in the village, and a few futile arrows sped. Running feet thudded, and I heard yelps of consternation. My allies were deserting me in panic.

But at this moment, when everything seemed lost, and the savages almost were among us with lance and war ax, Marbot was heard from in the copse on the right. The reports of the muskets of his party crashed out. So near were the Comanches, that he and his men could not miss. Every shot brought a warrior hurtling down from his horse.

"Tirez!" I cried to my own two Canadians in the hut.

And set the example myself. My loophole was at shoulder height, theirs near the ground as they lay prone. As I pressed my trigger, a great cloud of smoke sprang out, and with it immediately the smoke from the muskets of my two men. In the confined space of the hut the thundering discharges seemed deafening.

Vision was obscured momentarily, and we desperately reloaded our guns, hoping to be able to get in at least one more volley before the Comanches closed with us.

Then smoke cleared as I primed my flintlock and gazed out through my loophole.

What I saw was, perhaps, the most surprising sight of my life.

When last I looked, the Comanche array was bearing down upon the village at the full breakneck speed of horses lashed to the dead run, triumphant, bloodthirsty, apparently invincible, on the way to the massacre of every Neche.

Now, as if by some weird magic, all this was reversed. Every Comanche was in flight, save for a few prone figures which the guns from the copse and our hut had brought down.

With yelps of sheer astonished terror, flogging their horses, even forgetting their dead and wounded, they were in complete rout. Their array, a moment before so furious and victorious, had melted like a snow wreath in the sun.

For a moment I stared in astonishment. Then I understood what must have taken place.

The Comanches were brave, willing to encounter any danger they knew and understood: but they were savages so remote and unsophisticated that never before had they encountered gunfire. It was the sudden, utterly unexpected, thunder of the muskets, rather than their losses, that caused their stampede. Only in terms of what they could conceive could they interpret it: in some manner, they thought, the Neches had enlisted in their support the thundercloud and the lightning bolt, which meant the aid of the Indian gods themselves. The Comanches fled, not from death, but in sheer superstitious horror of the supernatural.

It was a victory, complete and astounding. In a few minutes not a Comanche was in sight, as they fled through the trees of the distant creek, and on beyond, not stopping to look back.

On the ground between their lurking place of the night and the village they attacked only a few prostrate figures remained: a dozen of the Neches, speared in flight or in the gully itself; six Comanches, dead or dying from musket shots, and two slain by Tokano and his men, who stood their ground in the melee that took place in the gully.

Tokano was wounded, with a spear thrust in his thigh, but he won great honor that day. Other wounded Neches also recovered in most cases. But those of the Comanches who still had life left in them were slain at once, without mercy: unless immediate death, rather than reservation for leisurely torture, can be accounted mercy.

Old Bernardino, who resolutely had held his own immediate band of warriors to their places at the river flank, even when the center of his line crumpled and fled, came to me with glowing eyes, and shook my hand. There was little to do now, except call back the women and children to the village and send out scouts to report on the Comanches.

6.

By evening the scouts were back. Not a hostile warrior remained in the country. For the time being, at least, the Neches were safe.

Once more, that night, I sat in Bernardino's lodge, where also the chief men of the village gathered to feast in honor of the white men who had saved them. Deeds were sung, particularly those of Bernardino and Tokano, and of my Canadians and myself.

This time formality was dispensed with and Bernardino spoke to me as an intimate. And now when I, observing this change in attitude, ventured to bring up the name of Padre Hidalgo, the old man nodded quite willingly.

"The medicine padre is a good man. He is the friend of the Neches," he said.

"He is near here?"

"No."

"I read a letter which he wrote," I said. "He told in it that he was among the Neches, and that he had a mission which he named San Francisco de los Neches."

"San Flasisko." He garbled it, but nodded.

"You know where it is?"

"Yes."

"Will you take me to it?"

"No."

"Why?"

"Nothing there. It is burned."

"Who burned it?"

"I do not know. I think the medicine padre."

"He burned his own mission?"

"It was a lodge with on top two crossed sticks." Bernardino illustrated by crossing his fingers. "It was of straw. It caught fire, I think, from a candle, when the medicine padre worshiped."

"Was he burned?"

"No."

Decidedly, to gain information from an Indian was like cauterizing a wooden leg, as the saying goes.

"Where is he?" I pursued.

"Gone."

Exasperating, but I persisted. "Gone where?"

"A long way off." Bernardino, with the edge of his palm, sawed the air in the direction of the south. "Back to his people."

"When?" I asked.

He considered. It was several moons ago, he finally said.

I thought to myself that the priest must have departed very soon after he wrote his letter to the Governor of Louisiana.

"Why did he go?"

"In the fire all his medicine things, his garments, the place where the cross stood, the cross itself, his books of thick writing—all were burned. He went, I think, to get more of these things."

Ah, this was an explanation. I began to understand that this mission had been abandoned, and why.

"But he did not come back," Bernardino went on. He spoke with an almost childish sadness.

"Do you expect him to return?"

"Not now. But we wish for it."

I considered all this. The Spanish mission no longer existed here, and we had made firm friends of the Neches, so that, in future, trade relations with them, if we chose to maintain them, would be good. Also, it was in our power to make an alliance with them so that France might, with boldness, look to this distance for a new frontier.

So much I had accomplished.

Yet I felt a sensation of the deepest disappointment. By no means had I learned anything of the Spanish plan. My errand was only half finished. I had no news to send Bienville concerning that matter which was so vital to him and me, and to France—the Spanish plan. In this I felt failure. I might have returned to the Red River and made my report, but pride and a sense of duty forbade that.

Somehow I must still in some manner seek to gain knowledge that would enable my people to prepare themselves if an incursion was forming in New Spain. Yet to approach New Spain, even its borders, was perilous, much more so to invade its territory. For a foreigner to enter the Spanish dominions was to court death, unless he by chance possessed all proper credentials and received a license from the authorities, none of which I had or could hope to get. I knew the Spanish law. It was specific on this point, and I knew also the grim jealousy with which that law was enforced.

Yet I could not turn back with my task unfinished. All at once a new thought stirred in me, heady and developing.

"If you want the medicine padre back," I said, "why do you not ask him to come back?"

"How can we?" returned Bernardino.

My thought took form with amazing rapidity and audacity.

"Send a deputation to the Spanish settlements with a petition," I said.

"We do not know how this petition is done, and we do not know the way," objected the chief.

With that my thought reached maturity.

It suddenly appeared to me that, greatly daring, there was here a chance for me to make an entry into the forbidden realms of New Spain, on an excuse plausible enough and so fraught with interest to the Spanish Church that with great good fortune I might gain the vital information Bienville sought, and perhaps be permitted—always assuming the utmost in good fortune—to return.

In that moment I made a decision, as a man sometimes makes grave decisions, without realizing fully its gravity, or the dread train of circumstances it would set in motion.

"I will explain the meaning of a petition," I said to old Bernardino. "Also, I will write it out in fair Spanish, so that you can present it to the authorities in New Spain. And, finally, I myself will lead you there."

Old Bernardino rose, and for the third time since I had known him, shook my hand.

There was little sleep for me that night. My men whispered and sniggered with their Indian mistresses, but this did not disturb me. A new obsession had taken possession of me.

Spain! I had no orders to go farther than I had done, but did I require orders? Looking back, I had an almost superstitious feeling that I had been prepared for this very moment, that my destiny had been guiding me to the step I was about to take. The failure of my project of the Natchez, my entanglement with La Demoiselle leading to my exile, Bienville and his words of loyalty that revived my almost lost devotion to my country and my King, the danger of the frontier to which I had been sent and the strange letter from the Spanish priest, my very journey to the Neches, all seemed to point in the same direction.

I spoke the Spanish tongue as a Castilian speaks it. I knew Spanish manners and customs. Ha! Was not a man entitled to think for himself, act for himself, when he had no direct orders contravening? I had a chance, a golden opportunity here in my hands, to do what no other Frenchman could do: enter the territories of Spain and return unscathed, if all went well.

There was risk, but also the auspices were such that they seemed most favorable. The challenge was grim, and I tasted the serious thrill of the knowledge of great danger, and with it a sensation of deep calm. I did not fear it. Instead I felt a kind of joy, a rather savage joy; it was, I believe, the recognition of the urge that every man feels deep within him—the urge that comes sometimes in his life to lay that life in pawn for something worthy of it.

I had been for a time forgetful, almost unfaithful to the dream I had gained from Iberville, the dream for which I had spent my youth, the dream of the greatness of France. I would now do something to further that dream. I meant to look back on it with satisfaction, and not with shame. I thanked God for sending me this chance to prove my courage.

The next morning I called Marbot to me.

"You will begin at once the march back to the Red River, taking the men and the furs we have bartered for," I told him.

"And you, Monsieur?"

"I go on."

"Alone?"

"Not alone. With the Neches."

"But—take me with you. These men will find their way back without me."

"No."

Marbot looked at me pleadingly. "In what have I offended, Monsieur?"

"In nothing. I place in you a grave trust."

He straightened. "I will do as you command."

"Here is a letter. I wrote it last night, and it is sealed. Wrap it so that it will be touched by no weather, and carry it on you at all times. You will go to the fort at the Natchitoches village."

"Yes, Monsieur."

"You will inform Jaccard that it is my will that he remain there with the men while you continue on to Mobile."

"I?"

"With this letter I give you."

"And for whom is this letter? The Governor?"

"By no means! Understand this most carefully. The letter is to be placed by you in the hands of the Sieur de Bienville—*at a time when none else shall see you*. Is this comprehended?"

"Most clearly, Monsieur."

"You will then return to the Natchitoches fort, to await there my return."

"But what if the Sieur de Bienville be not at Mobile?"

"Then you must destroy this letter and forget you ever had it."

"Yes, Monsieur."

"Swear it."

"I swear by my soul, that I will do faithfully your commands."

"Then *au revoir*, good friend!"

10.   "An Errand of Piety"

Four weeks later, on a dusty afternoon, having half swum, half forded the muddy Rio Grande, we halted and dismounted from our horses. On this, the south side of the river, we were in undoubted Spanish territory, and now I felt I was up against the rub, for very soon now my subterfuge would be put to the test, and I wondered if I could carry it off sufficiently well to convince the hawklike watchers of this Spanish frontier, when I encountered them. Although we had thus far seen no white habitations, lean cattle, wild as deer, had been visible, and there were other signs of settlement.

There were fourteen of us: old Bernardino and twelve of his most substantial elder chiefs, besides myself. The young chief, Tokano, who had distinguished himself against the Comanches, had been left in charge of the Neches village. Bernardino treated the "petition" which I had written for him in Spanish—using all possible and formal complimentary and pious expressions—with care amounting to awe, as if it contained some magical properties, carrying it in a bag of rawhide, gaudily painted in red and yellow designs and carefully waterproofed with buffalo tallow.

None of the Indians, however, had any actual realization of the true peril of the critical time before us, as I turned to them, having given the southward landscape a keen scrutiny.

"It is necessary that I make ready to meet the people of this country," I said to them.

They watched gravely as I took from a pack horse my portmanteau, and donned the mouse-colored leather coat and pantaloons, high soft boots, plumed hat, sword, baldric and sash. My toilet was a never-ending curiosity to the Neches: particularly my morning shaving—for I carried as always my razors and soap—the lathering of my face and the play of the glittering keen razor over it hardly ever failing to evoke expressions of amazement, and brown hands held over mouths, the Neches sign of surprise, when my face, washed clear, appeared beardless before their eyes.

Feeling now that I looked only half savage, I directed that we remount and proceed. Near where we forded the Rio Grande, a crooked watercourse ran into it, widening into a valley, and up this we took our way, the Indians following me without hesitation, their faith in my wisdom now so complete as to be embarrassing, since my faith in myself was far less.

Three hours we had ridden, when Bernardino, beside me, uttered a peculiar hissing sound. I looked in the direction he was pointing his arm. A defile emerged into our valley between two low ridges on our left, and, barely visible to a searching eye, a ragged yellowish fog showed briefly just above the nearer hill. Estimating the depth of the defile, it must be a considerable cloud of dust, and I was fairly sure it was made by a body of mounted men.

We drew up, the Indians huddled in a little knot about me, with the beginnings of apprehension as they studied the dust, which appeared, was lost, then appeared again, indicating a rapid progress of the makers. Presently a succession of riders swept out of the mouth of the small gorge. Spanish cavalry, without question—lancers.

An encounter such as this was not what I had planned, and it represented a serious danger, for every strange Indian was an enemy to the Spaniard, to be slain on sight unless some reason was given not to do so. If some hotheaded or vicious officer led that contingent, which now turned and galloped toward us, every plan of mine might be destroyed here at the very inception, to say nothing of the disaster which would overcome my charges, who had followed me trustingly here.

The Neches showed increasing symptoms of alarm. I must act, and act quickly.

"Bernardino, keep your people here, where they are!" I said to him, and drove my spurs into my horse's flanks. The Indians grouped where I left them, ready for instant retreat, but waiting to see the outcome of my meeting with the lancers.

In the oncoming troop were about twenty, and as I narrowed the gap between us I saw that the common soldiers wore flat-crowned hats and *corazas*, a sort of armor consisting of several layers of toughened bullhide, loose and sleeveless and hot, but capable of protecting the body from an Indian arrow, and perhaps even a spear thrust. All carried lances, and all were armed with swords or long knives of various kinds, while a few also bore ball-handled pistols of the old wheel-lock variety.

When perhaps one hundred paces separated us, I suddenly pulled my horse to a jolting stop, rose in my stirrups, waved in the air my hat with its red plume, and shouted, "*Viva España!*"

At once the leader of the soldiers threw up a hand. The charge slowed to a trot, then a walk, and the commander moved out ahead of his men.

I advanced to meet him.

All hung in the balance now, depending on what adroitness and boldness I could summon, and on the luck of the situation besides.

"*Alto!*" shouted the officer.

We both brought our horses to a stop, confronting each other. The conversation that followed, was of course in Spanish.

"*Por Dios!* A white man!" he exclaimed, almost incredulously.

I smiled. "I do not deny it."

"Who are you, and what are these Indians?"

He spoke with a coarse provincial accent, and I knew at once that my Castilian was much better than his, which gave me an advantage.

"The Indians are under my charge," I said, as if it were the most common thing in the world to be bringing strange savages into this area.

He was a burly man, his face broad, with a bulging forehead, short nose and heavy mustache, the skin deeply pock-marked. I guessed his age at about forty, and put him down as a typical subordinate, his mind heavy and slow, likely to hold grudges if offended, but afraid of making mistakes.

"They come on embassy," I added.

"Embassy?" He looked suspiciously past me at the chiefs to my rear. "Raiding, more likely! What are you doing with them? You are under arrest!"

My face did not change, and I spoke almost with condescension, as to an inferior. "You arrest envoys to the Governor of this province, and to the superiors of Holy Church?"

The question gave him pause. At once I followed up my advantage.

"I demand escort for myself and these chiefs, who are on a pilgrimage, seeking a mission from the reverend fathers for their people."

So confidently did I speak that he was impressed.

"You have not told me your name," he said presently.

"You have not told me yours," I answered haughtily.

"I am Lieutenant García Escobar de Herrera," he said.

"You are military commander of this district?"

"No. That is Don Diego Escalante de Ramón, Commandant of San Juan Bautista."

"Far from here?"

"Two leagues or such a matter."

"Then my business is with the Commandant, and not with a Lieutenant. Conduct me to him at once that I may make known my name and business properly."

The Lieutenant hesitated, liking neither my superb manner, nor my refusal to give my name. Yet mention of the Church seemed to influence him and my demand to see his superior was to him evidence of the genuineness of my mission.

"What about the Indians?" he asked, still suspicious.

"They will accompany us peaceably." I knew I had won my first skirmish and breathed an inward sigh of relief, for this might have ended very seriously. "I suggest that you warn your soldiers to treat them well, for they are chiefs of a powerful nation which looks to Spain as a mother now, but might as easily become her foe."

"An embassy?" said the Lieutenant. "We will see what this amounts to."

I beckoned forward the Neches chiefs. Herrera gave an order. The lancers fell into a formation surrounding us. For the time being, at least, we were prisoners.

It was, as the Lieutenant said, a short ride. On the way I spoke easily with him, as if I assumed that my party was being given the honor of an escort, rather than going under guard.

He, too, relaxed somewhat, being the type of man to whom arrival at any decision brings relief of mind, whether it be good or bad, indecision alone being the torment. He told me of himself, as if seeking to create on me a better impression than I seemed to have of him.

"I am on campaign," he said. "The Tobaso Indians have been raiding again, stealing horses and murdering persons they waylay. I ride to fight and punish these gentiles. At first I thought your Indians were of that tribe."

"You have struck these Tobasos?"

"No. My name has terror for them. They flee to refuges in the mountains and *barrancas* where horses cannot follow them, when they learn that Herrera has taken the field. A people of the rankest savagery, worse than beasts."

"Why don't you hunt out their villages?"

"They are too remote. No man knows where they live."

It seemed to me that this Herrera not only was a braggart, but no very enterprising campaigner, though I refrained from saying so.

A new interest, indeed, filled me. As we mounted a rise, a huddle of small *casas,* of adobe or of poles driven in the ground and plastered with mud, came into view, lying athwart the landscape as if a giant hand had cast a fistful of clay blocks haphazardly. Above them stood a church with two round towers, and to the right a small, high-walled fort. At the top of a low but steep hill overlooking the village was a white *estancia,* roofed with tile and surrounded by walls of its own.

"The mission, presidio, and village of San Juan Bautista," said Herrera.

"Whose is the *casa* on the hill?"

"Don Diego de Ramón's dwelling."

Almost as soon as we came in view a bell began to ring in one of the church towers and at the same time a trumpet blared at the fort. We rode through the village, where potbellied children stopped playing in the dust to stand and stare and broad-hipped women shrilled at each other while their men lounged with cornhusk *cigarrillos* and gazed at us with smoldering eyes. Everywhere were visible the small burros, inevitable transport of this country; countless currish dogs barked and yapped; and hogs and chickens wandered unconcernedly about the street and in and out of the houses.

Then the heavy timbered gates of the presidio swung open. We rode through and the gates closed behind us.

2.

"Dismount," ordered Herrera.

I turned to Bernardino, and spoke to him half in Spanish, half in the Neches tongue, putting all the assurance I could into the words, for the Indians' faces were filled with alarm.

"Tell your chiefs to get off their horses and rest in the shade there.

Have no fear. You will be well treated. Meantime, I must go and talk with the chief of this place."

The Neches indicated assent, dismounted, and took positions standing in the shadow of the wall, their robes wrapped tightly about them, to wait.

I glanced about. Within the enclosure of the quadrangle of thick adobe walls were the usual structures of a frontier fort: crude adobe barracks, a small headquarters building, and a little prison, the only structure built of stone, perhaps eight feet square, with an iron-barred window. A couple of ancient cannon, of the type known as *pedreros* because they threw rounded stones as ammunition, were placed in embrasures, one above the gate, the other on the side opposite. The soldiers I saw, wandering across the small parade ground, or stopping to stare at us, all appeared to be Indians of the Mexican type, slovenly and dirty in old ragged uniforms.

Then I saw a woman's figure whisk out of sight around one of the buildings, and a woman's face appeared momentarily at one of the barracks windows. Evidently the soldiers were permitted their wives or mistresses here, a custom rather universally Spanish.

There came the sound of a slap and a squeal. Some soldier was disciplining his woman for peering out at the strangers.

With Herrera I marched to the headquarters building, a title most imposing for a structure so unimposing, since it was flat-roofed and contained but two rooms. We entered. At a heavy and awkward table sat a man in a dark coat decorated with much tarnished gold braid. He was very grizzled, his face thin and deep-lined, his gray beard cut square across the bottom, his figure lean and spare.

I halted and bowed. The man inclined his stern head slightly.

"Don Diego," said Herrera, "I encountered this person and thirteen Indians two leagues from this place. He demanded to be brought here, saying he was an envoy on embassy. This I accordingly did, holding him and the Indians prisoner for your disposal as you see fit."

I knew this must be Captain Diego de Ramón. He asked a question in a voice harsh and dry. "What Indians are they?"

"I do not know. Some remote gentile people, I think."

The Commandant turned his gaze on me. "State your name, Señor."

"You are the chief officer here?" I countered.

A grim nod. "For these fifteen years."

"Then I have the honor to say that I am the Chevalier de St. Denis."

He stiffened. "French?"

I knew then that none of them had suspected I was an alien, and found a momentary satisfaction over the quality of my Spanish, which I have often been told has little if any accent.

"By birth a Frenchman, yes," I said. "By fortune and inclination, a citizen of the world."

"You have a *permiso* to enter Spanish territory?" His gray brows knit.

"None."

"How did you, an *estranjero*, dare come here without a license?"

"The Indians with me are of the Neches. They and I have come from their country, a month's journey north of here, on an errand of piety in which all good Christian Catholics should gladly join hands."

"Explain!"

"The Neches bear a petition to the holy fathers asking for missionaries to teach and convert them to the true religion."

The veteran's eyes narrowed and his brows bent into a still deeper frown. "Have they no priests in France?" he asked suspiciously.

"Assuredly there are priests in France. But these Indians are loyal to Spain, and especially to a certain Padre Hidalgo, who was once among them and for whose return they pray."

At the mention of the name Hidalgo, the Commandant's thin wrinkled visage changed slightly, and for a time he sat silent, as if thinking.

I studied him. He appeared to be in his late sixties, a man whose features showed a combination of intelligence and strong will, mixed kindness and cruelty, and perhaps a lack of education which kept him from fully developing his latent abilities. A Spaniard of Spaniards he undoubtedly was, who could kill without mercy, yet perhaps be a very good friend if he chose. I put him down as one of those remarkable soldiers of the Spanish frontiers, giving faithful, brave service to his King, receiving almost no thanks in return, grown old and gray in a vacuum of opportunity, living out his life and career in patience, and without bitterness toward his superiors who condemned him to this exile.

After a few minutes he said to Herrera, "Send someone to Padre Ambrosio, asking if he will be so good as to come here on a matter of importance." He then told me to be seated.

During the wait that followed, Don Diego conversed with me politely but coldly. I learned that he had established this presidio, supervising the very building of it, fifteen years before. His military authority extended not only over it, the mission adjoining it, and the town near it, but also over two other missions, San Bernardino and Nombre de Jesús, some distances away in different directions; and over several large ranchos belonging to Spaniards, as well as all the people, Spanish and native, who dwelt in this considerable territory.

He, meanwhile, learned only what I wished to tell him: that I was of good family, at present adventuring in my own behalf.

At this point a broad figure appeared in the doorway, and a portly friar entered, his head tonsured, a gray robe corded about his ample middle, and sandals on his large bare feet. He was, I was informed, Padre Ambrosio Quevedo, the *Custodio,* or as one would say, Father Superior, of the mission of San Juan Bautista and also the other two the Commandant had mentioned, and therefore possessor of considerable authority.

"So you come with the chiefs of the Neches," he said after the preliminary explanations. "But you must know the Neches dwell within the territories belonging by lawful claim to the King of Spain. How is it that you, a Frenchman, encountered them in those Spanish lands?"

Here at the outset was a mooted point: the old question of the disputed sovereignty of France and Spain. But I avoided the peril of debating it.

"A hunting trip took me afar into the wilderness," I said. "Thus I came upon them."

"Officially, as an agent of France?"

"Unofficially, as an individual in my own interests."

This was at least partly true, since I had no direct orders from Governor Cadillac to go to the Neches. Of the letter written by Padre Hidalgo to Cadillac, I deemed it best to say nothing, at least for the present.

Padre Ambrosio looked at me intently, as if to discover what equivocation lay behind my statement. He was an elderly, serious-minded man, whose large belly indicated a love of good food and soft living, with deep-set black eyes, a rather angular nose that went oddly with his broad fleshy face, and a large mouth inclined to lock itself tightly. I decided that while he indulged himself when luxuries were available, he also could deny himself if necessity or duty demanded, and probably was long accustomed to responsibility, perhaps stubborn and set in his ways.

"Why did these Indians speak to you, a Frenchman, of a Spanish priest?" he asked next.

"While I was in their village they were attacked by a savage alien tribe called Comanche. I aided them in the battle, which they won. Thereafter they regarded me as a friend. Their principal chief, Bernardino—a Spanish name and a Christian one, bestowed on him in baptism by that Padre Hidalgo of whom we speak—told me of the priest, for whom they have profound reverence and affection, and their longing to have him back. As a good Catholic I conceived it to be my duty to assist them in seeking the blessings of Holy Church."

Padre Ambrosio inclined his large head. "To forward the growth and power of Holy Church, which knows not bounds or rules of nations, and to foster the teaching of the true religion among the heathen, is always worthy of praise," he intoned sonorously.

I understood that the statement was general, and in no way a particular endorsement of myself, or of what I had done. A moment later he rose and made a significant motion of his head to the Commandant. The two of them stepped into the other room, while I sat with the Lieutenant and two soldiers who stood guard over me, knowing that my fate was being decided by that colloquy in there.

After a time I heard the tramp of the Commandant's boots and the whisper of the priest's sandals returning. For a moment they both regarded me fixedly, and I could not read from their expressions anything of how they were inclined toward me.

"Is there one among the Indians who can interpret?" asked Padre Ambrosio.

"The old chief, Bernardino, has a little Spanish," I replied.

The priest and Commandant passed out of the building, and presently I heard their voices, evidently addressing the Neches. Then there was a stir outside, and the gate creaked as it opened. From this I knew the Indians were being taken elsewhere for questioning.

Time passed, an hour or two, dragging as slowly as a heavy log. Herrera departed and the two guards did not speak. I fidgeted, my mind torn by speculation. What would the Indians tell? I reflected suddenly that I had spoken of my journey as a hunting trip, whereas it had been for purposes of trade. Would Bernardino mention this and throw additional suspicion on my whole venture?

This, which held me now, I realized overwhelmingly, was *Spain!* Spain of the grim Conquest. Spain of the unending cruelty of the Inquisition. Spain, to which human life meant little or nothing, when war or policy, or wealth or religious bigotry, were concerned. Spain, which still ruled half the New World and claimed more. Spain, forever jealous of other nations and hostile toward anything not Spanish. Spain, still dwelling in the memory of the days when Spanish arms were invincible and the Spanish word was law, not only in the Americas but over most of Europe also. Though Spain might not now be the terrible military power it was a century before, Spanish pride and Spanish ruthlessness still were forces to be reckoned with: and I was a prisoner to them.

Yet I studied to keep an outward appearance of calm. It was evident that the Neches were being given a far more than ordinarily close examination, perhaps with all manner of cunning suggestions to elicit from them information that conflicted with mine. The Spanish were noted for their craft, and the Indians childishly naïve.

Almost despairing I sat. At last I heard a voice outside, and a step, and the Commandant was back, alone.

He seated himself at the table and regarded me seriously.

"Your pardon, Señor, for this lengthy wait," he said. "We find it difficult to talk with the Indians, because only one of them has a few words of Spanish, hardly enough to express thoughts. But what we were able to get from them is a corroboration of what you have said."

I felt a great relief. I had forgotten Bernardino's scanty Spanish and that I myself communicated with him only because I had picked up some Neches words to supplement it. This was an unlooked-for measure of safety.

"Padre Ambrosio is still with them," he continued. I felt less secure. "He is trying to learn of the progress of Padre Hidalgo's work among them, the numbers of them ready to embrace the faith, and other questions necessary for the Church to ask, but with little success."

I felt better.

"I may say to you that Padre Hidalgo is well known here," the Commandant went on. "He was, in fact, one of the founders of this very mission, and is a friend of Padre Ambrosio, which disposes our *Custodio* well toward you. But I must also tell you this: though Hidalgo is held in esteem by some, in other circles he is less highly regarded, for various reasons. There are, therefore, difficulties here."

I nodded, without speaking.

"It is possible," he said next, "that there will be sufficient interest in this matter at Querétaro, the headquarters of the Franciscan order, that a priest will be assigned to your Indians. This, however, will take some time at best, and it may not be Padre Hidalgo himself."

Don Diego, with his dry voice and manner, seemed to be discussing the matter most frankly, from which I took hope.

"We cannot, however, keep the Indians here," he went on. "Padre Ambrosio will therefore send them back, perhaps tomorrow, with presents and a promise. He would dispatch a missionary with them, but he lacks authority. There are, as you perhaps know, politics even in Church matters. Padre Hidalgo, for example, is in difficulties with some of the ecclesiastical authorities now, because of what he considers to be zeal for the work of the Church, but which they see as lack of subordination. He carries the true faith to the heathen, but in directions unauthorized. You understand that the mission system must be advanced according to the policy of the government, else it will not receive government support. His mission to the Neches is an example."

"I understand the necessity." I nodded. The statement was, indeed, illuminating in a way he did not guess, for if what he said was true, there evidently was no immediate policy of northern aggression in Spain, and this was very much what I had come to discover. If I could return to Louisiana now . . .

The grizzled Spaniard glanced at me, his keen eyes gleaming under his brows. "All this, as you can see, affects you. It may be that the government and Church will welcome you for what you have done. On the contrary they may take the opposite position."

"I have no wish to remain here. I will return with the Neches," I said. "As I conceive it, my errand and my duty to the Church are completed."

"I regret," he replied, "but it is necessary that I detain you here until a decision is reached."

I was, then, to be held actually as a prisoner! For the first time I berated myself inwardly for my rashness in coming here. I was heavy as lead.

"Meantime," said the Commandant, "the Indians you brought are not satisfied. They wish to see you and converse with you, and Padre Ambrosio can get little from them."

"You mean you wish me to interpret for you?"

"That is it."

I made up my mind. After all, I had learned very little. Like it or not, I must trust to luck and see this thing through.

"Very well, let us go to them," I said.

The Commandant dismissed the guard, though he asked me to leave my sword in the presidio headquarters.

Together he and I walked across the village plaza to the church, and to a garden at the rear with a row of flat-roofed adobe tenements which constituted the convent of the priests. There, sitting under a large cottonwood tree, was Padre Ambrosio, with my Indians squatting about him.

At my appearance every savage came to his feet.

"Ho!" exclaimed Bernardino, smiling as if with relief. He shook my hand fervently.

Thereafter, I did as I promised, addressing Padre Ambrosio's questions to him in a bastard combination of Spanish and Neches, and giving him their answers. The burning of the mission, Padre Hidalgo's departure in discouragement, and other details were related by them, to his evident satisfaction. At the end I told them that I would remain here to look after their interests; but they were to return to their people next day, bearing gifts. Meantime a place would be provided for them to sleep, and food given.

Both Don Diego and the priest listened with deep interest, trying to follow the talk. At the end the Indians seemed fully convinced, and were led away to an empty building which was to shelter them, and given food sufficient to fill their bellies. Food and shelter are the chief concerns of a savage Indian, and for the present they were happy.

This done, I turned to Don Diego.

"I suppose it is the *cárcel* in the presidio now for me?"

He gazed at me in astonishment. "Prison? Señor, you misunderstand me! I have discussed this with Padre Ambrosio, and it is in both our minds that you are a good Catholic and a man of honor."

"I trust you are correct in both," I said.

"I have no wish to make your enforced stay unpleasant. So I ask for your word of honor that you will make no attempt to escape from here until judgment is rendered in your case."

"I do so give it," I replied.

For the first time a smile creased his face. "I will, of course, take the precautions that are my duty."

"I understand. A watch will be kept over me."

"Not necessarily the way you think." Again his face cleared with the dry smile. "If you will accompany me, Señor, it will be my pleasure to conduct you to my own poor house."

I stared at him in astonishment.

He made a rather courtly bow. "I ask you, Señor St. Denis, to be my guest—if you will so honor me."

Such was my amazement that I had to summon my presence of mind to express my thanks. From a prisoner I had in one breath become an honored guest!

3.

In the walk back to the presidio, where we got our horses to ride up the hill, Don Diego said calmly, "You are perhaps wondering?"

"Somewhat," I replied.

"I will be frank with you. A situation like this has never arisen before."

"I take it you will await some sort of directive?"

Don Diego nodded. "A rider left half an hour ago for Parras, capital of this province of Coahuila, bearing a letter setting forth the circumstances."

"The answer—when may it be expected?"

"A few days, perhaps; perhaps weeks. All depends on how occupied is the Governor, and what deliberations he must hold with the Church authorities." The veteran shrugged and waved his hands to brush aside an unpleasant subject.

I saw the situation rather clearly. Without warning I had appeared, a foreigner without a license to enter Spanish territory, which was contrary to law. Yet my errand was one that might be of great importance to the Crown; and my manner was so assured that it left strong doubts in the minds of these provincials as to how I should be handled. They were perplexed. It would hardly do to place me in prison: at least until higher authority ordered it. Meantime the Commandant and *Custodio* were prepared, no matter which way the cat jumped. If the reply from Parras was unfavorable, they could deal with me quickly enough. If favorable, they would gain credit by treating me with consideration.

I felt that the days, or weeks, during which I must await the decision on my fate, might seem the longest, perhaps, of my life.

When we rode up the barren hill to the white *estancia* on its brow, a *mozo** took our horses at the gate. We entered a wide courtyard, with stables and servants' quarters at one side, and before me was a rambling house with a wide carved door. At this portal, when we reached it, Don Diego bowed and motioned me to go in first.

"Señor, you are in your own house," he said.

A servant, a little Indian with an ugly, seamed dark face, wearing a cotton shirt and drawers, bowed before us.

"This man, Íñigo, will attend you. Consider him yours," Don Diego said to me. "He will show you to your room, where you may refresh yourself. *Comida* will be in an hour."

It was already near evening as the servant led me down a hall through the house to the rear, where we stepped out on a patio, enclosed like all other areaways, by walls. Here the building extended backward in two wings, partly sheltering the patio which was paved with flat flagstones and decorated with pretty flowering shrubs along the walls. Separated from it, by a lower barrier with a swinging gate, was a garden and orchard of citrus trees, giving a pleasing background of greenery with the yellow of the ripening fruit peeping through the leaves. Two Indians were working there, and it was obvious that incessant labor and a generous expenditure of water brought up the hill at considerable toil were required to maintain the pleasant little oasis. Without much question the life of the family extended in this direction where privacy and beauty went hand in hand.

Íñigo turned toward the wing at the right and I followed him across the rough flagstones. As I walked behind my guide, I suddenly seemed to feel, rather than hear, a stir and rustling behind the shutters of one of the windows looking out on the patio. Feminine eyes, I was almost sure, were gazing out at me from behind those shutters, with curiosity.

---

* Peasant

I did not know who the women were, whether of the Commandant's family, or servants: indeed, whether actually there were women at the window at all. Yet such is habit and instinct, that I found myself insensibly walking somewhat straighter, and was a little vexed and also a little amused at myself for doing it.

Our short parade soon ended. Íñigo ushered me through a door and into a sleeping room, quite large, with whitewashed walls, and a small narrow window, unglazed but shuttered, opening on the patio. Across one corner was a blackened chimney with a round hood for heating. Against the wall opposite the door a bed was built, with above it a crude carved wooden crucifix, four feet in length, the Christ hanging upon it gaunt and tortured, painted in raw colors to simulate life, with staring black eyes and black hair and beard, the ghastly red of blood from the crown of thorns and the five wounds seeming to stream down in a manner almost shudderingly realistic. Chairs and a table, made ingeniously of mesquite wood and rawhide, completed the furnishing. I perceived that my baggage had been brought up, with it even my sword.

For a time I luxuriated in a warm bath, then shaved again carefully, combed my hair afresh, and dressed in my green and gray velvet suit. With the baldric, sword, and sash, I hoped I once more presented a neat appearance.

Barely had I finished when the summons for *comida* came. Again I crossed the patio and entered the house. The servant who had summoned me indicated the way to the main salon, and I came to the door, then stopped.

At the far end of the long room stood Don Diego, in dark clothes with a high flared collar, knee breeches, and stockings, his sword worn at his hip in the Spanish fashion. But the surprise to me was the fact that with him were three women, since I knew the formalities of Spanish custom and the customary delay of introductions of feminine members of a household to a guest, until acquaintance was fully established.

With considerable ceremony Don Diego introduced them. Two were elderly: one thin and somewhat grim, her dark hair shot with gray; the other plump, with comfortable good looks and merry eyes. They were Doña Estrella and Doña Felipa, his sisters. The Commandant, it appeared, was a widower, and these kept his house for him.

The third, who shyly awaited her turn, was different. She was young, and sweetly formed, with a cloud of black hair and a pair of great startled eyes that, really gray, had the look of black as the pupil swam over the iris.

"Señorita Manuela Dolores Sánchez de Ramón, my granddaughter," said Don Diego.

The girl made a graceful curtsy, lowering her eyes; and I bowed to her, with perhaps a tinge of the extra, almost jocular, formality which an older man sometimes displays toward a very young and charming person of the opposite sex.

Before I could form any very complete impressions of these ladies, two other guests entered. They were Padre Ambrosio, looking benignly stern, and Lieutenant Herrera, obviously gotten up in his best, his coarse black hair plastered flat on his skull with some ointment, and smelling strongly of perfume. To each of the members of the household the man bowed, and gave a smirk to the girl. She appeared not to notice it. The smirk faded.

Almost at once we all went to the dining room, where we knelt to receive the blessing of Padre Ambrosio before we were seated. Thereafter we first tasted cakes and sweet wine brought by barefooted Indian women in shapeless dresses of unbleached cotton, and then the usual food of the country was set before us: a stew of meat and beans heavily seasoned with red peppers, *garbanzos*, and the flat thin unleavened bread made of maize meal called *tortillas*. An acrid wine washed down this fiery fare. It was not such as would have appealed to a dainty French palate, but I, who had prodded in kettles in Indian camps for my food, was hardly dainty. I made a good meal, although I felt it would take some little time to become accustomed to the extreme seasoning with which almost every dish was laden.

Conversation at first was polite, formal, and general. Knowing myself a prisoner, I yet conducted myself as if this hospitality was free and genuine, devoting myself to being agreeable, speaking lightly and pleasantly, with compliments for the ladies, and smiling replies to remarks addressed to me.

The girl sat opposite me, and I had a better chance to observe her. I guessed her age at eighteen or nineteen, and she was, I discovered, called by her second name, Dolores. She was an orphan, the child of a son of Don Diego who died when she was barely out of babyhood in a plague that took her mother also. She had been reared in this house by him and her two grandaunts, his sisters.

She kept her eyes on her plate and took little part in the talk, but I noticed that Herrera hardly took his gaze off her, and once or twice addressed to her elaborate compliments to which she did not reply. Was he perhaps a suitor? I found myself beginning to dislike the man.

That caused me to make a closer, though politely veiled, appraisal of the girl. She had beauty, I decided, of an elfin sort not common: although my type, for choice, was blond, I reminded myself. Nevertheless, I looked at her again, and again more than once during the repast.

After a time Padre Ambrosio said, "I ask your pardon for saying this, Señor St. Denis, but I wonder at something about you."

"What is it?"

"Your Spanish. You speak like a Spaniard, not a Frenchman."

"I should, since Spaniards, not Frenchmen, were my teachers. I dwelt for a time in Spain, where I was a member of the personal guard of His Majesty, Philip the King, at the royal palaces."

Their eyes opened at that.

"You have been in Madrid, then?" asked Don Diego.

"To be sure."

"Tell us—how would you describe—what are your impressions of our great capital?"

"Regal. Magnificent. Brilliant," I said.

About the table every face was intent with interest. The topic on which we had hit evidently was a happy one, for none of the persons present had ever been across the sea, and each of them was curious and eager to hear anything relating to the faraway, almost legendary motherland, from one who actually had been there.

"The Escorial," I went on, "which is the royal palace outside Madrid, is the eighth wonder of the world. It is immense, with nearly two thousand apartments, many courtyards, and four grand towers; yet with all its grandeur it is indescribably beautiful. The costliest woods and finest marbles of every color—brought from every country in the world —adorn its interiors. Its library is famous throughout civilization, and its galleries contain masterpieces beyond price. Its halls and gardens are decorated with magnificent statues, and its tapestries are unmatched anywhere. When the royal court is in residence there, it has pomp and magnificence not equaled, let alone surpassed, by any royal palace on earth, even those of Constantinople and Cathay—where, I am told, the Grand Turk and the Grand Mogul live in unexampled splendor. I could go on, telling you of this and the other royal palaces, including the noble Moorish pile in Madrid itself, but I fear I would weary you."

"It does not weary us!" cried plump Doña Felipa.

Even Doña Estrella's customarily stern expression relaxed in her interest. "You have seen the King?" she asked.

"Many times I have stood closer to His Majesty than I am to you at this present," I replied. "And I have spoken with him." I did not mention the fact that the last time Philip of Anjou addressed me, it was to dismiss me in disgrace for the affair of the two duels. Instead, I gave them a description of the royal personage which was perhaps more flattering than was deserved, but which these listeners heard with shining eyes.

"The people, what of them?" asked Don Diego.

"Aristocratic society in Madrid is brilliant," I told him. "The nobility of Spain is the most august in the world, the grandees polished in mind and manner to an incredible degree; witty, wise, proud, gallant, and with a national quality of bravery carried to the point of heroism."

I had a rapt little audience now as I continued to describe the grandeurs of Spain. And if I went a little farther than the strictest verity, and painted for them a picture somewhat overcolored, I can be forgiven, for they listened as if to a description of heaven itself, their pride in their Spanish heritage warmed and brightened by my words.

Formality was forgotten now, and they showered me with questions. One of these came, shyly, from Dolores, and it was the first time she addressed me directly.

"Are the ladies beautiful?" she asked.

"Divine!" I assured her. "Beauty in Spain is not an exceptional, but almost a universal quality. One sees about him more angels than there are in the skies above."

"The ladies are all—angels, then?"

So innocently naïve was the question that it brought a clap of laughter from the assemblage, in which I joined. She was confused, flushing with embarrassment; and the others, even kindly Padre Ambrosio, made it worse for her, laughing and teasing, as older people sometimes love to do with a pretty young girl.

It was I who came to her rescue.

"Do not let us laugh at you, Señorita," I said. "There is a proverb in Castile: 'Better a blush on the cheek than a stain in the heart.'"

Padre Ambrosio nodded approval at that, and for an instant she lifted her eyes gratefully to mine. I hastened to answer her question to stop further merriment.

"Not all the ladies of Spain are angels, I fear," I said to her. "In loveliness of face and form, yes. But, as elsewhere, some perhaps have failings of one kind or another. After all they are human, and every human being is prone to frailties, as I am sure Padre Ambrosio will tell you—even divinities in Spain."

At this there was another laugh, but not at the girl's expense. I thought that she was considering my words perhaps more thoughtfully than my light meaning deserved; and I wondered if she really was as naïve as she seemed. But she ventured no further queries, though she listened attentively while I answered continual questions from her elders.

By the time it was over, I felt there was a friendly warmth in the group, even to stern old Don Diego. The two grandaunts especially took interest, each in her own way. Doña Estrella plied me with questions concerning churches and shrines, and marriages and bloodlines of high personages, and etiquette at court and in the homes of grandees. Doña Felipa, less keen as to actual points of information, seemed enraptured by my few anecdotes of romance, my descriptions of balls and royal receptions, and what I could tell her concerning costumes, particularly of women of high degree.

Dolores was silent, but once or twice I found her wide eyes on me almost startlingly intent; whereat she instantly dropped them or looked away as if abashed. I found myself liking her and her youthful composure and modesty more and more.

Of Herrera only I was not certain. The Lieutenant seemed not to participate in the general interest. He alone did not laugh at the sallies, and he asked no questions. I thought his mind probably was too coarse and unimaginative to gather the full import of what was being said. The man lived in his immediate surroundings and the immediate moment: a brutish sort, who might be resentful because of the high hand I had taken with him when we first met; and might also be jealous of the center of the stage I occupied now, even to disliking the attention the little Señorita had given me.

But I discounted Herrera. The Lieutenant, whatever his feelings, was a subordinate, under orders. As for the Commandant, the reverend *Custodio*, and the ladies, I hoped and believed that I had succeeded, at least in a measure, in winning for myself a favorable, if not actually a friendly, regard from them.

4.

When I returned to my room at the end of the evening, Íñigo came forward, his hands folded before him.

"I have taken your things from the portmanteau, Señor, and hung them up," said the little Indian. "Such of them as need washing I will attend to. The boots in which you traveled I have cleaned and polished. The leather coat has stains upon it, but I think I can get them out, at least most of them, by methods the Indians use, if you will permit me to take it for three days."

I nodded.

"Wine is on the table," he went on.

Again I nodded.

"Does Your Worship desire anything else?" he asked.

"No. I will require nothing more from you before morning."

The Indian gave the *mozo* bob of the head.

"You may go to your own quarters for the night," I pursued.

He gave a gesture of dissent. "Oh no, Señor!" He seemed aghast. "I shall sleep in the hall—near your door——"

"I will not need you. You can go."

"I could not think of it, Señor! It would be a disgrace on this house if a guest were without a man at his call. Besides, Don Diego would be very angry with me if I left you."

At that I desisted. When I closed the door behind the servant I saw that Íñigo had brought a rug in which to roll himself as he slept on the hard tiles of the hall floor.

I sat down and swore deeply to myself. Íñigo, assiduous and omnipresent, I fully understood, was no mere stupid Indian servant. He was intelligent, even cunning. He had taken advantage of my absence to empty my portmanteau and hang up my garments, taking some for cleaning. It was a certainty that at the same time he had very thoroughly searched everything. A full catalogue of my effects would be reported to the Commandant.

Assuredly Íñigo had been assigned to keep a continuous watch on the "guest." Nor was he, in any likelihood, the only one. Besides Íñigo the entire household staff would have me under observation, and beyond these the presidio soldiers, the inhabitants of the village, even the priests of the mission. Any move I made, inside or out, would be noted instantly and reported.

Then I grinned. The good Lord has gifted me with a sense of humor, and this whole elaborate scheme had its funny side. It proved that my hosts were at their wits' ends in dealing with a man who must be watched and guarded like a dangerous enemy—yet treated like an honored guest.

Well, I would let the future take care of itself. With that I went to bed and slept soundly.

Next morning, as soon as I was astir, Íñigo knocked on the door to say that the Commandant would be pleased to have me breakfast with him. I dressed at once and went, and found Don Diego in a mood quite affable.

"You slept well?" he asked.

"Most restfully, *gracias.*"

We ate of fruits, chocolate, and cakes.

Presently he said, "Señor, my household takes kindly to you."

"I could ask no greater compliment," I told him.

Don Diego grinned dryly. "To be truthful with you, *amigo,* I had not at first intended to introduce you to my inner household—at least not at once. But you were—well—*seen.* Do you understand that? They say that women's curiosity is like San Elmo's fire, in that it appears without warning and cannot be slaked. But I say to you that San Elmo's fire comes and goes, while women's curiosity is everlasting."

I remembered the little stir behind the shuttered windows when I crossed the patio the evening before. Then I had aroused curiosity! I smiled.

"My womenfolk demanded that you be presented," he continued. "I demurred, thinking you might prefer your own privacy."

"On the contrary, I have never more enjoyed company than theirs."

"*Gracias.* In any event, and to make a long story short, I first refused, then temporized, and finally capitulated. When your women tell you to jump off a roof, pray that it is a low one, because sooner or later you will take that leap."

"I trust the jump in this case was not too uncomfortable," I said.

"It has been pleasing. My honored sisters are high in their praises of you. They say that your Spanish is so beautiful that it is hard to believe you are an *estranjero*—please forgive the reference, Señor—and that your manners and wit are charming."

"They are far too kind."

"As for myself," said the grizzled Commandant, "I find in you one whom I believe I would like to call a friend—of course within the limits of my duty. You appreciate that situation, I hope?"

"Most completely. One's duty and one's honor are the same, and are to be guarded with one's life."

"I was sure you would see it in this light," said Don Diego warmly. "And since we understand one another thoroughly, while we await word from Parras I beg you to feel free to come and go, anywhere within San Juan Bautista. And my house is honored by your presence."

I thanked him, and we went down to the church, to see my Indians off.

They were ready to start, with two lancers to escort them to the river, and their horses were well laden with gifts of blankets, ornaments, knives, and other articles.

But they were anxious about me. "You will come back to us?" asked Bernardino.

"After a time," I said.

"How long?"

"I cannot say. Let us keep each other in memory. Meantime, go and do not fear."

After that there came a somewhat lengthy ceremony, in which each of the chiefs in turn came up and shook me by the hand, with the word "*Texias!*"

They mounted. Bernardino lifted an arm and said a sonorous farewell.

I watched them go, and felt a sort of desolation, as if with their going the last link was severed between me and the world I had known.

11. *A Too Benevolent Dragon*

Although it was late in the year, the day had been hot, the wind dying early, and I took myself to my room at nightfall, fitful and ill at ease. In one day I had exhausted the possibilities of San Juan Bautista in interest and amusement, and found them singularly few and barren.

There was the presidio, and there was the mission, and there was the village of huts, and that was all. I wandered about, watched Indian men treading mud and water in a hole dug into the ground, for making adobe brick to go into an addition to the church convent; witnessed the drilling of a squad of awkward soldiers in the fort, with much yelling and abuse by Herrera; strolled through the village, being eyed with intense but shy curiosity by the women and children; talked for a time with Padre Ambrosio, with whom I was beginning to strike up a friendship.

This occupied my day. At the evening meal I did my best to be amusing and lavish compliments on the ladies, particularly the young and pretty one, Dolores. But I found it difficult, since my spirits were depressed; and so at the end of the *comida* I excused myself and retired.

Now I sat in my darkened room, thinking. Whatever I did, wherever I went, a sensation of tension oppressed me. Somewhere, between this outpost and Parras, rode a courier with Don Diego's report concerning me and my invasion of Spanish territory. No telling what decision might be made by the Governor, but until I knew, I could not rest.

My dark thoughts were interrupted by a tinkle of music from some stringed instrument in the patio outside, and then I heard a voice singing, so low that I could not understand the words, as if the singer were communing with herself alone. So young and light was the voice that I said to myself its mistress must be Dolores, the girl of this house.

I felt a desire to go out into the patio, but feared such an action might be taken as an intrusion.

Then, as if in answer to my unspoken wish, Íñigo knocked on my door.

"Señor," he said, "Don Diego requires me to extend to you his compliments, and say that if you have no more important employment, and feel so inclined, he would be happy if you would come and sit with him in the patio, where the night is cool and pleasant."

I rose. "Tell Don Diego I come at once."

When I stepped out on the flagstones it was full night, moonless, with only the stars in a clear dark sky to give a faint illumination. Yet I discerned on the far side of the patio a shadowy group, evidently the family, gathered outside to enjoy the balmy evening.

"Over here, *amigo*," said my host's dry, pleasant voice.

I walked over to where Don Diego was reclining in a hammock, the coal of his *cigarrillo* a spot of brightness in the gloom.

The women sat some distance away. I could make out the thin figure of Doña Estrella, the plump one of Doña Felipa, and the graceful form of Dolores, while a fourth shape, evidently a servant woman, sat on the flagstones. A cool breath of air fanned my cheek.

"The breeze is refreshing," I remarked, after I had thanked Don Diego for inviting me to join them, and had greeted each of the ladies with a proper complimentary salutation.

"One can depend on the breeze here after nightfall," said the Commandant, "even in summer when the days sometimes are very heavy. Tell me, Señor, you have inspected the presidio, what is your opinion of our fortifications?"

"The presidio is well planned," I said, knowing he had designed and built it. I did not add what my soldier's eye had seen: that the post could hardly withstand any kind of a well-organized military attack.

Don Diego seemed to read my mind. "You are asking yourself two questions, I think," he said.

"What two questions do you suppose I am asking?"

"Why the presidio is situated at the foot of this hill, which commands it. And why the walls are of adobe instead of stone."

"Those are, at least, interesting questions."

"I will answer them," said the Commandant. "This presidio is intended as a protection against Indians only. It is sufficiently strong to

defy a band of hostile raiders, although cannon would easily breach
its walls. It is placed where, in an emergency, it can be a quick refuge
for the people of the village. As for this hill, only a foe with artillery
could take advantage of this height. Against such a foe our great defense is our remoteness from any place whence such an expedition could
be launched against us."

"Most logical," I responded. "And especially so since I imagine this
is only a temporary frontier, and Spain will soon extend her borders."

It was a shot at random, said as if at a careless conjecture, but
I awaited his answer almost breathlessly.

"Who knows when that will happen?" said Don Diego. "We are ruled
by Viceroys, and each Viceroy has his own policy. In the fifteen years
this presidio has been established there has been talk at times of occupation of the country north of here, but except for the independent
effort of Padre Hidalgo, there has been no actual movement by either
the Church or the government. Yet the Texas territory, as all men know,
is the legal possession of Spain."

"That territory appeared to me most barren and inhospitable when
I passed through it," I ventured.

"Good only to raise goats, perhaps," he agreed. "Yet there is one
reason why sooner or later posts must be garrisoned northward."

"And what is that?"

He gave a short laugh. "Why, your people, the French, to be sure.
Are you not already on the Red River? When will you be seeking to
extend your hold farther south?"

"I do not think any such plan is in the minds of the French leaders,"
I said. "France and Spain are friends and allies."

"In Europe, perhaps. Never in America."

Don Diego spoke without rancor, as if it were something recognized
and accepted. At the same time I had at least a partial answer to the
question Bienville had asked. If this frontier soldier, knowing nothing
of upper-echelon policies, seemed so certain of a northward push by
Spain, the topic must be one often and seriously discussed in the capital.
Another thought, and an uneasy one: if officials here anticipated a
French aggression, might not a very serious view be taken of my own
presence in San Juan Bautista?

So uncomfortable was the subject that I was glad when Doña Estrella intervened. "War, presidios, politics!" she said. "Is there nothing else you men think about? Señor St. Denis wishes to relax."

"I find it very pleasant, here in this delightful company," I said, "for a man who has long been deprived of any family life."

"You have a family then?"

"Yes. I have not seen it for months, since I left Canada."

"A wife and children, perhaps? You have not spoken of them."

I smiled. "A mother and sister only. My father is dead. As for a wife, a man who marries must know everything—or nothing. I am in neither category. Thus far I have been too occupied to think of marriage, and have never found enough favor in the sight of any lady so that she thought of it."

Though I could not make out her face in the darkness, I thought there might be a faint smile on it in return for mine. "Perhaps you did not look closely enough to see," she said. "As to marriage there are two sayings: Love makes huts into haciendas and straw into silk. Also: A ship without a rudder has no port, and a man without a wife has no purpose."

"I agree with both, and I deplore my own misfortune." Again the subject had become a little too personal and uncomfortable. I sought to turn it away from myself.

"I heard a song a little time ago," I said. "The voice was charming. Could it have been you, Señorita Dolores?"

The girl hesitated, then answered, "Yes—it was I. It was nothing— I was only amusing myself——"

"I could not catch the words, but the melody was pretty."

She murmured thanks, seeming embarrassed by the compliment.

But her plump aunt, Doña Felipa, was not embarrassed.

"Our little Dolores is accomplished not only on the cittern,* which you heard her play, but also on the violin. Don Diego has ordered a harp for her from Vera Cruz, which she will master in due time, for she has great talent in music."

"Time can never deprive one of such an accomplishment," I said. "May I hear you sing again, Señorita?"

"I am not prepared—I—I had rather not——" she said.

---

* A precursor of the modern mandolin

Doña Felipa broke in. "Is it polite, my child, to refuse a request so courteous, from a guest of this house?"

"Please do not press her," I said. "I fear that I have embarrassed Señorita Dolores."

But I had forgotten the inflexible Spanish rule of obedience by a girl to the elders of her family.

"Give me the cittern," said Dolores. "I did not wish to seem ungracious, Señor. If you will have patience with my poor performance, I will try to sing something for you."

She took the instrument from the serving-woman who sat on the flagstones beside her chair. With a plectrum of horn she made a few experimental tinklings and tunings. Then she began to play, and sang, her voice at first uncertain, but growing in confidence:

> O traitor Night! O time of love when he
> Swore his devotion evermore to me;
> Night, thou art gone, and Day is here, alas!
> Deceitful he, with Night his love doth pass.
>
> Foe to my love, O Morn, why dost thou rise
> To witness tears so sad in maiden's eyes?
> He swore his love, but lover's oaths they say
> Like fickle sands are quickly blown away.
>
> I dry my tears as comes again the sun;
> One lover's gone? There'll be another one!

The song began somewhat mournfully, with a slow movement, but ended in a twinkling little lilt, like a laugh. I was delighted. The girl's voice was sweet though not strong, giving promise of greater richness later.

"An amusing sentiment," I said, applauding. "'One lover's gone—there'll be another one.' But I'll take oath, Señorita, that when your eyes work their magic you have only one difficulty with lovers—not keeping them, but getting rid of them."

The elders chuckled, but Dolores sat silent and motionless in the dark.

"You may indeed say so," Doña Felipa said. "And music is not our little one's only accomplishment. She dances divinely——"

"Oh, Tía, please——" the girl half whispered.

But the aunt went firmly on. "She takes lessons in polite Spanish, history, literature, and knows all the pious rituals of the Church, including the full calendar of saints' days, together with the proper observances of each. She can, with her own hands, prepare most delightful dishes for the table; sews and embroiders artfully; and knows how to manage a household and direct servants——"

"*Tía!*" the poor girl pleaded.

Don Diego chuckled. "Peace, Felipa. You disconcert the child. One would think you were extolling the excellences of something that was for sale, like a horse or a mantilla."

A moment's silence, then the thin sister, Doña Estrella, spoke. "You seem interested in music, Señor. Surely you are skilled in it yourself?"

"Hardly skilled." I laughed. "I have sometimes tried my hand at it, as a pastime. But not for months—and then only in camp, where men sang the sort of *chansons* that are liked by *voyageurs* and soldiers, but hardly by ladies."

"A song for a song!" exclaimed Don Diego. "You must let us judge for ourselves."

"I do not know any Spanish songs," I protested.

"Then a French one!" cried Dolores, who was gleeful at this turn. And she added, very prettily, "I have sung for you, Señor. Will you not sing for us in return?"

I considered. It is, after all, instinctive in me to please any company, and I felt especially so toward this. Furthermore, I enjoy music, and have found it a very useful accomplishment, especially where the ladies are concerned.

"I cannot refuse to return graciousness for graciousness," I said. "Compared with you, however, I am a very poor performer, Señorita. Furthermore, I am sadly out of practice. Yet if you ask for it, the penalty is on your own head."

They applauded a little in the darkness, and I went over to where she sat in the night.

"You are playing a cittern," I said. "May I borrow it?"

Mutely she offered me the instrument with both hands, her face upturned to me, its pale oval making her eyes seem greater in the starlight.

"Let me get the feel of this," I said, still standing beside her.

The cittern is a pear-shaped instrument, something between a guitar and a lute, with a thin neck bent sharply back, and four wire strings. For a moment I strummed with the plectrum, recalling the fingering.

Then I looked down at the girl, and a whimsical little inspiration came to me.

"You require from me a song," I said. "This night seems created for a serenade. May I pretend, Señorita Dolores—for this brief moment— that I am much younger, and very much handsomer, and beneath your balcony window singing this to you?"

The aunts and Don Diego laughed, and even the girl smiled a little.

I began a simple accompaniment, and sang, to a melody dreamy and half pleading:

> *Be not afraid, thou fairest, thou rarest*
> *That ever was made! Deny me not a kiss!*
> *Then shalt thou see the measure of pleasure*
> *I will have from thee. What hurt is in this?*
> *Then let us embrace and let pleasure be free;*
> *The world ne'er shall know how happy we'll be.*

I had sung it before, to various ladies in Quebec and elsewhere, with, I am bound to say, some success. When I concluded it, I knew from the expressions and hand clapping of my listeners that I had pleased them, even Don Diego.

Then I heard Dolores ask, "What does it say in Spanish?"

For a moment I wondered if the words of the song might be considered too bold in this company. But then I reasoned that a song is always its own excuse. So I translated—rather freely, and omitting some of the implications—apologizing for being unable to get rhyme and meter exactly in rendering it into the language of my listeners.

"It is a song I learned in my youth," I said.

Doña Felipa tittered. "His youth! One would think him a graybeard!"

"You are still young, Señor," said Doña Estrella. "The best part of your youth is before you."

The two elderly aunts seemed almost archly anxious that I should feel that they considered me young.

I did not respond to them.

"My rough voice is not to be compared to the sweetness of Señorita Dolores' tones," I said. "I would far rather listen to her—as I am sure all here would."

I returned the cittern, and she smiled up at me in the starlight. I thought her very lovely and pleasing then, and could not help hesitating for a moment beside her, standing and looking down at her upturned face.

Doña Estrella said, "It grows late. Let us go in, Dolores."

I came to myself, and stepped back. It seemed to me that the elder aunt had thought that brief moment when I stood close to the girl, and we looked into each other's eyes, too intimate and therefore improper.

It was as if a bar of some kind had been laid between us, yet my warm feeling persisted.

"Yes, Tía," said Dolores obediently. But I thought it was with reluctance that she rose.

I bowed to the ladies as they gathered their skirts and fans and departed, the Indian woman carrying the cittern. Don Diego also had risen to bow, with his grave courtliness. He now cast down his *cigarrillo* and trod on the coal.

"A pleasant evening," I said. "I shall regret when I must depart from this house."

"That, I pray, will not be for some time," said he.

We said our good nights and parted, and that night I found sleep a little difficult.

I remembered the probing questions of Doña Estrella and Doña Felipa's cataloguing of Dolores' accomplishments. That indeed did have the sound, as Don Diego said, of one extolling the excellences of something for sale, as a horse. Furthermore there was the coy insistence by the two elderly aunts on my *youth*. And I was *thirty!* It seemed they were most obviously trying to bracket me with that other whom they considered young—Dolores. And yet she was so much younger than I, nineteen at most.

I said to myself, Do not be ridiculous. You are a foreigner, poor, virtually a prisoner, certainly under suspicion, your future assuredly greatly clouded. They would not have such a notion concerning you.

And yet even a fool could see the signs, not very subtle, of matchmaking designs by the two aunts. It is a practice in which all women love to indulge, particularly old women. They seem to feel that a man who is free and unencumbered is some sort of a reflection on their sex, and they plot to remedy that situation as soon as possible, by tricking him into the arms of the nearest young suitable female.

The girl was, I conceded, attractive and freshly youthful, and it was always difficult for me to be completely cold to a charming woman. But I had enough experience of the sex, and their scheming, so that I shied away from this thought like a horse frightened by a blanket flapped in his face.

I had sufficient complications in my life already, certes, without becoming involved in something so full of pitfalls and snares as the plans of two old women for a possible husband for their grandniece.

In San Juan Bautista there was a sort of nightly ritual of clamor, which came twice during each night.

At moonrise, and again just before dawn, the little wolves of the desert called coyotes would come to the hills overlooking the town, and salute it with their shrill, quavering howls. That would arouse every dog in the village—and there seemed to be more curs than there were people—into a fury of barking. In turn this would awaken the game-cocks, of which each family possessed one or more, and they would join in the tumult with their shrill crowing. Lastly the burros, in every part of the place, as if feeling called upon to participate, would add their raucous and discordant voices to the general din.

Each time this occurred, it took an hour for quiet to settle down on the settlement again. I heard these "concerts" through from beginning to end, as I lay awake with my thoughts.

2.

Don Diego and I ate breakfast together next morning rather silently, it being the custom of the ladies to arise late.

"There is to be a flogging," he said. "I must go down, for as commandant I must witness it."

I rode with him, not to see the flogging so much as to get away from the house, where my thoughts were still difficult to arrange and manage. When we entered the gates of the fort, the garrison already was drawn up in double rank, and a man, naked to the waist, was being led to a sort of low rack of rough posts at the foot of the gallows, which the soldiers were facing.

Don Diego dismounted and at once marched across the parade ground, to take his position of command. I stood beside the headquarters building, watching the scene, which I could see very well from where I was.

The man to be punished, an Indian with a low brutish forehead and a face devoid of any expression, made no resistance, but allowed himself to be bound, spread-eagle fashion, on the rack—face *upward*.

Herrera supervised the binding, and ordered the ranks. Then he took his position slightly to the rear of Don Diego. A sergeant, with a whip of long leather thongs, came forward. With horror I now realized that the whipping was not to be on the back, but upon the bare, tender belly.

A command from Herrera, and the whip fell with a sharp crack, wielded with all the strength of the sergeant's arm. The Indian on the rack twisted and shrank, drawing in his belly until the ribs arched out about the straining cavity. Involuntary as the act was, it was equally futile. Again and again the whip fell, the keen crackle of it sounding each time as the lash bit into the flesh. Stripes appeared across the writhing abdomen, then the skin broke and blood trickled down the man's sides. His face twisted in agony, he shut his eyes tightly, but no outcry came from his lips.

Without expression the men in the ranks looked on. Fifty times I counted as the thongs of the whip whined through the air and cut cruelly into the body of the victim. At the end the poor wretch on the rack seemed almost unconscious, but he had not once uttered any sound.

I had seen floggings before; but never one such as this. Almost sick at the stomach I watched two soldiers untie the prostrate figure, and lift him by the arms, first to a sitting position, then off the rack. At once he collapsed on the ground, hugging his lacerated abdomen with his arms, his face covered with dust, blood running not only from the ghastly whip cuts on his flayed belly, but from a corner of his mouth where he had bit his lips and tongue raw.

A soldier threw an olla of water over him. The man began to crawl away, was helped to his feet, and staggered off toward one of the barracks, reeling as if he would fall again, but reaching the door at last, clinging to the wall for a moment, then disappearing within.

A command from Herrera and the ranks broke as the men went to their various assignments of the day.

Don Diego returned to the headquarters building, and I followed him into it.

"Why was the man flogged?" I asked.

"An example," he replied. "He was accused of theft by another soldier."

"What was the theft?"

"Oh—I know not. Some trifle. It was not the theft for which he was punished. It was his manner of answering."

"How did he answer?"

"He said nothing. He spat."

"Perhaps the charge was false."

"It does not matter. To spit as he did, when questioned by an officer, is an insult."

"The officer was Herrera?"

"Yes."

"Was there any witness to this spitting?"

"No. The officer's word is sufficient in such a case. You must understand that these soldiers are the scum of the world. Most of them are in the army for committing crime, it being common to sentence felons and vagrants to military service. They are cattle to be kept down by fear, else we would have mutiny. What you have just seen is one of the necessities of maintaining the rule of Spain in this land. These people understand the whip and the noose, but little else."

I found myself wondering at this host of mine, so pleasant in his household, so good a friend, yet ordering and watching coldly a flogging so devilishly brutal as that of the soldier. *This* was Spain—Spain the remorseless, Spain in which cruelty was as a bottomless pit. This was the part of Spain I disliked, the part feared by the world, and with reason: the Spain of the Duque d'Alba's Court of Blood in the Low Countries, and the Inquisition's dread and pitiless history.

And I, myself, was in the clutch of Spain. What would be the outcome of this?

Later, leaving the presidio, I visited the mission and had a glass of wine with Padre Ambrosio, to whom I spoke of the punishment of the soldier. The good priest was unsurprised and unshocked by the tale.

"I dislike the whip and deplore its necessity," he said. "But when it must be used, the belly is better than the back, for these people in their backs have no feeling. In New Spain the few must control the many."

"How few?" I asked with interest.

"Spaniards of pure blood number less than one fifth of the population."

"These rule all the others?"

"It is somewhat complicated, but I will try to explain. First, the highest positions in the country are all held by *European-born* Spaniards, who come from the mother country by appointment to authority in the colony. The viceroys, archbishops, bishops and governors are all of this class, which numbers less than fifteen thousand persons. I fear they are not loved, for they are somewhat arrogant. The lower classes have a name for them—*gachupines*—'wearers of spurs.' Governor Gaspar de Anaya, of this province, and some of his higher officials and judges at Parras, are of the *gachupín* class."

"What of Don Diego—and yourself—surely you are of pure Spanish blood?"

"Pure blood, true, but born this side of the ocean, and hence we are *criollos*. The *criollos* are the backbone of New Spain. Some of them are inheritors of immense wealth and even noble blood. Nevertheless, they are looked down upon by the *gachupines,* and hold a position inferior in the social scale. To the *criollo* only three professions are open—the Church, the army, and the law—and he can hope to rise to no great height in any of these pursuits. Because of this, many *criollos* are indolent and resentful of the privileged *gachupines.* We of the Church, I trust, having learned the lessons of humility, are least affected by such ambitions and considerations."

In spite of the last pious sentence I gathered that Padre Ambrosio did not wholly sympathize with this interesting caste system. But more was to follow.

"The third class of our people," he continued, "consists of those of mixed blood—the *mestizos*—who outnumber the pure whites by a considerable proportion. Some of these also are wealthy, but only the inferior posts of the army or Church are within their reach. Such a one is Herrera of the garrison, and also Padres Sulpicio and Marcos, the priests who serve under me here at the mission. Unhappily, the *mestizos* are often mistrusted by the Spaniards because of their Indian ancestry, while they are hated by the Indians, since in an attempt to deny their dark blood they are sometimes cruel and oppressive toward the natives."

"And the natives themselves?"

"The *Indios puros* are lowest in scale, while forming the vast majority of the population. They are ignorant, ambitionless, filthy, and sometimes rebellious. Yet one must pity them for they are the *tamanes*—porters—and do all the lowest, hardest, most ignoble toil on the *encomiendas*—the slave estates—often under the whip. They have souls, for which reason I am here to save them from hell; but because they have mentalities of children, they are exempt from the punishments of the Holy Office."

I know not why, but at that word a chill shudder passed through me, like that which, they say, one experiences when somebody walks across his future grave, and an icy hand for an instant seemed to constrict my heart. Perhaps it was some glimpse my soul had into the future, a glimpse my mind and eyes could not share, but which was transmitted to my body in that shiver and sensation of cold horror.

"The—Inquisition?" I used the word more familiar to us in France.

"We prefer to speak of it as the Holy Office," said Padre Ambrosio primly. "And bear witness that I hold it to be truly holy in its war against the works of the devil. It performs its sacred duties without fear or favor, and no matter how high the position of the accused, or whether he be *gachupín, criollo,* or *mestizo,* he pays the penalty inexorably if he is convicted of any of the crimes within its jurisdiction."

All this was said with the most sanctimonious fervor, and in such a way that I could not help feeling that the Inquisition was held in fear even by the priesthood, and even in so remote a place as this.

"What crimes?" I asked.

"Sorcery, witchcraft, apostasy, teaching the Mosaic Law, bigamy, blasphemy, and most important of all, heresy."

"And how are these punished?"

"Variously. Some by penance and fine, some by imprisonment, some by flogging. Sorcerers, witches, Judaists, and heretics die at the *quemadero* in the chief plaza of the capital, opposite from the viceregal palace and the cathedral."

The subject was a grim one, and after I left the priest, it stayed with me, preying on my mind. When I was in Spain in my youth, I was too light-minded and careless to be oppressed by the thought of the Inquisition, although I heard it mentioned once or twice, in whispers almost. No auto-da-fé, the name by which its pitiless public ceremonials of execution was known, had occurred in Madrid during my rather brief service in the royal palace guard there. But I had learned enough of it since that time so that now that I was confronted by it, I had that feeling of almost queasy uneasiness that comes with a foreboding of a formless dread.

I sometimes ask myself now why I did not in those succeeding days at least make an effort to escape. But then I know the answer.

In the first place I was under no likelihood of ever seeing the city of Mexico, where the Inquisition held its chief sway. At worst I might be imprisoned here, on the frontier, or at Parras, for a time. Furthermore I examined my conscience, and discovered that I had not gone to confession recently, and made all convenient haste to do so. I had only small sins to confess, for the reason that I had been nowhere that the opportunity for sinning offered itself since last I received absolution. Padre Ambrosio smiled on me, and I assured myself that I was a good Christian Catholic, and could probably name more saints than most persons. There could be no reason to fear that I would be singled out for attention when I was so insignificant and so remote. Yet Padre Ambrosio's sanctimonious primness in speaking of the Holy Office returned to me unpleasantly, because of the implications I could not keep myself from reading into it. Even between the orders of so-called mendicant friars there was an undercurrent of jealousy and ill will, and Padre Ambrosio was a Franciscan, while the Inquisition was armed and implemented by the Dominicans. . . .

But more important than this process of self-assurance and doubt which alternately I felt, the thing that kept me from any burst for freedom was a simple matter of honor. I had given my word to Don Diego that I would remain at San Juan Bautista until judgment was rendered in my case. Often I regretted that, but there it was. I possess, as I have said, a code of honor peculiar to myself, and the redemption of my given word is a part of that code. With that at stake I could not even think of escape, although had I been able to conceive of it, it might at least have given me something to do, even if it ended in recapture—and what must be faced if that occurred.

Don Diego sensed my tension. "You fret yourself without good reason, Don Luís," he said one day, using the familiar salutation he now employed toward me, with the Spanish pronunciation of my first name. "Governor Anaya is no doubt very busy with matters of moment. A delay such as this is perhaps the best sign that he considers the question concerning you of no great importance and will favor you. I beseech you, rid your mind of this concern."

It was advice easier to give than follow.

4.

Days passed. Time, and more than enough time, had gone for a reply from Parras, with still no word.

There came an afternoon when I was in my room during the siesta hour, awake and restless, for I had never been able to adjust myself to the custom of the afternoon nap. At length I stepped out on the patio, thinking to find myself alone.

To my surprise I saw, seated on a bench at the other side of the enclosure, a pretty figure. It was Dolores, reading in the shade, her dark head bent over a book in her hands.

The girl had interested me more as time passed. At first she was quite easily put out of face by my half-amused little flatteries, but later, as she became accustomed to me, she gave laughing rejoinders, so that a half-jesting camaraderie grew up between us.

What would you? She was a girl, with wit, and eyes of surpassing loveliness, and a form worth a man's dreams. I have never been insensible to lovely women, and so I secretly and smilingly carried on a little flirtation with her, as lightly as a bird touching upon a branch. It amounted to no more than pretty speeches, little gallantries, and a chance to test my charm on her, but it was better than doing nothing at all.

And all this without any real purpose. I confess that I have never been greatly troubled with conscience concerning women, but I do protest that I had no thought of harm to Dolores. On the other hand I had no thought, certes, of marriage either, for all my life I had avoided every lure women had set before me to trap me into that form of bondage and in my mind always ran the warning French adage: "Marriage is a covered dish which one has to chew until death."

More than once, however, I had wished I could sometimes see her alone, instead of always in company with plump Doña Felipa, who was her official *dueña*. There were dangers—those matchmaking aunts!—but even the strait-laced Spanish propriety could surely make nothing of a few minutes of harmless conversation alone with a girl in a patio. I should, perhaps, have awaited the appearance of the *dueña*, but in my boredom and to relieve my spirits I instead walked over to her.

"You make a charming picture, sitting there," I said to her.

She looked up from her book and smiled, unsurprised, so that I had a feeling that she had seen me come into the patio, and only pretended to be occupied with her book. At least she had not fled from me.

"Where is your—dragon?" I asked.

"My dragon, Señor?"

"I mean it jokingly. Your *dueña,* who guards you as the dragons of old guarded the fabled treasures men sought."

"Tía Felipa is taking siesta," she said with the faintest of smiles.

"Does she know you are out here alone, where something so terrible and perilous as a man can find you?"

"She does not think you either terrible or perilous, Señor."

"I am glad of that, for I am neither. But don't you think you know me sufficiently well to call me something less formal than 'Señor'?"

"What should I call you?"

"Luís is my name, which my friends use."

She considered. "I will try it—Luís. Yes, I like that—Don Luís."

"Only Luís," I smiled.

"Well—sometimes perhaps—when we are alone—then, Luís."

For some reason I felt absurdly happy at this concession from her. She smiled and made room for me on the bench beside her.

"What are you reading?" I asked. "A book of hours, I suppose."

Swiftly she put the book aside, half tucking it under her wide skirt on the bench opposite from me.

"You will not tell?" she said anxiously.

"Tell whom, Dolores? Doña Felipa?"

"Oh no. Tía Felipa, whom you call my dragon, likes *romanzas.* It is Tía Estrella whose displeasure I fear. She thinks such reading is—well, a waste of time—and a cause of idle and frivolous thoughts in a girl's mind."

"I would never think of telling."

"She would frown especially on *this.*" She took the book once more into her lap, and sat looking down at it almost contritely. "It is the story of Doña Catalina de Erazú, the one they called *La Monja Alférez.*"*

"Is a *romanza* about a nun worse than others?"

"Some—and Tía Estrella is one of them—consider that Doña Catalina

---
* "The Nun Ensign"

lived a wicked life, because she left the convent and wore men's clothes."

"And what do you think?"

"I—I am afraid that I think her life was—exciting."

She made this admission with such hesitation, and yet so frankly, that it struck us both as amusing, and we laughed out loud.

At once she put her finger to her lips. "Hush! Not so loudly. We must be quiet, or somebody will come with us."

Her manner was that of a charming conspirator, and the conspiracy was of the nature most flattering to a man—to be alone with him, without interruption by her *dueña* or anyone else. I felt a glow of pleasure at it.

"Tell me about your nun," I said, lowering my voice.

"Her pious family mistakenly made her take the veil, when she had no wish to be a nun," Dolores began. "After a time she rebelled against the discipline of the convent, and ran away." She gazed at me, wide-eyed. "That was very wrong, wasn't it?"

"Perhaps—but at least it was human," I replied gravely, but with a twinkle in my eye.

The girl seemed to relax as if she felt she had a sympathetic listener.

"She adopted men's attire," she went on. "That also was bad: but it was necessary, you see. Disguised as a man, she left Spain and went to Peru. There she became an *arriero*—a driver of pack trains—and wore a sword with which she became so expert that she killed several men in duels. Once she escaped execution for slaying a man only by revealing that she was a woman, a nun, and a virgin."

"So her sex saved her in the end."

"But what a humiliation, to be saved for such a reason, after all those brave deeds!" she exclaimed.

I was becoming more and more delighted with the beautiful play of her eyes and the animation of her young face. "It is humiliating to be a woman?" I smiled.

"No. But if she was going to be a man, she should die like a man!"

"A difference, I perceive. Was this the end of her story?"

"No, there is more to it. She was sent to Spain for trial, but the courts gave her a dispensation to wear men's clothes for the rest of her life. So Doña Catalina recrossed the ocean, coming this time to New Spain. She took up her old trade of *arriero*, and lived out her days. No man dared make sport of her, or cross her, for her skill with the sword remained with her to the day of her death."

"Now praise be to God that all women are not so skilled!" I exclaimed devoutly. "Do you envy her this life, Dolores?"

She thought a moment, then shook her graceful head. "No, I do not think so—Luís. Danger has not the attraction for a woman that it seems to have for men. She had freedom, to be sure, but also she had hardship, and a woman likes the luxuries of life. Furthermore, I think men's clothes must be very uncomfortable. The garments of women are much nicer and prettier, and I love nice and pretty things." Thus she prattled on, smiling at me. Then she said, quite seriously, "Furthermore, if I were a man, I would have to admire women. I much prefer to be a woman—and admire men."

This viewpoint interested me. "You admire all men?"

"Not all."

I grinned. "Lieutenant Herrera?"

She tossed her head. "By no means. He is stupid, and besides he is a *mestizo*."

"I think he admires you," I teased.

"I suppose so," she said indifferently. "He asked my grandfather for permission to pay court to me."

"Ah? And what did Don Diego say?"

"He refused, of course. Even if I had been inclined to him, it would not have been suitable."

"But have you other admirers? A girl so beautiful could not fail to have them."

"Not so many," she said quite candidly. "Men who are eligible—in Tía Estrella's estimation—are few in this country. None live here in San Juan Bautista. There are one or two sons of *rancheros,* but they are rustic and awkward, acting in a salon as if they were in a cattle corral. At Parras——"

"Oho! They ride all the way from Parras?"

"The Governor once did," she said with a little flash of pride.

"Anaya?"

"Don Gaspar de Anaya."

"He is a suitor of yours?"

"He was here."

"You refused him?"

"I do not like him."

"What is wrong with the high and mighty Governor of Coahuila? Is he, too, a *mestizo*?"

"Oh no, he is a *gachupín*. A native of Andalusia, in fact."

"Is such a one not desirable in marriage?"

"Tía Estrella thinks so. Tía Felipa also. But I do not. I treated him badly."

"Why?"

"He is too old for one thing. At least forty. And he behaves as if everyone is dirt under his feet—even Don Diego. And he appeared to believe he was doing me a favor by being interested in me." A spark of anger in her dark eyes.

"Hum," I said noncommittally.

"He is cruel also, and—and—soft and pudgy. Besides all this I am told he keeps mistresses—not only one, but two or three at the same time. Indeed on his *visita* here last spring there was in his entourage a sleek, bold creature who fawned on him and tried to patronize everyone else."

"And with this woman along, he paid suit to *you*?"

Again the flash of pride in her eyes. "When he saw *me* he sent her back to Parras. And swore he was through with her—with all her kind."

"This did not melt you?"

"I laughed at him, so that he went away angry."

"Bravo, Dolores! So you are rid of the Governor of Coahuila."

"I do not know that I am," she said thoughtfully.

"But you sent him packing, did you not?"

"Disdainful treatment sometimes only increases infatuation in men."

"You are very wise for your years." I paused, and then smiled. "Now that you have discussed men you do not admire, are there any whom you do admire?"

"I admire my grandfather, who is all things brave and honorable. And I admire Padre Ambrosio, who is kind and wise. And I—admire someone else."

"Who is he?"

"I will not tell you. I must go."

She did not need to tell me, and I felt a sensation of astonishment, mingled with tenderness. As she made as if to rise, I took her hand in mine.

"You are like a dream," I whispered, and I could not resist taking her hand to my lips.

"Please——" the girl said breathlessly.

"Stay but a little longer——" I found myself suddenly eager.

"Release my hand—please, please—Señor——"

"Luís."

"Please—Luís—if Tía should see us—oh, Luís—*caro*——"

The endearment came so suddenly, so softly, and so frightened, that I gave her back her hand. She departed with a swift, escaping movement that made my heart leap, and leap again when she paused an instant in the door to cast one glance back at me, searching, questioning, fathomless.

Not until I was back in my room did I regain fully my head. Then I cursed myself silently.

I felt I had overstepped the bounds of caution and good judgment with the girl, and this partly because she seemed to accept at full value everything I said to her. Most women I had known could play at the game of love as if it were a fencing match. But this one left down her guard, invited my thrust, offered no riposte.

The girl was entrancing, she excited me. That was admitted. An intrigue? A man of the world does not neglect his opportunities, and it might be too difficult to contrive something . . .

But I discovered, oddly, that the thought of intrigue in connection with Dolores lacked the appeal I might have expected. She was so innocent, so trusting, so willing to rely on my good faith and honor. Perhaps it was that the thing appeared too easy . . . difficulty lends a special enchantment to this sort of a game.

I asked myself, Am I in love with her? And I replied to my own question, No, certainly no. The thought is impossible. Assuredly I am not in love with her, but even to think of a seduction of her, in view of the generosity with which I have been received in this house, is treachery. Besides, an intrigue of this kind would be madness in my present dangerous and delicate situation. That is it. I am moved by considerations of safety, and of honor. Assuredly not love.

But I wished once again, and most heartily, after all this, that I had not given my parole to Don Diego. To escape from this place, for some reason, now had a certain added attractiveness.

5.

At the evening meal, Doña Felipa giggled at me and appeared to be more than usually arch toward me, which made me uneasy. But not until later did I realize how deeply I was involved in toils of my own making.

The fat aunt waylaid me in the hall.

"Don Luís—in here," she said in a whisper, with a flash of her dark eyes, motioning to a small alcove at one side. Rather unwillingly I stepped into the niche.

"I know everything!" she said at once, in a low voice but with much emphasis.

"What do you mean?"

"Ah, don't play coy with old Felipa!" She favored me with a nudge and a giggle. "You can trust me," she added.

"But I don't understand——"

"Ah yes, you do," she said. "Look at me. I am Dolores' *dueña*, but also I am her loving friend. She told me what you called me—her 'dragon.' That was amusing. But I am not such a dragon as you think. If I approve of a man, I will help him." She smiled. "And I *do* approve of you, Don Luís!"

"My profoundest thanks, but——"

"It is not too early for us to make plans! Between ourselves, I do not think Don Diego will be too difficult, if he is properly approached. You are of good family, as he himself says, even if you are French. You have won the hearts of this family. You are a soldier, and perhaps not too heavily endowed with money, but Dolores will bring you a very nice dowry. Her father and mother left her lands in Tamaulipas, and some household possessions of no little value, as well as a fund of ducats held in trust for her by Don Diego——"

"All this is very fine, but how do you know that——"

"I know very well that you are in love with our little Dolores. And—I tell you this for the ease of your heart, for such things are a torment to one who is not sure—she returns your love. So, since two hearts are in agreement, it becomes only a matter of arranging things."

"How arranged?" I asked desperately. "I am a foreigner—a prisoner whose fate is not yet even decided. And Dolores is so young——"

"It is proof of your kindness and love that you raise these considerations," she interrupted. "Of course she is young—she is at the time of life when a woman is at her most perfect moment, ripe to be plucked by some fortunate man! But you are far from old. A man does not become a man until he has passed the first simpering stages of extreme youth and seen a little of life. As for your present situation, I honor you for respecting Don Diego's feelings because of it. Nevertheless, I believe this matter soon will be resolved in your favor. Padre Ambrosio speaks highly of you, and has written to Querétaro concerning your services to the Church. So, you see, all difficulties will be blown away like a wisp of mist when the time comes."

"Doña Felipa——"

"Allow me to finish. You have not spoken to Dolores formally—of course not! Assuredly we know that you have the delicacy to follow the proper customs and first request of Don Diego, her guardian, permission to pay your addresses. But do not fear to ask him! Remember what I have told you—have courage! Now I must go."

Before I could stop her, or summon my wits to say anything that could possibly fit the situation, she left me.

The fat was in the fire, most definitely. That night I paced the floor —"trying to turn all the seams out," as the French say—and making poor business of it.

It was far from difficult to conjecture the course events had taken. I had not spoken to Dolores in terms of formal love, certainly not in terms of marriage. But she, most evidently, thought in terms of marriage, and so also did Doña Felipa. Without doubt the girl and her *dueña* had put their heads together, and to both their ingenuous minds there could be but one interpretation of my words and attentions.

I berated myself for forgetting the difference between the customs of France and Spain, particularly provincial Spain: the light tolerance of human frailties on the one hand, in contrast with the strait-laced propriety of a household such as this.

Here everything was taken to mean just what it said: there was no seeking for any subtle undermeaning. *Mort de Dieu!* The two of them, the eager girl and her no less eager matchmaking aunt, would expect me to speak to Don Diego, and soon.

Doña Felipa, her dragon! A dragon far too benevolent! Overgenerous with the lives and fate of others . . . curses on Doña Felipa!

12. *The Power of God, the King, and the Governor*

To be sure, I did not speak to Don Diego. But I felt that my position after my interview with Doña Felipa was acutely embarrassing, and it grew more so.

As for the two feminine conspirators, even though they received no sign from the Commandant that a conversation of the nature in which they were interested had taken place, they must have argued that this was but natural. Even had I already asked permission to woo Dolores, Don Diego would no doubt spend some little time in consideration of the various factors involved, before he gave final answer.

I dreaded confronting Dolores alone under the present circumstances, but I need not have feared. Since things had reached the present stage, her *dueña* thought it proper to be doubly vigilant. Yet I could not help observing that the girl took added pains with her appearance, wore her prettiest costumes, adorned herself with what simple jewelry she possessed, arranged her hair with utmost art, wore her tallest comb and finest mantillas, and assumed all the small graces that are instinctive and make women entrancing.

And she *was* entrancing. When she did chance to meet me—always in the company of her aunt—she was all starry-eyed, and fired a girl's pink signals in her cheeks. So young, so fresh, so openly in love was she that I would not have been human, if my heart did not go out to her somewhat. If things had been different . . . but they were not different. I put a button on my heart, as the saying goes.

What I did not count on was that such a secret could not remain with the two women.

Though they did not speak of it to Don Diego, nor he to them, it very shortly began to be whispered through the house that Señor St. Denis had fallen under the spell of Señorita Dolores. And from this rumors grew greater: that I had conferred with Don Diego (which I had not); and finally that permission had been granted to pay my addresses and Dolores and I actually were betrothed (which was farthest of all from the truth).

So toothsome a piece of gossip ran rapidly down the hill from the big *casa* through the settlement below. Women, patting their *tortillas* or doing their washing, gossiped about it; men in the plaza puffed their *cigarrillos* and discussed it; the priests in the mission shook their heads over it; and in the presidio the matter was given a thorough going over, first by the *cortejas,* and then by their soldier consorts.

2.

In the darkness of night I awoke, suddenly alert with that instant consciousness which the instinct of danger brings.

It was pitch black, too dark to see, but in the room was something— something that breathed.

"Íñigo!" I called out, for the servant slept in the hall and it might be he who had entered.

There was no answer.

Tensely I lay in my bed, trying to pierce the inky blackness with my sight. There was no sound. For a moment I thought I had been mistaken, there was nothing there after all.

Then I realized it was something else: *the sound of the breathing had ceased.*

It meant one thing to me: whatever that creature was in the black shadows, it had drawn in its breath for its spring.

My muscles tensed. Suddenly—I did not see so much as sense it with that sixth sense which comes in moments of deadly emergency—an intensification of the blackness seemed to brood over me.

By a movement instinctive and desperate I threw myself across the bed, falling on the floor on hands and feet, crouching naked save for my sleeping shirt.

At the same instant the blow came downward, a knife wielded with all the force of a heavy arm weighted with hate. But the point struck only the empty place where my body had lain an instant before, ripping through bedclothing and the mattress beneath.

Behind the bed I still crouched, peering into the darkness, knowing now that a murderer was with me in the room, bent on my death, for what reason I could not guess. I was helpless, nearly naked, weaponless, cut off from the door by the enemy who stalked me.

Who was that assassin hiding in the dark room with me? And where was Íñigo?

"*Quién es?*" I challenged, my voice vibrant.

My eyes were adjusting to the blackness, and now I could dimly make out the bulk of a shadow, no more. I gathered myself together, to leap, or flee, or do whatever instinct told me should be my next move. The shadow was coming slowly, but with deadly purpose, around the foot of the bed, and it was coming with the knife.

"*Quién es?*" I asked again.

No answer. Still I was cut off from all escape by the inexorable approach of the black assassin. I backed toward the empty fireplace, my knees bent, feeling the floor with my feet, body crouched.

"*Quién es?*" I called a third time.

Then the drama in the blackness of my room came to its climax as the dark bulk suddenly hurtled forward.

In the corner by the fireplace, I could not elude. Instead, with a fighter's instinct, I leaped to meet my assailant.

But I did it in my own way. I made no effort to grapple, to try blindly to reach for the knife arm, which could only have ended with my body ripped open, and my life spilled out on the floor.

Instead, I hurled myself sidewise, almost flat on the floor and rolling over as I went. Below the knees my body struck the legs of the oncoming killer. Taken completely by surprise, and carried forward more by his own momentum than by my force, he tripped, and with a terrible oath crashed on the floor beyond me.

Not for one breathless second did I hesitate.

Leaping to my feet, I threw myself toward the door, pulled it open, and an instant later was out in the patio.

"Íñigo!" I shouted. "Íñigo!"

At that instant a figure bolted from the door. It did not hesitate or turn toward me, but leaped the low wall separating the patio from the orange orchard, and was gone among the trees.

Lights flickered in the house. Don Diego, a blanket wrapped about him and a sword in his hand, was at the door with a candle. Heads clustered at windows, and I suddenly remembered that save for my shirt I was nude.

I stepped into the shadows. Íñigo appeared at my side.

"Where were you?" I demanded.

"I was sent for," he said.

"By whom?"

"One called to me that Don Diego wanted me."

"Did you see him?"

"No. I heard. I was sleepy. I went at once, asking no questions. Don Diego had not sent for me."

The Commandant came out into the patio and confirmed what Íñigo said.

"He came to my door, knocked, and asked what I required," said Don Diego. "I told him I did not send for him. Then we heard you call."

"Someone sought my life here tonight," I said.

They followed me to my room. With a candle lit and a blanket now about me, I showed the place where the blade had plunged into my bedding.

"It was not meant in jest," said Don Diego.

Then Íñigo gave an exclamation. *"Cuchillo!"*

He darted forward and from the corner beside the fireplace picked up a hafted knife, with an ugly, cruel, two-edged blade.

"He must have lost it when I overthrew him," said I. "That is why he fled, instead of again assailing me when he came out into the patio."

"Who could it be? And for what reason?" asked Don Diego.

I looked at the knife in the palm of my hand. "Could you discover to whom this belonged?"

Both Don Diego and Íñigo examined it. Both shook their heads.

"There are many like it in the village," said the Commandant.

"I would speak with you alone," I said.

"Leave us," Don Diego told the servant.

When the door was closed, I said, "How fully do you trust Íñigo?"

"With my life."

"He could not be bribed?"

"He would try to kill the one who offered the insult. Íñigo is no ordinary *mozo*. To him a trust is an honor. He would give his life to keep it."

"He went to you, without inquiring who called."

"Nay, when I send for one of my people, they come at once, and without questions."

With a shrug I looked down at the knife in my hand. "Then he who called knew this house and its laws. Will that be of help?"

"Perhaps."

"The man was big, heavy of body. Larger than most of the natives. Is there such a one who may have some reason for hating me?"

Don Diego looked me fairly in the eye. "Herrera," he said, "at one time had hopes of Dolores." He paused. "You have said nothing to me, Don Luís, but there is talk among the women along a certain direction . . ."

I returned his look squarely. "You know the circumstances, Don Diego. Until such matters are settled, I could not in honor broach such a subject."

He nodded his head, his eyes gleaming from under their grizzled brows. "I am glad to hear this from you, Don Luís. As you yourself said, honor and duty are one, to be guarded with the life. In the morning I will ask some questions of Herrera."

But in the morning Herrera was gone.

No man knew where, or why, but between sunset and dawn he had taken his horse and disappeared.

"I will report him as a deserter," said Don Diego grimly. "If I look him in the face again, he will have reason for regrets."

3.

Later I was glad that I was not at the *casa* on the hill when the lancers came. It was on a morning several days later, and I was sitting in conversation with Don Diego, when a sergeant and three men, uniformed in the red and gold of the elite guard, rode into the presidio and entered the headquarters office.

The sergeant saluted. "His High Excellency, Don Gaspar de Anaya, Royal Governor of Coahuila, is approaching this place. I ride ahead of him bearing orders."

Don Diego rose so quickly that it betrayed his surprise.

"The Governor? How soon?" he asked.

"Soon. Perhaps within the hour. He dispatched me and these men to execute his orders and warn you to prepare for his arrival."

"State your orders."

"I am commanded to arrest a certain alien, a subject of France, and hold him for His Excellency's disposal."

The Commandant glanced at me, his face a struggle of perplexity and concern.

I stood up. "It must be that I am he for whom you are looking," I said to the sergeant. "I am French by birth—though here as an envoy."

"Then it is my duty to seize you."

"I do not resist."

The sergeant made a motion and two of his men took my sword and placed themselves on either side of me.

"Lock him in the *cárcel*."

"Why?" asked Don Diego.

"The wording of the order was: 'Arrest him and place him in prison until I arrive.' So said His Excellency."

"It is not necessary. He will not attempt to escape. He can wait here. I will be surety for him."

"And will you also explain to the Governor why you see fit to disobey his direct command?" The sergeant's impudence showed how sure he was of his position.

Don Diego stood glaring, clearly at a loss.

"If it is an order," I said, "it must be obeyed. Do not concern yourself, Don Diego."

"Bind him," ordered the sergeant.

"Did the Governor also command that?" demanded Don Diego.

"Not specifically—but one always binds prisoners——"

"Do not *exceed* your orders, Sergeant!" rasped Don Diego in a voice that caused the soldier to fall back a step, with a new respect in his face.

"Don Luís, this is as great a surprise to me as it is to you," the Commandant said, turning to me.

"The Governor comes, himself personally, on my account, you believe?"

"No man can tell what is in the Governor's mind."

"I am ready, Sergeant," I said.

An hour passed. Two. I stood in the narrow little stone jail, gazing out through the bars of my window, and though I did not see it, San Juan Bautista was a scene of bustling activity strangely at variance with its usual sleepy appearance, preparing for the visit of the high dignitary.

Flags fluttered everywhere. In the village the Indian inhabitants grew busy sweeping the street. Soldiers furbished their arms and donned their best uniforms in the presidio. Even in the mission the priests prepared in various ways; for the arrival of the Governor was an occasion that touched every walk in life.

Suddenly a trumpet sounded a high, shrill call of warning. In the tower of the mission church a bell began to ring. Commands were shouted and the garrison of the presidio marched forth to escort the official into the town.

Don Gaspar de Anaya arrived in some little state, with lancers, a retinue of officials and secretaries, and a baggage train driven by *arrieros*, an eye-filling sight for San Juan Bautista.

Shortly after I heard all this bustle and stir, guards came for me and I was marched to the headquarters building. Lancers in the brave gold and red of the Parras garrison stood before it, the little pennons on their lances fluttering. One of them held a fine gray stallion, carrying a saddle and accouterments rich with gold and silver ornaments, carved brown leather, and bright silk embroidery—the Governor's horse.

Within, I was brought to a halt before the table, beside which stood Don Diego, looking sterner and leaner than ever. Frequently his eye went, with the grimmest of looks, to a burly figure beside the door. It was Herrera, attired now in the Governor's guard uniform. I understood how this sudden visitation had been brought about.

Don Gaspar de Anaya himself was seated. I saw before me a short, rather plump man, with full brown eyes and a small, full-lipped mouth, to which he sought to give an appearance of virility by means of a black mustache, waxed at the ends. He was far from an imposing figure, but he made up for it by the splendor of his garb: brocaded coat set off with gold buttons and braid, waistcoat of cloth of gold, baldric and sash red and gold, a sword with a hilt inlaid with gold, polished boots coming above his knees, golden spurs, and a wide hat pinned in tricorn form, heavily encrusted with gold lace and gay with a yellow ostrich plume.

"This is the man?" said Anaya when I appeared.

"Yes, Excellency," answered Don Diego.

"When did he arrive here?"

"A fortnight or more ago."

"And when was he placed in the *cárcel?*"

"Two hours since, as you commanded."

"He has been at liberty all that time? Be so good as to explain why he was not arrested as soon as he arrived at this place!"

"I requested instructions at once from Your Excellency," said Don Diego, "asking how to deal with him. Meantime, since he came on an embassy with chiefs of an Indian nation in a matter of interest to the Church, I took his parole and sought to treat him with consideration, until Your Excellency directed——"

"Consideration! The man is without a doubt a French spy. You should know how to deal with him without a directive—fool!"

At the epithet Don Diego straightened as if he had been slapped in the face.

"By Your Excellency's leave," I said, "I am no spy."

"You are a Frenchman."

"I am also a soldier who has served the King of Spain."

"Be silent!"

I closed my mouth.

Anaya surveyed me, scowling, one plump hand caressing the waxed mustache.

"A spy, without a question," he said at last. "Well, he will keep until morning. Herrera!"

The lieutenant, in his smart new uniform, saluted.

"Lock this prisoner in the *cárcel,* and see that he is watched by men of my own guard."

I had been taken neatly out of Don Diego's hands.

"I will judge your case in the morning, Frenchman," Anaya went on. "Prepare your soul this night, for the gallows is yearning for you."

I looked at him, almost grinding my teeth in my rage. The soft, flaccid little man—I could have torn him to pieces with my bare hands! For him I had nothing but a soldier's contempt; and yet he sat there, by grace of some influence at the royal court of Spain with all powers here, and with his armed men about him to enforce the authority he never would have been able to assert by his own character and strength.

I noted with detestation the waxed mustache, peruke, and other details of his costume and bearing that marked him as a fop, a glutton, and a sensualist. A bloated and slimy human slug, and I could do nothing against him!

They led me away.

4.

Herrera pushed me roughly into the tiny stone prison, shoved the door to, and locked it after me. Then he came to the small barred window and looked in at me.

"You can cool down here," he said gloatingly. "How do you like it?"

I did not answer him.

"You heard what His Excellency said." He made a motion, suggesting a noose about the neck. "I am led to believe that His Excellency does not speak merely to hear his own voice." He laughed nastily.

"At least *you* couldn't take my life," I sneered at him. "What a bungler! What a lily-livered coward! You have a new uniform, I see, but the Governor might think less of you if he knew you are too stupid and clumsy to kill a defenseless man lying asleep in his bed. And that you ran like a frightened sheep from that man, though he was bare-handed!"

I saw that it stung him. For a moment, looking at his hateful pock-marked face, I wondered if I had perhaps baited him to the point where he would come into my cell with his soldiers and do some cruelty to me.

But evidently he had his orders. He shrugged.

"Speaking of sheep," he said, "there is more than one way to skin a sheep. This is better. Tomorrow I will watch you strangle at the end of a rope, with satisfaction and no exertion on my part."

Then he left.

I paced the narrow, stinking little space between my stone walls. It was clear to me that Herrera, after he failed to murder me, fled from the justice he knew would be coming to him at Don Diego's hands, and rode hard for the one place where he felt sure he could obtain some sort of vengeance on me. His hatred was because of jealousy, for, as Don Diego said, he had set his mind on Dolores; and when he went to Anaya he knew he was surrendering any hope in that direction, for the Governor was interested in the girl also.

Yet he went, and it was a measure of his hate that he went: a hate he had kept well concealed, for though I knew he disliked me I did not dream of this mortal enmity he held against me. The sudden response of Anaya to the news Herrera brought was a measure also of that worthy's interest, for he was not one to ride a distance like that from Parras, without some mighty personal reason. It occurred to me that the dowry of which Doña Felipa had spoken must be considerable to inspire such an action.

So Dolores was at the heart of all this! With that I cursed all women, and even her. The Governor had promised me to the gallows on the morrow, and as surely as if she were to adjust the noose about my neck with her own hands, Dolores de Ramón was hanging me in the morning. For a moment I raged against her in my heart.

Then I sobered, and thought again, and faced the matter squarely. Was she to blame after all? No, it was I, and I only, who was to blame. Had I been content to leave well enough alone, it was likely that the indolent, neglectful Governor would eventually have taken the easiest action: allowed me to leave for the north, perhaps with a Franciscan priest or two, bound for the Neches, not much wiser than I had come, perhaps, but at least with my life.

But I could not leave well enough alone—oh no, not I! St. Denis, the "addicted to women," must ever be on the lookout for some feminine dalliance. Dolores was so young, so unschooled in the ways of the world: and I made love to her. Yes, secretly and smilingly, I lightly made love to her. Scamp that I was, out of sheer idle amusement I had neglected no chance to whisper in her little ear nonsense of the type that I did not mean, but which passed for coinage with her. I kissed her hand, offered her flowers, was attentive to her more than I even realized, now that I looked back on it. If I had not turned her head, there must have been something wrong with her—or me.

A sophisticated woman would never have taken seriously what I said and did. But Dolores *did* take it seriously. In her innocence, every word I said to her, no matter how light, went straight to her heart: this I now knew. Every compliment, she must have treasured. Perhaps she even remembered the very looks I gave her, and considered them over and over, as women do, what their meaning might be: though they may have had no special meaning at all. When I told her she was lovely, and protested that no other of her sex could stand beside her in brilliance of beauty—and that was one of my elaborate compliments, which had seen service on more than one occasion previously, and often had been laughed away by its fair recipients—she believed that I truly thought it so. And though she, in her honesty and humility, did not for one moment think it was true, it was enough for her, and gave her happiness, that I believed it.

Ah, poor little Dolores! Had it ever occurred to her that I might regard her merely as a pleasant diversion? No! Not for one moment: and had the thought occurred, she would not have owned it. To love and be unloved would be a disgrace that would crush her with shame.

A tenderness toward her came into my heart. I swore to myself that she should never know. If I died in the morning, at least I would do nothing to sully her belief in me. She would weep, but she could weep with pride. I repented the curses I had thought at her name.

5.

The day passed. I refused the food they brought me.

Night came slowly. Each time Herrera changed my guard, which was every three hours, he looked in on me through the window.

I had no inclination to sleep. About two hours before midnight a lance butt struck the door of my prison.

"Stand back in there," one of the guards said. Then, "When you are through with him, call me, Padre."

"Thank you, my son," said a voice I knew. A moment later Padre Ambrosio was admitted to my cell, and the door closed behind him.

I seized his hand with joy, for his was the first friendly face I had seen since I was locked in here. Then I understood the purpose of his visit and joy faded.

"You have come to confess me," I said. "Then the Governor is determined to hang me tomorrow."

"The power of God is supreme, but next to the power of God is the power of the King, and next to that is the power of the royal Governor," he said with a grim finality.

"No hope for me then?"

"We can pray, but short of intercession from heaven, I can see no hope. His Excellency is bitter against you."

"For what reason?"

"Let us sit on this bench, and I will tell you what took place this evening, so that you will know."

When he seated himself, he said: "To begin with, Dolores was frantic with tears and terror for you, when word of your arrest was carried up to the big *casa*. But Doña Estrella—who has a soft heart under her hard appearance—counseled her in this wise: 'Go to your room, child, and make yourself ready. More battles have been won by smiles than by long faces, and sometimes when men fail, we women must take charge.' The girl took this advice to heart, so that when Anaya arrived at the *casa*, she showed no trace of tears in her eyes, and was arrayed in her prettiest."

"To make an impression on Anaya!" I exclaimed.

"To use the weapons of a woman, my son. She detests Anaya."

"Why should he, who has all the women he wants, desire also Dolores?"

"She is a beauty, and she will be wealthy enough at her majority to be worthy of even the important time of the ruler of a Spanish province. Moreover, she flouted him in the past; and to make him dangerous, you must oppose him. In the news of Don Diego's friendly hospitality to you, which was brought to him by that dog, Herrera, he sees opportunity to break the Commandant, perhaps attaint him—unless Dolores and her dowry are given to him."

"He would abase her—never cease in his cruelties to her!"

Padre Ambrosio gave a sigh. "The Governor is capable of anything, even with a sweet child like Dolores. The *comida* this evening was by necessity a dinner of some state, to which I, as *custodio* of these missions, was asked. What I saw did not please me. A half dozen of Anaya's soldiers ranged along the wall behind him. He sat next to Dolores, at his own demand. The man is a beast. He spent the evening appraising the girl's figure and face, in a manner so offensive and fulsome that she grew embarrassed, and blushed, and could not lift her eyes. He sensed her shame and terror and was amused by it."

"Why did not someone denounce this?" I cried hotly.

"The Governor is the Governor, and his soldiers were behind him. All of us hoped, particularly she, that we could soothe his anger against you by tactful behavior toward him."

"And what next took place?"

"Anaya presently began to speak with her as if none of the rest of us were present, or as if we counted less than the dishes on the table. 'Señorita,' he said, with a smirk, 'look upon me as one who very deeply regards your welfare and happiness.' She did not answer. So he spoke again. 'You have been in danger, in evil company. I must tell you that the Frenchman is an enemy of Spain, the King, and all good Spaniards. He is a spy. Fortunately, we will soon be rid of him.'

"At this she looked up, with fear. 'Are you going to—to do something bad to him?' she asked.

"'He has committed the gravest of crimes,' Anaya said. 'Coming here, he imposed on the hospitality of this house, as a means to further his evil purpose. He would be imprisoned merely for coming here. But for coming here as a spy the penalty is death.'

"She protested then that you are no spy. He merely smiled and began asking her questions that must have been most painful to her. 'You do not know this man, Señorita,' he said. 'He has a devilish way with him, and I fear has so taken you in that you are no judge of him. Has he made love to you?'

"'No—not love—he has been most pleasant and kind——' she said.

"'Paid you great compliments?'

"'Perhaps——'

"'Kissed your hand often?'

"'Some few times.'

"'Sung to you?'

"'Yes.'

"'Embraced you?'

"'Ah, never! You should know that!'

"'I am glad the fellow has not gone so far,' said Anaya, 'but nothing he did would surprise me.'

"We all sat, still and mute as stones, watching him torment the girl we love like a daughter, helpless in our knowledge that he held the fate not only of Don Diego and his family, but Dolores herself, in his hands, subject to his whim.

"But Anaya was not through. 'This man has not spoken to Don Diego, I'll swear,' he said with a sneer.

"'Nay—I know not——' she said.

"'He does not intend to.'

"'How can you say that?' For an instant she looked up at him, speaking almost with heat, then her eyes fell again.

"'Because his purpose was never to marry you, but to ruin you,' said Anaya. 'He is a rake, a *seducero*, a satanic despoiler of innocent girls.'

"'That is not true! What reason have you for saying it? You do not know him! I do not believe it!' she cried."

I pictured in my mind the cruel scene: Anaya, with his lancers standing behind him, badgering the girl, and taking added pleasure in doing it before her helpless family. My heart burned with murderous anger.

"You torture me, Padre, with this description!" I exclaimed. "That poor, loyal child—why should she be subjected to a thing so brutal and so false?"

He gave me an odd look. "It *is* false then?"

"What do you mean?"

"Don Luís, you are a man of the world, who has met and known many brilliant and beautiful women who were worthy of your mettle. Why have you played with this innocent girl?"

"Played with her? I have but yielded her the homage that beauty and goodness deserve. I swear by every saint that no thought of harming her has ever crossed my mind."

"She is not used to this 'homage,' as you call it. You have given her to believe that you love her. And this to her means marriage."

I drew a deep breath. "Padre, I am not worthy of her. Yet if I had my liberty, and other things were less out of joint, so that I could do it freely and honestly, I would ask Don Diego for her tomorrow."

This I said partly because of the vow I had made to myself, that I would not shame the girl who trusted me. But I meant it also, although I had not yet at this time learned to love her, as I learned later, through my sad misfortunes.

Padre Ambrosio, however, took it as an avowal of love. "Now, I am glad to hear this!" he said. "I will confess to you, Don Luís, that I myself was skeptical. But both Dolores and Don Diego believe you to be a true man, and this I now believe also, praise be to God!"

He rose, and took a turn or two across the narrow floor. "I will tell you what else befell at the *comida*. The Governor spoke boldly, saying he would take Dolores away from this place, and make her mistress of his house at Parras—with her guardian's consent. At this he leered at Don Diego. You know the Spanish law, Don Luís. A girl cannot marry, before her majority, without her guardian's consent, and must marry the man he chooses for her, if he commands it. Don Diego saw himself ruined, and Anaya thought it would not be difficult to arrange matters with him, in return, perhaps for a little lenience toward him. Already, it was whispered, the Governor had promised Herrera the command of this presidio, and the possession of the Commandant's house.

"When Anaya said that, Dolores ventured a small protest. 'But—but

I am only a *criolla*——' she said, as if she hoped by this humbling of herself that he would think her not worthy of him.

" 'What difference does that make?' he answered. 'Does not the noble *Corregidor* of the city of Mexico have a *criolla* for a wife? A man may marry below his station, and a woman above it. The wife takes the title and standing of her husband.'

"She looked up at him. 'If I wed with you—will you spare Don Luís?' she asked.

"He grew hard and vicious. 'Then it is true—you do love him!' he exclaimed. 'There is a gallows for him in the presidio, and ropes are easy to come by for this lover of yours!' I thought he would rise from the table in his anger, and wondered what next would befall.

"But at this, Dolores' woman's instinct came to her aid, and she began to gabble at random, with all the shifts of a girl in a tight place at hand, half answering, half evading the question, giving the seeming of a promise without promising, appearing to deny without really denying, half turning the subject, half talking nothings—in short she gave him no answer at all, but gave him the impression that she was not subject to you in heart, and that she was free in mind to consider so glittering a prospect as being the wife of a royal Governor.

"So well did she do it that Anaya was convinced, and thought her won, so that he called her by an endearing name.

"Dolores ate very little, but the Governor made amends, ate for three and drank for a dozen. Presently he grew sportive, laughed loudly, and drunkenly ventured on heavy play, leaning over to pinch her cheek.

"But at this her fortitude gave way and she jumped up. Don Diego rose too, with a white look on his face like a drawn sword. Even Anaya saw that he had carried matters too far in this household, under his power as it was. He sat silent, glowering while Dolores fled to her room."

"Bastard!" I exclaimed, as he finished.

Padre Ambrosio did not even reprimand me for the word. "Don Gaspar de Anaya is a man who loves power," he said. "There is, moreover, a lust of cruelty in him. He is a notorious evil liver, who, so I have been informed, has carried on his warrings against the virtue of women not as other men do, through persuasion and courtship and wooing, but by the use of power, and pressure, and threat, for the mere pleasure of breaking them to his will, the more unwillingly they submit to him through their fear, the better he is pleased. He will use this method against Dolores and the Commandant. Don Diego is ruined if he does not turn over to the Governor his granddaughter——"

"But this is despotism! Is there no law? Has Don Diego no recourse?"

"Only one, and that is so remote and difficult as to be almost an impossibility."

"What is it?"

"A direct appeal to the Viceroy."

"Surely——"

"The Viceroy cannot be approached by a mere commandant of a frontier post, unless some important personage should provide the entree —and Don Diego has no such personage to whom he could turn. It would require an audience—a manifest impossibility—for a letter of complaint would be lost in the mass of correspondence which never reaches the Viceroy's eyes." Padre Ambrosio paused, and gave a heavy sigh. "You can see that our friends are at Anaya's mercy."

"And because they befriended me!"

"Do not blame yourself, Don Luís. They did rightly in giving you friendship. What they face now is injustice, and they must prepare themselves to face it, as many have done before them, and as you now face it. For already Anaya has condemned you, because you are an obstacle to him. That is why, my poor friend, I am here, to make ready your soul to meet God."

"Can the Church do nothing for me?" I asked. "It was for the Church I came."

"I would that I could say so," he replied.

A sudden thought came to me. "Padre, you are a friend of this Padre Hidalgo, the missionary to the Neches?"

"His best friend, Don Luís. We were boys together, postulants together, completed our novitiates together. Together, we founded this very mission. But he cannot aid you. He is in the capital now."

"I must tell you something, for your safety and his. Padre Hidalgo, in his despair, when no support would come to him from New Spain, asked help from France."

"What are you saying?" The priest seemed startled and shocked.

"He asked for the grant of a little food and some other small supplies, pleading the holy importance of his mission——"

"If this were known, it might go hard with him!"

"He perhaps is not even aware that the message ever reached its destination. You must inform him, so that if there is some way in which he can reconcile this act, he can proceed to do it. As for myself, rest assured I will never reveal it."

"Don Luís, my brother priest is very dear to me. This is the more reason why I would most gladly help you—if I only could!"

"Perhaps something may suggest itself," I said.

Then, on my knees, I said the things necessary to clear my soul, and received the absolution.

13. *A Point of Honor*

That night, after the priest left, I twice listened to the entire full chorus of coyotes-dogs-gamecocks-burros, which was a part of the nocturnal habit of San Juan Bautista, for I did not close my eyes in sleep.

Dawn came, with the early roll call of the garrison, and the men going to mess. At midmorning I heard the tramp of a guard, and the door of my prison was unlocked and opened.

Herrera and two soldiers entered, others remaining without.

"Bind his arms," said Herrera.

I made no resistance, and felt the cords fasten my wrists and elbows, so that I could not move my arms from my sides.

"His Excellency is waiting for you," said Herrera.

A full squad of soldiers escorted me. As we marched across the parade ground, I saw the gallows, with the whipping rack at its foot where the soldier had been flogged, and a chill went over me at the gaunt angular shape which threw its shadow on the ground. I had expected to be conducted to the headquarters; instead I was taken out through the gate. Anaya would judge me in the Commandant's house. We walked up the hill.

A good number were in the *sala*, where the audience was held. Besides the soldiers on guard, of whom, with my escort, there were a full dozen, I saw Anaya, sitting in the best chair, and Don Diego standing erect beside him, his grizzled mustaches and eyebrows seeming to bristle as with some suppressed inward fury.

These, however, were not what drew my attention. To one side sat the Commandant's family, together with Padre Ambrosio. Doña Estrella and Doña Felipa were serious and silent. And beside them, with eyes like those of a startled deer, was Dolores.

She gave me the faintest beginnings of a smile, then quelled it, but she did not speak or move her head. I looked away from her.

Anaya broke the silence. "Give your name," he said.

I did so. A secretary at a table took it down.

"You are a subject of France?"

"Yes."

"And are here as a spy and enemy of Spain?"

"No."

"You lie!"

I swayed one step forward, but the guards held me by my pinioned arms.

"By your criminal actions you have not only condemned yourself," Anaya said, "but you have brought into peril these people, whose ill-considered friendship toward you, you have abused."

"I have done nothing of the kind."

"You have wickedly and evilly imposed on the naïve confidence and childish fancy of Señorita Dolores de Ramón, for your own vile purposes."

"I deny it!"

A subtle look came into his face. "You wish to tell this assemblage that the Señorita means nothing to you?" he suggested smoothly. "That you have with her but conducted an idle flirtation, treated her as a plaything for your amusement, have no claim on her or she on you, in short are willing to forget about her entirely, and have no further communication with her, directly or indirectly, from now henceforth?"

I stood silent.

"A confession of this kind may work in your favor," Anaya went on, still in that same purring voice. "It may even save you from the gallows. Speak."

I looked at Dolores, sitting with her head hung and her eyes downcast, and the thought came to me that she was there at Anaya's command, for the very purpose of being humiliated through a public repudiation by me.

Bienville had accused me of being a romantic, and perhaps that was what dictated my next act. Whatever it was, though on looking back I can think of many things I have done of which I am not proud, I to this day feel some pride in what I then did.

"Has the lady, Señorita Dolores, asked that I do this?" I said.

"That has very little bearing on this matter. It is you who choose whether you live or die."

Again I glanced over at Dolores. Her eyes lifted and met mine for an instant, beautiful with pain. I said to myself that I had risked my life many times for causes far less worthy than this.

"Then hear this," I said. "It does not comport with the honor of a gentleman of France to forswear the love of a lady, until she herself has bade him to do so!"

A hush of something like consternation followed this audacious speech. Every eye in the room was upon me, except those of Dolores, who covered her eyes with her hands. In the faces of Don Diego and Padre Ambrosio was something akin to amazement and relief.

But Anaya said menacingly, "Do you understand what this means to you?"

"I understand that a gentleman does not barter the favor of a lady; and that no man with any honor of his own would even suggest it!"

The words were themselves insolence; but that was nothing to my manner and my voice. In my anger all discretion had left me. I scorned the Governor and spoke so that all knew my contempt. Anaya gasped as if I had struck him in the face.

"Take him away!" he half shouted.

The guards seized upon me, but I shook myself loose from them for a moment.

"Hang me!" I cried. "And if you do, you will follow me to the gibbet!"

"Enough of that!" said Herrera roughly.

But Anaya held up his hand. He regarded me with a strangely ferocious expression, yet as if he wished to know what lay behind that threat I had uttered.

"Ask Padre Ambrosio!" I said. "The arm of the Church is around me!"

Anaya turned to the priest. "Can you explain this madman's utterances?"

I saw Padre Ambrosio seem to gather himself, and I knew he had reached the decision to come to my help, whatever the risk.

"I am hourly expecting, Your Excellency," he said, "the arrival of a dignitary of my order from Querétaro, or direct written authorization of equal force, to embark on a work, for which our prayers are being said, of utmost importance to Holy Church and the King, in which this prisoner, Señor St. Denis, plays a great part."

"This man will hang as a spy!" declared Anaya.

Padre Ambrosio gave a short nod. "Your Excellency will do what in your wisdom you think best. It is not for me, a mere *Custodio,* to presume to advise you, for undoubtedly you have considered all aspects of the seriousness of the situation in arriving at your decision."

"What do you mean?"

"Surely Your Excellency knows that my reverend superiors, both here and in Spain itself, will be concerned over what happens to Señor St. Denis, inasmuch as he has presented what may be a peerless opportunity for expansion in a fertile field, populous with people waiting to receive the blessings of the true religion."

There was a stir in the room. Padre Ambrosio pyramided his fingers before him, and his expression seemed to be one of benignant, but entirely impersonal interest in the matter. "Your Excellency," he resumed, "will also be aware that His Grace, the Duque de Linares, Viceroy of New Spain, will himself be much concerned, and through him His Majesty the King, over this matter. For where missions are established and prosper, there go also the presidios and soldiers, and after them the towns and colonists, and so the dominions of Spain are increased and spread ever more widely, for the glory of God and the King."

There was a long silence. I thought to myself that Anaya had not considered that there might be such far-reaching ramifications in this question concerning me, and in peril though I was, I admired Padre Ambrosio's subtle approach to the matter, and the telling way he indicated its dangers to the Governor.

"You have certain word of this?" Anaya asked after a time.

The priest spread his hands in a negative gesture. "No official word —yet."

"But you expect it?"

"Hourly, as I told Your Excellency at the beginning. It was my duty to send to Querétaro and acquaint my superiors with full particulars of this most unexpected—almost I might say heaven-sent—development, on the same day that Captain Ramón forwarded it to you. But because of the *ladrones** which infest our roads, communication is slow and it requires much more time to reach Querétaro than Parras, because of the greater distance. Nevertheless, since Your Excellency did not see fit to take cognizance at once of the matter when it came to your attention—being, no doubt, occupied with other pressing duties—suf-

---

* "Thieves"—a phrase used for the robber bands of the time

ficient time has elapsed so that very soon I should receive my reply from my superiors. An official communication may have come to your headquarters at Parras already."

Anaya stared. His difficulty was that he had been formally notified of this Franciscan interest by a member of the order, and before many witnesses. The Gray Friars held mighty powers politically in the northern provinces, since they chiefly maintained the mission system on which the government so depended.

The Governor loved power, but he had the trait of those who deal in political matters: he could trim his sails with the best, and he was not one to squander himself at the bidding of a whim, or carry out an action for the sake of mere consistency, if the issues were inexpedient.

Now I watched his face and saw indecision struggling there. It seemed to me that he had little taste for embroiling himself with the Franciscan hierarchy, and I thought the battle half won: whatever happened, my life at least was not forfeit.

But I had fatally underestimated the man. Anaya was no mere fat fool. Beneath the soft flesh was a bitter will and a mind subtle and supple. To make him dangerous, as Padre Ambrosio said, one had to oppose him; and the greater the opposition the more perilous he became.

I saw a thought dawning in his face, followed by a pulse of triumph. "I am grateful for your counsel in this, Padre," he said. "Under the circumstances you have explained, I would not think of ordering him hanged, without conferring with the ecclesiastical authorities."

He left that hanging in the air for a moment, while about the room everyone waited, for his manner showed that there was more to follow.

"You say, Señor Padre," he went on, "that the Church is interested in this French dog? I shall deliver him to the Church. The Franciscans will not be more interested in him than the Holy Office!"

A gasp went up, and then a thin scream from Dolores. Doña Felipa was embracing her, seeking to comfort her. Horror was on Don Diego's face, on the face of Padre Ambrosio, even on the faces of some of the soldiers.

"Herrera, you will deliver this prisoner to the familiars in the city of Mexico. The charge: heresy. You will yourself remain to give such evidence as the tribunal desires."

In my ears seemed to be a roaring, and for the first time my knees weakened, so that the grip of the guards on my arms alone kept me from staggering under the weight of this awful condemnation.

"I am no heretic!" I cried hoarsely. "I am a true son of the Church."

"When you face the Inquisitors," he said, "the burden of the proof of that *will be on you.*"

2.

Before dawn next day we rode out of San Juan Bautista, Herrera, and my guard and I. There were four of the guards, all heavily armed, and Herrera had been chosen by Anaya to go as commander of the detail, because out of sheer malice he could be depended on to make the charges against me before the Inquisition so sweeping and severe that I stood little hope of answering them.

Now for the first time I felt despair. Again and over again, I wondered at myself, why I had risked everything to defy that pig Anaya, when I was at the mercy of the pig.

Strange, strange—and yet not so strange. It was not sheer vainglory that made me gamble. At the time I had thought very heavily on it, and I believed that if Padre Ambrosio came to my assistance, as he did, the Governor would not dare hang me.

The hideous manner of Anaya's escape from his dilemma—for it was a dilemma—had occurred to no one, to me least of all. Yet he had escaped, and at the same time fed his malice against me to the full, while avoiding any personal responsibility for my fate. The terror of the Inquisition hung over half the world, and I was in the clutches of that dread body. Not even the Viceroy would dare intervene for me now.

I knew enough of the methods of the Inquisition, how little was needed to set its terrible processes to work, how eager it was, in particular, to get its hands on a foreigner—*gabacho* was the contemptuous word for an alien, particularly a Frenchman—to make an example of him in an auto-da-fé, where the sentences of the Holy Office were proclaimed and carried out with pomp and publicity exactly opposite to the secrecy of its deliberations. The Inquisition was all-powerful, subject only to the royal will of the King, which was almost never exerted. It was not Catholic. It was entirely national and Spanish, a hideous device by which religion was made the vehicle of cruelty and oppression. It was repudiated with horror by every other Catholic nation, and by every Catholic outside of Spanish domains, yet it continued to flourish and because of its nationalistic quality, not even His Holiness, the Pope, had the power to curb or abolish it, however much he desired to do so. The Dominican fathers, elsewhere in the world, were justly beloved for their gentleness, humility, and the good they did; but the Dominicans of Spain, since they were the direct administrators of the Holy Office, were different from their brethren in other nations, being arrogant, pitiless, and dreaded as well as hated by the populace. Almost never was one accused before the Holy Office acquitted, and its penalties were carried out with abominations of cruelty and ferocity that shocked the rest of the world.

This was the horror that confronted me.

When we were some distance from the village, I turned my head for a last glance back. The earliest light was just touching the white *casa* on top of the hill, and I said to it a silent farewell, for it had begun to seem like a home to me.

It had been at first surprising, then painful to me, that nobody, not even Padre Ambrosio, had visited me in prison since I was condemned to face the Inquisition. But quickly it occurred to me that under the new terrible circumstances nobody would be permitted to see me except my guards.

I thought of Dolores up there on the hill, and rage was in my heart when I thought of her fate—condemned also, but to a lifetime of misery as the wife of the foul beast, Gaspar de Anaya. I hoped she might understand something of my motives in doing what I had done, and at least shed a tear for me.

Then I shrugged my shoulders. I must think of other matters. She was lost to me, for I knew her love for her grandfather, and that she would never permit him to suffer on her account, so that she was as good as Anaya's already. It is easy for a woman to forget a man who is no longer a part of her life; and certes I had been removed from her life as cleanly as if I were already buried. I had the charity in my heart to hope the girl would forget me as speedily as possible, and as completely as possible, for she had sufficient woe without a sad recollection. And I resolved by sheer will power to put her out of my mind.

After that I looked ahead and tried to adjust myself to my condition. I thought of escape, but I soon saw that it was utterly impossible. Our order of progression was as follows: Herrera rode ahead, his thick shoulders swinging to his horse's pace, with one of the lancers beside him. Then came another soldier, leading my horse by the reins. After us two more soldiers brought up the rear, each leading a pack mule.

The nag I bestrode was so poor and miserable that its selection for me was self-evident. To escape on it was impossible: the meanest horse ridden by any of the guards could overtake it in twenty bounds. To make matters more safe, my wrists were tied by a leather thong to the flat pommel of the heavy Spanish saddle, and the reins were in the hands of the man who led the animal.

But there was this curiosity: I had been forced to don my best attire, the green and gray velvet, with the hat and sash. Only the baldric and sword were missing, and these were carried in my portmanteau, which was loaded on one of the mules. When one was delivered to the Holy Office, a most rigorous inquiry was made into his personal possessions, and it would go hard with anyone who failed to make a full accounting, for anything of value was taken by the Inquisition treasury. For this reason everything I had was carefully itemized, one paper kept by the Governor's secretary, its duplicate given to Herrera to present to the familiars, and all these articles, including my clothing, and the money I still possessed and was permitted to carry in my own wallet were transported with me.

At noon we stopped beside a hut where there was a well, and Herrera had one of the soldiers unbind my wrists, so that I could drink a gourdful of water.

"You are most solicitous about me," I said to him with sarcasm, as I worked my fingers to get the blood back in them.

"More than solicitous," he replied with his unpleasant grin. "It is my duty—and even more my pleasure—to deliver you safely, and in the best possible condition, to the prison of the Holy Office."

"Yet you tried to murder me only a few days ago!"

"That was a few days ago. What will happen to you pleases me more than any quick death, by my knife or even by the gallows."

Shortly after that, I learned why I rode clothed in a manner that stamped me as a person of a class higher than the commonality of the country. The journey was a sort of triumphal progress. The man who rode with Herrera had a trumpet, which he played very badly. Nevertheless at each village Herrera sent him ahead, sounding his trumpet so that the people might come out and stare at the foreigner, who,

it was invariably announced, was being taken as a prisoner to the Holy
Office.

Sometimes the villagers gaped silently. But sometimes they cried out
at me:

"*Herético!*"

"*Gabacho!*"

Once or twice stones were hurled at me, where I sat helpless on my
horse, lashed by my hands to the saddle. But at this a soldier wheeled
out of line and rode over, using the shaft of his lance as a club to drive
the persons who threw the missiles into the *jacales*. I was to be delivered
"in good condition" and a stone cut in the head would not be looked
upon as such.

3.

That long journey has remained as a dreariness in my mind. First
there was the desert. There were days of this, working from tiny village
to tiny village, or even from water hole to water hole, where the water
was brackish and fouled by cattle and other beasts that drank there.
For most of the time we camped under the open sky, along the dusty
routes the Indians had used long before the Spaniards traversed them.
And when we camped my wrists were freed, but my legs each night
were fastened together by *grillos*—leg irons, locked with a key which
Herrera kept always in his possession.

Then came mountains: first, long hills, one beyond another, cuirassed
with flat slabs, motionless and barren; then growing to ridges more
rugged and ever more rugged; until we came to the true high mountains where peaks, the like of which I never before had seen, lifted
upward.

Those huge towering masses of rock awed me, making not only me,
but all mankind and its concerns seem antlike and insignificant in comparison. They made travel hard, too, for most of the defiles between
the great ranges were too difficult even for Indian paths, because they
had been cut into jagged *barrancas* by mountain torrents. It was necessary here for our party to turn aside and climb the great shoulders
above the canyons.

At first we would follow the narrow trail among jumbled boulders
and rock strata, tilted and twisted in the incredible architecture of nature. Trees—cottonwood, mesquite, and others—somewhat softened the

stark aspect of these rocks in some places. But quickly this chaos of the lower levels was left behind, and the steep mountainside, with the trail climbing ever upward, replaced it. The heights, even the great peaks, were barren for the most part, save for desert scrub growth, but sometimes in the loftier levels they carried a few gaunt conifer trees, not thickly standing but each separate, with its own shadow cast on the rocky soil.

Here the horses perforce went single file; and here, since it was difficult and inconvenient to lead my mount on the narrow crooked trails, Herrera for the first time caused my hands to be loosed, so that I could guide my own animal. We were sufficiently far along the way now, and my horse so slow and spiritless, that even I saw the hopelessness of any attempted dash. I would only have been recaptured, and bound again, and forced to submit to the old discomfort; for it is tiring to ride all day bound to the saddle by the wrists, when one is able to make only a few shifts of his position to ease himself.

Here we began, also, to encounter a trickle of traffic: burros laden with wood now and then; a small pack train driven by a couple of *arrieros*, perhaps; and more frequently the *tamanes*, load-bearing slaves, who went in gangs. The *tamanes* were dark and stooped from carrying burdens, short in stature, and almost naked, dirty sashes about their waists to keep their rags together, a thick padded affair on their backs and a strap across their foreheads, with which they carried unbelievable weights. Sometimes I saw them staggering along with a burden that would tax a horse, and they would keep going with it for miles with hardly a rest. Their stupidity, from this brutalizing work, was that of the lower animals almost, and their owners, the Spaniards, had nothing but contempt for them, and treated them worse than their horses by far.

There were occasions, in these great mountains, when our path climbed so high, and seemed so narrow as it made its way about some great cliff upon a dizzy shoulder, that for a man like myself, unaccustomed to mountain riding, the sight of the depths below, almost directly beneath me and blue with haze, and the thought that a stumble or misstep by my mount might send me whistling downward, falling through all that dreadful abyss, chilled the blood. I have little head for heights, but I kept my eyes on the trail ahead and the men riding before me, and in time learned that my horse, miserable beast though he was, could be relied upon not to fall or miss his footing, since he was as little inclined to make the resulting plunge as was I.

From time to time I noticed beside the path crude wooden crosses. These, I learned, marked places where wayfarers had been murdered by *ladrones*, who infested the wilder parts of the route. Relatives or friends of the dead placed the crosses at the spot, made of wood and by hand, and carved with the name of the victim, the date, and sometimes some pious phrase. Occasionally the crosses had faded garlands of flowers on them, hung there by some mourning woman.

Then, one evening, we came to a place where ten crosses stood clustered together. Herrera called a halt, and had a short conference with his men. Now I discovered that my escort of five men was not merely for the purpose of seeing that I did not escape. So heavy a guard was for insurance that our party would get through the bandit country in some sort of safety.

A little farther on, we came to a path leading downward from the traveled road. Herrera took us down this narrow way.

4.

In a steep arroyo we came by a small spring, where two young Indian women were filling earthenware ollas with water. Herrera rode over to them, saying something loudly to the girls, who looked up at him with frightened faces. They quickly placed the ollas filled with water on their heads, and led the way, with the superb carriage which such burdens on the head give, down the path to their village.

"The road ahead is dangerous," said Herrera. "We will wait here until another party comes, and join with it."

The village was a little larger than most of the settlements in this area; the huts built of stakes driven into the ground with withes interwoven among them and plastered with clay; the roofs of thatching, the floors of bare earth. A mangy goat or two wandered aimlessly about among these crude dwellings; a few lean chickens scratched here and there; a bowed old woman, bearing in her tattered shawl a few sticks for her fire, plodded slowly along; dusky children with eyes black as flies gazed at us in awe.

All the men of this village, save for the very aged, had been taken away to work on a gang which was building a road down the valley a few miles. They were not permitted to return home, but were herded at nights in a camp until the job was done, for this was part of an *encomienda* and these people slaves. So poor were they that they had barely what was necessary to keep life in their bodies, their fare *tortillas* of maize, which they ground in stone *metates,* and the red beans called *frijoles,* which they conserved with miserly care in sacks woven of cactus fibers.

In this village of women Herrera went around roaring his orders, and frightening the poor creatures out of their wits. No maize bread and beans for his party! He forced them with threats to catch and immolate some of their pathetically few chickens, which they served up unhappily to their uninvited guests, fearing the soldiers too much to disobey.

I pitied them: their helplessness and poverty, and the ill use to which they so meekly submitted.

They, on their part, pitied me. *"Pobrecito,"* they murmured among themselves, for the Indians knew the merciless nature of the Spaniards, and sorrowed for the stranger being taken to the capital for execution. But they did not express or show this feeling openly or in hearing of Herrera or his men.

The Lieutenant questioned some of the women, asking if there had been any word of *ladrones* in these parts recently. When they shook their heads, he seemed to gain confidence.

"I think the peril of the *ladrones* is greatly overrated," he said. "Travelers are likely to see a bandit in every ragged peon, an armed gang in each cloud of dust, and they beg for mercy every time a bush catches them by the sleeve. For myself, I have no fear of them."

I could not forbear asking why, if this was the case, we did not go on.

"Today?" he said. "Let me tell you this, St. Denis. For myself, there has always been in me a perfect fury for adventure and excitement. Swords and gunpowder, muskets and lances! Weapons in my hands, and enemies before me are all I desire!" He uttered this loudly, in a boastful manner, evidently to impress some of the Indian women who stood near, listening. "But I have *you* to think of," he went on. "There will be no fighting of *ladrones* this trip, because I want no accident to befall you."

His malice was so great that I did not answer him, and he went away to give further orders.

That night, with my *grillos* locked on my ankles, and one of the soldiers to keep an eye on me, I slept in a hut belonging to an old woman, who lived there with her daughter-in-law and her grandchildren, the men being away on the forced labor of the road building.

This grandmother had the deep-lined visage of the typical Indian, but the younger woman seemed to me charming. She was married, and had been for years, but she had not yet lost her youth, and she had small hands and thin lips, and an oval face, with the fine eyes that seem almost universal among the women in this country.

I sat and watched her making the two or three copper circlets on her wrists flash in the firelight as she patted the dough into flat *tortillas* for supper, tossing the corn dough from one hand to the other with swift and lovely movements in this most beautiful of household tasks. When the dough was flattened into a thin pancake it was placed on a flat heated stone and soon was baked sufficiently to be wrapped about boiled chicken meat mixed with beans and seasoned with red peppers, which was to be our repast.

Three children came in, a girl not more than six years old, a boy about four, and another boy just able to toddle. These were the offspring of the young mother and the grandchildren of the old woman. At once the little girl began to busy herself, fetching water and spreading mats, knowing full well she would be the last to be given anything to eat.

Meantime my guard, a swart, swaggering fellow named Pablo, attempted some sallies toward the younger woman. But if she could understand Spanish at all, she at least feigned ignorance of it, and the man presently desisted, lit a *cigarrillo*, inspected the *grillos* on my ankles to be sure they were well locked, and fell to scratching himself.

Presently the *enchiladas* were ready, served on baked clay platters to Pablo and me, while the family partook only of the cornmeal *tortillas*, with none of the meat and sauce to flavor it. In admirable silence they watched as we consumed what to them was a feast such as they hardly ever tasted. But the tiniest boy, as yet not fully trained in the Indian habit of self-control, looked on hungrily, following each bite to the mouth as if he were famished, tears starting in his eyes and the corners of his mouth turned down. For this his mother was ashamed of him and gave him a small slap; then she surreptitiously offered him her fingers to lick, on which some of the savor of the sauce remained.

I was hungry and could have eaten all my food and even more. But so piteous a spectacle was more than I could withstand. I knew that my hostesses had their pride, and to say anything about the children, or offer them something from my platter would have been humiliation. But I could at least pretend to be satisfied halfway through my meal.

I placed the platter on the floor, taking care it was on the side opposite from the guard, who might very well have decided to finish it himself. And presently the two little boys eagerly lapped up all that remained, licking the platter as clean as if it had been scoured.

But for the little girl there was nothing I could do. She stood humbly behind her mother and grandmother, her eyes great in the firelight. Already she had learned her lesson in life concerning the inferiority of her sex. She neither expected nor got a share from my plate.

Each night, in addition to my *grillos*, I was further secured by being fastened to my guard of that night by a chain from wrist to wrist. On this night for the first time I was glad of it. Pablo was forced to lie beside me, where otherwise he would probably have forced his attentions on the young woman of this *jacal*.

Perhaps, because of my presence, she alone escaped unwelcome attentions that night. I heard sounds elsewhere, running of feet, women uttering plaints or protests, though muted as if hopeless, rough male voices in peremptory demands, which unpleasantly indicated that the other soldiers were on the prowl. The women of this village had no defense and no recourse if Herrera's men wanted to make free with them.

14.   *The Santa Hermandad*

Next morning early, Herrera dispatched two lancers to go down the road and report if a traveling caravan was coming. These presently rode back down to the village to say that a strong party of *arrieros*, with their mule trains, was on the way.

It was lucky. I do not think the village could have subsisted us for a second night, to say nothing of the outrages committed by the lewd soldiery.

Herrera at once ordered the horses saddled and told us to mount. Before I left the hut in which I slept, however, I called to me the little girl and in her small palm pressed a copper *cuartillo*, a coin worth perhaps two French sous or an English penny. The wide-eyed ecstasy of the child seemed some compensation to me for the hospitality of the night.

But the mother found out about the coin, and came running after me, fearing it was lost.

She could speak Spanish after all, at least enough to express this fear, and it brought a scowl to the face of Pablo, my guard of the night, whose words she had seemed unable to comprehend the previous evening.

"My daughter, Isabelita, brought this to me," she said. "I fear it belongs to you, Señor."

I smiled. "It did belong to me. It belongs now to little Isabelita."

But Herrera snatched the coin away. "Put that back in your wallet," he growled. "Nothing is yours to give away, until the Holy Office decides on you." So the child was deprived of her coin.

We were mounted now, and Herrera gave the order, *"Adelante!"* Up the path from the village to the main trail he led the way, and at the top we waited until a few minutes later we heard the shouts of the mule drivers.

The lieutenant nodded. *"Buena dicha,"** he said, evidently relieved at the arrival of this contingent, because the *arrieros* as a class are known to be the hardiest and bravest, as well as the most trustworthy of the varied peoples of New Spain.

Presently we saw the leading *arriero,* riding at the head of his own train of mules. He looked like a ruffian, but a cheerful ruffian. From beneath his wide sombrero, which was covered with oiled silk, looked a face at once bold and merry, with a short thick beard and mustache, and further distinguished by a pair of round gold earrings. His strong figure, which was firmly seated in his saddle on an excellent horse, was clad in a close-fitting jacket of blue cloth decorated with a large number of bell buttons, and pantaloons of the same material, foxed with morocco and the outer seams decorated with lines of additional bell buttons. On his heels he wore Spanish spurs with rowels as big as a man's palm, having little steel ornaments at the sides, which tinkled. As he rode he gave a pleasant jingling sound with all the small bells of his costume. Altogether he was the most picturesque, as well as the showiest horseman I had seen in New Spain.

He drew rein and greeted us, and Herrera told him he wished to join the train.

"With all my heart," said the *arriero.* "There are three of us moving together here. Back of this poor train of mine is that of Andrés la Vaca, and behind him the train of Gustavo Orozco. Me, I am Hipólito José Terraza, whom they call El Risero."

Though he spoke of his "poor train," it was with obvious pride. Not less than thirty mules were in it, and it was driven by four *mozos,* all mounted, and armed with musketoons, as was El Risero—"the Laugher." The other two trains were about as strong. Altogether this combined caravan had fifteen armed men and perhaps seventy laden mules, a contingent numerous enough to defy most bands of *ladrones.* Nevertheless, the addition of the soldiers was welcomed by them, for these mountains sometimes were dangerous because of the robbers.

All three of the *arrieros* came forward and rode in company with Herrera, to talk with him, and from their glances backward, I supposed that part of their questions concerned me. So large a train and so many armed men awed any bandits that might have been watching from

* "Good luck"

their lofty fastnesses, and we experienced no incidents either on the road or in camp for the next two days.

On the third day after the *arrieros* joined us, Herrera came back and ordered my hands tied to the saddle again, and a guard to lead my horse, for the road improved and widened as we dropped downward toward a valley in which was the first town of any size since our journey began from San Juan Bautista.

It was a place called Cuencamé, where the main route from Chihuahua southward was encountered. That night the whole party stopped at a *mesón* which the *arrieros* frequented. My legs were fastened by the *grillos* as usual, and I sat in the courtyard, hemmed in by a stifling stench, watching a pair of gamecocks fighting an impromptu battle in and out between the restless legs of the horses and mules, while the *mozos*, engaged in unloading for the night, yelled and made bets on them. I was worn and discouraged, looking forward with misery to my future.

A voice said, "You are weary, Señor?"

I glanced up. El Risero stood beside me, wide of body but not fat, a good Spanish nose and chin modifying the Indian set of his eyes, and proclaiming the *mestizo*.

"Yes," I said.

The man in the dandified costume which jingled with its bell buttons, compressed, twisted, and coiled in his hands a rawhide *reata*. All at once he flicked open his hands, dropping the coiled rope on the ground.

I beheld what seemed to me a near miracle: the *reata*, twisted and dropped, had formed a design, beautifully intricate and perfectly symmetrical.

"You did that, knowing you did it?" I asked with surprise.

"A *roseta*," said El Risero. "Few can match me in the art."

He picked up the leather rope, twisted, coiled and squeezed it again, again dropped it. Another design appeared on the ground, a pattern of curves and leaflike spaces, exact and perfect.

"This is beautiful!" I exclaimed in admiration. "I have never seen such a thing before."

"Try it."

I rose in my shackles, took the *reata*, twisted and compressed it as nearly as I could in the manner I had seen, and dropped it. The rope was nothing but a flat, slovenly tangle.

"It is indeed an art," I said, smiling, and returning the *reata* to him.

For a few minutes the *arriero* remained beside me, continuing to throw *rosetas*, each different, each perfect.

All at once he spoke. "It is told to me that you are accused of being a heretic."

"So they say," I replied.

"Heresy is a crime that is execrable, meriting the severest punishment of the law."

"I agree. But I am no heretic."

"Ah? I wondered."

"I go to face the Holy Office because a woman on whom the Governor of the province of Coahuila had his eye smiled upon me instead."

"Aha!" El Risero nodded, as if this cleared a point in his mind. "A heretic, as I say, is an abomination. But a *gachupín*, such as this Governor of yours, is the enemy of all, and *gachupines* have been known to concoct false charges against those for whom they have ill will."

I nodded gloomily.

"I have been watching you," went on the *arriero*. "I do not believe you to be a heretic, for I have seen you cross yourself when some prayer or pious statement was uttered, as a good Catholic should. I will say further that I consider this Herrera a contaminated *cabrón*."

The word *cabrón*, though it has the meaning of a "he-goat," is in this country a term of vilest reproach, amounting to an obscenity.

Again I nodded, not speaking, but wholeheartedly agreeing with this judgment of the character of the Lieutenant.

"I have heard enough of Herrera's bragging in these two days to last me for my life," said El Risero. "And I feel sorry for you, because I believe you to be in unfortunate circumstances. But keep a good spirit. Chance may still turn in your direction."

Surprised and grateful, for I had heard few kindnesses on this journey, I thanked him for his sympathy.

"We of the people have no love for *gachupines*, or the dogs that follow them," he said.

With that, taking his *reata* in his hands, the *arriero* swaggered away, jingling with every step. I was left to puzzle in my mind over the reason for this extraordinary conversation. Why had the man gone out of his way to express friendship? Assuredly he had nothing to gain by it. The dislike of the *mestizos* for the ruling Spanish class might be the reason, but I thought it might be something else: the sturdy impulse of an honest man to befriend a victim of injustice and cruelty.

Next morning it took some time to get the mule trains readied for their journey, and I watched while it was done, with interest. It was a noisy process, with clouds of dust, shouting and confusion, and yet I saw in it a sort of rough orderliness after all.

Each mule had his own *aparejo*, a heavy and somewhat clumsy pack-saddle, held on the animal's back by a hair girth and wide crupper, the latter frequently embroidered with the name of the *arriero*, or even of the mule, and sometimes a couplet of poetry or some Spanish proverb. On one, for example, I noticed, *"Quién en un año quiere ser rico, al medio le ahorcan*—He who wants to grow rich in a year will be hanged in six months." An adjuration of honesty on the *mozos*, evidently.

The mules, when released from the corral where they had been fed, each walked directly to his own *aparejo*, which he evidently knew, and stood there patiently waiting to be packed. Once or twice a mule made the mistake of taking his place by another's load. The rightful animal, at this, gave a bray of rage, and delivered a shower of kicks that drove the interloper away, and to his own *aparejo*.

Meantime El Risero and the other two *arrieros*, in their showy costumes, stood giving directions to the *mozos*, saying how and on what mule should be put such and such bales, boxes, or other articles, overseeing the fastening of the cinches, laughing and shouting quips at each other. The loaded mules trotted off to one side, the ones being loaded stamped and sometimes shied. The courtyard was filled with noise and dust and the smell of animals and manure: the sights and sounds of caravansaries the world over.

When everything was ready, El Risero led off, riding at the head of his train, his mules following with his *mozos*, in ragged peasant garb, though armed, behind or on either side of the string of beasts if necessary. The other two pack trains, each with its master *arriero*, fell in order behind, and the caravan was on its way.

The *arrieros* are popular with the common people, for whom they constantly do favors. They are noted for their prodigious memories. Not only do they memorize every road, but also the paths and side trails that interlace the mountains, together with river crossings, springs, *lagunas,* sheltered camping sites, distances between every hamlet and town, and a thousand other details of their routes.

They are on good terms with everyone, and know everyone: it is even whispered they have friends among the *ladrones,* and certainly they seem relatively immune from attacks by the road bandits. For the common people, to whom they are loyal and universally obliging, they are carriers of countless small commissions. A half a hundred little purchases, such as a yard or two of cloth, medicine, *aguardiente,* a knife or machete, a cheap ornament, a package of *dulces* for the children, or any number of such insignificant things, are entrusted to each *arriero* by humble native men and women along his way, with a small coin or two paid in advance for the articles desired. All these the *arriero* keeps in his head, since he usually can neither read nor write, and none of them does he ever forget. In due time—perhaps months later—the cloth, medicine, earrings, or whatever it was, is delivered, and exact accounting made of the money entrusted, so that none of the commissions ever go wrong. Sometimes, too, the *arrieros* carry messages, and never are these messages forgotten, even to the exact wording.

2.

Our caravan, at last under way, started out southward from Cuencamé. Again, as we left the town I was released from the bonds that tied me to the saddle, and allowed to guide my own horse, for we were to do more mountain traveling.

A few miles from Cuencamé, a trail led off toward the right, and here El Risero drew up his horse, and the caravan halted.

He said to Herrera, "At this point our roads part, Señor."

I thought Herrera seemed surprised, and not a little out of countenance at this announcement.

"For why?" he asked.

"We are bound for Durango," said the *arriero,* "and this is the way to the great silver-mining city. You are for the capital, so you take the left fork, which passes through Zacatecas, and so to the city of Mexico."

Herrera looked doubtfully ahead, then back. It was obvious that he did not like this turn, and feared going on alone. Robbery is a national art in New Spain, and with robbery goes murder usually. Where roads are long and through wild, rugged country, and the police authority

more notable by its absence than by its presence; and where the natives have little hope ever of gaining anything from life, beyond starvation and misery, with labor, privation, and eventual death; and
where, moreover, most of them hate the tyrannical upper classes; it is
hardly a matter for surprise that many of them take to crime.

Their particular hatred is the soldiers, and many of the small crosses
I had seen by the wayside bore the carved designation that soldiers
had been ambushed and killed there. This Herrera knew.

But El Risero laughed at him. "The worst of the *ladrón* country is
behind you," he said. "You will be as safe from here on as if you were
in your own presidio."

At this Herrera summoned a more confident manner, and since there
was no alternative, we said farewell to the *arrieros*, and rode on while
they disappeared after a time around the side of a mountain on their
route to Durango.

Toward Zacatecas the mountains grew even higher and more rugged
than they had been in the earlier part of our journey, but we encountered at first no trouble, and Herrera became quite jaunty as we progressed rapidly toward the end of our journey where he could turn me
over to the familiars at the Inquisition prison.

The danger occurred suddenly and without warning, when we were
in progress along a very high mountain trail.

Herrera and one soldier were ahead of me, the other soldiers and the
pack mules behind. I had been having difficulty with my old horse,
which seemed near the end of his endurance, and was occupied with
keeping him moving at the speed of the rest of the cavalcade, when
Herrera suddenly drew up on the narrow path, turned his horse about,
and came back toward us.

"I have seen ahead some lurking men," he said. "They probably are
ladrones!"

I saw with contempt that he exhibited enough panic to justify my
opinion that he was a coward; and the others of the escort speedily
proved themselves no better than their leader. Those behind me turned
their horses about and began to retreat, driving the mules before them.
Ahead of me Herrera and the lancer who had preceded me also brought
their animals around, and now were pressing on me to turn also.

But I was at the moment in an awkward place, a particularly narrow part of the trail which everywhere along here was narrow enough and insecure.

"Let me come forward, so that I can turn about!" I cried to the two men ahead of me.

But the soldier ahead crowded upon me, Herrera right behind him, and with a yell comprised of terror and anger, pricked my old horse cruelly in the shoulder with his lance. Even Herrera, who wanted to deliver me "in good condition" to the Inquisition, forgot his purpose in the fear that now possessed him. If I went over the brink, it made no difference to him, so long as he saved himself.

My horse shrank half back on his haunches. In vain I tried to keep the beast from turning, but in spite of my efforts, and urged by the yells and another goading from the lance point, he began to edge about in a most precarious manner.

The path at this point rounded a cliff, overhanging an abyss that plunged fully five hundred feet straight down into the canyon below, and was so narrow, barely a foothold cut along the side of the precipice by the hoofs of countless mules and horses, that to turn about on it here seemed an impossibility.

Desperately I reined, trying to keep the old horse's head in the direction it had been, but he hunched around, holding up his head as I sawed on the bit, terrified and determined to make the turn however inadequate was the footing.

The moment was one of ghastly peril.

I saw that my gaunt beast, unable to keep his footing, would shortly topple over into the depths below. Instinctively I freed my feet from the stirrups, hoping that by a wild leap I might save myself from going over the precipice with my animal.

All at once the horse reared awkwardly on his hind legs. For one breathless instant I gazed down as the creature's forefeet, upraised, hung over the sickening gulf into which I looked. A dizziness like a vertigo swept over me. But so quick had been the movement that I was unable to act to save myself.

Another instant, and as if by some miracle the horse had swung about so that his front hoofs came down on the path in the direction opposite from that in which we had been heading a moment before.

For a moment the poor beast staggered, seemed to topple, struggled for balance, his very impetus about to carry him over the brink, down which stones and dirt from the edge of the trail bounded, kicked over by the hoofs that fought for a hold. I had no time even to pray. Every thought, every instinct, every breath, hung on the immediate instantaneous present.

One second—two seconds, each seeming like an hour—the old horse still clawed for footing.

Then he found it, was erect and stood trembling in every limb with terror, while I bowed my head over my saddle pommel in sheer relief.

But the soldier behind us was insistent. Again the lance point pricked, and my horse lunged forward. At a wider place in the trail I pulled to one side, and Herrera and the lancer went hurrying on past me, disappearing around the buttress of the cliff.

After a moment I urged my panting and still trembling mount after the soldiers who had left me.

As I did so, I heard a wild whoop. Then yells, musket shots, and groans.

An ambush! My companions were being murdered.

I pulled up my horse. Whichever way I went on this trail, I would die with the others, and I had no particular wish to die. Then it suddenly occurred to me that for the first time since I had been made prisoner, I was free to act for myself.

Immediately I dismounted and gazed downard over the brink of the precipice on which I stood. It was very steep down that way, but I could see some rough projections, and a few bushes and small trees. Perhaps a man might clamber down it. . . .

Over the edge I went, leaving the horse on the trail. Clinging to the rocky ledge, I felt with my toes for a foothold. A moment later I found one, and then another below. Now I was beneath the rim of the cliff, and there was some slope here so that I did not hang absolutely vertically. I began to work my way downward. Though the climb was long and hazardous, an active man, using crevices and occasional small bush growths for hand- and footholds, could make the descent.

The shouts and sounds above ceased. Whatever had happened was over. Perhaps the bandits had killed the soldiers: perhaps, on the other hand, the soldiers, who were well armed, had driven off the bandits.

It made little difference to me: whoever prevailed, they were my enemies.

All at once an enormous exultation came over me. I was free! For the moment at least I was safe. While I still clung to the precipice, feeling my way down at imminent danger of a slip that might land me in a broken heap at the bottom, my mind began to fill itself with speculations as to how I might put this unexpected occurrence on the road to my advantage. If I could only in some manner get a horse! Mounted, I might begin working my way northward, avoiding towns or cities, and with reasonable good luck—or perhaps I should say *unreasonable* good luck—I stood a bare chance of making my escape out of New Spain.

Then I became occupied with the problem of the descent, for I reached a steeper place on the cliff, with greater hazards, since the footing and handholds hardly existed here. Yet somehow I found a crevice for my toes, and edging downward along this, clinging like a lizard to the rock, I managed to make the final scramble, tearing my coat and bruising myself, but at last reaching the bottom, where trees and brush grew thickly and a small stream burbled pleasantly.

3.

There I stood, breathing heavily, and gazing upward: wondering how I had managed to come down that cliff, and what had happened to Herrera and his men, and which way I should go now.

A voice shouted, "*Alto!*"

At the command I turned and saw three men, grim and savage in appearance, with fierce mustachios and beards, all armed with musketoons.

Resistance was impossible. I raised my arms and tried to prepare myself for inevitable death.

"Bind him," said the leader. He spoke in Spanish and the two with him obviously were Spaniards and not natives.

This surprised me, for the *ladrones* usually were gangs of Indians, perhaps led by outlaw *mestizos*. But death, at least, did not appear to be immediate.

"He has a wallet," said one of the men.

"Take it," the leader commanded. He looked into it and seemed surprised. "There are gold pieces in here," he said.

My arms were lashed behind me with a thong, and then I was pushed and driven down the arroyo, scratching my face on the underbrush and hanging branches, toward a place where the canyon widened somewhat.

"Why don't you kill me at once?" I gasped.

"You will be tried first," said one of the men.

"So *ladrones* hold court on their prisoners?"

"You are not held by *ladrones*. You are in the hands of the Santa Hermandad."

The Santa Hermandad! Some word of that dread secret fraternity had reached me, in the form of gossip and conversations at San Juan Bautista, but I never had expected to confront it.

The origin of it was in Spain, where it began as a protection not only against outlaws, but as a check on the lawlessness of the feudal robber-baron aristocracy. Such were the benefits of its vigilance that the Kings of Spain gave it many privileges as well as the distinguishing title Santa Hermandad—Holy Brotherhood. Within the past fifty years it had been transplanted to the New World, dedicated to war against bandits, rebellious natives, and escaped slaves, and already had made a bloody record.

There was a question whether the Santa Hermandad was not more feared than appreciated by the people, because its powers were absolute, its sentences final. No report to higher authority on its decisions was required, and it could carry out its own executions. Those who fell into its hands never escaped if the slightest suspicion adhered to them. A hurried trial, an inexorable judgment, a quick shriving of the prisoner by a priest who invariably accompanied each expedition, and the condemned man was shot, garroted, or left dangling from a tree. Such severity was deemed needful to combat the lawlessness that jeopardized the safety of all New Spain; but it sometimes worked so quickly and ferociously that innocent men suffered death because of it.

I began to wonder if I were in any better case, captured by the Santa Hermandad, than if I had awaited my fate at the hands of the bandits.

My captors stopped me beside the stream, where trees overhung the water. I was allowed to stretch myself on the ground and drink, but the Hermandados stood erect, seeming to listen intently. All at once, from high above, came a distant cry.

"Ha!" exclaimed the leader of the men with me. "The signal! We have them!"

Almost at once there was a booming clatter of guns, the echoes rolling back and forth across the canyon. Wild cries, more gunshots, and then all was silent.

In the bottom of the canyon the three grim-faced Hermandados waited. They did not speak to me, although they talked among themselves in low voices. I sat with my back against a tree, too busy wondering what would be my fate to ask them a question.

An hour passed. After a time one of my three guards went down the canyon and disappeared among the trees.

More time passed. Then I heard voices and the sound of horses' hoofs, and the man who had left us reappeared, followed by a cavalcade of riders. This, evidently, was the main body of the Santa Hermandad.

At their head rode an elderly man with a short thick beard and dust upon his bushy eyebrows, from under which he gazed sternly about him. This personage dismounted, turned his horse over to one of his followers, and seated himself on the projecting root of a tree.

By now the tail of the procession appeared in the clearing. The last three riders were half leading, half dragging, each a wretched prisoner, whose wrists had been tied to the saddle leathers, and who came leaping and straining beside the trotting horses in their efforts not to be dragged off their feet.

"This is all?" the bearded man sitting on the root asked, when the three captives were brought before him.

"Yes," said one of his men. "We think there were about fifteen all told in the gang. Four were killed, we have these three, but the others, having too great a head start, escaped with the mules and the loot."

"What of the party they attacked?"

"All are dead, five of them. By their uniforms, they were of the élite guard."

"Was there upon them anything to identify them?"

"The *ladrones* had cleaned out their pockets and taken away their wallets."

"So there is no identification telling who they were and their errand?"

One of my captors pushed me forward. "Here, *mi jefe*, is a man we captured when he climbed down the precipice from above."

The grim bearded visage turned upon me with a lowering scowl. "You were of the party?"

"Yes, Señor," I answered.

"I will talk to him later," said the chief, and my guards drew me back.

"Padre, prepare to make a record, and then make ready to perform your duties," he next said.

I looked at the prisoners. All three were short in stature, dirty and ragged, Indians and almost as black as Negroes. They were brutalized and cruel, yet perhaps they had been driven to their outlawry by the life under which they lived.

Weapons were brought forward and dumped in a pile—an ancient arquebus, a musket with a broken stock which was lashed together with rawhide bands, a rather new musketoon, though rusty from ill care, knives, a spear, even a bow and quiver of arrows.

"These are all the arms?" asked the bearded man seated on the tree root, who obviously was not only the chief of the Hermandados but the judge of the captives as well.

"Yes, *mi jefe*," he was answered. "The other *ladrones* made away with their arms, and those of the soldiers."

The chief seemed angry. "We show less than sufficient zeal," he said sternly. "I am disappointed in this entire affair."

"The leader of the soldiers evidently caught a glimpse of one of our advance guards," he was told eagerly. "He thought we were of the *ladrones*, and retreated, falling directly into the trap of the bandits, who had been following him. It was for this reason that we could not catch them all at a place from which they could not escape."

So it was Hermandados that Herrera had seen ahead, and which caused his retreat!

The chief began to question the three prisoners, harshly and mercilessly. His queries were as to where they secured their guns, and who was their leader. The captives either remained silent as if they did not understand, or made frightened rejoinders in poor Spanish. Out of this came the information that their leader was one of those killed in the battle above, and the weapons they and their gang used were the result of a long collection, taken, like the weapons of Herrera's soldiers, from travelers murdered and robbed along the way.

"Verdugo!" the judge called.

A squat, harsh man, very wide through the shoulders, stepped forward.

"Over in that grove yonder," said the chief.

"*Si, mi Comandante.*"

The meaning of the word *verdugo* is hangman, and I wondered if this was the man's name or his title. The priest who had been taking down the questions asked the prisoners, and their answers, put his papers and pen and inkhorn into a scrip that hung from his belt, and accompanied the executioner's party, as the three condemned men, their arms pinioned behind them, were hustled off in the direction indicated.

Save for a half-dozen men detailed to go with the hangman and priest to assist in the execution, all the Hermandados remained in the clearing. Such hangings were too common to stir curiosity in them.

But I was curious, and I watched. The method was quick and merciful as possible, although it looked brutal. As soon as the priest finished his extremely brief rites, each condemned man was drawn up off the ground by a noose about his neck, the rope being carried over a branch of a tree. One of the Hermandados seized him by the legs and hung upon him, thus adding his weight to make the choking quick and complete. Death seemed to come almost at once.

Already, however, the leader on the tree root was occupying himself with other matters.

"Bring up the other prisoner," he said.

My captors pushed me forward and told how they had taken me.

"Your name?" asked the judge.

For a moment I hesitated, with the thought of giving them some Spanish name and relying on my skill with the language to carry me through on some plausible tale.

Then another thought came. "Louis de St. Denis," I said.

"Not a Spaniard?"

"No. I am a Frenchman."

"What is your affair here?"

"I am not a bandit——"

"That is obvious," the judge said impatiently. "But neither are you a soldier and those slain above were soldiers. Were you traveling with them?"

My thought took form. "Yes, I was traveling with them. They were my escort."

"Five élite lancers to escort you? For what reason are you of such importance?" The merciless glare of my questioner told me that this story was received with skepticism.

"I am an ambassador," I said. "I was being conducted to the capital to wait upon the Viceroy. When the *ladrones* attacked my escort, I escaped the slaughter by climbing down the cliff where I encountered these men in the bottom of the *barranca* and surrendered to them."

The bearded man looked me up and down, taking in every detail of my costume, the velvet coat and breeches of which were torn and soiled by my climb.

"An ambassador?" he said at last. "An ambassador from France?"

"No, from the Neches Indians, a powerful nation which seeks a mission from the Franciscan fathers."

"And yet you are a Frenchman!"

"I was born in a French province, but I have served in the army of Spain."

"Where?"

"In Madrid, as a member of the personal guard of His Majesty the King."

A new searching look. "Why did you not state this before?"

"I was given no opportunity to go farther," I said as calmly as I could. "Though I am French by birth, my deeds have benefited Spain, and the Franciscan order is greatly interested in me."

By now the man called Verdugo had returned from the hanging, looking very much as if he desired to add another to his list. With him were the priest and the others of his crew.

"I am Don Miguel Velázquez de Lorea, of the city of Querétaro," said the judge to me.

I had heard the name: this was the dread head of all the Santa Hermandad in New Spain. His reputation for mercilessness was well known.

"If you are of Querétaro," I said boldly, "you are conversant with the College of the Franciscans there."

"I am." Lorea snapped off the words as if he bit them in two with his sharp white teeth. Perhaps he had no great love for the Franciscans.

Nevertheless, I made another venture. "If you will take me there, this difficulty may be resolved," I said.

Then, rather breathlessly, I awaited his decision, for I felt that the fact that I was a foreigner would be almost as great a crime in the eyes of this man as if I were a thief.

"The soldiers killed by the *ladrones* were of the élite guard," I heard the priest at his elbow suggest.

It seemed to weigh in my favor, as if it partially confirmed my story, yet there was a period of several tense minutes while Lorea appeared to debate within himself whether to hang me or not. At last, however, he rose from his seat.

"Unloose this man's bonds," he said, "and fetch him a horse."

He gave a command, the whole troop mounted, and we rode down the *barranca*, leaving the dead *ladrones* swaying and turning around at the ends of their ropes in the grove of trees.

My chief captor rode beside me, and presently he began to chat with me in a friendly manner, so that I took heart from it, as evidence that I no longer was considered a common prisoner.

His name, he said, was Don José Calabanca. All members of the Santa Hermandad were of pure Spanish blood. He informed me that Lorea, since he had been head of the order, had captured and hanged or otherwise executed more than four hundred persons, besides punishing others by flogging or imprisonment, while releasing fewer than one hundred as innocent.

"There was something strange about the way in which this band of *ladrones* attacked your party," said Calabanca. "They evidently were following you, and may have been doing so for a long time, before your retreat threw you into their hands. Professional bandits usually do otherwise. What happens is this: as you ascend toward a pass, one man will step out from behind a rock and ask you politely to allow yourself to be looted. If you comply, you can go on, empty of pocket but unmolested. If you resist, the robber flees instantly, down the mountainside or into some convenient retreat. You proceed on in apparent safety, until you reach the pass itself. This usually is a narrow passage between rocks, and there a sudden ambuscade of muskets firing from either side, and arrows flying, awaits you to make an end to your obstinacy."

"Where am I being taken now?" I asked. "To Querétaro?"

"No. Don Miguel de Lorea is a devotee of the Jesuit order, and has nothing to do with the Franciscans, who are rivals of the Society of Jesus. He has, therefore, decided to send you directly to the capital, and to the Viceroy's palace."

BOOK THREE

The Hell of Holiness

15. *The Palace and the Plaza*

To my delight, Calabanca, my new friend, was assigned to lead the small escort of four Hermandados which conducted me to the city of Mexico. This was considered a sufficient number, because so great was the awe of the *ladrones* for the brotherhood that if they knew any of its members were in the vicinity they took great pains to stay in hiding or even depart for localities more distant. Within a few days, and without further incident, stopping at the best *fondas* or even at convents by night, we reached the capital, the city of Mexico.

With the most eager interest I viewed this center of Spanish power in the New World. It was a great city, assuredly far larger than Quebec, and already ancient before the Spaniards came, since it was the capital of the great Aztec nation before Cortés looked upon its walls and towering pyramids. I was, however, struck by the singular character of its arrangement: a bizarre combination of magnificence and squalor, stately buildings side by side in many cases with the most wretched huts.

The streets seemed a fantasy of shifting color: brilliant *rebozos* over white skirts, gaudy kerchiefs, tiger-striped *serapes*, white cotton garments, all passing back and forth against the soft pinks and greens and blues with which the adobe walls of the houses were colored. With this came the smells of the city: offal and sewage, pulque and sweat, manure and cookery. I saw that dwellings, which were small and mean, were mingled indiscriminately with the *cantinas, mesones* and even brothels; and that there were churches and convents numerous enough, it seemed to me, for a population far greater even than this. Churches, in fact, seemed to be the only structures of size and importance, until we came into the very center of the city.

As we approached this, I saw over the tops of buildings a great cathedral dominating with its two lofty gilded towers everything about it.

"That is the Cathedral of Mexico," said Calabanca with pride. "It is the greatest church in the Americas, and in all the world second only to San Pedro in Rome. A century was required to build it, and it was completed only about forty years ago."

Now we came out suddenly from the narrow streets upon a great plaza of outstanding interest because of the strange contrasts it presented.

"It is called the Zócalo," my companion said, "and it is the center of the city. Yonder, on the other side, you see the viceregal palace."

Across the space I beheld a building evidently of great extent. Although it was overshadowed by the adjoining cathedral, being no more than three stories in height, without towers or pinnacles save for small turrets of a castellate order at the corners, and a low belfry in the center of the west façade, its front filled the entire eastern side of the plaza.

"There are within it four courtyards," said Calabanca, "each communicating with the others and surrounded by the building's wings. Facing us, at the front, are the windows of the *Audiencia* and other tribunals, with all their offices. The apartments of the Viceroy's household are adjoining the official wing and facing in on the same court, while behind are the mint and the quarters of the palace guard. The rest of the building is devoted to apartments of officials of the government in residence, together with attendants of the court in an official capacity, chapels and priest houses, and archives and storage rooms."

I observed that the two principal entrances of the palace were immense doors, fully a story in height, and that all windows were protected by bars of iron. It was a fortification as well as a palace.

But Calabanca continued, "The large building of stone on the south side of the plaza, opposite the cathedral, is the municipal building, which contains the offices of the administration of this city, the police guards, the records, and the apartments of the *Corregidor*, who is the chief magistrate. Beyond it is the municipal warehouse."

All the structures pointed out were imposing, but alas for this magnificence! The great square, aside from these, was surrounded by mean, almost miserable structures of adobe, while the plaza itself presented a most extraordinary appearance.

We were riding along the western side of the square, and I saw there was an open space in which stood a large gallows, a whipping post with the irons ready to take the wrists of the victim to be flogged, and a curious platform like a stage, built of stonemasonry and surmounted by an iron post.

"The *quemadero,* where heretics are burned, and common criminals executed," explained Calabanca calmly. "It is a sight when an auto-da-fé is held here! The whole population comes to see, for it is considered a lack of zeal for the faith if any man remains at home because he shrinks from the sight of the punishment inflicted on those who have defiled the true religion."

I took another look at the grisly iron post. From its top a chain was suspended, at the end of which was an iron collar, the so-called *jugum,* to be locked about the neck of the wretch who was to be burned to death. In spite of myself I felt a shudder go through me. Spain assuredly took a back seat to no other nation in its instruments of punishment.

But though I gazed upon the *quemadero* with horror which I tried to conceal, nobody else seemed to pay any attention to it; and the whole plaza beyond it, to the street before the palace and cathedral themselves, was occupied by a spectacle of filth and squalor. Through the years it gradually had been occupied by a collection of ramshackle structures, so that now it was completely filled. Some of these were of flimsy wood; others, even more despicable, of *tulés* thatched with palm leaves or straw. All housed booths where merchandise of one kind or another, ranging from jewelry to food, was sold.

"What a pigpen!" I exclaimed. "Why do the authorities permit it?"

"You mean the *cajones?* They are pretty crowded, I must admit," said Calabanca. "Hardly room to move between them. Once or twice an effort has been made to expel peddlers from this plaza, to beautify it. But each time the outcry was so great that the idea was abandoned. Yet I believe it must be done one of these days. Not only is the place a firetrap—one spark might set the whole thing into a roaring volcano of flame—but its people are not of the most wholesome sort. The peddlers are ordinary lower-class people, but among the booths are always to be found also the *léperos.*"

The phrase was new to me. "This signifies leprosy?" I asked.

"Oh no. Victims of leprosy are called *lazarinos.* You will be seeing them near the cathedral. The word *léperos* signifies good-for-nothings, and is applied to the idle and dissolute, chiefly *mestizos,* who engage in drunkenness and mischief, shunning any useful occupation: a treach-

erous, light-fingered gentry, ready to steal anything and devoting themselves to carousing, gambling, cockfighting, and occasional brawling."

We turned along the street paralleling the north side of the plaza,
and approached the immense cathedral. It was of grayish stone, very
richly ornamented with carvings and statues, but of a solid, ungraceful
architecture, which I, who prefer the Gothic, found uninspiring.

Before the cathedral's doors were swarms of beggars who infested
the pavement. I had seen beggars before, but never such a profusion
of squalid misery as here. In every form, the crippled, blind and dis-
eased were present, from sickly and distorted childhood to decrepit and
palsied age. One, a veritable living skeleton, deformed in a disgusting
manner, with a face of bluish, ashy paleness, the sex of which could
not be identified, was carried in the arms of a strong Indian man, who
laid it outstretched, perhaps taking a share of the pittances it received
as it held out its shriveled and skinny arms to every passer.

Armless and legless creatures, their rags arranged so that their condition was shockingly visible to every beholder, besought alms in strident
and piteous tones. Mothers held up deformed, rickety, or sightless children imploring a copper coin for their miserable offspring. Wretches,
with legs and arms contracted and twisted, peered with bloodshot eyes
and haggard faces at us as we passed, and when one of them received
a gift, his countenance was lit by a gleam of satisfaction almost dia-
bolical. The clamor of their cries rose in a discordant babel.

Most disgusting of all, however, were the *lazarinos*. Leprosy is a disease unknown in Canada, although I had seen cases of it in Europe.
Here, however, it numbered its victims in hundreds, and many of them
were before the cathedral. No disguise, no concealment of their repul-
sive distortions was attempted: on the contrary, the full exposure of
their loathsome and hideous deformations was the aim of each of them,
so that their appearance caused the nerves to quiver.

Calabanca glanced at them indifferently as we rode past.

"Leprosy is present always among the poor," he said.

"Look at that dreadful fellow!" I exclaimed. "He has no nose and his
fingers are gone."

"One cannot be squeamish in a large city," Calabanca replied. "That
lazarino is in the later stage of the disease."

"Is not this disease to the last degree contagious?" I asked. "Why
are these allowed to mingle freely with the people of the city?"

He shrugged. "It has been the custom since time began. I believe the ill is contagious only by contact with those in its most advanced stages. What would you do, let them starve? They cannot do any work."

I was glad when we were past the cathedral. But now we approached the viceregal palace of gray and red stone, its innumerable windows looking out on the plaza, and the red and yellow flag of Spain flying above its small belfry tower.

To my surprise we did not turn down the front, but continued toward the rear of the massive structure.

"Where are we going?" I asked.

"To the palace guard," replied Calabanca.

"But my business is with the Viceroy!"

"I regret, Señor, but I was instructed to place you in the custody of the guard."

"What, am I to be a prisoner?"

"You are a foreigner, and without a passport. Until you receive one, you must be held in custody. I assure you it is nominal only, and I think not for long. I myself will go at once to the office of the secretariat, and report on your case, your business, and the circumstances under which we encountered you. Have patience."

I was silent. It was my first intimation of this turn in my fate, but there was nothing I could do about it.

When we came to the rear of the large edifice, I saw the entrance which led to the guard quarters, with soldiers standing before it, or wandering idly about.

A startling cry came suddenly from above: *"Centinela alerta!"*

I glanced up quickly. In a sort of sentry box built out from the walls directly over my head was a soldier who had uttered the shout.

Instantly the cry was taken up by another, situated farther along the building, and so it was repeated by one after another, until I could faintly hear the long-drawn shout echoed from the farthest walls of the palace, returning after having made the complete round of the huge building to the place where it started.

"A device to keep the sentries on the alert," said Calabanca.

We dismounted, and following my guide, I entered the portal, stepping over the recumbent forms of a soldier or two who lay drowsing on the pavement, rolled up in coats or blankets. Within I found myself in a large court, surrounded on all sides by the buildings which were soldiers' barracks. Over one strong and gloomy door I read the word *Castigo*.* It was the prison, where I presumed I would be lodged.

But instead I was conducted down a passage somewhat like a cloister, opening in alcoves on the courtyard, until finally we entered a room where my name was taken in a book by an officer with a morose scowl, the date placed after it, the name of Calabanca and the Santa Hermandad, and notations made when several other questions were asked.

"You are a foreigner without a license," the officer growled at me.

"Don José Calabanca has told you that I am no common wanderer," I replied. "I am a soldier, an envoy, a man of influence. I have served as an officer in the royal palace guard of the King of Spain. And I have come here for a personal interview with His Grace, the Duque de Linares, Viceroy of New Spain."

The officer's face changed slightly. He glanced at Calabanca.

"If what you say is true, Señor," he said, returning his gaze to me and with a voice less harsh, "your stay will not be long, I am sure. I must hold you however until I receive further orders. You understand how this is so?"

"I understand a soldier's duty, Captain."

"We will seek to make your stay as comfortable as possible." He turned to a soldier on duty in the room. "Take this man to the priest's quarters. He will be under guard, but show him no discourtesies."

Calabanca bade farewell, in a friendly manner. "I must return to Querétaro as soon as I make my report. *Adiós*," he said. So we parted.

The residence of the priest, who was chaplain of the soldiers, was temporarily vacant since that personage was absent on a visit to a neighboring city. There were two rooms: a bedroom and a small chapel. That night, following the luxury of a warm bath, I slept in the priest's comfortable bed, after a supper which was the same eaten by the Captain and his family, I was told. Thus far matters had progressed not too badly. At least no charge of heresy hung over me, and I was not consigned to the prison of the Inquisition. I hoped that the charge and the danger both had died with Herrera in the mountain pass high above Zacatecas.

---

* "Punishment."

2.

But the incredible took place next morning.

In the middle of the forenoon I heard voices somewhat raised, and the door of the priest's quarters was thrown open.

I saw the Captain and a soldier, and with them a man of about my own age, with a handsome, swarthy face, in which the clear whites of his dark eyes seemed the whiter by contrast, and which was given a look almost Mephistophelean by a mustache and short forked beard, both jet black.

I could hardly believe my senses. I *knew* him, though not in a dozen years had I seen him, and in that time continents separated us: Don Beltrán de Córdoba, the friend of my youth, with whom I had sported and laughed in the Madrid days, long, long ago!

For a moment he stood, hand on sword hilt, his gaze very straight and direct. And then he smiled, showing wonderful white teeth.

"It *is* you—Luís!" he exclaimed.

"Beltrán!" I cried.

A moment later we were in each other's arms.

"Ah, what luck, what fortune!" he said, when we had sufficiently expressed our unabated affection. "I am here as *ayudante* to the Viceroy, coming over last year on appointment. It was by chance only that I was in the office of the secretariat, and overheard a man reporting on someone he had escorted for the Santa Hermandad to the capital. I paid, indeed, little attention to his answers to routine questions, until the name St. Denis caught my ear."

"'St. Denis?' I asked him. 'You are sure of this—he is a Frenchman?'"

"'Yes, Señor,' the man said."

"'It can't be!' quoth I. 'No—impossible! Not the Luís de St. Denis I knew!'"

"'He is called Don Luís,' said the Hermandado."

"I pondered . . . the name is not so common, and when I learned that you were here on some mysterious embassy, it occurred to me that it was exactly the sort of thing you might be involved in. So I came to see!"

There are moments in life of pure joy, and this was one of them. We both laughed in sheer delight.

"It is worth everything, just to see you, and hear you speak in the superb manner of a grandee of Spain!" I exclaimed.

Superb it was, indeed, and now Beltrán turned on the Captain. "Release this gentleman at once, Rodríguez!" he commanded. "To treat one of such consequence in this manner is an outrage!"

"Yes, Your Worship," said the Captain, and added hopefully, "I am sure the gentleman will tell you he was given all consideration here."

"True." I nodded. "I have no complaint on this score."

"But to be locked up like a felon!" cried Beltrán. "Captain Rodríguez, I am surety for this man. He goes with me."

To be free was like breathing life again. Rejoicing, I left the garrison quarters with my friend, and together we walked along the street, asking questions and retracing our divergent careers since last we saw each other. While I was in the Canadian campaigns, it developed, Beltrán had fought in the Peninsular defense against the invading English, in the Spanish army commanded—ironically—by the bastard son of an English King, the Duke of Berwick.

"A bitter man, but a great soldier," said Beltrán. "Berwick, natural son of James II by his mistress, Lady Arabella Churchill, sister of the Duke of Marlborough, was of course Marlborough's nephew and shared something of that military genius's ability. He was bitter against the English, both because of his father's dethronement, and the shame of his own illegitimacy, and fought them like a mad bull. We beat them well at Almanza and drove them out of Spain—all but Gibraltar, which they still hold."

"You distinguished yourself, I'll wager!"

"At least I was decorated, and given this appointment, which does me well since my father, the old Conde, indulges me with a liberal income from two of his estates."

"Of all men in the world, to have you here, at this place, at this time!"

We had walked almost the length of the rear side of the viceregal palace, when we reached a door before which stood a guard. The man presented his musket at the sight of Don Beltrán.

"As a member of the court I dwell here," he said, leading the way up a stair to the second floor and opening a door. "Bachelor's quarters." He smiled, and with some complacency, for the rooms of the apartment were richly furnished.

"You have never married?" I asked.

"Never. It will be time enough when I come into my inheritance. And you?"

"No wife."

"But are no celibate, I'll swear."

I laughed. "I once asserted I was."

"How was this?"

So I told him the story of La Demoiselle, and how I escaped entanglement with her matrimonial plans. As I finished, I said, "And oddly enough, I have actually been a celibate, since that moment, though not by wish: rather by lack of opportunity."

"You have not seen a tempting woman in these months?"

"One. A lovely little thing with tiny feet, the divinely graceful form of a nymph, and eyes of beauty unsurpassed by any of her sex it has been my fortune to behold. She loved me."

"Ah? But not enough to give herself—for love alone?"

"I do not know," I said, my mind going back and dwelling upon Dolores. "She may have loved me enough for that. In fact I think she did. She would have given me what I wished, if I had asked it. The odd thing is I could not bring myself to ask it."

"You, Luís! A loveless life is to a woman worse than death, and you were never behindhand in rescuing the fair from such fate."

"To you I know it seems strange: to me it does also, when I think back upon it. She was very young; she trusted me. And there is a French saying:

> *Marrying her whose virtue you've destroyed*
> *Is paying for a luxury enjoyed.*"

"Hum. You contemplated marriage with this one?"

"Hardly contemplation, so much as a thought in the back of the head. I think I loved her too—in my own way. But no matter. If this had ripened further, there is no telling which way it would have gone. But the fruit remained unpicked—at least for me. Because of her, I am here."

"Tell me, Luís, the whole of it."

For a moment I hesitated. Should I put my life in this man's hands? Beltrán was my friend, always had been my friend! I could trust him as I trusted myself.

But then the fear which never left me that the Inquisition might in some manner still reach its devil's claws out for me stayed me. It was not lack of trust, but rather because knowledge of this secret would be a danger to him. Should he harbor one sought by the Holy Office, knowing that he did so, he would be caught in the same mesh that caught me.

So I did not tell him the whole truth. Instead I sketched the tale of Don Gaspar de Anaya's jealousy, his desire for Dolores, and his act of spite toward me, sending me a prisoner to the city of Mexico, to face trial for entering the Spanish realms without a *permiso*.

At the end he said, "You say the escorting soldiers were killed?"

"Every one."

"Then there will be no accusation and no witnesses against you. This is most fortunate! The worst that can be said of you is that you lack the *permiso*, and this you can easily explain by the loss of your baggage in the attack of the *ladrones*. But what about this girl Dolores?"

"Lost from my life. I do not think I will ever see her again. For all I know she is by now the wife of Anaya—that was the immediate prospect when I was sent south under guard. She had an inheritance he was greedy to get his fingers on."

"Anaya—Anaya—I believe there is some sort of a dossier on that man in the records here. Complaints, I think. I will look them up for curiosity. But you are well out of this whole affair. What are your future plans?"

"I have none."

"Will you remain here?"

"That only fate can decide."

"Why not?" asked Beltrán. "What has France done for you? After your years of risks and rigors, you are nothing to France, the victim of the spite of a treacherous woman. Do you owe France anything when France considers that she owes nothing to you? Is it just that after your services and sacrifices you should be a pawn for a woman's caprice? Lord of earth! Is it not a man's right to work for his advantage when all others turn their backs on him?"

"I am a Frenchman."

"You are the dearest of all the friends of my life. You speak the Spanish tongue better far than most hereabouts. You know Spanish manners, and you understand the Spanish mind."

I stared at him. "In what you say there is some truth."

"You are ready to embrace opportunity if it offers?"

"I think so. Yes, surely."

"It is well said, and I am happy." Beltrán warmly seized me by both shoulders. "I myself will obtain for you a *permiso* to remain here—as *ayudante* it is only necessary for me to present the written paper, which His Grace will sign on my recommendation, usually without even reading it." He paused, stood back, and surveyed me with some particularity. "You are a soldier—what else?"

"Nothing else—save that I have some facility with tongues—and know how to deal with savage tribes——"

"Just the thing! The Viceroy has need of someone—anyone!—who can go into an Indian village without precipitating a new war—as our officials seem perpetually to be doing. New Spain needs pacification, not bloodshed. There are tribes like the Mixmecs in the south and the Yaquis in the west with whom a man like yourself might do more than a dozen regiments of soldiers. And New Mexico itself is still restless, though the great revolt of the natives there was put down fifteen years ago. There are gentile tribes like the Apaches——"

"And a new threat, the Comanches, whom I encountered on my journey here."

"Exactly. We must obtain a private audience with the Viceroy, present your petition in behalf of the Neches Indians for a mission, describe to him your abilities, and obtain from him a commission, as *enviado oficial*, dealing with savages and with them making treaties, which should be worth a most comfortable salary to be paid you by the treasury of New Spain!"

"When can I see His Grace?"

"That depends. The moods and actions of rulers are hard to predict and the Duque de Linares is almost as absolute here as is His Majesty in Spain. We will have to make arrangements—but in the meantime you will live with me. It will be like the old days in Madrid! There is much to amuse you here—you are in the capital of the entire New World. Confess that it is grander than any city on this continent—even in your own Canada?"

"I am forced to admit that it surpasses even Quebec."

Beltrán nodded again, with his gleaming smile, as if well satisfied. "It also possesses a very elegant society, living on a scale almost like that of Madrid. We have not, of course, the royal court, but the Viceroy's court possesses some splendor. We have our musicales, balls, entertainments, receptions, state dinners, and events of less formal but sometimes more enjoyable nature. You will see. I myself will introduce you to the grandee world of Mexico. But wait——" He gave me another look. "You must have proper garb. To say the best of it, your clothes show signs of wear."

I glanced down at myself. The green and gray velvet, once so fine, was torn and stained, with buttons missing here and there. "Signs of wear" was a mild term for it.

"You have no money, I suppose?" he said.

"I did have. A purse containing, as I remember, thirty louis d'or, and a few silver livres——"

"You were robbed?"

"It was taken from me by the Santa Hermandad."

"Is this so? Excellent! If the Santa Hermandad took your money, you may depend on it that the purse has been deposited with the provincial treasurer, and not shy by a single copper, for that organization is noted for its scrupulous handling of all money matters. Perhaps the man who brought you here carried it in his baggage. I will inquire in the morning, and regain it for you. You will at least be able to outfit yourself. Meantime—but no, you have the advantage of me by three inches in height and at least as much in girth of chest. Otherwise I would lend you some garments. As for lodging, you will be my guest, at least until we can find you a commission and you can establish a place for yourself."

"But my dear Beltrán! I cannot live on your bounty!"

"Tut! Would you not do the same for me if the conditions were reversed?"

He could always have his way with me, and he spoke now so winningly that I could only surrender, reflecting that such a friend comes but once in a man's lifetime.

That night we feasted, and had wassail, attended by Beltrán's servant, a grave man of middle age named Manuel, who wore the red livery that I remembered was of the Córdobas, from my old days in Madrid. And so I began my life in the capital of New Spain, with the great happiness of finding the lost companion of my youth.

And yet not then, or at any time later, was I free from a gnawing apprehension that continually beset me. I was no longer a prisoner.

I had a friend who appeared to be close to the Viceroy's ear. No charge stood against me here. But for all this I felt that I was surrounded by peril. I was a foreigner, and therefore a marked man, the subject of suspicion if I made the slightest false move; even, perhaps, should I make no mistakes at all. But how long would it be before some untoward incident might recoil against me?

A sense of urgency oppressed me: I must, somehow, escape from this place, and as soon as possible. If there was no one with a present accusation against me in the capital, there always was the threat of Anaya in his northern province. Presumably he now thought me dead, but it would be only a question of time until word might reach him that I had escaped the massacre by the *ladrones*.

If it did, I could well assure myself that his enmity would be in no wise abated.

This was a reason why Beltrán's plan to obtain for me a commission as envoy dealing with wild Indian tribes so lifted my hopes. For the position itself, and even the salary of which he spoke, I cared nothing, except inasmuch as they were a means to an end.

That end was escape! I considered every possibility. Having just come down the trail from the north, and having experienced its perils, the *ladrones* that infested it, and perhaps even more dangerous to one like myself, fleeing alone, the grim Santa Hermandad that patroled it, I thought to myself it would be desperation indeed that would send me out on such a wild flight as that.

Beltrán's idea was infinitely better. As an official, with an escort, I could travel to far distances in comparative safety, and thence, perhaps, make my bid for freedom.

Meantime I still had my task: the discovery, if possible, of the grand Spanish plan as regarded the north. If I could carry that back with me, all these travails would be well repaid. And because of this, I must for the present curb my anxiety, and run the risks which the passage of time must bring me, in hope that I could at last bring a full and satisfactory report to Bienville.

Because of all this, I felt like a wild creature caged. Yet I must assume the lighthearted manner of a carefree guest, and prepare myself to do everything in my power to avert all suspicions or resentments, while at the same time watching for any chance, ready to embrace any opportunity that might take me out of New Spain, back to my own land.

3.

Next morning Beltrán returned from the offices of the *Audiencia* and placed in my hand my purse. I counted the money. As he had said it would be, the tale was exact.

"We must exchange this French coin into Spanish," Beltrán remarked. "One *doblón,* called also *onzo de oro,* equals four of your louis d'or. Four *pistoles* make up one *doblón,* and one *pistole* is equivalent to two *escudos,* sometimes called ducats. There are eight *reales* to each *escudo.* Therefore you can—roughly, of course—keep your values as follows: a *pistole* is about the same as a louis d'or, and a *real* the same as a livre. You will soon become used to the valuation of other coins, especially the *cuartillo,* which is one fourth of a *real,* worth about two of your sous, or one English penny. But enough of this. Manuel will go to the changer's, or see to it for you. And by the way, you yourself will need a man. I have already told Manuel to look for one, and while he is on this present errand, he will be on the watch for someone suitable."

He delivered my purse to his servant, and the latter departed.

"Manuel can be depended on," Beltrán said. "I brought him from Spain; he is one of our family retainers, and served the old Conde, my father, before he served me."

Thereupon he brought forth a written paper and flourished it.

"Your *permiso,*" he said with triumph. "It was as I said—His Grace put his signature to it without hesitation. You are safe now. There will be a court reception tomorrow night. The Viceroy makes it a practice to exhibit himself to his court at a reception each week, and to the populace in a public procession each month, except during Lent. He is extremely zealous in all matters religious—in fact, between ourselves, I sometimes think His Excellency spends too much time at Mass and too little at his administration. He is an old man, and depends on me for more and more of his work, while he devotes himself to pious conversation with the priests and monks. You will see for yourself, for I will present you to him tomorrow evening. At least with this *permiso* you can come and go wherever you please."

An hour later, when Manuel returned with the money, converted now into Spanish coins, apologizing for the tenth deducted by the changers, I went out with Beltrán to equip myself with clothes. Under his conduct this was a simple matter, for he took me to his own tailor.

"I am his best customer," he told me as we entered the place. "As I said before, my father, the old Conde, indulges me, and I am a prey for fine clothes—it is like an avarice in me."

In truth it was, for while I was purchasing one decent enough outfit, dark red, which suited my complexion well, he in the meantime ordered two complete costumes for himself.

I paid the tailor, donned my new garments, and stood forth for his appraisal.

He nodded, with an approving glance.

"Ah, Luís," he said, "you are a figure to draw the eye—especially if it be the eye of a woman. What a head! Almost fiercely handsome—and your own hair, I would not change that. The peruke is by no means as universal here as in Europe. The Viceroy, to be sure, affects one, and so do many of his courtiers, including myself, who are newly from Spain. But many of the important men of this colony keep to the old styles, and in you it is brilliantly effective—you are splendidly individual!"

As we walked back to his apartment, he continued in this enthusiastic but far too kind vein, and presently said, "Speaking of women—does this celibacy which you declared to the Governor of Louisiana continue indefinitely?"

I shrugged. "Not necessarily, I think. Although it does not concern me especially."

He smiled at me. "You do not object, then, to feminine companions? Charming ones?"

"But never! Charming ones especially!"

"We will meet a lady of my acquaintance, and through her others. She will be pleased to know you, of that I am certain—but no poaching, mind!"

He laughed, and I with him.

"She is . . . ?" I asked.

"Yes, I will confess it to you. We have been lovers now for two months, and are devoted. Especially when her husband is away from the city, which fortunately is frequent."

"The same old Beltrán!"

"And the same old Luís!"

We slapped each other on the back, and roared with such mirth that anyone seeing us might have been justified in assuming that we were intoxicated: which, indeed, we were, but not with wine.

4.

When we reached Beltrán's quarters, his servant, Manuel, was waiting for us, with a strange man.

"Señor," he said to me, "I have brought this person for your inspection. I think he will do very well in service for you."

The newcomer was in his middle thirties, with a large smooth face, a long sly nose, somewhat plump in figure, and dressed very shabbily, though he swung a ragged cape rather jauntily over his shoulder. I judged him to be an adventurer. He stepped forward and made me a bow, which for stateliness and flourish was remarkable in one so down at heels.

"I hold it a privilege," he said in a voice curiously orotund, "to pay my respects to Your Worship."

"What is your name?" I asked.

"Achille Zorro."

"Achille Zorro," I repeated. "A name obviously concocted. Achilles the hero, and Zorro the fox. Now what is your real name, my friend?"

"It is my real name," he answered, unabashed. "More real than the name with which I was christened at birth, for that name was given me without my consent, while this one I chose for myself. It is, furthermore, a professional name. Know that—in spite of these rags—I sometimes make a most impressive appearance, am treated like a prince, and have soldiers and servitors in my train."

"By this," I said, "I am to understand you are a stage player?"

"Precisely, Señor. And without vanity I can say that I have played many important roles triumphantly, being chiefly and justly popular as a lover in high tragedies. I die so beautifully in the last scene that every eye in the audience is wet with tears."

"If you are such a success, why do I now behold you so shabby?"

"A frank question, Señor, and I welcome it. I confess that at the moment I am tolerably poor. My mistake was in leaving Spain, where the stage flourishes, and coming to this land where the populace is too ignorant and poor to patronize the theater. For this reason Achille Zorro, master tragedian, is a man without an occupation."

"It is evident that you left Spain somewhat hurriedly. Perhaps the authorities there are still seeking for someone under the name you so conveniently discarded?"

"If so," he said, with a true tragedian's sigh, "the charge against me was unjust, for the tavern keeper—Oh, that contaminated liar!—doubled, nay, trebled the score against me, as I could have proved."

"If you could prove it, why fly the country?" I asked.

"You must know, Señor, that he who has the most gold has the most justice in court. If such a man as I were to appear, without a single bit of silver in my pocket before the tribunal, yet with every word, line, leaf and passage of the Bible in my favor, and on the other side, against me, was one as rich as that innkeeper—so long as he had the gold, I might appeal to my holy book in vain, until it and I were tired of walking around each other, for justice I would never obtain."

He paused, with a look so injured that in spite of myself I smiled, and saw Beltrán equally amused, because the fellow was so patently a rogue.

But he continued, "So, since a ship was just hoisting sail to leave Cádiz—where this difficulty of mine took place—and was bound for New Spain, I incontinently boarded it, signing as a would-be colonist."

"How long have you been here?"

"One year, Señor. Twelve months. A long time to make a living by one's wits."

"Can you find no work for your hands?"

"Work?" He was horrified. "The idol of thousands of playgoers in Spain, laboring with his hands like a common peasant?"

"It is better than having nothing—not even a wife or a good suit of clothes."

"Ah, but I do have a wife. Young and passably good-looking. Yet I am none the better for it, so capricious is my fate."

"How so?" I glanced over at Beltrán and saw he was as filled with inward mirth as I, seeing where this would lead.

"She was a dancer in a stage company in which I played," Zorro explained. "I married her, knowing what dancers, and in fact all actresses, are, hoping she would not let me starve. As bad luck would have it, she was the only one in the entire troupe who was incorruptibly chaste! Can you conceive of it? One virtuous woman in twenty, and she fell to my lot!"

"And so, instead of supporting you by—by her lack of virtue—you must support her, *with* her virtue?"

"Not so, Señor. I left her behind me in Spain. We have parted for good, for I cannot abide ingratitude."

At this both Beltrán and I laughed aloud, and yet there was something so ingratiating and humorous about the rascal that I could not help liking him, and his very airs were amusing.

Achille Zorro, however, seemed wounded by our laughter. With a bow, to which he contrived to give a suggestion of coldness, the devotee of the tragic muse stood back, wrapping his cape about him.

"Have you any qualifications beside 'dying beautifully in the last scene'?" I asked.

His austerity departed. "Ah yes, Señor," he said eagerly. "I know clothes and how to wear them, in spite of the state in which you see me. In addition, I am an excellent cook, an agreeable companion, and am filled with tact and dexterity, so that if you perchance should have occasion to wish some secret message delivered or other mission of a delicate nature, you can depend on my discretion——"

"As to these 'missions of a delicate nature,' that is neither here nor there," I interrupted. "I am unacquainted with any ladies in this city."

"Ah, but a gentleman like Your Worship undoubtedly will soon discover an interest of this nature——"

"Enough of that. It is more to the point that you yourself know what to expect from me. Are you aware that if you follow me you may often find yourself on the frontiers of this country, in positions of danger?"

He gave me a stare, then said, after a pause, "If you expect this to affect me, Señor, you are wrong. Indeed, it is an added attraction to a man of my caliber. Having depicted, to the satisfaction of many audiences on the stage, the character of an adventurer, I have a desire to try a little of the real thing."

"You mean that you enjoy danger?"

He threw out his chest. "I lust for it! I have some knowledge of handling weapons from my stage playing. You will find me, Señor, a veritable two-bladed sword of a man, as well as a most cunning concocter of stratagems."

"I shall hope to be able to concoct my own stratagems," I told him. "If you know the other duties of a valet, that is all I ask. I will employ you on that understanding. You will begin at once."

5.

I know not whether it was that I once more stood decently arrayed, with a few gold pieces remaining in my wallet, or whether it was that I once more had a retainer in attendance on me, or whether it was the assurances of Beltrán that all danger was over for me and my own eagerness to believe them, but all at once I felt a great uplift of optimism. I had severed the links that connected me with San Juan Bautista and all the perils stemming from the ill fortune I had experienced there, and I was quite willing to accept, and did accept—for the moment—the assurance in my own mind that the greatest danger at least, the dread of the Inquisition, under which I had suffered, was laid to rest.

I remember that I was very light of spirit, and smiled at Beltrán like a boy.

He smiled back. "You need only one thing more," he said. "A sword to complete you, for all gentlemen carry at least dress swords in this city."

"Then I will get myself a sword," I said. But at that a rueful thought came. "It must be something quite modest, for the present at least. My wallet is grown very light."

"You can always call on me for such money as you may need until we arrange a permanent post in the government for you——"

"No, Beltrán. I am already too deeply under obligations to you. Tell me where there is an armorer, and I will look at his stock. So that the blade is good, I can at least for the present do with a hilt of plain iron. The cost of a rapier these days is all in silver pommels, cross guards, and basket hilt, and the fighting steel none the finer for all this frippery."

But at this, Zorro, my new man, offered a suggestion.

"Have you thought, Señor, of the Baratillo?" he asked.

"The Baratillo—what is that?"

"The name comes from its merchandise: cheap. It is a special section of the Zócalo, over at the end opposite from the palace, where goods can sometimes be bought at very low cost. Some of the articles are gewgaws, but also at times one encounters articles of real value, which can be obtained—by a shrewd bargainer such as myself—for a tithe of their real worth. I have once in a while seen excellent weapons at some of the booths in the Baratillo."

"Why are they so cheap?" I asked.

"Perhaps because they are mysteriously come by—some call the Baratillo the Thieves' Market—I do not suggest the *ladrones* of the highways—yet it might be worth our while to try the place."

It seemed so reasonable that yet that evening we went to the market place. It fascinated me: a noisy, disorderly, incessant movement, swirling among the close-packed *cajones* and *ramadas,* on which the benignant towers of the cathedral and the impressive sweep of the palace seemed to gaze askance. Merchants and mendicants, priests and peddlers, prostitutes and pickpockets—*gachupines, criollos, mestizos* and *Indios*—old and young, men, women and children, rich and poor, rubbed elbows and wandered about without discrimination among the booths. It was a bizarre combination of din, stink, ugliness, and beauty —this last, in particular, where the flower booths ranged. Ladies of high degree had their sedan chairs set down, to bargain over some article, perhaps standing beside native girls, sometimes very pretty, who came swaying along, musk-scented.

But all at once a momentary silence fell. I saw two black-clad figures with white crosses on their cloaks passing through the crowd, which fell apart to make way for them, and a whisper went around: *"Militi Cristi!"*

It was my first sight of members of the "Soldiers of Christ," better known as familiars of the Holy Office—that is, members of the "family" of Saint Dominic, although not actually belonging to the order itself. They are the armed lay brothers of the Inquisition, its agents and spies as well as its police. Never do they go forth, unless two of them go together, and never are they without arms. This pair passed on through the lane formed for them by the people, silent, stern, looking straight ahead, on what errand no man could say, but leaving a cold sense of dread even in the hearts of the most devout, for it could never be anticipated where they might strike next, or why.

Not until they had left the Zócalo and gone on did the crowd once more resume its movement, and the cheery noisiness which was normal with it.

Zorro and I traversed the entire plaza, coming at last to a collection of booths across which the very shadow of the gallows seemed to fall, for the sun was low in the west—the Baratillo. He went among these places where merchandise of various kinds was displayed, with great confidence, I following. Presently he stopped at a booth, and said, "*Compadre*, my master is looking for a sword. What have you for us to see?"

"Swords, Señor?" said the peddler, a shifty-eyed rogue if I ever saw one. "They are difficult to come by, and most costly——"

"Come, come!" interrupted Zorro. "You are not talking to a *ganso*,* my friend. I was not born yesterday, and I have been in the Baratillo before this, and more than once! The *espadas*, quickly!"

He snapped his fingers. For a moment the peddler stared at him, then reaching under the counter he drew out three or four rusty old knives and machetes.

"This is all I have in the direction of which you speak," he said.

"Nonsense!" snapped Zorro. "What do I have to do to convince you? We are not cutting sugar cane or mesquite. We carve men!"

I stood at a distance, watching them wrangle for some little time, with many gesticulations and increasing heat, until they were calling each other by names which would have meant immediate mortal battle in France. And then, gradually, they seemed to arrive at some understanding, the personalities grew less pointed, the voices became calmer, and in the end the keeper of the booth displayed three swords.

At once Zorro took them and brought them over to me. "Look at them, Señor," he said in a low voice, "but if any of them strikes your fancy, do not give any sign but just tell me which one it is, and leave the rest to me."

I glanced down at the three weapons, and almost gasped. One of them was my own—the very sword I had carried all the way to New Spain, which had been taken from me when the *ladrones* made away with the pack mules after killing Herrera and his men. Thus quickly did stolen merchandise reach this market from the robbers of the roads. For a moment I debated denouncing the peddler, and claiming my property on the grounds of theft. But in an instant I realized how inadvisable that would be. It could only result in an uproar, and an investigation of the circumstances of my loss of the sword. Even if I were able to convince the authorities of my ownership, the matter would be traced back to the incident on the high pass in the mountains, and from

---

* "Goose"

there, who knew where else? It might even be pursued all the way
back to San Juan Bautista, with the disclosure perhaps that I was
charged there with the crime of heresy!

So I kept my face from showing my excitement, and said to Zorro:
"The French sword was once mine—try to buy that for me."

At once he returned to the booth, and began an elaborate bargaining
for one of the *other* swords. He had no intention of buying it, but his
purpose was to make the peddler believe it was the one desired, and
after a long argument, to settle on the blade I really wanted, as an
inferior substitute, which he would be willing to take if the price were
very much lower than was being asked for the one over which he was
arguing so loudly.

It would take time: perhaps half an hour, for this kind of business,
which was largely compounded of acrimony and haggling, until a fish-
wife would have been ashamed to participate in it.

I turned away to look about, and as I did so, the sun now near the
tops of the mountains to the west silhouetted a figure that brought me to
a sudden halt. Wide sombrero, short thick beard and mustache, gold
earrings, gaudy garb of jingling bell buttons—he was Hipólito Terraza,
the *arriero* with whom we had traveled, him they called El Risero, the
Laugher.

But he was supposed to be in Durango, six hundred miles away! I
gave another quick glance. There could be no mistake. It was Terraza,
and he must have followed me here: immediately, too, for I had now
been only two nights in the city.

At once I wished I were somewhere else: or he were—preferably in
hell. He was not looking at me, but stood in profile, his beard thrust
out, his attention on something in a different direction. Quickly I
turned, and stepped around a booth, placing it between myself and
him, hoping that he had not seen me.

This man knew me as one being transported on a charge of heresy!
He had discussed the matter, not only with Herrera, but with my very
self. He was the link in the chain, connecting me with Anaya and his
malignity, that I had hoped was destroyed—and it was only necessary
for him to tell what he knew, and I was doomed!

As rapidly as possible I began making my way through the maze of
narrow lanes between the *cajones*, heading for the palace. I did not
even stop to tell Zorro to cease bargaining for that accursed sword, in

which I now had lost all interest, but left him violently disputing with
the peddler.

After a little of this twisting among the booths, I began to breathe
more freely. The *arriero* probably had not seen me; or if he had, he had
not recognized me. I promised myself that once I got back to Beltrán's,
I would not again go into a place so disreputable as this plaza, where
the dangers were so great, and so little realized by me until now.

But as I walked I seemed to hear, as if within my head, a faint jingling sound. It was like the bell buttons on El Risero's clothes, and I
glanced about quickly and apprehensively.

No, he was not there. It was my imagination playing tricks on me.
I resumed my progress, hastening my steps a little. Again I seemed
to hear that jingling inside my head. I zigzagged, purposely changing
my course. Still I heard the maddening sound as of distant little bells.

All at once I halted. The *arriero* was just ahead of me, apparently
examining a display of fruit on a counter. But I was sure he was watching me out of the corner of his eye. The jingling was not my imagination
after all—he had been pursuing me through the labyrinth of the market.

I stepped aside, to go around the rear of the booth, and found myself in a small alley formed by two of the *cajones* standing back to back
with barely room to pass between them. As I started through, this the
comedy—if such it could be called—came to an end. Into the narrow
alley, from the other side of the booth where he had been standing,
sauntered the *arriero*. We both halted, confronting each other squarely,
for the moment alone in this small space.

"Good evening, Señor," he said calmly.

"You have been following me. Why?" I demanded.

He gazed at me silently for a moment. "I wanted to assure myself
it was you," he said.

"For what reason? And why are you here, instead of in Durango,
where you said you were bound?"

"One can change his mind."

"If you want money, I have none."

"Have I asked for any?"

A sudden thought came to me. "You turned off, to let our party go
ahead! It was after that when the *ladrones* began to follow us! *You*
set them on our track!"

He regarded me steadily, without speaking.

"You are one of them!" I exclaimed.

He drew himself up. "*Adiós*, Señor."

"Wait," I said, "you have not told me what you wish of me——"

"You have called me a *ladrón*," he said in a tone so full of dignity and a sense of injury that I was struck by it. "Let me leave this thought with you, Señor: speaking without thinking is shooting without aiming."

He turned and went swaggering off, his bell buttons jingling, while I looked after him, for the moment at an utter loss. I also turned about, and wandered rather aimlessly among the booths, my mind filled with the most fearful conjectures. At least one man was footloose in the capital who knew my secret. El Risero! But what would he do with it? Sell it, perhaps, to the informers of the Holy Office?

He had been affronted when I accused him of being a *ladrón*. Considering that, I could not, for my life, really believe that the man was a thief. He had been friendly to me, and I had, in my surprise and disordered thinking, repaid that friendship as soon as I saw him again, by insulting him. If he needed a motive to denounce me to the Inquisition, assuredly I had furnished him with one!

I began to wish I could find him again, to offer him an apology and try to make amends, but where should I look for him now, in this labyrinth? The Baratillo! That was where I first saw him: perhaps he had returned there.

As rapidly as I could walk I hurried in that direction, the high gallows and iron post of the burning place a landmark above the tops of the booths. In a few moments I was there. But El Risero was not to be seen.

Zorro, however, was. He came hurrying to me.

"Where did you go, Señor?" he said. "I have made a fine bargain for the sword you wanted. Give me three *escudos* for the whole thing, scabbard and all. I assure you, you would pay ten times as much at any armory."

As I paid over the coins to him, and he went to get the sword, I reflected that he knew values, certes, for he had almost exactly estimated the price which the weapon originally had cost me in Quebec.

On the return through the Zócalo, I kept a continual lookout for the *arriero*. I did not see him anywhere.

I said nothing to Beltrán of my encounter in the Zócalo, for that would
have entailed explanations and I would have been forced, perhaps, to
end up by revealing to him the whole devil's nest of troubles that beset
me. I wish now that I had told him then. It might have made a difference, for I think he would have counseled me to leave the city at once,
and helped me to obtain a horse and equipment to do so. On the other
hand, there is no telling in what difficulties it might have involved him.
At any rate, it is past: one cannot recall events and alter his past decisions, however he may wish it.

He examined the sword when I displayed it to him. "French!" he
said. "French blades are very good, although of course there is nothing
to equal our Toledo manufactures, which are world-famous."

In this I agreed, for the Toledo swordmakers have a secret in the
making of steel, and workmanship that has made their blades a standard wherever weapons are carried and used.

I am of a nature that does not believe in nursing apprehensions over
unformed dangers. El Risero, though he had been wounded by my
aspersion, had made no threat against me, I remembered, leaving me
with that injunction about "speaking without thinking" which I now
began to interpret as more sorrowful than angry. I persuaded myself
that he might not, after all, do me harm, and hoped I might see him
again, to learn more from him.

Meantime, Beltrán, after we had supped, began to prepare for the
Viceroy's reception which was to be held that night, and bade me to
do so likewise, for I was to accompany him.

At about eight of the clock we left his apartment and walked around
the palace building to the front. With nightfall the city had taken on
a different aspect. The Zócalo was dark, its booths closed and locked,
and its ugliness, dirt, and squalor, softened by the shadows, seemed

less apparent. At the same time all the windows of the cathedral and the palace were ablaze with lights, giving new charm and magnificence to those impressive structures.

Here and there, afar in the city, I heard the tinkling of guitars or the wail of violins, and with them tenor voices singing softly, yet with passion, love songs of which the Spanish people have an innumerable variety exceeded by no nation on earth, not even France. It was pleasant and rather beautiful.

I commented on it to Beltrán. "As in Spain, I notice, lovers salute their adored ones with song."

"Yes," he said. "But there is a difference here. Serenades are not always necessarily expressions of love in the sense of passion. Here in New Spain they may, on occasion, mean no more than a compliment to the lady thus serenaded."

"An elaborate compliment!" I exclaimed.

"Perhaps. But these people love music, and it has become a custom. There are musicians always for hire, who make their living by assisting in these night concerts beneath the windows of ladies. As I say, it is not always an avowal of love. I have serenaded a lady for no reason more important than that she was gracious enough to have me to a dinner. It goes on so frequently that nothing is thought of it."

"Then I think the custom most pleasant," I said. "Your city by night is as dreamy with distant music as it is harsh with the noises of the streets by day."

Before the great door leading to the wing of the palace devoted to the sittings of the Viceroy, a long succession of coaches was discharging passengers.

"The high personages make it a point to arrive by coach," said Beltrán, "no matter how short the distance. For example, the *Corregidor's* dwelling is less than a square away, but he will come by coach like the others."

We entered the building in quite a stream of people, all richly dressed, and were announced, like the others, by a major-domo with a stentorian voice, as we came to the large ballroom. I observed that considerable magnificence attended a sitting of the Viceroy. The place was brilliantly lighted with candles, of which hundreds sparkled in the chandeliers and along the walls. Already many of the persons of the court, gentlemen and ladies, were present, moving about, speaking with each other, while a line was awaiting turns to express compliments to the Viceroy.

"We will pay our respects at once," said Beltrán.

Within a few minutes, for none was allowed to speak more than a few words with the Viceroy, I found myself before His Grace, Don Fernando de Alancastre, Norona y Silva, Marqués de Valdefuentes, Duque de Linares.

"Your Serene Grace," said Beltrán, and presented me.

I bowed, and was struck with a sensation of disappointment as if I had been cheated. The Duque de Linares appeared anything but the figure of majesty and power I had imagined. He was a very pale, long-faced man, wearing a white peruke of exaggerated style rising in two puffs high above his forehead and falling almost to his elbows. His coat was of cloth of gold, very richly frogged and decorated, and he sat in a magnificent chair on the dais, with beside him the Duquesa, a woman so fleshy that her corsets creaked audibly when she breathed, but fairly covered with jewels. He favored us with a nod, and we passed on, while persons of rank who followed us continued to approach him and received the same cold unsmiling acknowledgments.

The Viceroy and his wife seemed to be alone on the dais, in spite of the stream of courtiers who bowed before them, and the soldiers ranged behind them.

As we drew off to one side of the room, Beltrán commented on some of those greeting the ruler of all New Spain.

"This is Pedraza, the *Oidor*, who has charge of the finances," he said. "The little fellow in snuff-and-butter is Hernández, the painter, who is making a portrait of His Grace; now you see the *Corregidor*, Don Baltasar de Lanciego, Conde de Queiroz, and his wife, the Condessa."

"His wife?" I exclaimed. "She looks much too young for him."

"Ah yes. Don Baltasar married when he was past sixty, and has now been wedded for more than five years to Doña Joya."

"Joya?" The word for "jewel" struck me.

"It is a nickname. Her true name is María Teresa, a very common name. Someone called her Doña Joya, I suppose because she is very pretty and sparkling, and it has stuck. She prefers it."

"Joya suits her." I gazed with admiration at the *Corregidor's* wife, who was coming back from the dais, accompanied by her husband. She was tall, very gracefully made, with a laughing face quite beautiful at

the distance from which I was looking at it, and her hair, crowned by
its mantilla and high comb, was blond, almost red—she was what is
called a *rubia,* rare and sought after in this land of brunettes.

But her spouse, the old Conde, was a displeasing contrast to her. His
nose was huge, and rough as if scarred by some disease. His dress,
though richly expensive, could not disguise his debility, and he walked
with a limp.

"Don Baltasar suffers with the gout," commented Beltrán.

"How could a woman so young and beautiful bind herself in marriage to a man like that?" I asked.

"It is for the very reason that she is so beautiful—with no other
assets," he told me. "She is a *criolla,* and her family is poor. When the
Conde took a fancy to her, it was her chance to make a really good
marriage, and her parents therefore made the arrangements. I am not
sure that she greatly desired the union, and perhaps she went to her
marriage bed reluctantly. But at least she is a *Condessa* now, one of the
great ladies of the city."

I thought of Padre Ambrosio's account of that dinner at San Juan
Bautista and Anaya's expressed determination to take Dolores as his
wife, explaining that she would be uplifted to his rank and title by such
a match. I supposed by now she was the Governor's wife, and I wondered if she, too, "went to her marriage bed reluctantly" to use Beltrán's
words. I was sure she did; and though I had made every effort to put
her out of my mind, I felt a burning of pain and anger within me at
the thought.

Beltrán interrupted this. "Ah, they are coming this way," he said.
"I will present you to them."

The old Conde, on closer inspection, was sunken-cheeked and
wrinkled, his eyes, with their slightly clouded irises, seeming to be held
in red eyelids that almost stood apart from their cavernous sockets. He
bowed slightly at the introduction, but said nothing.

The Condessa now that I saw her near at hand, seemed very lovely,
though her beauty was not perfect. She had a short upper lip, and was
inclined to plumpness: not too much so, but sufficient to give her figure
a voluptuousness of curves. A sumptuous woman, appealing directly to
the sensual instincts of a man.

She gave to Beltrán a smile like a flash in a spangle. But her look at me was perfectly expressionless as I murmured my compliments. Then the couple passed on.

"They are about to dance," said Beltrán. At the far end of the room an orchestra was tuning its instruments, and the central floor was being cleared. About the walls were chairs for the ladies, the gentlemen remaining standing.

"As I remember, you are very light on your feet, Luís," said Beltrán.

"Out of practice," I replied, preferring to watch.

"Then excuse me, for I see someone with whom I must speak."

He departed across the floor, and I saw him conversing laughingly with a gay, dark little creature. I surmised this must be his lady of present interests.

Now the Viceroy and his Duquesa arose, and advanced to the floor. It was a signal for the first dance: a minuet, since His Grace traditionally opened a state ball, and this was one of the few numbers he considered of sufficient dignity for his participation.

The couples soon took their places, and I saw Beltrán lead the dark little lady out. But my attention was more engrossed with Doña Joya, who sat just across the room. She had been besieged by at least a dozen men, and at last she accepted one of them and went out. Thereafter she was in every number.

The minuet as danced in the Viceroy's court was a perfect expression of an age in which deportment was most carefully cultivated and polish meant everything. Its movements were slow, its bows and curtsies graceful, its pauses were traditionally filled with compliments of a smiling nature by the gentlemen and polite coquetry by the ladies. In its ceremony, beauty and bravery of attire, and its stylized chivalry and courtesy, it was beautiful.

But when it was completed, I thought that a thrill of relief ran through the assemblage. The Viceroy and his mate took their seats once more on the dais, and the numbers thereafter, except for an occasional quadrille, were the old, beautiful open dances that Spaniards loved: modeled on sex coquetry, the movements full of foray and feint, lure and repulse, escape and surrender. And the wife of the *Corregidor,* always attracting the eye with her fair head, was like a star in each one of them.

At an intermission Beltrán came to me and asked me to accompany him across the floor. There he bowed before his partner, and made a most elaborate presentation.

She was Doña Gertrudis Valverde y Mendoza, and her husband Don Pedro was, I discovered, the inspector general of the military forces of New Spain, at this time on a *visita* to Culiacán, on the western coast.

She was very petite and pretty, with flashing eyes and a waist most slim and graceful. At once she was interested in me.

"You are the friend of whom Beltrán speaks so lavishly!" she said. "But why are you not dancing?"

I made a lame excuse. "I have no entree, and I have forgotten the Spanish dances."

"Entree! With whom would you like to dance?"

My eyes went down the line to where Doña Joya was conversing with two courtiers.

"She?" asked Doña Gertrudis. "But we will arrange it!"

"I dance too badly."

"That I doubt," she said. "In any case Joya dances well enough for two. And she has glanced over here twice. She is curious. I think she would agree to a dance with you, since you would form for her a diversion, because you are new while she knows everyone else."

By now, however, the figures were forming for the next dance, and Gertrudis and Beltrán left me. I stood by the wall, fascinated by Doña Joya. It was a fandango, and the gentlemen sprang to their places, while the ladies seemed languorous and light, beating time with their small heels, seeming to invite and tease. The music began, and as I watched Doña Joya I felt the rhythms pulsing in my body. She danced magnificently, seeming in turn to lure and retreat, advance and turn away. All at once the music stopped. Each dancer remained as if frozen in the exact position he or she was thus caught, arms overhead, bodies bent, a foot even at times in air for the next step. A breath or two, and the music struck up again, the dancers bounding once more into full life, the castanets rattling, the men imitating the sound by snapping their fingers; whirling, pursuing, turning, spangles glittering, smiles gleaming, eyes sparkling and flashing, it was a scene quivering, glittering, animated, passionate and seductive.

At the end Doña Gertrudis and Beltrán returned to me, and there was a breathing space, for the number had been almost violent.

"I spoke to Joya," said Doña Gertrudis. "The next number will be *la gavota,* similar to the French gavotte, but with Spanish variations. You will not find it difficult to adapt yourself, and she will not refuse if you ask her."

It was surprisingly easily managed. I conducted her out for *la gavota,* with a little apology in advance. But I found her as Beltrán and Doña Gertrudis said: wonderfully skillful. She lured my body to answer her own with deft emphasis of her movements, imparted to me the most sensuous pleasure, invited me with half-closed eyes and parted lips, was mine for the moment, working her magic of coquetry on me alone.

My heart beat faster. But when the dance was ended, she changed all in an instant back to formal reserve.

"You dance divinely!" I exclaimed with delighted enthusiasm. "I have never known a partner more magnificent." My voice was slightly unsteady.

"Thank you, Señor," she said, and her politeness, cold and impeccable, quenched my warmth, and brought me back to myself.

At once she was borne off by another partner, and standing against the wall I alternately watched her, in a *seguidilla* with a polished young officer, and Beltrán whirling through the lively dance with his flashing-eyed little Doña Gertrudis.

I did not wish to dance again. But Beltrán and Doña Gertrudis would not hear of such a thing. At their insistence she herself was my partner in a quadrille that followed, and in which I could hold my own.

"How do you like our Joya?" she asked me, as we formed the figures.

"She dances wondrously."

"That is all you have to say?"

"She is like fire in the dance, like ice when it is over."

She gave me a laughing little look. "That is her way. I am led to believe that she can be warm enough, when she chooses, with the right one. And it does not take a dance to do it."

I thought that over. "What has happened to the *Corregidor?*" I asked suddenly, for he was not in view.

"Oh—he? He does not dance. I might almost say he does not count—with her. There is a card game in another room, which he invariably joins. He leaves her alone much of the time—too much of the time, perhaps. After all, with his age and his gout, Don Baltasar would make but a poor figure on a dance floor, don't you think?"

I thought to myself he might make an equally poor figure in a bed.

At the end of the evening, when Beltrán and I were leaving the ballroom, from which the Viceroy and the Duquesa had long ago retired, we chanced to encounter the *Corregidor* and Doña Joya at the door.

I gave her my best bow. She looked not at me, but *through* me, as if she did not see me, as if I did not exist.

2.

"We will begin today our siege of the Viceroy," said Beltrán next morning.

"And what do we do?"

"You will wait in the reception chamber with the others seeking private audience. I, who will be with His Grace in my official capacity, will try to gain a hearing. We may not succeed today. We may not succeed for many days. But it is the only way of seeing him."

So I sat in that chamber for a day, and then another, and in the end for a full week. And as I did so, I watched those who came and went, officials, soldiers, and personages of importance seeking favors. Two of those I saw interested me especially. Both were clerics, both were past the prime of life, both were full of pious actions, and both wore the robes of the Church. Yet otherwise how different they were!

One was tall and personable, stout and smooth, his skin soft as a woman's, his robe, his ring, his cross, and his slippers all in accord. His hair was silvery white and though he affected a humble bearing, pride could sometimes be seen in his look and manner. For he was the Most Reverend Archbishop of New Spain, Rafael Celestino de Solveira, a prince of the Church and a true courtier.

He was famous for his smile, his politic manner, and his ability to make himself agreeable to those with influence and power. In particular he had studied women, as all courtiers must, knew their changeable nature and caprices and how to forestall them, and that the easiest way to power is through the women of the powerful. For this reason he paid constant attention to the old, fat spouse of the Viceroy, never wearying of flattering her and pretending that her opinions—although she was in reality most vague and vapid—were important to him. This it paid him to do, for Archbishops had in the past been elevated to the great post of Viceroy itself, and due to the age of Linares there might conceivably be a change at an early date, whereupon another Archbishop might be considered, especially if he were recommended as successor by the retiring Viceroy, through the influence of the retiring Viceroy's wife. Solveira did not overlook temporal chances in his spiritual world.

The other holy man was in many ways a contrast to the Archbishop. Though only of medium height he gave the impression of being tall, because of his gaunt frame and face, which bespoke the life of an ascetic. Where the Archbishop smiled often, this man smiled almost never. His visage was dark and deeply lined, and it fell habitually into expressions of sternness that were the hallmark of his character. Where the Archbishop's robe of purple was rich and ornate with lace, this man's robe was of harsh serge—a white cassock and scapular, and a sinister black mantle. Where the Archbishop was accompanied usually by a retinue of several priests and pages who laughed and chatted with those in the reception chamber while their lord was in conference with the Viceroy within, this man was accompanied always by two only: armed attendants, dressed in black, and with a white cross upon their bosoms and backs, who spoke to no one.

I will not forget the thrill almost of terror that went through me when I first saw this man in the same room with me, and learned who he was: Esteban de Pulgar, the Grand Inquisitor of New Spain, accompanied by two of the familiars of the Holy Office.

Whenever his eyes chanced to rest on me, if only for a moment, I half shivered, wondering if the look was of suspicion, or if perchance he had some word of the false charge made against me by Anaya. But his gaze always passed on, and he said nothing to me, nor took any notice of me, and as time passed I could breathe more freely even when he was near.

I learned that the Grand Inquisitor was said to be a model of his kind. He was most diligent and fervent in his zeal for the truth of the faith as he saw it, for the salvation of souls, and for the extirpation of heresy. Tireless and intrepid, he was coldly earnest and never allowed himself to be inflamed with wrath or indignation.

He was known to be unmoved by either prayers or blandishments of any who sought to influence him. In doubtful matters he was circumspect, not ready to yield credence, merely because a thing seemed probable; for he said that a probability was not always true. On the other hand he did not obstinately reject the improbability either, for it often turned out to be fact, or so he stated. This enabled him to believe stories that it would be almost impossible for logic to swallow, in arriving at a verdict that convicted a culprit.

His certainty that he, of all people, knew what the truth was, made him terrible, for it was absolute. He had forwarded the Holy Office's reputation for zeal, which had been made by the numbers it convicted and punished, by whatever means; and in pronouncing judgment on a culprit he never showed any emotion, whether of pity or anger, but in his face preserved invariably the severity of justice, making him seem something less or greater than human at such times.

Yet this man sincerely believed in what he did. As a judge, he held that it was his duty to vindicate the faith and avenge God for the wrongs inflicted on Him by misbelief. But on the other hand he considered himself a father confessor, striving for the salvation of the wretched souls perversely bent on perdition. If an offender pleaded for mercy, and unreservedly submitted himself to this spiritual father, Pulgar would sometimes grant him grace. But *grace* meant several things: pardon complete, pardon in part, or most important of all— from the viewpoint of the Inquisitor—a state of acceptance with God. The first two forms of grace, being least valuable in the mind of the holy tribunal, were rarely extended.

I learned of the Inquisition's contention that God himself was the first Inquisitor, and the condemnation of Adam and Eve was the first model of the Inquisitorial process. God judged the first man and woman in secret, the learned men of the Holy Office said, thus setting an example which the Inquisition was bound to follow, especially since it thus was enabled to "avoid the subtleties which criminals would raise in their defense, especially at the suggestion of the crafty Serpent." God, it was pointed out, called no witnesses, but this was because of the confession of Adam and Eve, and ample legal authority was cited to prove that such confessions, however obtained, were sufficient to justify the convictions and punishments.

It was enough to make me shiver almost, for it seemed blasphemy for men, even those of the Holy Office, thus to compare themselves with God, wielding irresponsible powers which nothing short of divine wisdom would prevent from being turned by human perversity into an engine of the most deadly injustice. Released from all restraints of publicity and unrestricted by the formalities of the law, the proceedings of the Inquisition were purely arbitrary.

Though the Grand Inquisitor Pulgar repelled me, at the same time he fascinated me with the same sort of horrible fascination a snake is sometimes said to exert over its prey. There was still a sufficiency of injustice in France, God knew, but at least the Inquisition long ago had been abolished from within its borders. That it still persisted in Spanish territories, with its terrible functions uninhibited, was a fearful indication of its power.

I tried to reassure myself that I was not in any peril from the Inquisition, but the fear never left me, and sometimes I awoke at night with it. That man El Risero: he had every power over me if he chose to use it. I realized now that only if I could gain powerful support here could I be safe, and the days that I waited fruitlessly for the always deferred interview with the Viceroy seemed endless.

3.

It was one day a week later, when I was alone in the apartment, since Beltrán was on duty at the palace, and there were to be no audiences that day, when my man Zorro came to me with word that someone was waiting in the hall to see me.

"Who is he?" I asked.

"Señor, I do not know him, but he is a priest."

What would a priest want of me? I said, "Show the padre in."

In a moment he stood before me, a dark, club-jointed, tense man, in the habit of the Franciscans. The hair of his tonsured head was coarse and black, and though he could not have been less than sixty years old, there was scarcely a thread of white in it. From under prominent brows his dark eyes, which were set rather closely together, wandered swiftly about the room, taking in every detail, before coming to rest on me. I recognized that glance: it is the instinctive and ever restless look of one accustomed to the wilds, where constant observation is a necessity for safety or success. The same look can be seen in all white foresters and all wild Indians.

"You are Señor St. Denis?" he asked me.

"Yes."

"I wish to speak with you alone."

At my nod Zorro departed to the servants' quarters, closing the door.

"I am Padre Francisco Hidalgo," said my visitor.

My heart gave a great bound of apprehension, as I thought of what this might portend. So this was the priest I had sought so long and vainly!

But how had he learned of my presence in the city, and particularly of my connection with him? It could only have come to him from San Juan Bautista, through Padre Ambrosio. But if Padre Ambrosio sent him word of me, presumably he knew I was still alive and in the capital, instead of dead with Herrera's men. That meant that others also would probably know.

The false accusation of Anaya hung over me suddenly like the sharp edge of the headsman's ax, ready to fall: for if the Governor had knowledge that I was here, he would most assuredly forward the charge of heresy anew, and the charge alone was sufficient to send me to the Inquisition dungeons. I felt an involuntary perspiration break out on my forehead. I believe I am as brave as most, but the horror of that fate is enough to chill the stoutest heart.

"What do you want of me?" I managed to say at last.

"I wish to thank you," he said.

I warily watched him, to see where this might lead, for the Spanish priesthood is noted for its subtleties, and he might be attempting to trick me into some statement that would condemn me.

"For what?" I asked him.

"For forwarding the labor I attempted and in which I failed, among my dear children, the Neches Indians."

So he did know!

"I had word of this from my dear friend, Padre Ambrosio," he went on, speaking with great earnestness. Then he added, in a low voice, "That letter of mine to the French Governor, Señor—it was the last hope of one who humbly, if perhaps unwisely, desired to carry on God's work."

He spoke almost pleadingly, as if to win me to his cause, and I knew all at once that Padre Hidalgo was as fearful of his fate as was I of mine.

"I believe you," I said to him. "As to the letter—that it reached its destination and was read, and therefore brought me to the Neches and thence to New Spain, is known to only three men in this land: Padre Ambrosio, you, and myself."

He nodded, regarding me most narrowly with his close-set eyes, as if he tried to read my thoughts in my face.

"It was by accident I learned you were here," he said. "I am chaplain to the palace guard——"

"It was *you* whose apartment I occupied for a night when I was first brought here!" I exclaimed.

"Yes. If it was a comfort to you, I am happy. I was absent in Toluca, conducting services there at a church during the illness of its priest. Only yesterday I returned, learned you had been, in a manner of speaking, my guest, then your name, and that Don Beltrán de Córdoba had taken you away."

"Which brought you here."

He nodded. "Some time ago I received a secret letter from Padre Ambrosio——"

"Concerning me. So, Padre Hidalgo, we are, in a manner of speaking, rowing in the same boat. Each of us, though innocent, can be adjudged guilty of a grave offense: you of perhaps treasonable correspondence with the French authorities, I of heresy in which there is no iota of truth."

Again he nodded, and I saw him gulp, the sign of extreme nervousness.

"Since you learned of my presence in the manner you say," I went on, "it is probable that in San Juan Bautista they believe I am dead with the guards who were conducting me here. Unless you reveal that charge against me which Padre Ambrosio disclosed in his letter, I need not for the present at least fear such an accusation here. On the other hand, unless I tell it, none need ever know of your letter to the Governor of Louisiana. A bargain, Padre: keep my secret, and I will keep yours."

"I assent," he said, "and my conscience permits this, for Padre Ambrosio stated in his letter that the charge of heresy was false, and that you are a true and loyal son of the Church."

For a few moments we stood silently gazing at each other, two men who by the irony of fate held each other's lives in our hands.

Presently he said, "What do you propose to do here?"

"I hope for an audience with the Viceroy, looking to a commission as a negotiator with Indian tribes, in which I am skilled——"

The keenness of his look sharpened. "On the far frontiers?"

"That is where the savages are most troublesome."

"I believe, Señor, that I can forward that hope."

I studied him, and it occurred to me that he was anxious to get me as far away from the capital as possible; even though he believed that, given opportunity, I would escape back to French territory, which I had secretly resolved to do. But I would be glad for such help as he might give me.

After a moment he said, "I must make you understand how you have benefited me. I was under great censure for my losing effort in the Neches country; and for this reason was relegated to this humble garrison chaplaincy. But when Padre Ambrosio sent a message to Querétaro, describing your arrival at San Juan Bautista with the chiefs, and sending their petition for my return all written in fair Spanish, my superiors learned how fruitful my mission really was. I am again in favor, and will be given important responsibilities again, perhaps even being sent back to the Neches, since it seems most probable that a full and well-organized effort, with military backing, will be extended in that direction."

So the northward thrust of Spain was being planned after all, and I had much to do with setting it under way!

"In his letter, Padre Ambrosio dwelt at some length on your influence with the Neches, who would not go back to their own country until they had seen you and been reassured by you. He said that your assistance was absolutely necessary for success in accomplishing the project of Christianizing them." Padre Hidalgo paused. "You make friends easily among the Indians?"

I nodded. "So I believe and have cause to think. It is because I perhaps have some understanding of the savage mind, which makes it possible to meet them on their own ground of thinking."

"A valuable asset," he said. "One that I, too, try to cultivate."

"With success, Padre, as the mission to the Neches proves."

"I thank you." He gave a slight smile. "My interest is not entirely unselfish, for I feel pent in the narrow confines of a chaplaincy, but at least it is sincere. And examining my conscience I cannot see how it is contrary to the cause of God and the King if I can do something to arrange a meeting between you and the Viceroy."

"I have sought this vainly for a long time."

"Let us see what the Church can do. My superiors of the order of St. Francis have brought all this to the attention of the Archbishop, and the Archbishop is bound by duty to interest himself in the expansion of the missions. The Archbishop, I have heard, has an interesting line of influence with the Viceroy. *Adiós.*"

With that the strange man departed, the white crown of his tonsured head gleaming in its circle of black hair. In considering all that had been said and what he had hinted, I was sure he was friendly to me, and might help my fortunes. But there was also the unpleasant fact that now there were two men who knew of the charge hanging over me: Padre Hidalgo, and El Risero, the *arriero.*

4.

I related everything in this interview to Beltrán, except that I omitted the mutual secrets concerning each other which the priest and I held.

"This is wonderful!" he exclaimed. "You will receive your summons now, and soon, because I know how these matters work. The Viceroy will act on a suggestion from the Archbishop, who will be prompted by the Franciscan hierarchy, which in turn will be actuated by Padre Hidalgo."

Sure enough, two days later we received word that I was to be admitted. We were prompt.

As we entered the Viceroy's inner chamber, past the guards, the *Oidor,* or chief auditor, was just bowing himself out. The Duque de Linares stood beside one of the windows which looked out over the plaza, smoking a long thin *cigarrillo.* I observed that the chamber was splendidly furnished and decorated with hangings of tapestry and several paintings, among which the portrait of the reigning monarch of Spain was especially prominent. In this place the Viceroy conferred with his officials and others of importance sometimes quite informally, in contrast with the extreme stateliness and punctilio observed in his public appearances.

Beltrán and I halted just within the door, beside which a secretary sat at an escritoire, writing. Other than this man, Linares and ourselves were the only persons in the large room.

Presently the Duque turned and regarded us, allowing a stream of smoke to issue from his mouth and nostrils.

I was struck by the intense pallor of his narrow face, made still narrower in appearance by the exaggerated white peruke which hung down almost hiding his cheeks. His eyebrows were extremely light, almost sparse, detracting from the expression of his eyes; and his mouth, though wide and full-lipped, displayed little evidence of force and vigor. He was spare and fragile-looking, with a perceptible stoop as if he were yielding to the approach of the infirmities of ill health or age, and at times his head gave just the faintest suggestion of the palsied nodding of an old man. On this day his garb was of black velvet, handsomely decorated on the cuffs and down the front of the coat with elaborate gold embroidery in floral designs, and set off by a gold-hilted court rapier, in a gold-chased silver sheath.

"Don Beltrán," he said, speaking in a high, rather weak voice, "what is it that brings you here?"

I stood wondering how it was that he did not know our errand, since I certainly had been officially summoned. Then I saw his vagueness, and it came over me that he perhaps had forgotten all about the summons. It caused me to reflect on the strangeness of fate that placed such a man in a position of power second only to that of the King.

Beltrán bowed. "Your Most Excellent Grace, it is my honor to present Señor Don Luís de St. Denis. This is the gentleman of whom I told you, who is more skilled in dealing with the gentile tribes of savage Indians than any other."

Without replying, and moving rather listlessly, the Viceroy walked to a chair beside a richly carved round table, on which were a gold-plated reading stand, a splendid decanter filled with wine on a silver tray with some glasses, a box of the long thin *cigarrillos* he preferred, some writing materials, and a small white alabaster statue of Santiago de Compostela, the patron saint of Spain.

"Wine," he said fretfully.

At once Beltrán, as if accustomed to such an order, stepped to the table, poured a glass of wine, and set it before the Viceroy with a bow. Linares took a sip, looking vacantly across the room as if daydreaming.

Presently, however, he said, "State your business, for I am engaged shortly to have my usual discussion on matters of doctrine with two learned doctors of theology, monks of the Carmelite convent."

"I will allow Señor St. Denis to speak for himself," said Beltrán.

At this, I said, "Most Noble Highness, if you will indulge me I will try briefly to explain my ideas and purposes."

He looked up at me, and I met his gaze fairly and levelly.

All at once he said, "Ah, you appear to have a bone in your neck!

You look me in the face. I sometimes wonder if people of this country have any spine at all, for they seem to be unable to hold up their heads, and continually scan the floor. Very well, I will hear you."

"I need not tell Your Grace," I said, "that this realm of New Spain is threatened at all times by the hostility of savage tribes, and placed under great expense to carry on wars against them. If these tribes could be dealt with diplomatically, so that they would consent to live in peace and receive the teachings of the Church, it would save great treasure and many lives, while extending the influence of the Spanish Crown to areas it has not yet been able successfully to reach."

He frowned. "This is nothing I do not already know. To what does it lead?"

"I am fortunate in possessing one or two traits which you might find useful along these lines, in forwarding such understandings with savage Indian tribes," I said. "I have, first of all, a small gift of tongues——"

"Ah yes." The Viceroy nodded. "Don Beltrán tells me you are of French birth, yet in your Spanish I detect no trace of usage or accent which would indicate that you are other than a Castilian born. What other languages do you command?"

"Aside from French, I speak and write English. I also have acquaintance with many Indian dialects and can pick up almost any native tongue within a few days. For example, in a short stay, I was able to talk freely with the Neches Indians, so that I was able to bring them to the borders of New Spain seeking reestablishment among them of a Spanish priest."

"All this is very interesting," said Linares, "but talking to an Indian does not mean disarming him."

"Except for the Iroquois, who are so inflamed by the English that no impression can be made upon them," I replied, "I have never been among a savage people who did not listen to me and accept friendly guidance from me."

"This is large talk! Very well, what do you propose to do?"

"If Your Grace will permit me to serve you in an official capacity, I intend to work among Indian tribes to pacify them and avoid wars."

"And for this, what do you want in return?"

"Appointment by you as an *enviado oficial*——"

"At what salary?"

I looked him in the eye. "One hundred Spanish ducats a month, and sufficient funds to enable me to buy presents to give to savage tribes I visit."

He looked at me as if I were mad. "This is unheard of!" he exclaimed. "A hundred ducats? Why, that is as much as is paid to some of my most important officials—Don Beltrán, my *ayudante,* for example!"

I did not look at Beltrán, who had himself suggested this figure to me. Instead, I spoke with the utmost courtesy, yet without any suggestion of asking less.

"Your Grace need only consult the costs of the army——"

"That is exactly what I have been doing!" Linares exclaimed testily. "You saw the *Oidor* who went out of this room as you came in? He had just finished auditing the military expenses of the past quarter. At this rate, the treasury will be bankrupt!"

"Do you not see?" I said. "You campaign against the hostile tribes on the frontiers, and the campaigns are invariably wasteful, since even when victorious they achieve no lasting result, but bring about a fitful peace soon broken again. If I brought one of these warlike tribes—only one—into peaceful submission, your treasury would save many thousands of ducats on that one tribe alone, to which the small salary and expenses of my office would be as nothing."

He pondered for a few minutes, making with pen and ink small arabesques on a sheet of paper.

"But how do I know you can accomplish these things?" he suddenly asked, putting down the pen. "You want money: it is the first request of everyone. And you want it without any kind of a guarantee of performance. Why should the royal treasury risk such expenditures on you?"

"Because in turn I risk something more valuable."

"What?"

"My life. Every time I go into a hostile Indian village."

Again he was silent for a time. Then he said, "I will consider the question, and discuss it with my council."

Beltrán's eyes met mine, and in both looks was disappointment. I could imagine what cold water would be thrown on my proposal in a meeting of the Viceroy's council, by men who had no knowledge of me or interest in me. This was fatal to my project.

But just then there came an interruption.

The door opened, and we all turned to behold the Viceroy's wife entering the room.

Linares rose quickly. "Why—Eusébia, heart of my heart, what are you doing here?"

She came toward him with short, quick steps, her feet very tiny considering her weight, holding the train of her dress of blue and gold over an arm to facilitate her walking. Save for those little feet, she appeared to me more like an old fat peasant woman, none too bright, than like a Duquesa of the realm, in spite of her necklaces and other jewels.

Linares, however, seemed to think quite differently. "Here, *querida*, take this chair and rest yourself," he said, himself drawing forward the seat and taking her hand as she sank into it. He looked at her with anxiety in his face, for what reason I could not guess.

For a moment the corpulent old lady puffed, because she was too tightly laced and had come hurrying. Beltrán and I stood mute, and of course rigid, as she fanned herself vigorously with a magnificent hand-painted fan, her corsets creaking.

"You hastened too much. You must remember to move more slowly. Catch your breath. There is no reason for worry," the Duque kept saying in a low, soothing tone, holding her hand in one palm while he patted it gently with the other, meanwhile gazing into her face with concern. She lifted her eyes to his.

It struck me forcibly: that picture of two old people, full of affection and devoted to each other, seeming oblivious to everyone else in the room. Later I learned that Her Grace was in bad health, subject to dizzy spells, and that the physicians were gravely concerned over the condition of her heart. In spite of her age and her fleshiness, she was beloved of the Duque and he of her. To see them forgetting rank and titles, the thin, failing old man, and the gross, sick old woman, in that scene of simple human affection and concern, turning to each other as if the rest of the world did not exist for either of them, somehow touched me, as at once sad and sweet.

After a moment this changed, when the Duquesa caught her breath. She sat up, ceased to fan herself, and His Grace, releasing her hand, stood erect instead of stooping over her, though he remained beside her and still gazed at her with the closest attention.

"You have not yet told me, *querida*, why you have come," he said.

She took her eyes from his face for the first time, and looked over toward Beltrán and me.

"Who is this gentleman, Fernando?" she asked.

"Why, Don Beltrán de Córdoba——"

"Oh yes, of course I know Don Beltrán," she said. "But the other?"

"He is Señor St. Denis."

"Present him, Fernando."

The Duque at once became apologetic. "Forgive me, my heart," he said. "You came in so suddenly that I fear I lost my manners. Señor St. Denis, I honor you by presenting you to my beloved wife, Doña Eusébia, Duquesa de Linares."

"I am honored indeed," I said, with my best bow.

"Is this the man who will forward our missions in the north?" she asked.

The Duque gave her a quick look. "What do you know of this, my beloved?"

"I am not as stupid as you think, Fernando," she replied.

"Is this what brings you here?"

"Yes."

"Eusébia! Have you been scheming with the Archbishop again?" He said this smilingly, but she replied quite seriously.

"Scheming? What a word, Fernando! And when we seek only to further the work of God! I am surprised at you for using it."

"I only jested," he apologized gently.

"I know. You are always teasing me. And I know also that no one is more concerned in forwarding the holy work than you, dear Fernando. As for His Reverence, to be sure I consulted with him, thus learning of this situation. The order of St. Francis, to which I owe many obligations, needs the services of Señor St. Denis; and so, also, the Archbishop tells me, does the realm of New Spain."

"If the Franciscans are so eager for him, why do they not pay his salary?" asked Linares, a trifle sulkily.

"You know they cannot, having no provision for such," she pleaded.

"I cannot employ an official, such as is suggested, without discussing it with the council, and receiving sanction——"

"Oh, Fernando! Please speak sensibly. You can do what you want and you know it——"

"You must understand that I have my responsibilities——"

"Oh, Fernando, do not speak so crossly!" The old lady's eyes began to wink, and two large tears welled up in them.

"Oh no, *querida*—there, don't weep," said the Duque hastily. He drew a lace handkerchief from his sleeve and began with the utmost solicitude to dry her eyes. "Do not worry, heart of my heart, it will be exactly as you wish. There—that is better—come, I will accompany you back to your rooms, for you must rest; and I am to see the Carmelite fathers."

He assisted her to rise very tenderly.

But the old lady was not as vague as she seemed. "First," she said, "give the order, so that you will not forget——"

She knew his weakness, and His Most Noble Grace, Don Fernando de Alancastre, Norona y Silva, Marqués de Valdefuentes, Duque de Linares, Viceroy of New Spain, as obedient as any other doting husband, dictated to the secretary the order which made me *enviado oficial*, on the exact terms I had asked, and on which, actually, I would have been most happy to compromise by half.

Then he led his old wife away, murmuring to her, as she smiled at him, while Beltrán and I bowed to them as they went.

"A most unusual intervention," I remarked when he and I were on the way back to his apartments. "And a providential one, too," I added, "for until Her Grace arrived, I thought my proposal was lost."

"The Archbishop is a most wily politician," he answered. "Knowing that the one person who can have her way with His Grace is the old Duquesa, he has devoted his time to cultivating her with flatteries and attentions, and when there is some issue in which he is interested, he can usually induce her to plead its cause with her husband. Linares and she are almost childishly devoted to each other, and he can refuse her nothing, especially if she weeps. The Archbishop must have made this appointment for you, and saw to it that Doña Eusébia would be there too. This is most impressive, Luís, for it indicates a very deep interest in you on the part of the Church; and that can only be because of your influence with the Neches people. I can almost certainly predict that within a few weeks there will be an expedition, both religious and military, organized to march north for the occupation of the Texas country by both missions and presidios."

17. *The Wife of the* Corregidor

With the Archbishop and the Franciscans sponsoring me, and with an official appointment from the Viceroy—the pay of which began at once—I now felt, for the first time, that matters were clearing up for me; and that I need no longer be very fearful of the danger that had been with me every minute since I arrived in the city, crouching, as it were, in the dark, ready to spring upon me—the menace of the Inquisition.

Enabled now to relieve my friend of the burden of entertaining me, I took rooms in a house near the southern end of the rear of the palace, but across the street, which though not so luxuriously furnished as Beltrán's, were still sufficiently good for me.

As for my plans, I thought them already pretty well set. I had only to wait. Presumably, the ecclesiastical authorities were eager to begin carrying their missions into the Texas country, and especially to the Neches, with whom I figured so strongly. I supposed it would not be long before an expedition was organized, which I would accompany in my new capacity as *enviado oficial*. Once I reached the frontier—and I would trust myself to be well mounted by then—I could make my break for freedom, going through the Neches country, where my superior knowledge of the geography would stand me in good stead, and so back to Louisiana.

And I would take with me the most vital kind of information: the certain knowledge that Spain was on the march to the north at long last. It was exactly what Bienville desired of me, and though I still had not as many details as I would have liked, I conceived it was my duty to get it to him as quickly as possible.

Meantime, I sought to carry on my life exactly as if I intended to be a resident of New Spain for all time. Every day, of course, I saw Beltrán, and usually we dined together at night. Occasionally we gamed in one of the large and luxurious rooms of the palace given over to cards and dice. Gambling, I discovered, is the national curse of New Spain, seeming inborn in everyone, whether Spaniard or Indian, and indulged in from the highest nobles to the miserable slaves on the *encomiendas*. Women, and even children, gamble as incessantly as the men. It seems as essential to them as food: perhaps more so, for a native frequently risks his entire month's subsistence on a turn of the cards, a roll of the dice, or the spurs of a fighting cock. Frequently I saw gambling on the very steps of the cathedral, and there were many booths and spaces in the Zócalo devoted exclusively to one of the many forms of this pursuit.

I myself played conservatively, since I could not afford heavy plunging; but Beltrán lost a good deal more money than I liked to see. This he took lightheartedly, seeming not greatly to care.

But as weeks passed, with no evidence that anything was being done about that combined operation of Church and state to the northward in which I was concerned, I began to fear that the usual inertia of official action in New Spain had set in, and that it might be a long time before anything definite would take place. With that the sense of false security in which I had been living vanished. In its place acute anxiety returned.

I said nothing of the state of my feelings to anyone, not even Beltrán, but a mounting fear built up in me. How long could I continue an existence so precarious as this of mine in the capital, without making some mistake or encountering some untoward incident that would place me, a foreigner, in deadly peril, through the suspicion or resentment I might unhappily arouse somewhere? And this was to say nothing of the risk that Anaya might discover that I still was alive, and press his charges anew. I began to realize how weak was my prop when I thought the Franciscans or even the Viceroy could save me should the Inquisition reach out for me.

One day Beltrán told me that we were invited to the home of his *corteja*, Doña Gertrudis Valverde y Mendoza, her husband being away again on one of his inspections. There, insofar as my state of mind would permit me, I had a pleasant little dinner, and found my friend's dark-eyed inamorata as charming as I had thought her when I met her at the Viceroy's ball.

With his devilish handsomeness I could not blame Doña Gertrudis for being in love with Beltrán. During the dinner, which we three had alone, she betrayed this by fond looks, and giving him her hand under the table, though she tried to preserve at least an appearance of decorum before me. She asked me a few teasing little questions of the kind women love to ask, which I parried smilingly. Knowing they would be in each other's arms the minute I left, I excused myself early, and went home so that they could be alone together.

Beltrán was grateful for my tact in this respect, and told me so next day.

"What with one thing and another, I did not get home until cockcrow," he said. "Now, what do you think of my Gertrudis?"

"She is most sweet and beautiful," I answered. "And most fond of you."

He nodded. "She is wonderful. We talked about you."

"Indeed? I cannot think of anything on that subject that would make conversation of interest between you and your charming lady."

"On the contrary. She is interested in you because you are my friend, and observed that you seemed abstracted and rather quiet. This she attributes to loneliness. Hating loneliness herself, she is very sympathetic, and even had suggestions."

"I am far from lonely," I said. "I see you every day. And what I observe about me here is most interesting——"

"That is not the kind of loneliness to which I—or Gertrudis—refer. A man needs the stimulation of women. It is not natural, Luís, for you to go about as you are."

I shook my head. "I do not require feminine associations. The thing that is destroying me is idleness. If only something would happen—some occupation for me! I am not accustomed to doing nothing, Beltrán! It appears to me that matters here move as slowly as a glacier. Action—even danger—would be a welcome relief from this long monotony!"

This outburst, which really reflected my great uneasiness, was taken by Beltrán merely as an expression of boredom. He listened sympathetically, nodding his head.

"A small love affair would help break this monotony and give you something to occupy your time and mind pleasantly, and perhaps excitingly," he said. "Do not forget that love is an art practiced among the hidalgo and grandee classes here, just as it is among the courtiers of Spain—or of France."

"But love affairs lead to difficulties——"

"Not necessarily." He smiled. "Remember your days in Madrid? Spanish women are perhaps as susceptible as your French ladies, but they are far more careful of outward appearance. A lady here, even though she is in love with a man, must know that he is discreet, and that her affair will be conducted with all proper precautions, before she consents to become his *corteja*. This circumspection safeguards the lover as well as herself."

"All most interesting," I answered, "but I see no opportunity to put it into effect."

"Have you forgotten Doña Joya, the Condessa de Queiroz, with whom you danced?"

"How could I? She is exquisite."

"When next you see her, why not bow to her, as if her appearance is at least not unpleasant to you?"

"I have done so."

"What did she do?"

"She looked straight through me at the wall behind me."

He was amused. "That is to be expected," he said, as if reassuring me. "Bow when you meet her again."

"And be snubbed once more?"

"This lady, Doña Joya, is one to whom the admiration of men is as necessary as the air she breathes. And she may not be as insensible to you as you appear to believe."

"On what do you base such an idea?"

Beltrán gave me a smile which for sheer satanic brilliance few could equal—short jet-black forked beard, flashing white teeth, merrily wicked eyes.

"My little Gertrudis is as sly as she is gay and sweet," he said. "She knows Doña Joya and has talked with her. I assure you the matter is at least a possibility—if it interests you."

I understood. Like most charming women who have themselves done a little straying, Doña Gertrudis was in sprightly readiness to help another of her sex along the same path. As for Beltrán, his interest was in me, and what he thought would be a diversion to ease my ennui.

"Of course—any man would be interested," I replied. "But would this not be most dangerous?"

"Not very dangerous, I think." He glanced at me quizzically. "And if you need some practical reason to overcome your reluctance in your own mind, Doña Joya *could*, if you won her, be of great value to you. Customs here are much the same as in Europe. One gains influence through those he knows. You win the esteem of a courtier; if he has the proper connections, he makes you acquainted with a minister; the minister takes to you, and through him you reach the Viceroy."

"I have reached the Viceroy—through you."

He shook his head. "Not through me. Through a Franciscan friar. You would be cooling your heels yet for all I seemed to do for you. And in this connection, one of the quickest ways to reach the mighty is through a woman."

I feared any additional complications in my already uneasy existence, yet my own experience in court circles told me there was much in what he said. So I listened to him.

"Doña Joya's husband," he went on, "is the *Corregidor* of the city of Mexico, one of the most important officials in the realm, and an intimate of the Viceroy."

"And for that very reason his wife probably is incorruptibly chaste, while he is probably most jealous. Of all the nuts to crack, why offer me this?"

"You do not understand the true situation, Luís. Gertrudis assures me that Doña Joya feels some strong resentments against her husband, which might incline her toward a lover and a dalliance, if the right man approached her in just the right way."

"Resentments? Ha! Of what nature are these resentments?"

"For one thing, the old *Corregidor* is a *gachupín*—as they call us who are from Spain—and he seems never to have allowed her to forget that she is a *criolla*, from a poor family, too, and that there still is a social gulf of sorts between them. He is, furthermore, too old and decrepit to have any active interest in her, except to show her off as an attractive possession. This wounds her feminine pride, and she feels cheated as well, for all these Spanish women are creatures of desire and passion. She revenges herself on him by flirtations, about which he does not seem to care a fig. Gertrudis is of the opinion that it might be possible to lead Doña Joya into transgressions far more interesting than mere flirtations, if only to revenge herself on her husband for this indifference. Does not the problem intrigue you?"

Again he flashed that devilish smile at me.

"I can hardly believe this," I said doubtfully. "She seems to me to be most cold and virtuous."

Beltrán laughed. "There is a saying to remember: About money and a woman's virtue, don't believe half."

It was a challenge which I confess was tempting to me, for Doña Joya was a woman any man might covet, and if she wished adventure of the sort, it would be a pleasure to assist her in it.

2.

Although Beltrán was half joking when he suggested the "practical reason" to overcome my "reluctance"—since from his old knowledge of me he did not think I really needed any such reason—in actuality it was that, more than any other thing, which caused me to embark on what followed.

I was restless with increasing anxiety to see affairs move toward the object I desired. If any kind of an expedition was organized to leave the capital, I would not be too censorious about it, so long as I could go with it. It need not even go north, I decided. Anything to get me through the *ladrón* country. If it took me to either coast, I might find some opportunity to slip away from the Spanish authorities on a ship or fishing boat.

But in the present doldrums into which matters had fallen, nothing of this kind appeared in prospect for a long time. Unless—well, a little prodding of an old husband by a young wife, and his suggestion to an intimate, the Viceroy, might possibly facilitate matters.

In this mood I began my first little essays toward a *rapprochement* with the lady, Doña Joya. And very soon I discovered that such an approach was a far more difficult matter in New Spain than it would have been in Canada or France.

The object of my interest seemed always to be under guard. Not only was her home swarming with menials, but when she appeared outside of it, she was usually either in her coach or with her husband. On a few rare occasions, such as when she visited one of the jewelry stalls in the Zócalo, she might be accompanied only by a woman, but this one, middle-aged and plainly dressed, with a severe expression, evidently was her personal maid and *dueña*.

I bowed to Doña Joya on the street. I smiled at her when I encountered her in one of the halls of the palace. In every way I sought to show her that she had aroused my admiration. But with each effort she seemed only to grow more distant, to behave as if I did not even exist.

Discouraged, I spoke of this to Beltrán.

"My friend," he smiled, "have you forgotten your Madrid days? No Spanish lady of degree is going to respond openly to such signals as you have given her. Yet the signals are of themselves valuable, since she cannot have failed to observe them. The admiration of men is what the ladies live on, and do not think your charmer is insensible to your admiration. To a Spanish woman outward decency and the appearance of virtue are all-important; but the same woman may not be obdurate to your suit, if she is certain it is close and secret. It is time you thought of the next step."

"What is that?"

"You should try to find an intermediary. An intermediary is all-important in a case of this kind." For a moment he thought, then went on, "It must, of course, be a woman; one in whom Doña Joya has confidence and unreservedly trusts. The difficulty is that few women unreservedly trust any other woman in a thing of this nature. For example, though she and Gertrudis are friends, it would be unthinkable to ask Gertrudis to approach her."

He left me to consider that and I, after consideration, had a thought. Zorro! The rascal might be the very man for such a problem. He had boasted of his skill and discretion in matters of a "delicate nature."

That night I called him before me. The master of the tragic muse, when I explained my situation to him, gave me a forthright reply.

"I appreciate your confidence, Señor," he said, "and will undertake to see what I can do. Give me a little time for investigation."

The next morning but one, while he was serving my breakfast, Zorro said, "I have found out this much, Señor: the key to the Condessa is her maid, whose name is Ysabel, and who, I am informed, knows Doña Joya far better than does the old *Corregidor*, who is too much occupied with his cards and his wine and his cronies at the court, and is past the age when his young wife's brilliant charms have the overpowering attraction that they have to a younger man."

"How did you discover this?"

"There are two worlds, Señor: the world of the great, in which you live; and the world of the servants, in which I live. We have our gossip and information just as you have, and we have friends who will aid us, just as you have."

"This Ysabel—I know her even less than I know her mistress," I objected.

"That is our problem. Ysabel is devoted to Doña Joya, and will not gossip. It is for that precise reason that she will be of use to us. We must discover what acquaintances she has. Leave this to me, Señor."

Another day passed, and again Zorro had news.

"Our Ysabel has a bosom friend," he told me. "She is an elderly widow, Señora Eleanora Cadóz, and I have sure information that Ysabel visits her frequently, almost daily, for they are intimates."

I nodded. "Now that we know of this Señora Cadóz, what next?"

"An approach must be made to her. She is in straitened circumstances, so I think that a small gift of money might easily enlist her help. For after all, most women are delighted to forward affairs of the heart, and acting as a go-between—for a little financial reward—is a common enough practice among a certain class of women in this city. Let me visit this Señora Eleanora, and at least sound her out."

I agreed, and waited with growing interest. Two days passed. I saw Doña Joya setting out in her coach, and as usual made her my best bow, receiving as usual only her chill profile as a reward. On the third morning, however, Zorro was most complacent.

"It is as I hoped," he told me. "I have seen Señora Eleanora, and she has consented to talk with you. As a matter of fact, she is waiting now at her house, which is only two squares down the street from here."

Somewhat reluctantly—for thus far I had rather been pushed into the affair and it ran contrary to my usual plan of procedure—I allowed Zorro to conduct me to a small house of adobe, tinted yellow with water paint, within which, sitting by a fireplace in which she was cooking, was a woman, fat and venal-looking, about fifty years of age, and evidently a *mestiza*.

Zorro introduced her as Señora Eleanora Cadóz, adding that we had come on the business he previously had discussed with her. She looked at me with silent suspicion until, after a few words of conversation, I placed in her plump hand two gold *escudos*. Then, gazing at the coins, she gave a sly grin and promised to help me, suggesting that I return the next day.

On the way back to our lodgings, Zorro was jubilant. "Do you observe

how adept I am in matters of diplomacy?" he crowed. "Mark my words,
she will have Ysabel there. Already our first obstacle is as good as overcome. Tomorrow we shall see it triumphantly surmounted!"

"*We?*" I exclaimed. "You expect to accompany me?"

"Of course, Señor! I must go with you. With all modesty, I must say
that I am without a peer in the perception of the niceties and the
arrangement of those little nuances of behavior that are so esteemed
by the ladies. I assure you that I am a positive necessity to you."

I thought it over. Inasmuch as the interview was ostensibly to be
with a serving-woman, and since I was not fully conversant with the
local rituals in this sort of affair, I decided that I would permit him to
go with me.

"Now, first of all," he said, "we must purchase a gift."

"For whom?"

"This woman of the Condessa's."

I shrugged, but in the end entrusted to him a little money, and
saw him off to the Baratillo, where he said jewels could be bought as
cheaply as he had obtained my sword.

That night Beltrán dined with me, and we dined well, for Zorro was,
as he had promised, an excellent cook. The rascal brought me a ring
containing a small emerald, for which he said he paid four *escudos*—
the exact amount of money I gave him, by the way—and which he
assured me would bring at least five times that in any legitimate place
of business. Though I suspected he got it for less and pocketed the
difference, the bargain was obviously good enough, so I said nothing.

After dinner he ventured to discuss our procedure of the morrow,
while Beltrán looked on, a wineglass in his hand, and his eyes dancing
with mirth.

"We must approach our problem with dexterity and flexibility," Zorro
said. "And you, Señor, must forget your French coldness and formality."

"*French* coldness?" I had to smile at that, for it has never been one
of the things of which my nation is accused.

"With all respect," Zorro continued, "there are degrees of skill in love-
making. The Englishman's wooing is a block of ice, that freezes as it
beats into submission its victim; the Italian's is hot water, sometimes
too scalding and frightening away its object; the Frenchman's is dew,
glittering but carrying little authority and apt to be flicked away as

drops too unimportant for notice; but the Spaniard's is wine, exhilarating, charming, delighting her to whom it is poured forth."

Beltrán clapped his hands with a laugh. "Bravo, my good Zorro! As eloquent a testimony to the Spanish art of love as these ears have ever heard!"

I joined in the laughter, and Zorro bowed as if he were on his beloved stage, receiving the plaudits of an audience.

"In your conversation with this Ysabel, Don Luís," he went on, "bear in mind that she is the key to our problem. Woo her, almost as if she were the one you desire. Women take pleasure even in such vicarious courtship as this. You will win her as much by your manner as by any hope of reward."

Beltrán gave a nod. "Most true, Luís," he said positively. "I see that you have an excellent preceptor. I myself can testify that Zorro is on very solid ground, up to this point at least. I confess that I am immensely diverted by the whole affair, and I hope you will not keep from me, as your friend, your progress in its successive steps."

"That I will promise you," I said. "But I have the feeling that half the city is looking on at what in my poor judgment should be conducted between two persons alone—he and she, who are most intimately concerned."

"If I had anyone to wager with," said Beltrán, "I would hazard fifty ducats, this very minute, that Doña Joya is as good as had."

3.

I was by this time so interested that I was determined to go as far with the matter as I could, if only to see where it led me.

The following morning, when Zorro and I went to Eleanora's house, we found there a woman whom I recognized as Doña Joya's companion and maid, whom the widow introduced to us as Señora Ysabel Serna.

She also, it developed, was a widow, and somewhat younger than Eleanora, though still far from young, with a face that might have been pleasing at one time, but now was faded, and lined with that expression of severity which chaperones the world over habitually assume.

While I gave her some compliments, she surveyed me closely, and came directly to the point.

"Señor," she said, "I am wax in the hands of my beloved Eleanora. She has implored me to befriend you, and because of her I would most joyfully do so, if it were in my power to make you happy. But, sad as I am to say it, I do not believe I can do anything for you."

"Would you but try?" Remembering Zorro's coaching I put into my words as much feeling as I could.

She gave her head a little shake. "If what Eleanora tells me of the state of your heart is true, I am sorry for you, Señor. I don't think you realize what you have undertaken. Assuredly it is the most difficult enterprise of your life. My mistress is a paragon of virtue, and is, furthermore, filled with pride and propriety."

I was not a little dashed, but at the moment my eye chanced to meet that of Zorro, who gave me a little smile and a lift of the eyebrows. At that I took courage.

"I beseech you, help me, Ysabel," said I, making my voice as pleading as possible. "I would rather you deceived me than deprive me of all hope!"

I took both her hands in mine, as if with emotion, and at the same time slipped into her palm the ring Zorro had purchased. She felt it, grasped it, placed it in her lap. As if looking down in meditation, she managed to get a glimpse of it by slightly opening her hands. Quite evidently pleased by it, she raised her eyes.

"I am truly affected by your unhappiness," she said.

"If you only knew how deep is my heart's anguish!" I said.

"One should never give up hope, Señor. Remember the saying: Between a woman's Yes, and her No, one cannot put a needle's point. My mistress, as I told you, is most virtuous. But after all, even virtuous women have eyes and ears wherewith to see and hear, and hearts wherewith to feel, and there be, I assure you, few honest women who are not sometimes a little weary of their trade."

"Are you telling me—there is a possibility——"

"I will say this to you, Don Luís. My mistress has her burdens to bear. Her husband, the *Corregidor,* is near to seventy while she is only twenty-six. They sleep in separate apartments, eat at different hours, and sometimes do not see each other—so divergent are their pursuits— for days at a time. I do not think there can be any passion between them, and this is sad, for she is young, and most beautiful, and at her age she cannot help being lonely."

"Ah, if I could do something to banish that loneliness!"

"I will be on your side!" Ysabel suddenly exclaimed, as if coming to a decision. Then, as if to justify herself, "I do this only because I wish for my dear mistress' happiness, and I do believe that if she had some little interest to warm her heart it would make her happy."

"You uplift me!" I cried.

After that, having thanked her most earnestly, I departed with Zorro. On the way back to our quarters, he held forth.

"An excellent beginning," he said, "and I must compliment you, Señor, on your histrionics. You might make a capital actor; although perhaps not with sufficient depth to qualify you for the heavier tragedian roles."

I smiled rather wryly to myself at being thus patronized by my servant.

"We have done the preliminary scouting, which precedes the skirmishing, which in turn precedes the battle," he went on. "Having established an agent in the camp of the enemy, we can proceed to advance against her outposts."

"Ah! And what is the next step in this Spanish plan of attack?"

"Next we serenade her."

"A serenade? Out of the question! For one thing, I am not in practice, either of voice or instrument. For another, I know no Spanish songs——"

"I do not expect you, Señor, to tinkle a guitar and sing under her window yourself. It is better if you *provide* the music. There are many voices and hands skilled in music for hire——"

"*Madre de Dios!* In another two days, it seems, all of New Spain will know of this enterprise of mine!"

"You are restive as a roweled horse, Señor," he said soothingly. "And since you are French, I understand it. But believe me, it is the way we do things here. The *caballero* gives a little concert, and shows himself so that when his lady glances out of her window—as she invariably does—she sees who it is that thus honors her."

"What about her husband, the *Corregidor?*"

"The *Corregidor* probably will be occupied at the palace with his usual game of cards. But even if he learned of it, he would consider it no more than a gallantry, and yawn over it. There is no lady of charms but has her serenades. We consider it one way of complimenting the fair—like sending her flowers, but perhaps a little more emphatic."

I knew, of course, the stylized customs of courtship so dear to the Spanish heart, but I could not help grumbling.

"I do not like it," I said. "You spoke of this as a battle: it is more

like a siege, and a protracted one at that. In France we dare the direct
assault upon the battlements. A lady has at least the right to see her
suitor face to face, and if he serenades, it is his own voice she should
hear, however bad it may be."

"I beg you to try this, Señor. Your lady will prefer it, I assure you,
since she is Spanish, not French. It will give her, moreover, a chance
to study you and come to some conclusions about you. She knows you,
of course?"

"I sometimes wonder. We have met; we have danced together."

"But she has given no hint of favor?"

"She looks through me."

"An excellent sign!" he exclaimed. "It is high time we tried the serenade."

I thought to myself, These Spaniards are wonderful!

4.

Beltrán strongly seconded Zorro. "Put yourself in this man's hands,
Luís," he said. "I could not do better myself."

So, with many reservations of mind, I began what to me was a most
curious routine: a routine in which I, who presumably was in pursuit of
the lady, did almost nothing for myself, but only looked on with increasing exasperation, while others went through their paces for me.

That night, feeling much out of place with having my *affaire d'amour*
forwarded by so many, I found myself on the street beneath a window
on the upper floor of the *Corregidor's* dwelling, which Zorro assured
me looked out from Doña Joya's boudoir.

As master of ceremonies, the tragedian first placed me where the
moon's full light fell on me, in the middle of the street. Then he arranged the musicians to one side—a guitarist, a violinist, and a tenor.
Lastly he himself took to the concealment of the shadows and gave
the signal to begin.

A love song arose. I did not sing. I stood apart, feeling a little ridiculous, but assuming as well as I could the attitude of one plunged
in hopeless melancholy, as both Beltrán and Zorro had instructed me.
There was no sign from above. When the musicians finished their little
program of two or three songs, we departed, I paid them, and Zorro
and I returned home.

By appointment, next day, I met Ysabel, but this time I did not take Zorro with me.

"How went the serenade?" I asked her.

"My mistress, I believe, was entertained," she said.

To me this had a tepid, unfavorable sound. "Did she know who it was that gave the concert?" I asked.

"I ventured to inquire if she was not curious who thus honored her, and she answered quite coldly that she had not the slightest interest."

"*Sangre de Cristo!*" I exclaimed in disgust. "It appears we have wasted both time and money!"

But at this Ysabel changed her tune, and eagerly cried out that I was too easily disheartened, and that I must remember that her mistress habitually hid her real feelings in all things.

"I happen to *know* she looked out of the window and saw you," she went on, "so she does know who serenaded her in spite of what she said. She is only dissimulating. I warned you this would be a difficult matter, but what a prize she is, Don Luís! Worth striving for!"

I grunted, still not satisfied.

"Eleanora, my love," she said, "is there in your garden a perfect rose?"

"I believe so, Ysabel."

"Then let me have it. It will be a token from Don Luís!"

I understood that the solicitude of the two women, and their eagerness to smooth over the difficulties, was because they expected, if I were successful with the lady against whom they were plotting, to receive a reward. To whet this appetite I gave both schemers a bit of money, and promised to return next day at the same hour.

I kept my word, and found Ysabel waiting, seeming quite filled with enthusiasm.

"We progress famously!" she exclaimed when she greeted me.

"Truly? Doña Joya is beginning to show some interest?"

"Of course not! What do you expect?"

"Then why——"

"Listen to what occurred. In my zeal for you, I had the temerity last evening to tell my mistress—though I was certain she knew it full well—that I had found out who gave the serenade the previous night."

"What did she say to that?"

"'I have no curiosity,' she told me. 'Many *caballeros* have expressed their passion for me in this manner, and I have never inquired further about them.' To this I said, 'But, Doña Joya, this is no ordinary *caballero*.' She looked at me. 'No? Who is it then?' she asked." Ysabel gave me a significant look. "Observe, Don Luís, this was her first sign of curiosity—and yet I am sure she is burning with curiosity, and that, knowing who you are, she is eager to hear more about you!"

I glanced at her impatiently. "Well?" was all I said.

She went on with her story. "I said, 'Why, it is that very famous stranger, who is received at court, the friend of Don Beltrán de Córdoba—the French soldier and adventurer, Don Luís de St. Denis!' At that my mistress turned on me sharply and asked if I had been peering through the lattice. I denied it, saying I would not be so bold. 'But I met him on the street today,' I told her, 'and he introduced himself to me. Ah, Doña Joya, there is not such another figure of a man in all New Spain! That face of a handsome savage! That well-turned leg! That superb height! Those shoulders!'"

"Hum!" I said, clearing my throat in some embarrassment. "And did—did she—what did she reply?"

"To be frank, she seemed vexed." Then seeing my face fall, Ysabel added hurriedly, "But I know quite well she was not! At first she said, 'Spare me these rhapsodies about a man who is of no interest to me.' But a little later she asked, 'What did he have to say to you?' There, Don Luís, you see a woman's curiosity and instinct breaking her down!"

"Continue," I said, with no change in my face.

"I told her, 'He gave me this, and besought me to tell you that he considers you loveliest of all God's creatures, that he adores you, and begs for your friendship and the privilege of speaking with you.' With that I gave her the rose from Eleanora's garden."

"She accepted it?"

"Yes, she took it, and for a moment looked at it. Then she cast it on the floor and trod on it. 'This is impertinence!' she exclaimed. 'If ever you encounter this bold fellow again, tell him to carry his caterwaulings to someone else who will think more of them than I!'"

At that I rose angrily from my seat. "Let us forget the whole thing from this instant!" I said.

But again Ysabel was all eagerness to placate me. "Not so fast!" she cried. "Keep in mind that when a woman's lips say 'It is enough,' she looks at you with her eyes, and they say, 'Again.' It is the nature of women to disdain those who love them—at first."

I hesitated. "Well, is there anything left for me to do?"

"Yes! Oh yes, indeed! You must write a letter for me to take to Doña Joya. Write it most pathetically, telling her of your anguish at her coldness, and your despair. By this she will feel triumph because she has made you suffer. Women are that way, and having made a lover suffer, they next become inclined to him. Do not be afraid to use poetic, even extravagant phrases. Vanity is on your side, so extol her beauty— a woman's beauty is her perdition, and sometimes the perdition of others."

"A letter? What if she shows it?"

Ysabel laughed. "I fear you know little of women, Don Luís. In one thing only can they be trusted—the secret of being admired."

I thought for a moment. Having gone thus far, I might as well go a little farther. So I sat down and wrote the letter as directed.

In it I did my best to put the passionate feeling Ysabel had enjoined, and my woe because I could not approach nearer to the beautiful Doña Joya. I sighed, inkily, over the divinity of her charms, and my own desolation, and all this I mingled and larded with compliments.

When I had finished, I feared I had overdone matters. No person, not even a woman, in her right senses, would accept such a sea of twaddle and believe the writer meant it. But when Ysabel read it she cried out that the letter was too cold—I must write it over, putting into it still more extravagant protestations of my undying devotion, and further apostrophes to her transcendent charms.

This time I was certain I had gone too far. But to my surprise Ysabel nodded approval over it.

"Ah, Don Luís!" she said. "You should use your pen more often in such matters as this, for indeed you have the gift of saying that which goes closest to the feminine heart!"

5.

So the matter dragged itself along, and I had the curious sensation of being on the side lines. I knew I was in pursuit of Doña Joya, and she, presumably, knew it also. Yet neither of us had spoken to the other, and I had seen her only once—at a distance—since the whole thing began. With each succeeding day I grew more and more dissatisfied with this unsatisfactory arrangement, and less convinced it would achieve anything.

But when again I saw Ysabel at Eleanora's, later in the week, she was smiling, and assured me that all was going wonderfully.

"Doña Joya not only read your letter—she kept it," she said.

"Kept it? Tell me instantly!"

"The evening after you gave me the letter, I said to my mistress—as if thinking of it by accident—that I had met you on the street. At once she asked what you said, if anything."

"Ha!"

" 'Don Luís stopped me,' I told her, 'and asked in a sad and hopeless tone if you received the rose he sent you. You may believe I was ready for him! I called him a scoundrel to his face, and told him you despised him and never wished to be reminded of him again. You should have seen him! I left him stunned by my contempt—and yours!' "

"This, I suppose, pleased your mistress."

"Not exactly. For a time she was silent, looking off into nothing. At last she said, 'I am glad you put that man in his place. But really, Ysabel, I am sorry you were so rude to him. A maid ought always to be polite to her betters.' "

"The first sign that she is relenting!" I exclaimed.

"But listen further," said Ysabel. "I answered her, 'I only followed your instructions, Doña Joya, but thinking back on it, I agree it was rather cruel, for Don Luís seemed cut to the heart. I must say, however, that he is at least constant: the feelings you have inspired in him must be very strong indeed.' My mistress gave me a quick look. 'Why, what happened?' she asked. I answered, 'He waited for me and on my way back again spoke to me, most politely apologizing. Then he handed me a sealed note, and disappeared. I glanced at it and saw it was addressed to you. Since it is, no doubt, an apology in proper form, I brought it, thinking you should have it.' "

She paused and I, all impatience, urged her to go on.

"Give me time to catch my breath!" said Ysabel, smiling at this eagerness of mine. "My mistress took the note and read it. At once I saw her face go rosy. Then she said to me, 'I am out of patience with you, Ysabel, for taking any communication from him. However, this is, as you thought, a most abject apology. The creature comes crawling for forgiveness, as he should! But such humility only increases my contempt for him. If you ever see him again, I command you to have nothing to do with him, and by no means bring me anything more from him.' "

I stared at her. "Then I suppose the whole thing is over?"

"Don Luís," grinned Ysabel, "do you not yet know that women resist in order to be conquered? Observe that she did not describe to me the *true* contents of the letter, which both you and I know! She pretended it was an apology, as I suggested to her. Furthermore, she did not throw it away. She crumpled it, as if angry, but kept it in her hand, and still had it when I left her. I will wager a new mantilla she since has read it over in secret more than once or twice. Tell a woman she is beautiful, and the devil will repeat it to her ten times!"

"If only I knew! This suspense is unnerving me!"

"We make progress, I assure you! My mistress is young and charming, with an old husband, and without love. She needs love and she needs admiration, from such a man as you. Whether or not she at present acknowledges it to herself, the need for these things will grow on her, as she ponders it—and take my word for it, she will ponder it more and more unceasingly. You must have patience and wait."

"Wait for what?"

"The next move is hers. She will say something or do something on which you must be prepared to follow your advantage."

"How will I know?"

"Am I not working in your interests? That man of yours—Zorro—he appears to be a fine fellow, and discreet. Let him be your messenger, to and from me."

"Ah, Zorro?" I gave her a look, then smiled to myself. The rogue evidently had not been idle.

This time there was no pretense by Ysabel that she was moved solely by concern for her mistress' happiness. I gave her another present of money, rather handsome this time, and promised to have Zorro keep in touch with her.

18. The Riot of the Women

I have made love to not a few women in my time, but this was the strangest of my wooings, and it was increasingly distasteful to me. My instinct is to seek the secret personal approach to a woman: subtle if possible, audacious perhaps, perhaps guileful at times, even desperate when necessary, but at least a he-to-she personal adventure for both of us.

Here, however, I had now expended almost a fortnight during which others conducted my love affair for me, and in that time I scarcely laid eyes on the object of my desires, had never spoken to her. The formality of this Spanish way left me impatient, so that I was ready to throw aside all restraints and intermediaries, and carry out my own assault on Doña Joya's citadel, boldly and directly, win or lose, as a Frenchman should.

And yet, for all of its unwieldiness, the process had achieved something for me, as I was to learn. I did not dream, however, of the explosion that was about to take place, which would bring matters to a crisis in a manner as terrible and uncontrollable as the eruption of a volcano.

I was to have dinner with Beltrán that evening, and left my quarters to go over to the palace building, when I heard outcries that caused me instead to hasten along the south side of the great structure toward the plaza, from which the sounds seemed to come.

The street down which I hurried bounded the south side of the Zócalo—the plaza—beyond the palace; and facing that great square filled with booths and huts, looking north toward the cathedral, were two stone edifices of three stories each, the municipal warehouse and just beyond it the *Corregidor's* residence, with the municipal governmental offices.

In front of the warehouse I saw a crowd of Indian women, milling about, complaining, and shouting, some of them with anger.

It was the regular practice, to which I was accustomed, for a long queue of women, carrying baskets, to form daily in front of the warehouse doors and pass before the counters where they were given corn. This was because a serious shortage of grain had occurred, due to an almost complete crop failure in the great central valley. Maize, the chief staple of the natives, was so scarce and high priced that the Viceroy ordered all supplies impounded and distributed equally to those who applied for it, hoping by careful conservation to make the corn last until more of it could be brought in from the outlying provinces.

This evening, however, the warehouse doors had been closed, and the women remaining before the building had empty baskets.

Presently, with shrill outcries and insulting remarks, shouted evidently at the officials within, the women began to disperse, streaming off in different directions, their faces sullen and angry.

Wondering what had taken place, I stopped where a number of men had gathered on the street corner, and my eye wandered to the *Corregidor's* residence beyond the warehouse, where I had serenaded Doña Joya. Just then one of the men in front of me turned toward me to leave. When I saw his face I almost gave a start.

It was the *arriero* called El Risero. He had been completely out of my mind, for I had convinced myself that he must long since have left the city with his mule train on one of his errands of transportation. But here he was: and here also was again the threat of that peril which he represented to me.

He saw me. For a moment he hesitated, then he came up to me. My first thought was an honest wish to set matters aright between us.
"I have tried to find you, El Risero," I said to him.
"For what reason?" he asked.
"For making a hasty and ill-considered remark, which I wished to explain to you, retract, and make apology for."
He looked me up and down, and I was struck once more by the bold hardihood of his face with its short beard, and his strong figure.
"The retraction and apology first," I said. "Then, if you care to hear it, the explanation."
He waited.

"In a moment of surprise I accused you of being one of the *ladrones*," I went on. "As soon as I said it I regretted it, but you left me so quickly that I could not tell you so. I now offer my regretful apology, for whatever else you may be, El Risero, I am certain that there is about you nothing dishonorable, and I make no shame in confessing that I was hasty, and ask your pardon for so offending you."

His face, which had been stern, cleared.

"Why, Señor, I thank you for this!" he said. "It is most handsome of you, and the pardon is freely given. And now that it is over, let me say I do not really blame you for thinking what you did, which is why I was not very angry with you."

"You understood what was going on in my mind?"

"To a degree, yes. You found, in the Baratillo, your own sword—I saw you examining it when your man brought it to you. A moment later you espied me, standing not thirty feet away. The connection was obvious, though wrong, for I did not know that sword was in the booth until it was brought forth."

I nodded. "That was part of my thinking. But there were also one or two other questions. As for example, why you told Herrera, the lieutenant, that you were going to Durango, when obviously you did not. And why, so very soon after, the *ladrones* pursued and attacked us. Do you not see how I was puzzled?"

For the first time he grinned. "An *arriero* knows many kinds of men, Señor. Most of them are of the lowliest orders, and there is a saying that there is no choice in a poor herd. But I do favors, and sometimes the favors are requited. I conceived the belief that you were unjustly charged that day I talked to you in Cuencamé. That the charge was a piece of spite work by a *gachupín*, Governor Anaya, gave me additional incentive to help you, for I have no love for the *gachupines*. As for your Lieutenant, there is another saying: Dress a monkey in silks and he is a monkey still. Perhaps I *did* drop a bare hint, at a place in the town where the hint might reach certain ears. And perhaps I *did* turn off— the other *arrieros* were indeed destined for Durango, and it was a convenient excuse to let your party go ahead."

"So the *ladrones*, having received the hint, took up our trail?"

"They hate the soldiers, Señor. But the understanding was that the *civilian* prisoner—which was you—should be spared. Robbed, yes—you cannot ask *ladrones* not to rob—but spared. You understand that?"

"I think I do."

"When I followed, next day—for my business really was here—I found some native men just finishing the graves. They said they had buried the soldiers and some others, including a robber or two who were killed when some of the Santa Hermandad overtook them. I asked if any of the party attacked survived, and they said no. From this I supposed that by misfortune you were dead there also. I regretted it, and came on. Then I saw you and was glad. I followed you, to inquire about you. What ensued you know."

"And am deeply sorry for."

"No matter. Words and feathers are blown away by the wind. As to anything I know of your past status, Señor, be assured that nobody will ever discover it from me."

"A thousand thanks."

For a moment we looked into each other's eyes, and our mutual liking returned.

Then his face changed, and grew dark.

"This is an evil thing here." He jerked his head in the direction of the warehouse, which had now been entirely deserted by the women.

"What happened?" I asked. "I have just arrived."

"They stopped issuing corn to the women. There will be pinched bellies in the native quarter tonight."

"Why did they stop it?"

His eyes seemed to blaze. "Because the *gachupines* have taken it all! There is none left for the poor. If I could, I swear I would destroy every dog of a Spaniard in this poor country of ours!"

With such passion did he speak that I wondered. "What reason have you for such bitterness?" I asked.

"There are many," he said grimly. "I will tell you only one, since it is a story well known, but it in itself is enough. Señor, you are looking upon a man who is the son of a *gachupín*—a most notable one, though now dead, Don César de Zúñiga, *hacendado* of a great estate in Sinaloa. There was a girl on his estate, a native girl but pretty, and just ready to marry a man she loved, when Don César saw her, took a fancy to her, and had her carried off and brought to him. He kept her as a prisoner and his unwilling mistress for three months, then tired of her and cast her out. The man she was to have married sought the life of Don César and was himself killed. The girl gave birth later to a child, a boy, begotten in her by Don César. That child, Señor, stands before you now. The girl was my mother. She died, never having had a husband, because of this wrong committed against her. Does this give you some understanding of my feeling?"

"It does, my friend," I said soberly.

"I must go, Señor," he said. "But let me say this to you: It is the hungry hound that hunts, and the populace of this city is hungry. Trouble is breeding, and I beg you to stay out of it."

El Risero strode away in the direction of the native quarter, and I, thinking deeply, turned back toward Beltrán's place of residence.

2.

That night, as I ate with Beltrán, I heard the other side of this vexed question. He was unusually silent at first, drinking more wine than was his usual custom. I respected his mood for a time, but at last asked the reason for his moodiness.

"What is it, Beltrán? Has something occurred at the palace that is adverse to you?"

"No, not that," he said.

I gave him a close look. "It has something to do with me? You hesitate to tell me? Do not fear—I am capable of hearing it."

He smoothed his short beard for a moment, then said, "I'll tell you what worries me, Luís. It's the famine. Have you noticed discontent in the city?"

"Yes," I said. I told him of the disturbance at the warehouse and something of what El Risero had said to me.

"That's it!" Beltrán exclaimed. "These people are too stupid to see what is being done for their benefit, and the exertions His Grace is going to for them. What ingrates! Dogs—cattle—swine!"

"How did things come to such a state?"

"In confidence," he said, "I fear the Viceroy himself is to blame. It is as if a strange malady has seized him, rendering him unable to act. He is caught up in a network of meshes. He fears doing anything that might incur the displeasure of the King. His age and weakness hamper him also. And his courtiers, in addition, keep him in a maze of intrigue, pulling this way and that, until he knows not where to turn. Flattery—by far the subtlest of poisons—blinds him to his best course and keeps him blind."

Beltrán paused, and looked at me seriously. "If you want the truth, the worst of them is old Don Baltasar, the *Corregidor*. He is a combination of senile inefficiency and senile guile. He will do nothing to make better the administration of the city, while he yet continues to assure the Viceroy that everything is as it should be. If there is trouble growing out of this, it is the *Corregidor*, and others like him, too occupied with their pleasures to devote time to their duties, who will be to blame. Give me a chance, I say! If I were *Corregidor* things would be different around here, I assure you! And it *could* happen! One of these days the King's council is bound to discover the inefficiency here. When it does, do not forget that the Córdobas have friends and influence in court also!" He hesitated. "But this is ridiculous," he ended bitterly. "We are faced not by a future, but by a present situation."

"Do you think there is danger of an outbreak?" I asked.

"Nobody can tell. The Viceroy keeps his subordinates, including myself, in the dark. Belatedly, he has at last sent for additional troops from Vera Cruz, but they cannot arrive here for days."

"Surely this threat is not immediate?"

"It may be. In this city are more than one hundred and forty thousand persons, of whom the vast majority are natives of Indian blood, illiterate, ignorant, addicted to the drinking of pulque, hardly ever thinking or even trying to think from one day to the next, more childish than adult in mind, but capable of great fury and destructiveness, if ever aroused and given leaders. Against these can be opposed only the palace guard—one company of infantry, less than one hundred men."

"But you yourself said the natives would have to have leaders."

"They have them. We have a considerable population of *mestizos*—of mixed white-and-Indian, or Negro-and-Indian blood. Some of these are reliable and hard-working, but among them also are criminals and others notorious for being lazy and dissolute. They are well named *léperos*—rascals. These are the troublemakers. They incite the natives to discontent by denouncing the government, and even charging that Linares is speculating in corn, withholding it from the populace until it rises in price, which simply is not true. But it is a dangerous accusation and I think the *léperos* deliberately foment an outbreak in hope that it will afford them a great chance for plunder."

"But the Spaniards? Aren't they armed?"

"Oh, of course every Spaniard of the better class has his own weapons, but they are few in comparison to the rest of the people, and they have no organization for action in time of danger."

"Then why, of all times, did they cut off the supply of corn to the women?"

"They had to. The distributors have been giving each woman only a little corn day by day, enough to support her and her family, because the supply was so small. Today the supply ran out before all could be served. With the *léperos* whispering to them that they are being discriminated against, things appear to me to be at a critical stage."

He seemed so gloomy that I sought to rally him. "I agree that it does not look too well," I said, "but cheer up, Beltrán! Is there a cloud or two in the sky? Very likely it will all clear away. The new corn supplies will shortly arrive, and with them the troops from Vera Cruz. I have seen situations that seemed worse than this which amounted to nothing. Let us have another glass of wine and talk of pleasanter subjects. Tell me what you and Doña Gertrudis have been doing lately, and I will report on the regrettably slow progress of my own suit."

But this, which ordinarily would have started Beltrán into amused conversation, did not seem to interest him now. Usually so full of quizzical advice and humorous suggestions, he did not respond.

By this I knew the gravity of the situation was perhaps greater even than he had intimated.

3.

Nevertheless, I did not expect matters to come to a head as quickly as they did. When I returned to my own rooms at the end of the evening, Zorro mentioned the trouble.

"There may be excitement at the warehouse tomorrow," he said.

I was far from apprehensive, only curious. "If so, I want to be where I can see it."

"I know the very place," he told me.

"Where?"

The tragedian smiled a smile notable for its sly roguishness. "Since you told me to keep in contact with Ysabel, the Condessa's maid, I have been improving my time somewhat."

"Truly? In what way?"

"Ysabel has conceived an admiration for my person, in which, I think, her good judgment need hardly be criticized." The rascal preened himself.

"You seem quite well satisfied with your own appearance," I said dryly.

"There are those by the hundred—nay by the thousand—who have agreed with Ysabel, when they saw me in my performances on the stage."

I smiled. "If this woman admires you, what do you think of her?"

"She is something older than perhaps I might have fancied," Zorro said, "but she has some good qualities. She is amiable, by no means cold-natured, and above all grateful."

"For what is she grateful?"

"When a woman reaches a certain age, how often does she gain a lover? There is a saying that a woman is wiser in autumn than a man in the spring, and this refers to affairs of the heart when she is in the autumn of her career. Ysabel knows enough to be thankful for the chance the good God has given her."

"I sometimes think you are a greater rogue than I knew, Zorro."

"There is another side to having a *corteja* like Ysabel, who, let us confess it, is no longer beautiful. It is an axiom that a beautiful woman is paradise for the eye, hell for the soul, and purgatory for the purse. My Ysabel, counting her good fortune, makes no demands."

I laughed. "I thank you, good Zorro, for this philosophy in cynicism. But where does all this lead?"

"To this, Don Luís. Ysabel's bedroom—in which I have spent some pleasant hours—is immediately below the sleeping apartments of her mistress, in the *Corregidor's* residence. Her window overlooks the street before the warehouse. There is a back entrance—I know it well. If I ask her I am sure she will permit us to come up and view whatever takes place from this room, for she will do anything to please me."

"There might be some danger in this."

"No, Señor. Her mistress never descends to the servant quarters. If Ysabel is not in attendance on her, she is summoned by a bell worked from a pull cord above. She will, however, probably be in attendance, leaving the coast clear for us."

"I should like such a place of vantage. But when will you arrange it?"

"Tomorrow morning. Ysabel and I have a regular meeting place. It is in the cathedral. She is very devout and attends Mass every day. I, who am not so devout, have taken to attending it also. Often she and I have schemed amorous meetings while the priests and choir solemnly chanted the ritual. I will see her there, and you shall have your point of vantage."

I suddenly snapped my fingers, with a laugh of pure exultation and joy.

"At last, at last!" I cried.

"What is it?" he asked, as if he felt an unpleasant premonition.

"Does Doña Joya also attend Mass?"

"Sometimes."

"Then if her mistress is with your Ysabel, I shall see her! For I will go to Mass with you tomorrow morning!"

"But——" Zorro sputtered a protest in consternation. "This is most precipitate——"

"Peace!" I said to him. "For half a month, my good Zorro, I have stood aside and watched the snail-slow Spanish method of conducting a love affair, which takes infinite time, goes to infinite trouble, and comes to infinitely nothing! Let us see now how a Frenchman conducts an *amour*—and I promise you that, whatever the outcome, you will at least not die of old age before something happens!"

4.

The Cathedral of Mexico is immense, its spaces so vast that three separate full services can be held in it at the same time. In the night families from the country sleep on its floors, and throughout the day penitents crawl on their faces from the doors to the foot of the main altar.

Zorro told me that Doña Joya favored one of the lesser altars in one of the apses, and next morning as Mass started, I was there with him, although he was still filled with misgivings.

It was during the *Kyrie eleison* that he nudged me. I felt a thrill of eagerness, for now that I had decided to take a direct personal hand in the pursuit to which I had so long been devoted, I began to feel a new excitement concerning it.

Two women had just entered: Doña Joya and her maid. They knelt, the servant dutifully placing a cushion for her mistress, and began going through the great measured ritual of the service.

I observed that Ysabel was on the lookout for Zorro. When she saw him, she also marked me. She must have whispered to Doña Joya, for I was sure the latter stole a glance at me under the cover of her mantilla.

Before the last Gospel I left the cathedral and was waiting at the door when the two women came out with the crowd after the dismissal.

When Doña Joya saw me, she stopped, lifting her chin.

I bowed low to her. "Most beautiful Condessa, may I speak a word with you?" I asked.

"For what reason?" she demanded haughtily. "If it is a matter of business my husband, the Conde, attends to all of that. I can think of nothing else on which I would speak with you."

She said this in a manner so lofty that I knew it was part of the armor all women assume before they are sure of the state of a man's heart. I also knew it was my task to disarm her.

So I ventured to look her in the eyes with a little smile. "I chanced to observe that you are unescorted. Have you noticed what is taking place near your dwelling?"

Her eyes followed mine across the square. During the service in the cathedral a mass of basket-carrying women had gathered in front of the warehouse, long before time for opening it, evidently fearing another shortage like that of the previous day. It was an unruly, pushing, angry mass, the women shouting and fighting among themselves, and crowding each other so that the officers in charge of the distribution were finding it difficult to make ready for it.

"If I may be so bold," I said, "a strong arm might be of service in case there was danger that such a lady as yourself might be jostled by those clamorous people."

She glanced at me from the corners of her eyes. Then she nodded. "I see what you mean. Thank you, Señor."

After her acceptance of my offer, she showed no hesitation, but walked with me across the Zócalo, through the alleys between the booths, where already a crowd was loitering to watch the happenings at the granary.

"Come up here with me, Zorro," I called. "Condessa, if you will be so good as to follow close behind, we will clear a path for you."

With little ceremony I began to do so, striding forward, pushing people roughly out of the way, Zorro beside me following my example. There were curses and objections, but we clove a way through the mob, the two women following close behind us, unmolested.

When we reached the door of the *Corregidor's* house, I gave Doña Joya another bow.

"I think you are safe now," I said.

She looked at me, then at the crowd of women. "What are they going to do?" she asked.

"I do not know. But there may be some strife here. I advise you to go within."

She turned her eyes on me again. "I must thank you, Señor," she said.

"If there are thanks, it is I who owe them to you. I am most deeply honored to be of service to one whose beauty and charm captivate every heart, including my own."

She drew herself up. "You exceed yourself, Señor."

"Do not take me wrong," I said earnestly. "That I admire you so devotedly does not mean that I do not respect you as a lady beyond all reproach. I aspire to no more than your friendship—which I most humbly beg."

She lowered her eyes. "You are a spendthrift with compliments."

"I mean them with all sincerity."

At the moment a new series of shouts arose and the crowd which overflowed from the warehouse past the front of the *Corregidor's* dwelling swirled angrily.

She drew back. "It is dangerous—isn't it?" she asked.

"Again I urge you to go within."

For an instant her eyes dwelt on me, without any change in her still face. Then she said, "You have been courteous, Señor St. Denis. Perhaps you might care—to watch?"

"The crowd? From what place, Condessa?"

"There is a gallery which immediately overlooks the street. Will you?"

"With the utmost pleasure!" I said joyfully.

"Your servant can remain in the quarters of the household staff. Ysabel, precede us."

She placed one hand on my arm, lifted the front of her wide skirts with the other, and we went together, hardly speaking, up two flights of wide stairs.

When we reached the hall above, we could hear renewed shouts in the street. For the first time her face became animated, as if she now felt the excitement she had repressed before. She turned to me.

"Come, to the gallery!" she cried, almost gleefully, and led the way, her maid following us.

5.

We came out on the balcony in time to see the beginning of the riot. Increasingly, anger and excitement had grown among the native women with their baskets. Now, suddenly, a score or more of them, led by a fierce chocolate-skinned virago, instead of waiting their turn in line, rushed forward to the granary and began trying to help themselves to the corn by reaching over the counters for it.

"Back! Get back!" shouted the officer in charge, a lean man with a deeply lined visage, who wore a tricorn hat and a sort of uniform.

His shouts were vain. The women pressed forward, almost upsetting the counters in their avidity for the grain.

All at once the officer seized a whip of thongs called a *látigo,* and began to lay about him.

Over backs, arms, and heads, indiscriminately, the whip whistled and cracked. Back shrank the women, some with the welts of the lash on their faces.

"Ah!" I exclaimed. "The whip was a mistake!"

"What else could he do?" asked Doña Joya. "The sluts deserve it!"

"You will see. They will only be doubly furious."

She was beside me, and I felt her hand as if unconsciously, take my arm. It was a tacit acknowledgment that my fortnight of courtship at a distance had borne at least this much fruit: the formality she had erected between us was forgotten in the excitement of the happenings below.

With my arm I pressed her hand to my side, and she did not withdraw it. In this intimate manner, standing very close together, we watched what followed.

"Look!" I exclaimed. "Their anger has grown hotter. They are rushing forward again!"

The virago who seemed to be the leader was shouting something to her companions, and now they pressed determinedly toward the counters. Again the whip cracked as the officer wielded it with all the strength of his arm. But now it seemed to have no effect. Sullenly, taking the lash across their backs and even their faces, the Indian women struggled to get at the corn.

"This is dreadful! What will he do?" cried Doña Joya. I was faintly surprised that her sympathy seemed almost entirely for the official, and none of it for the hungry women. But the thought soon passed.

In desperation, when his whip proved ineffectual, the man in the tricorn hat seized a walking staff, and with it began to rain heavy blows on the head and shoulders of the chocolate-colored woman who was leading, and her companions nearest her.

The act showed his panic, for its brutality could not fail to provoke the mob to its fullest wrath, with the disastrous consequences he feared.

"Oh!" cried Doña Joya, I think in horror.

A blow, delivered with all the official's might, struck the leading woman on the head. Dropping her basket, she gave a cry of pain, clutched her head in her arms, and fell to the ground.

Aghast, the other women halted. Voices rose in consternation and fury.

"María Copaña!"

"María is down!"

"Our María—she is killed by these *cabrones!*"

"Get her away from the cruelty of the accursed dog of a Spaniard!"

"Beasts! Devils! Bastards born out of wedlock of wanton mothers!"

Brown hands dragged the prostrate woman back from the doors of the warehouse. She was moaning feebly, blood running down her face.

"To the cathedral! To the holy father!" cried the voices.

In amazement we watched as the crowd of women picked up the injured María, carrying her on their shoulders, and rushed across the plaza through the aisles among the booths of the market place—a mob nearly two hundred strong, heading for the palace of the Archbishop on the cathedral grounds.

Doña Joya shivered. "They are like animals. I—am afraid," she said.

"They are only women," I soothed her. "There is not a man in that entire crowd. They cannot do much."

I did not tell her what was in my mind: that where the women are inflamed, the men soon catch the same fire.

Before the archepiscopal palace the women for a time milled about, calling for the "holy father" to come out and hear their complaints. The Archbishop, however, appeared to be unwilling to see them in their state of excitement. One of his attendants came out on a balcony above the crowd and seemed to be making an effort to appease it, but the Archbishop himself made no appearance.

"They're going to the palace now!" I suddenly exclaimed.

Balked of laying their wrongs before the Archbishop, the Indian women, still carrying the injured María, streamed over toward the doors of the great edifice on the eastern side of the plaza. No effort was made to prevent them from entering, and they filled the lower halls, clamoring to see the Viceroy. When they tried to climb the stairs, however, guards with muskets stopped them.

Thereupon, once more, the whole wild crew, hair streaming and voices raised in angry cries, rushed to the archepiscopal palace. By the time they reached it, the injured woman they carried was dead: partly from the blows on her head, but also partly perhaps from the rough treatment she had received at the hands of her own friends, in being carried back and forth, injured as she was. The women laid María on the ground and shouted for the Archbishop to come forth and see the murder that had been done by the warehouse officials.

This time I saw the Archbishop actually make his appearance, on the high balcony: a distant purple figure to us in the gallery of the *Corregidor's* residence. He lifted a hand in the sign of the cross, and some of the women below fell on their knees.

But the Archbishop was a Spaniard, one of the hated *gachupines*, and he had never taken the trouble to familiarize himself with the native patois. This made it difficult, for he had to use an interpreter. Through this intermediary he attempted to tell the women that he grieved for their sorrow; and that he had sent a message to the granary officials asking that the Indians should henceforth be treated with more consideration.

Only half understood as it was, the Archbishop's utterance nevertheless carried the prestige of his holy office, and thereafter the women dispersed for the day. I noticed that thus far not a single man had participated in the entirely female demonstration.

Throughout this disturbance, which took more than an hour of time, I had watched from the balcony with Doña Joya's hand tucked tightly in the crook of my arm, her face beside me, her interest as fascinated as was mine in the exciting scene.

When the women scattered, she at last withdrew her hand, and stepped a little away from me.

"I am glad it is over," she said. "And I must thank you again, Don Luís."

I felt a sense of pleasure at this use of my given name.

"I trust it is ended," I replied. "If there is further trouble, will you remember one thing, Doña Joya?"

Her eyes seemed to veil. "What?" she asked in a low voice.

"That I will gladly venture my poor body for your protection. Only call for me. I will be at your door at once."

"I will remember," she said, and gave me her hand.

I kissed it, and departed with the heady feeling that I had taken a long step toward what I desired.

19. *Fire and Storm*

The following morning the city appeared to be quiet, and after I rose and breakfasted, I went across the street to speak with Beltrán. There was a double guard at the rear entrance to the palace, but I was recognized by one of the sentries and permitted to enter.

Beltrán was up, sitting in a dressing gown and having chocolate, with an expression of weariness on his handsome face. When he saw me, he rose and half embraced me.

"I am glad to see you!" he said. "I was so occupied yesterday, being in attendance on the Viceroy throughout the day, that I had no chance to learn where you were or what you were doing."

"I believe I can take care of myself, my friend," I laughed.

"It is not that. I was not concerned over you, but it is good to have someone with whom to discuss matters. His Grace was greatly upset yesterday, taking a grave view of the disturbances. Last evening he ordered Don Baltasar, the *Corregidor,* to investigate the complaints of the women and punish the distributors of the corn, if they were guilty."

"What was Don Baltasar's report?"

"He treated the matter lightly—more lightly, I am sure, than it deserves. It had, you see, interrupted his écarté game in which he was then engaged in the palace lounge, and so he sent a subordinate to look into the matter. When this messenger returned, the *Corregidor* came to the Viceroy, and stated that the charges of the Indian women against the officials at the granary were false, and that it was no more than a drunken affair of the natives."

"They are not false," I said. "I myself witnessed the beating of the women, and the blows that caused the death of their leader."

"You? Where were you?" asked Beltrán.

"In the balcony of the *Corregidor's* house, directly overlooking the scene of the disturbance."

"Caramba!" my friend exclaimed. For the first time he showed mirth, slapping me on the shoulder. "You have progressed so far? And how do you find the divine Joya?"

"Charming, of course."

"I knew it! You always were a lucky dog with the women. You are to see her again, I suppose?"

"I greatly hope so. She has promised that if trouble arises once more she will send for me."

"Excellent! It is a sign that she looks favorably on you." Beltrán paused. "I hope that the trouble is over. The Duque has taken precautions. He has ordered that in the future one of the *oidores* shall be present at each distribution of corn, to make sure that complete fairness is observed. At the same time he gave instructions to the commander of the palace guard to see that the arms of the soldiers are in good order, muskets kept loaded, pikes issued, and ammunition distributed. Also that a double day-and-night guard be maintained with nobody admitted to the palace quadrangle without proper credentials. I will not conceal from you the fact that he was not a little shaken by the manner in which the women invaded the palace yesterday afternoon and tried to rush up the stairs to confront him."

Beltrán smiled fleetingly at this, and I grinned also at the thought of how the outraged women must have appalled the weak old gentleman who was the Viceroy.

"Today, however," he went on, "things seem peaceful, so much so that Linares, following his custom, will go to the convent of Santo Domingo, this afternoon, to converse with the holy fathers."

2.

I was less optimistic than Beltrán that the trouble was really ended. When he went to his duties, I returned to my quarters and called for Zorro.

"Have you a sword?" I asked him.

"No, Señor."

"But you say you can wield one?"

He hesitated. "To speak truthfully, I am skilled only in the kind of fencing that one does on the stage."

"Hum. It is possible that you may have a chance to put this stage training to a more practical use."

"You—you do not expect that we will be involved in—in any fighting?"
Zorro half stammered.

I looked at him closely. The fellow seemed to have gone slightly pale.

"I hardly think there will be any actual swordplay," I said to quiet
his fears. "Nevertheless it is well to be armed at times like these. Can
you get a weapon?"

"Perhaps."

I gave him some coins, and he went forth, returning after a time
with a short heavy cutlass, of the type coming into use among seamen
for hand-to-hand fighting. It was stiff and ill-balanced, but he seemed
well pleased with it, and wore it with all the airs of which he was
capable.

I did not go on the street until later in the day. Zorro, however, wandered forth in the middle of the afternoon on some tomcat errand, I
suppose. It was toward evening when I was startled by shouting and
some gunshots. At once I called for Zorro. He had not yet returned,
but in a few minutes I heard him running in the hall, and he burst in
with excitement.

"Don Luís!" he cried. "I have just conversed with Ysabel. The people
are threatening to riot again, and she gave me a message to you from
her mistress, saying that Doña Joya greatly wishes you to come to her."

"We go at once," I said.

It was only a few minutes' walk to the *Corregidor's* house. I had
expected to see a crowd before the public granary, but to my surprise
there was nobody there. When we cleared the palace wall, however,
and emerged upon the Zócalo, I could see where the trouble was brew-
ing. A dense mass of people had gathered among the booths of the
plaza, the sound of many voices rising, as men shouted and gesticulated.

"These are not all women today!" I said a little grimly.

The street, however, was clear, and we reached the *Corregidor's*
house, to which we were immediately admitted. With Zorro I climbed
the stairs and found Doña Joya and Ysabel waiting in the main *sala.*

I went up to her and saluted her hand. She seemed pale and
frightened.

"I came as soon as your word reached me," I told her.

"And I am glad you are here!" she said. "The Conde is gone; he was
home late last night and was recalled to the palace early. There are
only servants here, and it is a relief to have a strong arm and a sword

beside me. I hardly slept last night. Through all the dark hours I seemed
to hear the cries of those women. This afternoon it seems worse than
yesterday. Oh, *what* is going to happen to us?"

"Nothing, perhaps," I said. "What has created this new excitement?"

"Tell him, Ysabel." She looked to her maid.

"There is a complete failure of supplies at the warehouse," Ysabel
said. "As I understand, only about five hundred *fanegas** were received,
hardly a drop in the bucket for so large a populace. When this was
known, it caused a rush by the native women, each trying to be first,
and in the wild milling one of them stumbled, or fainted, or otherwise
fell to the ground, being trampled by the crowd of women until she
was severely injured. Up to that time the men had refrained from taking
any part in the disturbance, because by Indian custom only the women
carry the corn and they only went to the warehouse. But now the men
at last took a hand. One of them carried the hurt woman on his back
out into the plaza, where he laid her down. They are there now, and
some of them must have firearms, for we heard shots."

"Probably only to vent their anger," I said. "Let's take a look."

Once more we stood in the balcony. In the plaza I saw the dense
crowd of angry natives gathered about the injured woman and the man
who had carried her there. He was displaying her, shouting a loud
harangue.

I gave an exclamation. "That is no native! I know that man!"

"Who is he?" asked Doña Joya, beside me.

"An *arriero* I once met."

The man who had carried the woman from the warehouse to the
plaza, and was now proclaiming that her hurts had been caused by
Spanish tyranny, was Hipólito Terraza, him they call El Risero. I remembered his hatred of the *gachupines,* and his reason for it. If the
natives lacked a leader, I suddenly thought, they had one now in him.
And knowing him I said to myself that this might turn out far worse
than I had thought.

"He is a *mestizo,* with great courage and considerable capacities," I
added. "He will bear watching, that one!"

Zorro gazed at the threatening mob, obviously impressed.

"What animals!" he said. "Will they turn against us, do you think,

_____
* A *fanega* equals about a bushel and a half

Don Luís? There seem to be a great many of them, and they appear to be in a most unpleasant humor."

"Perhaps their noise is less dangerous than it sounds," I answered. "They may content themselves with gestures and yells. If we stay where we are, I do not think they will disturb us. What, did you not tell me you were a two-bladed sword of a man, Zorro? Are you afraid of these people?"

I said this more to quiet the fears of the women than for the benefit of Zorro. But as he listened to my assurances, the tragedian grew visibly more erect, his chest puffed out, and his voice strengthened.

"Fear them?" he said. "Who speaks of fear? It is most fortunate for those savages that they do not have to brook my fury! Were my violence aroused I would tremble for them! I would teach them a lesson they would not forget!" He gave a look at Ysabel and struck an imposing attitude.

"You need not deny yourself that satisfaction," I suggested slyly.

"What is that, Señor? What do you mean by that?" Zorro gave me an uneasy side glance, as if to read a hidden meaning in my words.

"If you have some deed of desperate valor to perform," I said, "and really want to teach those people a lesson, I am sure if you descend to the plaza you will be accommodated, for the poor ignorant creatures are not aware that we have with us such a champion at arms."

Zorro blanched slightly. "No. No, Señor. I—I have no personal resentments against them. It—it would only be cruelty—for me to launch myself on them. I will spare them."

With this magnanimous declaration he stepped back against the wall. Ysabel gave him a glance of some contempt.

But already a new alarming development in the plaza turned our attention that way. As if to give endorsement to El Risero's declamation against the Spaniards, the poor woman on the ground at his feet gave a last whimpering cry and died.

It was like a signal. The woman's friends took her off, but now the blood of the mob was up. Across the plaza it charged, overturning some of the booths as it went, the figure of the *arriero* at its head, and on its outskirts, here and there, the furtive *léperos* egging the natives on.

The doors of the palace were this day closed and barred. Before them the crowd formed thickly, uttering threatening shouts, some of their insults hurled directly at the Viceroy, who was supposed to be in the palace, although at the moment he was some distance away, being still at the convent of Santo Domingo.

I learned later that the Duque was at prayer in the convent church when the tumult arose outside. He got up from his knees and hastily went to the rear of the church. But as he was preparing to return to the palace, a terrified friar came running in, saying that the streets were filled with rioting natives who were armed and threatening. At this the Dominican fathers prevailed on Linares to remain where he was, in the convent, believing that the natives were in such profound awe of them —since the Dominicans represented not only the Church but the Inquisition—that they would hardly desecrate the place, which turned out to be the truth. Because of this, however, the Viceroy was absent from the palace throughout the great uprising that followed, which was the reason why such confusion and lack of decision was displayed by the authorities, for none had the official right to take his place in issuing commands or deciding on plans of action.

Meantime the yells and shouts of the crowd before the palace grew louder and more threatening. All at once stones began to fly, hurled at the building, smashing windows and splintering wooden balconies.

"Oh, look—the soldiers!" cried Doña Joya, who was by my side.

On the roof of the palace a squad of the guard appeared.

"Are they going to fire on the crowd?" I asked, more to myself than to her. She did not reply, standing fixed, her eyes wide as she watched the drama before her.

I saw, rather than heard, the officer in command give an order, my soldier's eye marking the way he stiffened and threw back his head at his shout, although the uproar of the mob drowned the sound.

His men brought their muskets to their shoulders and at another command a cloud of smoke burst forth from the guns, with the multiple reports of a small volley.

Now the mob displayed the customary cowardice of mobs. Back, back it swirled, leaving some of its members prostrate and writhing on the ground, and retreating in panic to the Baratillo or the cemetery of the cathedral.

"Those men have been shot!" exclaimed Doña Joya, gazing at the figures on the ground. But I shook my head.

"No," I said. "That volley was without balls—of gunpowder only. It was to frighten the crowd, nothing more. Those people you see were knocked down and injured in the flight. See, some of them are getting up already, and limping away. The others will soon discover that no real ammunition was used against them. Look—there is one who did not flee!"

One man stood alone before the palace in the space the others had left vacant. El Risero sturdily refused to run. Now he was beckoning his fellows to come back. As quickly as I, he had understood the harmless nature of the volley fired by the soldiers.

"That man is more dangerous than all the other thousands behind him," I said seriously.

Already, indeed, as the mob realized that the shots were harmless discharges, it began to surge back to where the *arriero* stood. And gaining confidence, again in the manner of all mobs, it interpreted the failure of the palace guard to use musket balls as a further sign of weakness on the part of the authorities.

I could hear some of the yells and cries:

"Death to the Spaniards and *gachupines!*"

"Death to those who have all the corn and are killing us with hunger!"

And with these threats more personal:

"Death to the *Corregidor!*"

"Death to the Viceroy and all who defend him!"

It was now half past six o'clock in the evening, and though hardly thirty minutes had elapsed since the rioting began, the plaza was filled with the populace. I estimated that not fewer than ten thousand persons, mostly natives, surged back and forth among the booths, always spurred and encouraged by the stealthy *léperos* who moved among them, giving them new outcries to shout, mouthing new grievances, fanning new hatreds.

And in that whole mass perhaps one man alone had any clear idea of what he was doing. I believe that El Risero, in his burning hatred of the Spaniards, that day thought the time had come when the downtrodden people could overwhelm and destroy their oppressors, a revolt which, if successful in the capital might spread throughout New Spain. And though he had behind him nothing in the way of an organization, but only a chaotic mass of men who, angry as they were, still hardly knew the full extent of what was happening, he managed to rally them into some sort of cohesive action by sheer force of his personality. That day, although I was against him and his purpose, I admired in my heart the manhood of the great *arriero*.

3.

At this moment began an episode which showed how really ugly the situation had become.

The doors of the cathedral suddenly opened, and from it issued a procession: acolytes, censers, priests, choristers, and the Archbishop himself, with his ecclesiastical attendants, canopied and robed, with all the sacred symbols of crosses and images to impress the populace. Belatedly the Church had decided to intervene in an effort to restore order.

Watching from the balcony I saw the faces of the great crowd turn toward the advancing procession. I had observed the devoutness of the natives here, displayed at times in ways almost extravagant, such as lengthy prostrations, the penitent covering considerable distances by progressing each time only the length of his body, until he reached the doors of the cathedral and at length the foot of the altar. The passing of a robed priest or monk was enough to make every person in sight bow his head, the men removing their sombreros in reverence.

"If anything will quiet that mob, this is it," I said to the woman at my side.

"Surely they will listen to the holy father," she said, as if prayerfully.

Onward advanced the procession, the Archbishop on foot beneath his canopy, uplifting a cross in his hand, while before him went his high cross-staff, with the crucifix turned so that he faced it as it preceded him.

For a moment the crowd quieted, as if undecided what it should do in the presence of so sacred a demonstration.

Then came a high, loud yell:

"They are *gachupines* too!"

It was the voice of El Risero, and the cry came at the exact moment to crystallize the mob's spirit. Instead of prostrating themselves, men began to seize stones and other missiles and hurl them at the procession, meanwhile yelling and advancing menacingly.

A robed priest went down just in front of the Archbishop, struck on the head by a stone. Others winced from less serious blows.

It was too much for the priesthood. To a man, including the Archbishop himself, they turned and ran in undignified panic back to the cathedral, kirtling up their robes about their legs to give them greater speed, and losing all semblance of rank or precedence in their race for the doors of the great church. The injured priest, who scrambled to his feet after the others fled, was the last to arrive. As soon as he was inside, the great cathedral doors were slammed shut and presumably barred.

Up to the very entrance surged the crowd. But this was as far as it went. No desecration was committed on the building, and no effort was made to force the doors.

"Luís—this is sacrilege!" cried Joya at my side.

I noticed that in the terror and excitement of the events we were witnessing, she had as if unconsciously begun to speak to me intimately by my first name, dropping all formal titles of address.

"That was a bad sign, Joya," I said, taking her hand to reassure her as much as I could, and she permitted me to keep it.

Having chased the Archbishop and his retinue into the cathedral, the mob was returning to the palace in a dark threatening mass.

Once more stones and other missiles, including arrows, began to rain on the building, which already had sustained some severe damage.

Suddenly I saw the front portals open, and a platoon of the guard filed out, led by Captain Rodríguez himself. They formed in a line before the portal.

"I warn you to stand back! Disperse!" shouted the Captain.

The crowd, its clamor momentarily subsiding, allowed him to be heard clearly. But, encouraged by its numbers, it began at once to press forward.

"This time we will shoot to kill, using lead!" cried the Captain.

I nodded approval. "It is time for soldierly action," I told Joya. "Otherwise the mob will get out of hand worse than it has."

The soldiers brought their muskets to their shoulders. At this some of the crowd who were in front, began struggling to retreat from those menacing leveled gun barrels. Behind them, however, the pressure was too great, and whether they wished it or not the persons in the forefront were borne forward toward the line of soldiers.

"*Tiran!*" ordered Rodríguez. But the roar of the mob now was so loud, that only his soldiers, and those of the crowd who were nearest him heard it.

The long, rippling crash of the volley thundered out, and the front of the line of troops was hidden by powder smoke.

Real terror now took such possession of the front ranks of the crowd that they actually forced those behind them to recede for a moment. But in another moment it was again noticed that nobody had been wounded.

"The Captain ordered that volley fired over the heads of the rioters!" I exclaimed. "Now, why did he do that? It is exactly what he should not have done! If he fired at all, he should have done execution!"

Joya gave a little wail and clung to my hand.

I was only too right. Instead of being routed, the mob was now visibly encouraged by the second discharge which proved harmless. Upon the soldiers who were desperately trying to reload their muskets, the populace rushed, howling, led by El Risero.

Loading the cumbersome firearms required time, and before they could be recharged, several soldiers were on the ground, felled by stones or arrows, and the rest were in full flight for the shelter of the palace.

"Those poor fellows—they are shut out!" cried Joya.

The doors of the palace had been opened to admit the soldiers, but as the crowd approached they were shut again. Not all the soldiers succeeded in getting within. Those who were shut out beat on the doors with their fists, imploring that they be admitted, but their pleadings were not heard, or else were ignored.

In another moment the mob had swirled over them, clubs and knives rising and falling. Every man who was shut out, including those wounded in the bombardment of stones and arrows, was murdered mercilessly.

I turned to Joya and found her staring in half-hypnotized horror.

"I think you had better go within," I said to her. "See that all the doors and windows are securely locked, the shutters closed. There is no telling what may happen next."

"Will they attack this place?" she said.

"If they do, we will do our best to defend it," I answered her.

She gave me a look and went within with Ysabel and Zorro. I remained for the time being on the balcony watching the terrible drama that now developed.

Wild with triumph and fury the rioters raged about the palace, smashing everything possible; thundering against the doors with logs used as battering rams; some few, having taken the muskets of the slaughtered soldiers, experimenting with discharges from those weapons.

None of this was effective. The building was of stone, provided with loopholes for musketry and embrasures for cannon—of which there were none. Its doors were of heavy timber, reinforced with iron and strongly barred, its windows heavily shuttered and defended with gratings of wrought iron. The palace was, in a word, a fortress, and with resolution could be defended.

But to my amazement resistance within seemed almost nothing. Not a shot was fired from the loopholes. Yet the thick stone walls of the edifice were in themselves a defense difficult for men without siege weapons to break into.

I looked for El Risero, and after a moment I picked him out. He had withdrawn from the aimless surging about the palace, and was talking most earnestly with a few men he had gathered about him.

In a moment I saw what he was proposing. There was a rush for the nearer booths in the plaza, which were constructed of the most combustible materials. Carrying the debris to the palace, the men heaped it in front of the doors and set it ablaze.

The doors were to be burned down!

Fires leaped up, flaring furiously, and I saw that it would go hard with those inside the beleaguered palace.

But at this moment a diversion occurred that immediately occupied the interest of the crowd to such an extent that the defenders were able to open the doors and scatter the blazing debris, quenching the flames.

4.

Up to now El Risero had, by his almost unaided efforts, managed to give some sort of cohesion to the movements of the rioters. Had he kept his leadership the result for which he hoped—the destruction of the *gachupines* and other Spaniards—might have been brought to pass. That he did not keep the leadership was no fault of his.

The diversion which took matters out of his hands was caused by the *léperos,* who found that what they had been waiting for at last had arrived: the opportunity for plunder.

While the doors of the palace were being fired under the direction of the *arriero*, some members of the crowd had gone to the other end of the plaza, and built a blaze about the foot of the gallows and pillory, as a gesture of resentment at these symbols of oppression. And this precipitated the remarkable event that followed.

Sparks from the burning gibbet and platform, carried by a slight wind, set one of the nearer stalls of the Baratillo section in flames. As if this were some sort of a signal, a scene ensued which I found it hard to believe was occurring before my eyes.

It was now between seven and eight o'clock in the evening and darkness had fallen, yet almost in a moment the whole great plaza flared up in a tremendous conflagration that made every object stand out as if it were day.

"To the stalls!" came the cry.

Into the market place surged a sea of humanity, attacking first the booths where cutlery was sold, and snatching from them knives, machetes, and iron bars to use as clubs, and for prying open doors or windows.

With that the flood was loosed. Chaos came!

Friend or foe, innocent or guilty, man or woman, there was no difference now. Robbery and rape, fire and blood—the people became maniacs of greed, lust, death, and destruction. Dying men groaned and women shrieked as they were borne away by ravishers. Falling structures crashed, flames leaped skyward in great showers of burning sparks. In the lurid light the furtive figures of the looters could be seen flitting in and out among the still unburned booths, or disappearing into the dark streets and alleys of the city, laden with plunder.

Now began one of the most incredible aspects of the riot, some of which I observed myself from my vantage point, and some of which was described to me later. Mixed in the rabble were many of the owners of stalls, who did not dare openly protect their merchandise and other property, yet were unable to look on with indifference as it was swept from them. Merchants yesterday, they became robbers now: and they might as well rob themselves as be robbed by their comrades!

They joined, therefore, in the attack on their own stalls, being sometimes first to enter and if possible seize and carry to a place of safety some of their own property. Others, pretending to be resigned at being despoiled, seemed to encourage the pillage of their stalls: after which they stealthily followed the plunderers, and as soon as they were alone with them in a dark street away from the plaza, by a sudden blow or deadly thrust, not only left the robbers in bloody death, but relieved them of their loads.

Save for these hundreds of looters, most of the crowd of thousands for a time seemed almost hypnotized by the sight of the spectacular conflagration in the plaza, staring at it silently, or leaping and howling like apes at the scene of destruction, but otherwise doing little.

One sight I saw which I will not forget. Standing alone, illuminated by the light of the flames, was a figure that I thought tragic. El Risero, having lost control of the mob, was gazing at the spectacle of insane and senseless destruction, with his head bowed like that of a man in profound dejection. He knew he had failed. For a moment he stood thus, then with a gesture of despair, he left the plaza, walking rapidly away and disappearing into the city.

Shortly after that, the rioters seemed to remember again the objects of their hatred.

Standing high in my balcony I heard a cry fraught with menace that all at once became intensely personal to me.

"The *Corregidor!*"

I saw the crowd turn, and rush roaring toward the house from which I was watching. Now I at last stepped within, shut the doors to the balcony, barred them, and hurried to the room where Joya, her maid, and Zorro were peering in terror through the shutters.

Joya turned to me, her face white. "They're coming—for us!" she cried.

And at the same time Zorro exclaimed, "Look! They're bringing wood to set fire to this house!"

"Calm yourselves," I said. "This structure is of stone like the palace and will not yield to ordinary fire. They intend to burn through the doors. But we may prevent that. Meantime, stay away from the windows—"

The crash of a heavy rock hurled against the wall gave point to the words, and Joya and the two servants shrank away.

I ran down the stairs, and found some servants gathered in a frightened little knot in the hall. Blows and the thudding shocks of logs smashing against it resounded from the door. Then I heard another sound—the rustle and rattle of dry palm fronds, sticks, and *tulés* from some of the booths which had thus far escaped the general holocaust, being heaped outside to be set afire.

At one side of the door was a small peephole, and I looked through this. Outside I saw a black mass of people, a torch suddenly illumining savage brown faces. Then I saw a fiercer, brighter glow as the heap of combustibles was set ablaze.

"Come help me!" I called to the servants. "We must thrust open the door and throw that burning mass away!"

They cowered back against the wall of the hall, too terrified to obey.

All at once I heard a new yell outside. Gazing through my small opening, I saw a rush. Someone in the mob had discovered the *Corregidor's* coach and mules. There were shouts and jubilant outcries. A moment later the coach appeared in my orbit of view, with the mules hitched to it. Men crowded about it, cramming it with straw and palm fronds. In a moment this mass was set ablaze, and the coach driven out into the plaza, the mules galloping without a driver.

Yells, laughter, the mad outcries of the bull ring rang out as the poor beasts, wildly affrighted, dashed about the plaza. Followed by their blazing equipage, the mules sought repeatedly to escape from the flames, but each time they were driven inward by the crowd that surrounded the plaza. At last, in sheer wild panic, they bolted toward the very heart of the vast conflagration, and disappeared, perishing in the incandescent flames of the burning stalls.

But meantime, by bullying, almost beating them, I managed to get the help of three or four of the *mozos* in the hall. Together we unbarred the door, and by main strength thrust it outward.

Too occupied with the spectacle of the frightened mules and their flaming coach to interfere with us, the crowd hardly noticed that we pushed back and scattered the blazing heap of kindling outside the door. Water quenched the places where the woodwork was burning. Then we shut the door and barred it again.

I turned and looked about the hall.

On the stairway, gazing down at me, her hand at her throat, stood Joya, with Zorro and Ysabel behind her.

"Something must be done!" I said. "If they return—and they will—there will be no second good fortune to save us!"

5.

Thus far I had watched the terrible spectacle of violence in a manner curiously aloof, as if I were an onlooker not personally involved in it, rather pitying the people and hardly blaming them for their behavior. But their excesses, capped by the cruelty of the burning of the mules, suddenly changed all this to anger.

"Is there a back exit from this place?" I demanded.

Some of the servants nodded, and mutely pointed.

"Luís—are you—going to desert us?" asked Joya, almost in a whimper, as if she believed her last hope was gone.

"No, I am not leaving you!" I answered. "But I hope to do something to save you—all of you!"

I looked at Zorro. "You have a cutlass. Come with me," I commanded.

He came down the stairs, going pale but not daring to disobey, and stood beside me. A moment later the two of us were in the walled patio at the back of the massive building, shielded from the great leaping illumination in the plaza by its bulk. None of the rioters had as yet reached the rear of the structure.

I felt suddenly a spark of a different excitement, almost happiness. Here was action at last! Battle, perhaps—danger—even death were just around that dark corner. It was as if a great breath of cold, clear, fresh air had been taken into my lungs long accustomed to breathing only the warm, enervating atmosphere of passiveness and stagnation.

We left the patio by a gate, and by an alley reached the street.

"Who are those?" I asked suddenly.

Clustered together beside the wall, a dark group of men was gazing out into the flaming plaza.

Then I saw. These were Spaniards, gathered together and watching, all armed, yet inactive simply because there was nobody to lead them.

I drew my sword, and a moment later was among them.

"*Caballeros!*" I cried. "Has your courage failed you? It is time these curs were punished!"

Faces turned to me, at first surprised, then growing attentive.

"What has happened to the Spanish steel of heart and blade that conquered a thousand times its numbers of infidel dogs in this very city under the heroic Cortés?" I continued. "Have you lost the bravery of your fathers? No, by the Crucified! I can never believe it!"

In the light of the roaring flames of the plaza I saw their faces grow stern, their hands fall on their sword hilts.

"What are we waiting for?" I cried. "*Adelante!*"

The shout seemed to galvanize them. Out came swords, like slivers of light, and forward we moved as if we were one.

Having completed its amusement with the mules, the mob came roaring back to the *Corregidor's* house. But suddenly we burst from the throat of the dark street, a compact little body of men, charging directly at the center of the oncoming mass.

I was in the lead, and I was glad that my sword was a soldier's cut-and-thrust weapon, instead of the rapier of the courtier, which has no edge but only a point, and loses advantage in a melee.

Among my Spaniards were some pistols and a musket or two, and from these shots crashed out. This time the flying balls did not not go over the heads of the mob, but directly into its thickest numbers, bringing down men where every leaden missile struck.

Behind me somebody raised the old war cry of the *Conquistadores:* "*Cristo y Santiago!*" and the swords began to play.

That night I fought in a white fury, slashing right and left through the ruck, like a man with a scythe. Indians, half-breeds, outlaws, robbers, murderers—whoever they were—none was as tall as I, or with such a reach, or impelled by such rage.

Behind me came the Spaniards. The Spaniard is proverbially brave: it is the national virtue of his race. And these Spaniards were stirred to a peak of fury and hatred almost mad, by the events of the past hours. They were willing to die, desired to die, almost prayed to die, if dying each could take with him his full quota of foes. And men who go into combat welcoming death as if it were a lover have a certain advantage over men to whom death is a horror to be shunned and fled from.

We were few in comparison with the hordes confronting us, but all of us were skilled with the sword, whereas our enemies were armed with knives, clubs, a few spears, and a few captured guns which they hardly knew how to load or shoot. In a wedge we fought, I at the apex, the Spaniards following, and we hacked and hewed a path of blood, like a scythe through grain, leaving the dead and dying scattered behind as we clove our way deep into the crowd.

I remember, in that hour, that I felt that I could have carved those human brutes before me with a dagger or a club, with a flail or a whip. As it was my arm wielded a sword that whistled through the air, then went more quietly through the flesh.

Into the very heart of the mass our charge carried us. The fight became a rout, a butchery. Retreating before us, the mob found itself running into the volcano of flame it had itself created in the plaza. With that it scattered, and in utter panic flight streamed off on each side before our wedge of swordsmen who knew no wish but to kill.

It was then that I called a halt and wiped my blade. The rioters were gone: melted like mist before the first display of resolution and real resistance they had met. And the tragedy was that such resolution and resistance would have cowed them in the very beginning as it had cowed them now, and would have saved that whole day of terror and destruction.

My Spaniards gathered about me, as I glanced back. The trail of huddled prostrate forms we had left reached all the way back to the *Corregidor's* house, marking the wake of our storm through the mob with our avenging swords. Some few moaned or twitched, but for the most part the slashing blades had done their work so well that the fallen lay silent and stiffening.

"How many of us are down?" I asked.

A quick count.

"Don Tomás is not here."

"I do not see Camado."

"Julio! Where is Julio?"

So went the calls and questions.

Perhaps a half dozen had fallen out of the thirty who began the charge.

"I do not see my man, Zorro," said I. "I gave him a sword, but the best Toledo blade cannot make a hero out of a coward. He seems to have had no stomach for this fight."

The riot was over, the rioters dispersed. I led the way back toward the *Corregidor's* house, my men looking at the prostrate bodies, seeking their friends. One after another these were found, two dead, the others hurt but living.

All at once I halted beside one prostrate form.

"Zorro!" I cried.

He lay with a great gash in his breast, from a spear thrust. Beside him was the cutlass he had carried, and I saw it was stained with blood. So Zorro had not been a coward after all.

I knelt and lifted his head, but already the stricken man was far on his journey, looking out on another world with the strange astonished glance of death.

"Help me!" I implored.

It was but a little way to the *Corregidor's* house, and two of the Spaniards assisted me in carrying him there, where we laid him on a bed.

"Is there a priest?" I asked.

There was none.

But poor Zorro was past this in any case. He died, without effort and with a simple dignity that was better, perhaps, than any of the "beautiful deaths" of which he had been so proud on the tragic stage.

6.

As I pulled a sheet over Zorro's face, I saw Ysabel at the door.

"He is—dead?" she asked.

I nodded. "A good death. A brave death!"

"No death is good!" she wailed. And she knelt beside him weeping, calling over and over his name to ears that heard her not.

I left her with him, and went out into the hall. There, again on the stair, was Joya, white as if the emotions she had undergone had drained her for the time being of blood.

She held forth a hand. "Luís——"

Slowly I mounted the steps to where she stood, and lifted the soft fingers to my lips.

Then together we went to the floor above, her own apartments.

"I watched you," she said, almost in a whisper. "Through all that dreadful battle—lit up by the terrible glare of the fire—I watched you only! My heart was in my throat every minute! How you slew them! You were braver than any man I have ever known—more terrible——"

I was too weary to respond.

In her own room she brought me a basin, and into it poured water from a silver ewer. Then she stood beside me with a towel, while I cleansed myself of the blood and grime, attending me as if in duty bound.

After that she gave me wine. I drank, and the strength seemed to flow back into me.

I looked at her. She seemed to me all at once very desirable, half leaning against the wall, her hands behind her, her body curved at the hips, her bosom half exposed under the lace of her bodice, her brows so delicately arched, the blond richness of her hair.

In all that terrible day no word had passed between us of love. No word, indeed, had ever yet been spoken between us formally of that which was in my mind.

But now I set down my wineglass and walked over to her. She half shrank, her eyes falling, but I took her hands from behind her and compelled her to look at me.

"Joya," I said, "it is now—or never."

Suddenly all shrinking ceased. She lifted her head, and gazed into my eyes with a look of such reckless, almost desperate passion, as to make my heart skip a beat.

"Luís—it is now . . ." she said.

20. *Women: of the Flesh, and of the Soul*

I do not know that I would ever have succeeded with Joya had it not been for the riot, the fire, the danger, and the violence of that night. Is there some hidden chord in women on which cruelty and death play, arousing in them a special kind of lust? Or is it some blind female instinct to recreate the race when they see many men die? I only know that at such a time some women seem to lose all ruth or scruple, and forget every restraint.

I think Joya's instincts were excited by the terrible explosion of events; and perhaps by the way I came to her after the fight in the street, still bloody, sweating, and with my eyes still flickering with the flame of battle. Her nature for that hour craved me, a combination of ecstasy, and cruelty, and fear allayed; with a fervency that proved to me the saying that when a Spanish woman unleashes her passions, it is like a storm, wild and fierce as a cataclysm of the elements.

She even expressed something of this to me, once during the night as she lay in my arms, and looked at the red shifting lights cast on her window by the fire raging in the plaza.

"You have had me as if I were a woman of the streets," she said. "As if I were one of those women who were carried away screaming to be ravished by the rioters; had me as if I were a *puta*, a bought woman, or as if you raped me; had me shamelessly, with lust, with force, and with triumph. And this is the way I wanted it tonight!"

She spoke half musingly, as if putting it thus into words gave it some secret added savor, and for some reason it repelled me to hear her speak in a manner so abandoned. Then I excused her in my mind with the thought that she was beside herself with the excitement, and hardly knew what she said; and after all, she was assuredly most choice. . . .

I spent the most of that night with her, in the enjoyment of her enhanced by the luxury of her own bed with its perfumed sheets.

It astonished me that the old Conde did not in all that time return to his residence. But when I spoke of this to Joya, she laughed.

"Probably he is afraid to come home, in the night and with the city in uproar. As for me, his wife, I am sure he has hardly thought of me. Don Baltasar is an old man, Luís—too old for any woman. His age enables him to regard me with feelings almost completely detached, as if I were a puppet, playing out some sort of a farce for him. Even if he knew of it, I do not think he would grudge me my game here with you in this bed, so long as it did not become an open scandal that would reflect on him."

I was inclined to share this conclusion of hers: but later I found that we had hardly been fair to the *Corregidor*. In the absence of the Viceroy from the palace, he had thought it his duty to remain there, sitting in an informal junta, or council, made up of such responsible officials as were present, to try to deal in some manner with the crisis confronting them.

Toward morning I left Joya for more than an hour, because a fire, spreading from the municipal warehouse which was now in flames, had gotten into the eastern wing of the *Corregidor's* building—that part of it given over to the municipal offices and archives. I directed the servants, forming bucket lines and removing documents and records to places of greater safety. Before we quelled the flames this part of the edifice was severely damaged, but at least we kept the blaze from the residential wing.

When, after this last interruption, I returned to Joya, she was up and dressed in a silken wrap, and the house was so full of smoke that we coughed and wiped tears from our eyes. Windows and doors must be opened wide to allow fresh air to come in, and love-making was therefore ended for us by necessity. But by this time we had both slaked our fever, and since I had made sure no further danger threatened her, she kissed me and I left her to go out on the street.

It was now near to four o'clock in the morning. I saw smoke rising in billows high above the roof of the northern wing of the palace, nearest to the cathedral, and the windows of that portion of the great building were luridly red from flames within. Many men, including soldiers in uniform, were fighting that fire, which had broken out because of sparks from the plaza, and I went there to help.

I did not sleep that night. Throughout the dark hours bands of armed Spaniards patroled the streets, while efforts continued to bring under control the conflagration in the palace building, and also in some of the smaller structures about the plaza. Toward dawn I encountered Beltrán, in command of one of the patrols. He looked worn and weary.

"What a horrible night!" he exclaimed. "If you will believe it, Luís, the confusion and terror in the palace should have shamed any Spaniard. It was I who suggested sending the soldiers forth against the mob. And I was sorry I did so, for after the council decided on this, the members grew so fainthearted that they ordered the men to fire over the heads of the mob! What poltroonery! I begged that they be allowed to shoot into the crowd—otherwise it would be an empty gesture. I offered to lead the guard myself. But I, a mere *ayudante*, was overruled, for the council attempting to order affairs in the absence of the Viceroy was composed of men of the highest rank like the *Corregidor*, the supreme judge, the chief *Oidor*, and others of the kind. So they sent the soldiers out to be massacred—a senseless, useless sacrifice of those poor men!"

"I saw it," I said.

He gave me a look. "But you, Luís—I have heard about you!"

"Concerning what?"

He laughed. "Do not stand there looking as if you did not know hay from straw! Your friends, whom you led in that charge on the mob, have not been exactly silent about your exploits. No empty display of arms by you, was it? From their telling you were a combination of Roland, Bayard, the Cid, and Death himself!"

"Oh, that," I said, with some relief, because for the moment I actually thought that the report of my night with Joya was abroad. "You know enough of men who are excited and filled with enthusiasm to discount what they say, Beltrán. Among those of us who fought there was no choice. If there was a hero, he was my servant, Zorro, who though he was afraid, fought bravely and died fighting."

"You are too modest always, my friend." Beltrán smiled. "It was the crucial stroke that broke the mob and saved the whole city, perhaps, from destruction. But we'll talk about it in the morning. Breakfast, say? In my rooms, since you tell me your servant is gone—and too bad it is, for he was above all things amusing. Now I must be on my way again with this endless patrol."

I nodded and returned to the palace fire, which was now nearly quelled.

So passed the night.

2.

The sun rose upon a mass of smoldering ruins in the plaza, and upon the bodies of the dead, which lay scattered among bundles of loot that had been dropped by the mob in its flight. All the fires about the Zócalo were out, but the wing of the palace in which the records were kept was badly damaged, the flames progressing so far back that before they were quenched, the barracks of the palace guard had to be evacuated and the prisoners released from the jail, for safety. Later, however, the soldiers were able to return to their quarters.

I breakfasted with Beltrán, neither of us having closed our eyes; and a haggard, smoke-stained, unshaved, weary pair we were.

"The Viceroy, who remained in the Dominican convent throughout the night, returned to the palace this morning," he said.

"Is there any report of the regiment from Vera Cruz?" I asked.

"I do not know. But I think present danger of rioting is over. A large *conducta* of wagons laden with corn is approaching the city from Cholula and more is on the way. Distributions start again at once. With their bellies full, the people will be less restive. The patrols must continue, of course, until the troops arrive from Vera Cruz."

I nodded, remembering El Risero's words, *It is the hungry hound that hunts.*

"Meantime, there is news," Beltrán went on. "We have a count of the casualties. More than a hundred persons are dead, including the soldiers who were massacred, and the rioters who were killed by you and your Spaniards in your fight last night. Many others are injured, either by wounds, or burns from the fire. Prisoners are being brought in. One in particular, the ringleader of the uprising, has been apprehended. He was denounced—by a traitor among the very people he had been leading—and was arrested as he tried to escape from the city this morning. He gives his name as Terraza. I would not care to be in his shoes, let me tell you."

"Where is he?"

"In the dungeons of the Holy Office. The judges of that tribunal assuredly know better how to extract a confession than any others."

"With what is he charged?"

"That will not be known until the verdict and penalty are announced."

"He will be tortured?"

"Undoubtedly."

My heart gave a great leap of consternation. Terraza—El Risero—under torment! He might—nay, almost certainly he would—reveal his information concerning me, since one of the impositions placed upon a victim put to the Question in the torture chamber was that he must name any heretics, or suspected heretics, of whom he had knowledge.

"What of this man?" Beltrán asked, noticing my expression.

"Nothing," I said. "I chanced to meet him—that is all."

"Do not mention this to anyone else," he said seriously. "It is an ill thing to be called as a witness in the proceedings of the Holy Office."

So the old terror was upon me again.

It grew, as in those next days I saw the dreadful brutality with which punishments were inflicted on those adjudged guilty of participating in the riots, until I lived in such apprehension that I hardly knew one peaceful moment, day or night.

The executions began on the afternoon of the very day after the night of the riot. As their first act, the authorities rebuilt the gallows that had been burned down. At the foot of this new gibbet, as soon as it was completed, three Indians accused of helping set fire to the palace were shot to death. Afterward their right hands were cut off and nailed to the gallows tree.

Hangings and wholesale whippings followed during the week. Eleven natives and one *mestizo* died by the noose, and another *mestizo*, who died of his wounds in prison, was also hanged to expose his body on the gibbet even though life had already departed from his poor corpse.

Each day, moreover, a large crowd gathered to look on as men, and not a few women, had their backs or bellies cut to ribbons with the lash until they were raw and streaming blood. At least forty were thus whipped, some dying under the lash.

But the climax came when it was announced that on the ninth day after the riot, the prisoner, Hipólito José Terraza, would suffer death by burning at the stake, in a special auto-da-fé arranged by the Holy Office for this purpose.

He had been found guilty of the crimes of sorcery and heresy. Only sorcery—communion with the foul fiend and the use of the devil's black magic—it was solemnly stated, could have enabled an *arriero* who was virtually a stranger in the city, so to gain control over the minds and passions of the masses as to conduct such an uprising as he had led.

As to the finding of heresy, I learned there were two counts. First, Terraza was adjudged guilty of treason against the King of Spain, which was rebellion against God, under the interpretation of the Holy Office that the King, by divine right, was God's representative on the throne. Second, he had *criticized* the Holy Office. The accusation set forth that "during his examination the accused said things against the Holy Office, its mode of process, and its purposes, that were manifest blasphemies of the first and most culpable order, and a sin upon a matter of faith, revealing the heretical spirit of the accused and his bitter hatred of the Holy Office."*

That mere disapproval of the Inquisition and its ways could be twisted into a conviction of heresy, with the terrible punishment involved, increased my own feeling of clammy dread. Almost hourly, I began to expect that I might see the arrival of the black-garbed familiars looking for me.

But they did not come. And when the Sunday of the execution arrived—invariably the autos-da-fé were held on Sundays or other feast days of the Church, so that more people could witness the spectacles—I concluded that even under the torture El Risero had not named me, and blessed him for it.

At dawn that day the crowd began gathering. A sort of grandstand had been erected for the officials and nobles with their families, and there were two special daises, one for the Viceroy and his retinue, the other for the Archbishop and his attendants. The commonality, however—men, women, and even children—stood in dense masses to watch the proceedings.

I would have given everything I possessed, and more, to be absent; but I must witness the execution, for suspicion might attach to anyone, particularly a foreigner, who who did not do so, as evidence of sympathy for the victim, culpable and punishable. So with Beltrán I sat in the stands and watched the horrible spectacle that followed, with a face that betrayed no expression of any kind, though keeping it so was the hardest thing of my life.

Just before the hour of the execution, the Viceroy and Archbishop, with their parties, arrived and were seated in their daises, from which

---

* A historic wording of this very finding in one of the recorded proceedings of the Spanish Inquisition, in which criticism of *itself* was ruled as heresy, to be punished by the rigor of death at the stake.

the best view of the stone platform and iron stake could be obtained.

I looked—yes, the old *Corregidor* was there, and with him his wife. I had not seen Joya since that night we spent in each other's arms, and now, almost curiously, I watched her mount the dais, clad quite charmingly in a dress of lace and silk, as if for a *fiesta*, seat herself calmly, greet a feminine friend, and begin to talk with her, with a giggle, behind her fan. That she could be calm, much less laugh, at such a time, peculiarly shocked and repelled me.

Now came the procession: first the Grand Inquisitor and his subordinates, followed by the officials and familiars of the Holy Office, a full muster of Dominican friars, and lastly, closely guarded, the prisoner. He was wearing the hideous yellow shroud called a *sanbenito*, painted with figures of the devil and representations of burning flames; and on his head was the cap of derision called a *coroza*. In his hands he carried a candle of green wax, supposed to represent the three theological virtues: the wick, faith; the wax, hope; the flame, charity. It was to be noticed that the flame of charity, or mercy, was quenched.

Poor, broken El Risero—he was not the Laugher now! Too well had the torturers done their work on him, for he obeyed as if mindlessly everything he was told to do. Very feebly he walked, and I was sick at heart to see that once stalwart figure so reduced.

The Grand Inquisitor, Esteban de Pulgar, himself delivered the sermon from a special pulpit, after the Viceroy, the officials, and the entire great crowd had said in unison "Amen," to the oath of respect for the supreme jurisdiction of the Holy Office which was read out to them. It was a long sermon, taking most of an hour, filled with fanatical invective and bolstered by lengthy texts. Once, glancing at Joya, I saw her smother a yawn, and shift her position impatiently, as if she wished they would get on with the proceedings.

Through it all the victim stood before the pulpit, but I saw him seem to stagger, so that the familiars upheld him from sinking to the ground, when the last dread words of the harangue were pronounced:

"The Church of God can do no more for you, Hipólito José Terraza, since you already have abused its goodness! Therefore, we cast you out from the Church, and we abandon you to the secular justice!"*

---

* The usual formula of the sentence. The Holy Office was careful of its wording. It did not say it *delivered* its victim to the secular justice, for delivery suggests activity in the matter. It merely *abandoned* him—washed its

After that the wretch was forced to mount the stone platform, and the whole great assemblage leaned forward the better to see. Though the dais was at some distance from me, I glanced again at Joya. Her attitude seemed to indicate eagerness, almost avidity, as she waited for the final act in this tragedy. It was not different from the attitudes of almost all the others, but in her for some reason it sickened me.

About El Risero's neck was locked the iron *jugum*, its chain connecting him with the top of the post. Three iron bands were passed around his body, confining his arms and legs, and holding him tightly to the stake.

Until the very end I hoped that the severity of the sentence might be mitigated, as sometimes happened even with the Inquisition, by strangling the prisoner to spare him the agony of the flames. But there was no mercy here. An example, an object lesson, was to be made of him so that it would never be forgotten by those watching, that they might live in terror of it.

I cannot dwell, even in my mind, on the death of that brave man. Three cartloads of dry wood were heaped about him, and after some time spent in prayer, the mass was set ablaze. At once the flames roared up. Not even the stoicism of the sufferer could prevent him from twisting about and giving vent to some horrible animal cries. But so fiercely did the fire mount that he died within a few minutes. Yet the body was seen among the flames for nearly half an hour in spite of the intensity of the heat, before it fell to pieces and was consumed in the incandescence.

I felt ill. I wanted to retch. And yet, with the sternest rigor, I forced myself to sit still beside Beltrán. To this moment the memory of that dreadful scene lingers with me as a horror. . . .

3.

During all of this I had made no effort to see, or even communicate, with Joya in her home. Yet had I really wished to do it, I could have found the time somehow. Actually there were other reasons why I shunned her.

I had from her what I desired, sought, almost gave my life for, yet

hands of him—sanctimoniously refusing to take responsibility for what the secular justice next did to him.

the night with her left me with a sensation of disgust: at her, at myself.

As early as the very next morning after the riot, when I was making arrangements to give poor Zorro a decent burial, an old proverb came to my mind: A woman is attractive only as long as you have not yet had her.

But was this true of Joya? No, as a woman of soft, seductive, perfumed, clinging flesh, she was still alluring to the senses.

It was something else: an odd reluctance. In that night of fire and blood and lust there was nothing between us of that which gives poetry to love. We might as well have been two animals rutting together. Curiously, I was secretly shamed by it.

And yet why? By no means was this the first time I had taken a woman for mere sensual gratification; and she me. It is an old story with one who has had affairs of this kind. Without love I had bedded women before, and that they did not love me gave me no special concern, mentally or emotionally, so long as they satisfied me otherwise.

Seeking the answer for this, I even asked myself if I might perhaps be getting old? Had I passed the time of the heats and passions of youth, and was now becoming introspective, the years chilling my blood?

But thinking of that night with her, I could not in honesty say that I had shown any sign of weakening ardor; nor, I think, would she be able either to think it or say it of me.

No, this was not the final reason why I could not bring myself to return to her. It was something hidden deep within me, which I would have considered an inconsistency somewhat odd in the nature of one with my past, had I understood it then.

But I did not understand it: that was to come later. I put it down instead to two things. First, I misliked in her the cruelty which was inflamed into passion by the slaughter in the plaza, and which later was exemplified by the avid eagerness with which she leaned forward the better to see and sense, when they set the flames to poor El Risero. In this she was agog, beside herself. Yet, to be fair, so were countless others, women as well as men, in that crowd.

Second, I meant nothing to her. I was certain of it. She had used me when she wanted a man to release the pent emotions in her. I merely happened to be handy at the moment. Any man who was available, perhaps, would have served her just as well. There was no heart in

WOMEN: OF THE FLESH, AND OF THE SOUL   365

her, and she would throw me over as lightly as a wilted flower when it suited her to do so.

I even reasoned—as men will—that she would perhaps be glad if I stayed away from her, now that the episode was over. Yet there was a factor on which I did not reckon, although, certes, I should have known enough of women to take it into account.

Beltrán it was—cynical, sympathetic Beltrán—who brought it to my attention. I had found difficulty in obtaining a suitable man to replace Zorro, and we were, an evening or two after the riot, discussing the problem, while I bewailed the loss of my servant. And that reminded us both of Zorro's services in promoting my pursuit of Joya.

It had not escaped Beltrán, who had followed the affair rather closely, and knew I had spent most of that night at her house, that something most interesting must have happened between the *Corregidor's* wife and myself. He knew Joya, and he knew me.

So, when he asked the question, I told him all that occurred, feeling that I wronged neither her nor myself by trusting to his discretion. He listened, then asked what next I planned to do. But on this I had not made up my mind.

I think Beltrán kept a rather close watch on me in the next days, although he said nothing more on the subject to me for some time. It was the Monday following the auto-da-fé when again he broached it.

"The *Corregidor's* house is undergoing repairs," he began, indirectly.

I indicated that I had noticed workmen busy on it.

"The office wing was nearly destroyed," he continued.

To this I assented.

"Have you been over to see it?" he asked.

"No," I replied, "I have not been near the place."

He gazed at me as if in surprise. "In this time you have not seen Doña Joya?"

"Except at a distance, no."

For a moment he was silent, then he said, "Do you not think you should at least have made a 'thank-you call'?"

"What do you mean?"

"It is our custom that when one has been regaled at a feast or otherwise handsomely entertained, he calls upon his hostess with a present of flowers or some other gift, to express his pleasure and gratitude.

You must admit that you were both regaled and handsomely entertained by this lady; and in a manner infinitely superior to a dinner or even a ball."

"I suppose," said I reluctantly, "that is true."

"You are making a mistake here, I am afraid," he pursued. "She is a woman who is in a position to do you harm if she chooses."

"I do not think you understand the matter," I countered. "It is my belief that Joya cares nothing for me; perhaps is most glad that I do not annoy her, now that she has had what she wants of me."

"There is a difference," he said with a little smile, "between a woman throwing a man over, and a man throwing a woman over. Whatever her motives, Joya has *given* herself. And once having given herself a woman expects—nay, demands—that it permanently affect the man, leave its brand deep in him. If it does not thus intensely take possession of him— however little it may mean to her—it becomes a sore wound to her vanity, and she may come to hate the man. Knowing this, it is well for a man, after an affair with a woman, to continue playing the lovelorn gallant to her, at least until this pride in his mistress is assuaged. Convention suggests that if anybody is to be thrown over, it is she who must be given the opportunity to do the jilting."

He had spoken truly, and I realized that I had been unwise not to follow this course with Joya. But still I did not approach her. The longer one fails to make his accounting to a woman in a matter of this kind, the harder it becomes to face the music.

But it could not go on forever. Two days after this last conversation with Beltrán, we each received a formal written invitation to a musicale which was to be held at the *Corregidor's* residence later in the week.

Many others, of course, were also invited. But I knew that the invitation was to me a personal summons that I hardly dared refuse; and also that some time during the evening I must confront Joya and explain myself. Beltrán agreed with me in this; and we decided that we would arrange things so that when I met her, it would be alone.

With no very pleasurable anticipations I accompanied my friend at the time set to the *Corregidor's* house. As he had said, it had been under repair since the fire, and a temporary wall now cut off the ruined eastern wing from the dwelling portion of the edifice. In spite of this, however, the penetrating stink of burned timbers hung on the air as we mounted the stairs to the *sala*.

Already a considerable assemblage of guests had arrived; for there had been little activity of a social nature since the riot and this occasion was looked forward to as a beginning of a return to normal life. At one end of the large room was a small platform for the musicians; at the other a long buffet, with wine and various confections and delicacies for the guests. To overcome, I suppose, the still lingering smell of the recent fire, the place was filled with sweet perfumed flowers, to which incense sticks added their scent in a combination of odors rather overpowering, yet not entirely unpleasant.

I beheld our hostess, seated on a divan, in a pale yellow gown with jewelry of jet, the colors making more vivid and striking her undeniably handsome blond head with its high comb in the back. Very gracefully she was receiving those who came up to pay respects.

Behind her stood her husband, the old Conde, looking not a little like a white-peruked vulture, with his great beak of a nose, and his red-lidded eyes. As I approached he gave me a little absent nod, hardly seeing me; and then turned to join the conversation of a group of his elderly cronies a little distance away, with whom he was forming a table of piquet for the other room. The vagueness of his glance assured me that he had no suspicions concerning me.

Joya's eyes, as I moved toward her, rested on me for a single moment. Then she turned to a couple before her with a gracious smile and greeting. There had been no smile in the look she gave me, and I braced myself for what was coming.

The couple passed on, the Conde was with his friends, and the two of us were for a moment alone, as I bent over her perfumed fingers.

"So you deigned to accept our invitation, Señor?" she said with a biting note of sarcasm. I noticed her formal address, and that though she seemed to smile, her eyes were cold.

"Deign is hardly the word," I said. "It is an honor to come to this house."

"Perhaps you have some excellent reason for not having availed yourself of this honor of which you speak?"

I recognized the symptoms, and thought of the adage: Woman is like your shadow; follow her, she flies; fly from her, she follows.

"With the city in such disorder," I explained, "I have taken part in the patrols."

"This has occupied you twenty-four hours of each day?"

"Not all: but there are times when one must sleep."

"I was informed that the Vera Cruz regiment has arrived."

"It has. Two days ago."

"And with its coming the civilian patrols ended?" she pursued.

"With its coming, yes," I said lamely.

"Then you have had some other reason for avoiding me?"

There, it was out: the direct challenge, and the demand for an explanation; an explanation that already, before I made it, would almost certainly be rejected, no matter what I said.

"I had no intention of avoiding you," I began. "Rather, I thought you might perhaps be pleased by my absence. If I was wrong, I will be most happy to come to you again—if—if—you will permit me——"

"If I will *permit* you!" she flared, the pretense of a smile faded now. "Have I prevented you these two weeks? And you have not even taken the trouble to dispatch a note! Do not attempt to excuse yourself for this affront! The door was open. It is closed now—and you may regret it!"

I had no reply. Almost at once her eyes went past me and the trained smile of the practiced hostess came again on her face, as she spoke to some newly arrived guests who were approaching.

Dismissed, with an angry question and something like a threat hanging in the air, I stepped aside, berating myself for my clumsiness. Now I remembered that I had paid my suit to Joya, in the beginning at least, for the very selfish reason that I hoped to gain her influence to further my affairs: although I swear I had forgotten that original, unadmirable aim, in the sheer excitement of the pursuit, once it was launched. Instead of a friend I had made an enemy of her, one who might do me great hurt.

I wondered if I could make some amend. But trying to placate an angry woman is like taking the stopper out of a phial of some violent effervescent acid: it is apt to boil over and dangerously burn you. So, since the music was about to begin, I took my place near Beltrán, who stood behind the chair of his Doña Gertrudis.

Not once during the evening did Joya again appear to notice me, or speak to me, although she passed among her guests in the intermissions, chatting and laughing with them. When we said good night at the end, she hardly seemed to hear my thanks; but to Beltrán she gave her hand to kiss, and a brilliant smile, and a pretty word as to her pleasure in him as a guest.

On the way home, I said, "I suppose you noticed?"

"Her coldness to you?" he asked.

"Yes. Everything is exactly as you predicted. She is furious."

He shrugged. "Dealing with such a woman is like thrusting your hand into a bag of serpents, on the chance of snatching an eel."

"She will hardly confess about me to her husband, the *Corregidor*," I said, half to myself.

"She will not have to do so," he replied. "Merely by concocting some excuse for detestation—such as an imaginary affront—she can coax and nag and weep, until he, who above everything else loves his ease and peace, will out of sheer weariness do everything she asks against you."

"By my cursed stupidity I brought this on myself!"

"No matter. Let us not put the plow before the oxen. Not what has happened, but what we should do next is of account."

"If only something would take me away from here!"

"Exactly!" said Beltrán. "And I think the time is favorable to set such a thing to going. The report of your deeds the night of the riot—I refer only to your deeds with the *sword*—has come to the Viceroy's ears. I saw to that. He looks upon you now with favor, and I believe he will consent to an audience, in which you will take part, together with the Archbishop and the Franciscans, to plan and authorize a missionary and military expedition to the frontier. That would at least take you out of the city long enough for Doña Joya to cool her rage a little, and perhaps listen to reason when you return, if she is approached carefully."

He spoke so confidently that I felt almost jubilant when I said good night and went to my lodgings. If the Viceroy took early action—before Joya could inflame her husband sufficiently to oppose me in the council—I might soon be on my way northward toward the border. I imagined myself already making my final escape, and riding for Louisiana and the protection of France.

4.

Beltrán said it would take at least a day or two for an audience of
such importance to be arranged, and I spent the next day in idleness.
Not yet had I found a servant; wherefore I must either cook for myself—
a thing I detest—or eat in one of the *mesones,* of which the city had
many, all of inferior quality, the food running strongly to beans and red
peppers.

Toward evening, therefore, I went out, and presently found myself
traversing the street just north of the burned-out plaza, passing the
cathedral, before which the usual horde of beggars already had resumed their clamorous sway. A blind child drew on my pity, and I
gave the mother a copper coin: then hurried on, for the beggars, like
gulls which swoop when one of their number is given a bit of bread,
came swarming with outcries for alms, turning to imprecations and
curses when I refused to give all what I had given one.

To rid myself of them I walked westward. The sun was near its
setting, and I saw a man standing alone near the far end of the Zócalo,
where the gallows loomed above the stone platform and iron stake of
the auto-da-fé. He was, evidently, a *rústico,* new to the city; and he
was staring at the heaps of charred debris in the plaza, and at the
grisly device for roasting a human being to death.

The peasant figure was short, in the *mozo* garb of white cotton shirt
and drawers, a wide sombrero on the back of the head, and rawhide
sandals on the feet. Even as I neared the man, I had a curious premonition. Then he turned, and I stopped stock still in my surprise.

The face, gazing into mine at a distance of no more than ten feet,
was the ugly, dark, deep-lined countenance of Íñigo, the Indian servant
of Don Diego de Ramón, Commandant of San Juan Bautista!

For a moment his expression was one of astonishment as great as
mine. Then, like a flash, it changed to overpowering fear.

Whirling about, the little man ran wildly away, as if from the devil.

What was Íñigo doing here? Why did he run at the sight of me?

A thought came. *Dolores!* He might give me news of Dolores!

With that I set out after him, and I swear that so greatly did the
thought of her possess me, that it was not until later that I came to
realize the dangers Íñigo represented to me.

It is undignified to gallop down a street, even a street nearly deserted in the evening, but there was nothing for it. If that was Íñigo, I must somehow stop him, question him, discover his errand in this city. Grasping my sword by its scabbard to keep it from entangling my legs, I ran.

And in panic Íñigo fled. His legs, however, were short, while mine are long. Very quickly I was overtaking him, reaching out for him. But my snatch at his shirt tail missed, he doubled like a rabbit, and dodged into a narrow alley, I close behind him.

Ahead of me his white cotton figure twinkled: then suddenly stopped. He had chosen a blind alley and come up against the end of it.

Knowing I had him cornered, I halted.

At once he fell on his knees, crossed himself several times, and began pattering out prayers.

"Holy Mother of God, preserve me!" he quavered. "Most Sacred Virgin of Guadalupe, preserve me!"

I said, "Íñigo!"

"Go away from me, leave me I beseech you! By all the saints, by my soul, I swear that I never did anything against you——"

"I do not intend to hurt you," said I.

He looked up and said in a trembling voice, "But you—are you not—Señor St. Denis?"

"Assuredly."

"Then—you are dead! You *must* be dead! Oh, why do you pursue me? Holy Mother of God——"

I laughed aloud. The fellow thought I was a ghost!

"Get up, Íñigo," I said. "I am St. Denis, but I am far from dead. Observe—I am still panting from the race you gave me. Does a ghost pant?"

As if this homely suggestion reassured him somewhat, he slowly rose from his knees, peering at me with eyes almost starting from his head.

"But—but—you were murdered by the *ladrones!*"

"*Ladrones* killed Herrera and the others. I alone escaped," I told him. "Here—feel my arm—it should convince you that I am flesh and blood."

Very cautiously he reached forth a hand to touch me—with one hesitating finger. The solid contact seemed to convince him and he ceased quaking.

"It is indeed you, Señor? And you are well? I am delighted!" He grinned with relief.

"Now," said I, "tell me what brings you to this city."

"I came with my *maestra*."

His *maestra*! Could it be Dolores? Or one of her aunts?

"Which *maestra*?" I hung on his reply.

"Señorita Dolores."

"She is here—in this city?"

"Yes, Señor. We arrived only this afternoon."

"Where is she now?"

"At the *fonda* called Las Cruces, behind the cathedral grounds."

Knowing she was so near, I felt a sudden great longing to see her, and that was the first intimation I had of what she really meant to me.

The Spanish have a saying: The cure for love is land between. It seemed to have been the opposite with me, for love for her had been growing, almost unrealized, in my heart.

Another proverb better fitted the case: Absence is to love what a wind is to fire; it puts out a little one, and fans a big one. Mine, certes, had been fanned into flame by being separated from her.

"Íñigo, I must see her," I said. "Take me to her."

Very willing he was now to do my behests. He led the way out of the alley, though I kept on him a sharp eye, for it now came over me that this man knew I was accused of heresy, and it was imperative that he be made to keep silence. At the rear of the cathedral grounds we found the small inn he had named, second rate and not very clean in appearance.

That Dolores should be staying in such a place seemed to me shameful, but at least she was here! Like a thirsty man approaching water, I anticipated the sight of her.

But all at once I wished I had not come.

As Íñigo and I entered the inn, we looked down a hall that opened into a small patio at the rear. There, as if framed by the doorway, clearly outlined in the late evening light, I saw Dolores, dressed in white. And with her a man.

Her hand was on his arm in a gesture so intimate, and she was smiling up in his face so fondly, that it was very evident there was something more than mere friendship between them. What right had Dolores to be with such a man? And without even a *dueña* to watch over her! Who was he, anyway?

To myself I thought savagely that he was far too old for her; and then I realized that he was about my own age. I marked also that, much as I instinctively disliked him, he was handsome in a soldierly way; also that he seemed very sure of himself with her, bending his head down toward her as she smiled up at him.

So immersed were they in some deep discussion, their voices so low, that their words did not come to me, nor did they notice my presence.

Beyond doubt he was a suitor; and from all appearances a successful one. Were they married? No, Iñigo spoke of her as *Señorita* Dolores. What had happened to Anaya and his intentions upon her?

Jealousy burned in me, and yet I reasoned with myself, rather despairingly, that I had no right to feel resentment, or judge her. She believed me dead. And she was made for love, ready for love. It would scarcely be human for her not to turn to another. Yet in spite of this I found myself illogically angry with her. As for the man, I felt I could kill him there in the patio, where he stood smiling with such damnable assurance down at her upturned face.

But this would never do. Never before had I felt such jealousy over any woman. I must not show it now. I would have turned back silently and departed without ever letting them know that I had been there to spy on their intimate little scene, but at the moment Iñigo called out.

"Señorita!" he cried. "I have found Señor St. Denis. He is here!"

After that I could only step out from the darkness of the hall into the evening light of the patio. The two turned. In their faces was a look as if they could not believe what they had heard and now were seeing.

With a little cry, Dolores turned for refuge to the man. He took her in his arms and she hid her face on his shoulder, while he regarded me fixedly. I measured him. He was a complete stranger to me, yet I judged him a swordsman. If he had wronged her . . . perhaps we might yet settle the difference between us over this girl, here and now.

After a moment he said, "Come, *querida*, we must greet this gentleman."

In a muffled voice, as if she feared to look, she said, "Is it—is it really—*he?* If it isn't—if this is a mistake—don't let me look——"

"At least it is someone," he replied, "though I do not have the honor of his acquaintance."

Slowly she turned her face to me again.

At first she said nothing. Then, leaving him, she moved toward me, gazing at me as if to make sure, until she came up to me. With a little helpless gesture she held out both hands to me. I took them.

"Luís, oh, Luís!" she cried.

And all at once she was clinging to me, sobbing.

"It *is* you—my heart—my beloved!" she cried, and over and over thanked the Holy Virgin. "It is really you—alive and yourself! Oh, Luís —*caro*—it is beyond my wildest dream—and yet how I have prayed for this. It is true—it *is* true?"

I hardly knew what to do, looking down on that graceful, dear, dark head bent on my shoulder. But I knew that I loved her and in a manner that I had never loved any woman before.

If she needed protection she should have it, and I would pledge my life for it. My arms tightened about her, and I looked across at that man standing beyond in the patio.

He read my look and seemed slightly amused.

"Dolores," he said, "will you not introduce us?"

At that she seemed to come to herself. "Oh——" she said, drawing away from me, but not far. "I have not been kind or polite——"

By the hand she drew me toward him.

"Don Juan," she said, still with a little sob in her voice, "this is Don Luís de St. Denis."

"The Don Luís concerning whom I have heard so much?" he asked, with the same little smile.

"Yes, Luís—my Luís!" she cried, as if she exulted. "And, Luís—this gentleman is my *tío*, Don Juan de Ramón, the youngest son of Don Diego Escalante de Ramón, my dear grandfather."

An uncle! This altered matters, and my bow was as deep and cordial as his.

"Don Luís," he said, with dignity that reminded me of the Commandant, his father, "we are well met. For if a tithe of what this now starry-eyed little creature, my niece—who has been so desolately unhappy—be true, I am most proud to know you."

"The honor is mine," I replied, "when I meet any son of Don Diego de Ramón." I smiled at Dolores and held up her hand, which was still tightly clasped in mine. "But as for this one—whom I worship—take even that tithe of what she said with a pinch of salt, for I fear she is far too disposed in my favor." And I kissed the hand.

"Nay, but my honored father has a like opinion of you," he said seriously. "And Don Diego is no mean judge of a man. For that matter, when they told me how you defied death rather than renounce our sweet Dolores, my heart warmed to you, as did the hearts of all our family."

I could not reply to this, for it touched me. And though the act of which he spoke was not entirely unworthy, I felt humble that they should clothe it with nobility so much greater than it deserved.

5.

That evening we dined together at a small *mesón* not far from the inn. Don Juan, I soon saw, was a younger Don Diego, and, like his father, a Spaniard of Spaniards. From sheer relief at discovering that he was no rival of mine for Dolores, I liked him perhaps better than I would ordinarily like a man on such short acquaintance.

As for Dolores, sitting between us, she appeared very thin, and showed evidence of weariness, her face seeming to be all great lustrous eyes. Yet she was so ecstatic in her happiness that she imparted a glow to us who were with her.

"Íñigo says you arrived here only this afternoon," I said.

"Yes, it has been a long journey and wearisome to Dolores," answered Don Juan. "We heard about the riot and the fire, from some people who passed us on the way north while we were on the road."

"What terrible destruction!" said Dolores. "And were there many deaths?"

"Both during and after the riot," I told her soberly. "I am glad you were not here to see it. There was an auto-da-fé—but I will not go into it. Please tell me all about yourself. It seems almost a miracle to have you here. I had thought you married—to Anaya."

She gazed at me almost with indignation. "Did you dream I would consent to wed that man—or any man—after your sacrifice for me? Oh, Luís, if you did you very greatly mistook me!"

"I only knew he desired you—and would use his great power—to——" I broke off.

She bowed her head. "Don Gaspar did desire me."

"Yet gave you up? It does not sound like the man."

"I will tell you the whole story," she said, looking up again. "After they—they took you away—Don Gaspar came to me and seemed to expect that I would then go with him to Parras. But I said, 'Excellency, I cannot come.'

"He appeared not to believe me. 'What is this?' he said. 'Why do you say you cannot come?'

"I sought not to offend him—for the sake of my grandfather, who already was in disfavor—but yet I had to speak the truth. 'Because, Excellency,' I told him, 'I will never wed any man, if it so be that I cannot wed Don Luís.'

" 'But he is condemned!' he cried out. 'He is already a dead man! Would you bind yourself to a corpse, when you can be the bride of a Governor of a province?'

"I still endeavored to be gentle and politic, though I hated him. 'Excellency, hear me,' I said. 'Don Luís is the lord of my heart, and for that reason I can never be your wife.'

"With that his choler rose. 'But you *will* be my wife!' he almost shouted at me. 'I will see that Don Diego commands it!'

"Then I said to him, 'Even if Don Diego, my grandfather and guardian whom I love, should command it, I would kill myself first!' "

She paused for a moment, and I pictured the scene: the timid, almost pleading girl; the bullying man. And the thought of her inflexible constancy almost choked me with emotion. Now—now at last—I understood the real reason for the aversion I felt toward Doña Joya. It was the presence of Dolores in my heart, so deep that I did not even know it then, and the comparison made by some instinct unexpressed within me, between her and that wanton creature of perfumed flesh.

"Don Diego—what did he do?" I managed to say.

"When Anaya confronted him, and he heard what I had said, Don Diego refused to assent to the marriage. Anaya first made promises of promotion and favor; then he raged, shouting insults. My grandfather stood grim and silent, but did not yield one whit either to promises or rage."

"What greatness!" I exclaimed. "And he did this knowing that most surely Anaya would do him injury!"

"He knew it," she said. "The Governor departed, saying the last of the matter had not been heard. Nor was it. A few days later word came that you and those with you were—dead—murdered by—*ladrones*——" Her voice trembled and tears came into her eyes. "I was so broken with grief that—that it was some time—before I understood what had happened to my grandfather——"

She fought for control. It was her uncle who took up the story.

"That is the reason why we are here," he said.

He explained that he was in garrison at Chihuahua, where, like his father he was a Captain in the army, when a messenger came urgently summoning him to San Juan Bautista. He rode at once.

"When I arrived," he went on, "I learned that a *fiscal* advocate had come with an escort, and laid charges that Don Diego had appropriated to himself moneys of the Crown, advanced for the maintenance of the garrison and presidio of San Juan Bautista."

"That is a lie!" I said hotly. "Don Diego is a man of flawless honor!"

He gave a little nod. "A lie, of course, Don Luís. My father has made an accounting for every *cuartillo*. Yet he was removed from command and ordered to remain under guard in his house, while formal charges were put through the courts in Parras. Such is Anaya's power that I fear there is little doubt what the courts will decide. Don Diego will be adjudged guilty, imprisoned, his rank taken from him, his property confiscated, himself and our whole family ruined."

"I brought this evil on you!" I said miserably.

"Not so, Don Luís. You have acted in all respects as a gentleman of honor should. It is that pig, Anaya, who caused this disaster. And that pig, Anaya, will squeal if we can obtain justice."

"And you are here seeking that justice!" I exclaimed.

"I conferred with Don Diego, and made extensive inquiries about Anaya," he nodded. "That man is as crooked as a scorpion's tail, his record is full of injustices and peculations. But the difficulty is bringing any charges against a provincial Governor to the attention of the Viceroy—too many influences can be brought to bear against it. Nevertheless, I had a bill of particulars drawn. I needed, however, a direct witness to go with me to the capital. Since neither of my aunts was capable of such a journey, and since Don Diego was confined to his house by order, it was Dolores who came with me."

Now many things were explained, and finding Dolores, which had seemed such a miracle, was not so very much of a miracle after all. I remembered Padre Ambrosio's words: *The Viceroy cannot be approached by a mere Commandant of a frontier post, unless some im-*

*portant personage should provide the entree—and Don Diego has no
such personage to whom he could turn. . . .*

They had come all this weary distance seeking what Padre Ambrosio
considered an impossibility: an audience with the Viceroy. It was their
last hope.

"We took advantage of a *conducta* that was making its way here, to
get through in *ladrón* country, for there were only three of us—Dolores,
Íñigo, and myself. As you can see the journey was hard on Dolores—
she is very weary."

"Not now," she protested.

But my heart misgave me at her thinness, although her eyes were
beauty unsurpassed.

"If we can only reach the Viceroy!" Don Juan exclaimed.

"Perhaps you can," I said. "And for once I may be of use to you.
I have a friend, Don Beltrán de Córdoba, who is *ayudante* to the Viceroy. He told me there was some sort of a dossier on Anaya in the government files—perhaps others have made complaints. At any rate, through
him, if we are fortunate and use the right moves, we may gain an
audience——"

"It would be the greatest favor—I cannot express how important——"

"No favor at all, Don Juan. I have profound regard for Don Diego.
And I loathe that cur, Anaya. I would do it for myself—if it were not
more important that I do it for you—and for this lovely one, who deserves everything good from everyone, myself most of all."

Beneath the table Dolores felt for my fingers, in a warm little squeeze
of gratitude and love.

After that the talk turned to what to her was important: she demanded that I give an account of my own adventures. This I did, making it as brief as possible, touching on such humorous episodes as I
remembered, and bringing my story up to the present without any un-
necessarily harrowing details.

But at the end, I said seriously, "From all this, you see that I am
still in some jeopardy. If word went about that I had against me this
accusation of heresy, however false it is, it would be most dangerous for
me."

"Trust us," said Don Juan. "Íñigo also will keep his tongue."

From Dolores there was no word, only a shining look of loyalty.

So, with the needful backgrounds sketched in, we turned to the present for the moment and tried to forget both past and future. Merely to look at Dolores, and hear her speak and laugh, gave me a rare and poignant happiness. And my mind went back over the devious lane of my life, which had led up to so fair a garden.

I found myself completely enamored of the perfections of her grace and loveliness, the sweet play of expression in her face, the lustrous highlights of her eyes; and in this was something new to me, not only a great outreaching of my heart to her, but a kind of tender awe I had never felt toward a woman before.

To myself I swore that I would forever keep in mind the things I had done of which I was not proud, that I might always remember to atone for them with increasing devotion to her.

At the end of the evening, when we parted at their *fonda,* she lifted her face, as naturally and expectantly as a child, to me. But somehow I could not touch those lips with mine—not yet. So I kissed her hands, and rather brokenly spoke of my love, and my unworthiness, and my gratitude. Then I left her promising that I would come again in the morning.

It was a promise I did not keep.

21. *The Audience of Torment*

That night, walking back to my home, I felt greater happiness than I could remember. This love that I knew for the first time was overwhelming, crowding out all other thoughts, and filling me with ecstasy such as I would not have believed possible before.

Everything was right. We would be married: she would be mine. But not until I let her understand fully the strange, complex, inconsistent, sinful, repentant creature a man can be, and received her forgiveness. For the moment I forgot the complexities that beset my life, but as I reached the corner of the street where my lodgings were I remembered there were problems still to solve. Before I rested I would go to Beltrán and enlist him in the cause of Dolores and her family.

So I turned up along the rear of the palace, instead of crossing over to where my rooms were. As I neared the door leading to Beltrán's apartment, I chanced to notice a figure lurking across, near my door, which suddenly dodged into an alley nearby.

It seemed to be one of those worthless *léperos*, but I thought nothing of it, for I was armed. There were, in fact, two soldiers on sentry duty at the door of the palace. They saluted me as I entered, and I forgot the lurking man.

Beltrán, still up, received me gladly. I told him my news, and he questioned me eagerly about Dolores and her uncle.

"I have every reason to think that you can see the Viceroy no later than tomorrow," he said. "The Franciscans are making the appointment, and the Archbishop will be there also. At that time you will be able to make the request for an audience in behalf of your lady and her family. The Viceroy, I think, will listen to you, for he is strongly disposed in your favor. Meantime I will indeed go into that record on Anaya——"

This was all he had time to say. He stopped, for there was a knock on the door.

A moment later his servant came in, pallid and stammering with terror.

"God have mercy on us, Don Beltrán!" he cried.

"What is the matter, Manuel?"

"They have come! They are here!" The man chattered so that he was incoherent.

But he did not need to be more explicit, for at that moment six black-clad figures, armed and grim as death, burst into the room.

Both Beltrán and I sprang to our feet. His face went set and white. He could not have known that it was I for whom the familiars of the Inquisition had so suddenly come.

"Which of you is Luís de St. Denis?" one of them asked.

I gulped. "I am he."

Without a word two of them seized me while a third locked iron gyves on my wrists.

I stood as if paralyzed while this was going on. What was most frightening, in its way, was the manner in which Beltrán, my devoted friend, was behaving. I knew he would gladly risk his life for me. But now he said not a word. This was the *Inquisition*. He dared not lift a finger, and that was the measure of the terror in which the institution held him and all the people of Spain.

Silently they marched me out into the street. Looking across at my own door it flashed through my mind that the lurking *lépero* I had seen must have been a scout or spy, placed there to warn the familiars of my return, so that they could arrest me.

The Plazuelito—the "little plaza" of the Inquisition—is all that separates the Dominican convent from the grim Casa Santa—the "Sacred House" of the Holy Office. It is some distance from the palace, and in all that walk through the dark streets not one word was spoken to me by my guards.

One question kept beating, like a heavy refrain, through my mind. Who had denounced me?

Had Anaya renewed his charges against me? It was hardly likely. If he had heard of me, perhaps through some report of my actions during the riot, the distances were too great for him to have acted so soon.

There was El Risero. Perhaps, after all, he had given my name under torture. Yet I could hardly believe it.

Doña Joya—had she in some manner learned of it? She would be malignant and cruel enough to use such knowledge against me. Yet how could she have known?

There were three others in the city who had knowledge on which the Inquisition might have acted: Dolores, Don Juan, and Íñigo. But this was unthinkable.

One last possibility remained: Padre Hidalgo. Yet of all things Padre Hidalgo would wish least that I reveal to the Inquisition his letter to the French Governor. No, he could not be the one.

I was at a loss, and it made more absolute the despair I felt as I found myself being ushered into the dark structure where the Holy Office held sway.

The entrance to the place was unwholesome. A friar at a table opened a huge book that might have contained all the names in the city, dipped his quill and wrote by candlelight.

"Name?" he asked.

"St. Denis," one of the familiars answered.

"Accused or witness?"

So they even imprisoned witnesses here!

"Accused," the familiar said.

He did not say of what I was accused, and I waited to hear the question asked and answered. But the friar only made a notation and said, "Put him in Number Seven in the lower tier."

The familiars began to search me.

"Do it carefully," said the friar. "By some means the prisoner in Number Three this morning obtained a cord and deliberately strangled himself slowly. When he was found he was dead. He is now howling in hell: but the cell guard who allowed him to take his own life is occupying that selfsame cell. A new jailer is in charge on that tier."

As if this incident of suicide made them doubly suspicious of me, the familiars searched me thoroughly, even roughly.

"Here is his purse," one of them said at last. "Also his sword and belt. That is all we can find. His other effects are being seized from the rooms he occupied."

"Take him away," said the friar.

I was prodded forward, down a stair of stone. If I had any thought of making an escape from this place, I speedily saw how hopeless it was. Guided by the new jailer, my guards and I went down two narrow flights of steps into a passage so dark that even with the horn lantern the jailer carried, we fairly groped our way.

Two men could scarcely walk abreast in it. Its walls, ceiling, and floor were of stone, and of a slimy dampness, as I ascertained by feeling with my manacled hands. In that brief walk we passed several strong iron-barred doors. Within one of them I heard a voice cry out as if in supplication to us, but the others were silent. Yet I was sure that every one of them was tenanted.

We halted before an iron cage door similar to the others, and the jailer's key grated in the lock. My wrists were freed of their irons, and I was pushed into the cell.

From within came so appalling a stench that I held my nose. Then I realized I must become accustomed to it, and desisted.

By the faint glimmer of the lantern at the door, I made out two things: near the door itself was a small pannikin with water in it; and at the back there appeared to be some sort of low pallet, with a heap of rags on top. Rather than trust myself to that vile couch, I resolved that I would sit or stand up all night.

The iron cage door closed, the key grated again, locking it, and the familiars with the jailer went away down the dark passage.

In spite of its slimy coldness, I sank down on the stone floor. Resting my back against the wall, I stared into the total blackness with numb hopelessness.

How long I sat thus, I do not know. I was brought to full consciousness by a sound—a combination between a whistling sigh and a groan.

Such a sound I had never heard before. It is impossible to describe: no beast of the wild ever made it, nor any living man I had known.

All atremble, I came to my feet.

Could it be . . . that the spirits of the dead came back to this unholy of unholies, where once had lain the tortured bodies they had inhabited?

The hair rose on my head. I stared about me this way and that, trying to make out in the blackness some shape, *any* shape, and seeing none.

Again it came: the dreadful, whistling sigh.

Now I located it—the pallet! What being crouched there, waiting perhaps like a vampire to prey on me while I slept?

Then I heard a voice. "*Agua!* Water! For the love of God, water!"

It was a man, a living, suffering, human creature!

I groped to the pallet. In the darkness I could barely distinguish that the being on the bed was terribly emaciated, and my exploring hand revealed that his hair and beard were wild and tangled. Near the cell door was the pannikin. I brought it and lifted the head of the other, who drank from it eagerly.

"I thank you," said the man, when he lay back.

For a long time there was silence, then he said in a feeble voice, "Who are you?"

"I am called St. Denis," I told him.

"Accused—witness—or familiar?"

"I am accused, of what I do not know. But you say 'familiar.' Are they imprisoned too?"

"Sometimes, as spies, to gain the confidence of prisoners and trick them into confessions. But it makes little difference to me who you are. I am not long for this world, for which I bless the merciful God, who will take me from these merciless men."

I stood silent, wondering what to say.

The creaking voice began again. "I am Pedro de Antigua, and I was, on the day I was brought here, in my fortieth year. How long it has been I do not know, but if you could see me, you would think me an old man, in his eighties at least. That is what the Inquisition has done to me. And why? Because I saw the burning of a girl, a child no more than fourteen years old, accused of witchcraft. In my horror I cried out against it—and they brought me here to repent of that pity I felt."

Another long pause. Then, "Have you said aught against the Inquisition?"

"Never, to my knowledge," I said.

"Listen to this . . . O wretched man . . . from one who has learned it . . . through suffering——"

The sighing voice broke off. I listened intently.

After a time I said, "Señor Antigua—are you asleep?"

"Not asleep . . . dying."

"But—you were going to tell me——"

"Oh . . . yes. On your soul . . . never confess to anything . . . never . . . allow them to trick you into . . . contradicting yourself. For contradiction . . . they rule as perjury . . . and perjury will deliver you to the torturers. . . ."

That was seared into my mind as if by a hot iron.

The rest of the night Pedro de Antigua lingered. He died in the morning. The guards who took him away said his disease was prison fever. I was now the sole tenant of the cell.

2.

The worst thing about awaiting trial in prison is the uncertainty and dread; and this is especially grave for one who is awaiting trial before the Inquisition. The very name of the institution is of such terror that the mere mention of it is enough to pale the average person, who fears it worse than he does the devil, even when he is free and innocent and has no reason to think he will ever be brought before it.

As I lay in the cell, after they took the body of Antigua away, I suffered all the apprehensions of which my imagination was capable, for I knew the power of the Inquisition, and something of its methods of prosecution and judgment. I did not know the charge against me, or my accuser, it being one of the rules of the Holy Office that this information be withheld from a prisoner, as well as the names of the witnesses who testify against him.

My mind was occupied by alternating gusts of rage, of speculation as to what manner of trial would be employed against me, of despair, and sometimes even of hope. Surely, I said to myself, someone would intervene for me. There was Beltrán, and perhaps even the Viceroy, who had thought well of me since the night of the riot, might interest himself. But this was quickly succeeded by the dull realization that nobody, however powerful, interfered in the affairs of the Inquisition.

For three interminable days and nights I lay in the cell alone, seeing nobody except the jailer who each day brought my ration of poor food and water. I could tell the days from the nights only because the darkness was a little less intense during the hours when the sun shone on the earth above my dungeon.

On the fourth day I heard the tramp of feet in the passage, voices, and my door was unlocked. Before me stood five men: the jailer, and four familiars in their black uniforms, armed with swords and pikes.

A lantern was held to illumine my face, and my eyes, accustomed to the dark, blinked.

"Prisoner," said a voice sternly, "do you consent to behave peacefully and gently in your appearance before the court of the Holy Office?"

I stared. What did this mean? What could I do?

Then I nodded.

"Hold out your wrists," said the same voice.

One of the familiars began to lock the gyves once more on me.

"This is not necessary, Señores," I said. "I have agreed to go peaceably and gently."

"Be silent!" came the rough order.

Manacled, my head bowed, I marched as commanded down the narrow stone passage with my guards. Presently we ascended the stair, crossed a hall, were passed through an iron-grilled door by other guards, and came at last to a small vestibule, hardly larger than a closet.

It opened into a large room, and though I could not see into the other room because of a screen that separated it from the vestibule, I heard voices, evidently in low discussion of something. In spite of myself, my flesh crawled at the sound; for those speaking could be none other than members of the dread tribunal, and this that I was about to enter was the court chamber of the Casa Santa of the Inquisition.

Presently a voice said aloud: "Produce the accused!"

Prodded by my guards, I walked forward and entered the judgment hall.

Simplicity, barren simplicity, was its one great distinguishing feature. Bare walls, unornamented by a picture or relief of any kind; windows paned with thick glass which admitted light but forbade the eye to see through, and barred with iron; a few wooden benches without backs, including one fairly in the center of the room; the black-clad familiars, with their pikes, at the doors, and standing guard over me; and at the far end, the focus of everything, a high stand on which sat the judges, clad in their habits of black and white.

On the highest seat was the president of the tribunal, with just below him three lesser judges. The president I recognized, and shivered inwardly at the recognition: Esteban de Pulgar, the Grand Inquisitor of New Spain. But Pulgar's gaunt visage showed no return recognition.

The three sitting below Pulgar I took to be the usual officers at a hearing: the diocesan ordinary, the *fiscal* advocate, and the notary to take down what might transpire. Before them on a special table stood a tall crucifix, two green candles alight, and the Gospels on which witnesses were sworn. Save for these, the familiars, and myself, there were no other occupants of the chamber; for the sittings of the Inquisition are secret, its proceedings never revealed, save for the final judgments.

All three lesser judges, like the president, however else their appearances might attract or repel, were marked by a clear-cut look of intelligence. They were chosen men, skilled in technicalities, deep in knowledge of the most devious tentacles of the law, setters of traps for the wretches brought before them, schooled in the single art for which the Inquisition is famous—conviction of the accused, no matter how.

"Prisoner, state your name," said the friar at the right of the three below the president's high desk. He was, I learned, Fray Nuño de Palma, the *fiscal*, a man of intense cunning, chosen as prosecutor because of his skill in every trick of casuistry.

"Louis Juchereau de St. Denis, chevalier of France, and envoy to His Grace, the Duque de Linares, Viceroy of New Spain," I replied.

Pulgar frowned. "Your name only was asked. Do not volunteer other information to this tribunal than the answer to its questions, on peril of being charged with contumacy and willful disobedience to this court."

To the notary, he said, "Strike out the title and office the prisoner has volunteered, but leave in his nationality."

Absolute silence reigned in the room save for the scratching of the quill as the notary obeyed these instructions. Meantime the judges and guards all regarded me with icy sternness.

Presently the *fiscal* said, "With the divine assistance of Our Lord and His Holy Mother, we require you to speak the truth in these proceedings, for the welfare of your conscience. Kneel, and swear with your hands on these Gospels that you will answer with exact truthfulness all the questions that shall be asked you."

To be forced to my knees in this manner was a subtle step in the process of abasing me, yet I must obey. I knelt and gave the required oath. Thereafter I was permitted to seat myself on the small bench upon which the Inquisitors looked down from their elevated stand.

The questioning now began, and at first it was of a nature that surprised me, because of its mild and almost kindly nature.

Particulars such as my birthplace, age, date of my confirmation, and military service were inquired into, all of which I answered truthfully, since there was nothing to hide.

Then came a question, apparently innocent. "Who is your confessor?"

At once I recognized its deadly motive. If I had not been to confessional regularly, it might be distorted into something enormously incriminating, by interpreting my failure to observe my Catholic duties as an evidence of heresy or even apostasy.

Yet I must tell the truth, since the facts would be too easily established to risk equivocation even had I desired.

"My confessor," I said, "is Fray Ambrosio Quevedo."

"Of what church?"

"*Custodio* of the Franciscan Mission of San Juan Bautista."

"When were you last at confession?"

I thought back. "Two months ago."

There was a long solemn silence at that. Pulgar said to the notary, "Take down the name of the Franciscan Ambrosio Quevedo, that we may question him concerning this statement."

Then he said to me, "Have you heard anyone speak of matters such as those of which you are accused?"

I was astonished at the vagueness of the question, but I was to learn that this was the habit of the Inquisition. Questions were purposely vague, because if precisely questioned the accused might in his answers confine himself to the matter of those questions, whereas if the inquiry was in general, clouded terms, he might in his replies betray other matters, or persons, hitherto unsuspected.

I answered, "I do not yet know of what I am accused."

"The Holy Office has as its sacred duty the inquiry into many mortal sins," said Pulgar. "Consult your own conscience. Have you been guilty of adultery, blasphemy, usury, or any heretical act, or treason against His Most Catholic Majesty, the King of Spain?"

"Of the last I cannot be accused, since I am not a subject of the Spanish realm, and cannot therefore commit a treason against it."

They consulted among themselves. Thereafter Fray Palma, the *fiscal*, took up the questioning. "You have not answered all the items of the question put to you," he said.

I considered the items. Adultery—my accursed luck with women! Blasphemy—my unbridled tongue! Usury—never. Heresy—if I had committed a heresy I did not know it. But if I admitted any single one of these things, I was doomed.

So I answered, "I cannot remember having committed any of the

THE AUDIENCE OF TORMENT 389

sins of which you speak, and if I have done them, I have confessed them and received absolution, which erased them from my mind as from my soul."

"You do not remember?" said the *fiscal* grimly. "It is well to bear in mind, Prisoner, that there are ways of stimulating memory."

How well I knew! I remembered El Risero, broken and feeble, as he went to the stake. But I maintained my silence, though my heart continued to sink until I thought it was in the heels of my boots.

Yet after that threat, the examination reverted to the same smooth and treacherous method as before. The questions, like all questions at trials of the Inquisition, left the essence of the matter aside, shut out the possibility of the essence being revealed, were designed only to form a channel through which the judges wished my answers to flow, so as to lead to the desired result: a fatal admission and a conviction of guilt.

As soon as I tried to say anything that did not fit in that aim, I was cut off. I felt, as all who are questioned by the Inquisition invariably feel, perplexity as to why some questions were put to me. Over and over they were asked, in different ways, and I was at the extreme of tension, trying to answer them, and yet—bearing in mind the dying warning of Pedro de Antigua—seeking also to keep my answers from conflicting with each other.

Sometimes in that long afternoon I wondered why these men were taking such pains. It was as if they were practicing a kind of condescension, or even a courtesy, by going to these lengthy recourses; for I was in their power, and they could compel me to answer whatever they chose.

Late in the day, Pulgar came out with a question: "Do you have knowledge of any *fautor* in this case?"

"I do not know what a *fautor* is," I said.

There was a moment's silence then the *fiscal* said, "*Fautor* is a word in the law meaning those guilty of concealing or defending heretics or persons accused of heresy. Is there anyone in this city who has knowledge of the accusations made against you, and who has not informed the Holy Office of this knowledge?"

At that moment my heart seemed to stop beating. I could face death for myself. *But that question involved Dolores!*

It was, I knew, heresy to criticize, however mildly, or even dissent from, the actions of the Holy Office. Now it appeared that it was also heresy to impede the Holy Office in any manner, or on any pretext, such as by withholding from it information.

The horror burst upon me that Dolores was under the shadow of such an accusation. Never in the history of man has such complete and cruel power been invested in any body as in the Spanish Inquisition. And if it ever were revealed that Dolores knew of the charge made by Anaya against me—even if that were not the charge on which I was directly brought here—she might be brought to this very courtroom, tried, perhaps tortured, and condemned.

Sweat as cold and dank as the onset of death came on my forehead and cheeks, and with it a worse despair than I had ever felt.

When I was put to torment it would not be myself but *her* of whom I must think. How would I resist it? How long could I maintain my resolution under agony? Would I break, and for cessation of anguish gasp out her name, and the names of her uncle and servant? Ah, God, there could be no easy way out for me now! If I died under torture, I must keep *that* secret locked within me!

They were waiting. "I know of nobody who has knowledge of any charges against me," I said, my voice almost choked.

"Are you sure of this?"

"I am sure."

Now Pulgar spoke. From the desk before him he lifted a paper and glanced at it. Evidently it was some formal notation.

"It is clear, Prisoner, that you conceal the truth," he said in a voice cold as the stones of the dungeon. "I adjure you, by the Holy Trinity itself, to cease employing dissimulation."

"I can only say what I said before," I insisted.

"How can you deny your guilt?" he exclaimed. "Can you not see I have the proof before me? Speak, since you perceive that I know!"

What the document was, I had no idea, but he spoke of *my* guilt, which made me think that for the present at least he had turned from the subject involving her whom I loved. I shook my head, and managed to repeat my last words, though with all hope gone.

The Inquisitors held a short, low-voiced conference among themselves. Then the *fiscal* said, "Prisoner, do you persist in contumacious denial of what is known to be true?"

I could not answer.

"Speak!" he demanded.

"I—do not deny what I know to be true," I said. "But I cannot say what I do not know to be true."

The *fiscal's* scowl returned. "Are you aware of your fate if this tribunal abandons you to the secular arm?" he asked.

I knew. Torture, before death. I nodded assent, not trusting myself to reply.

All at once Pulgar spoke again. His manner had changed, becoming winning, almost sweet and soft.

"Look now," he said, "we pity you, and we want you to tell us the truth, everything that preys on your conscience, for we are anxious to expedite this affair in your interest."

A long silence followed, for I was unable to reply.

Pulgar's expression grew stern again. "You still obstinately refuse to confess any of the things that have been asked you?" he said. "We will give you time to consider your conduct. If you do not repent and reconcile yourself to the Church and God, though we deplore pain, the next time this tribunal devotes its attention to you, it will be in the Audience of Torment. Take the prisoner away."

With my guards about me, I stumbled from the audience chamber.

3.

But this time I was not conducted directly down to my cell.

Instead they took me aside, to a low-ceilinged room, lighted only by guttering candles and by the glow from a sort of forge for heating iron implements. Its walls were decorated with rings, rivets, chains, manacles, and other instruments of this place. Two men stood by the forge, masked, naked to the waist, with leather aprons: the sworn tormentors.

"Look about you, Prisoner," said one of my guards. "Here are the engines designed to extract the truth, no matter how unwilling the subject."

My blood ran cold as he showed me in turn the instruments of torture: the *garrucha*, or pulley, which is the torture of the hoist; the *escalera*, or ladder, the torment of water; the *potro*, or rack; and the *cauterio*, or burning. With gusto he explained each of these, forcing me to stand before them and contemplate them as he discussed their various hellish functions in inflicting agony.

I thought I was to be put to the torment by one of these means at once; but it was not yet my time. This was a step of almost fiendish subtlety, designed to terrify the mind and break down the will, by the workings of anticipation and imagination before the day of the actual audience in this ghastly room.

Having put me through this, the guard told me to sit. I obeyed, taking my seat before a sort of anvil, and in obedience to a command placed both my feet upon it. The two half-naked men came forward, one of them taking from a hook on the wall a pair of fetters consisting of two ankle rings connected by a short chain of heavy links.

To struggle against this was useless. I submitted to it, while my heart seemed to sink to new depths.

The rings were of malleable iron, strong enough, yet capable of being bent by heavy blows of a hammer, and that was the manner in which the openings were closed after they were placed on my legs. They had, furthermore, holes in the flanges, fitting together at the ends, and through these, rivets were pushed and hammered flat, thus sealing the openings. All of this was done with such noise and grimness that it was plain the chains were expected to remain on me for life.

Thereafter I got to my feet again, and found my step confined to about half a pace, no more, while my chains clanked dismally with every movement.

I was for the moment too furious to feel despair; furious enough, I almost felt, to eat the links that chained me. Yet I forced myself to maintain a calm expression, though I felt like shedding tears from that very rage. I now considered myself cut off from any hope, unless by a miracle.

We returned to my cell. Descending the narrow, slippery stairs, I was concerned lest I stumble, because my chains would have tripped me and sent me headlong.

Within my cell another chain was brought and I felt a lock clamped to the fetters that bound my feet. Not only was I confined by the irons on my legs, but I was fastened to the wall of stone by a ring set into it at the floor.

They finally took the manacles from my wrists, and left me locked in the cell. I sank to the floor, exhausted in mind and spirit. This, it seemed, was the capsheaf of my misfortunes.

4.

That night, in spite of apprehension and hopelessness, sheer weariness overcame me so that I slept for several hours.

I awoke to find that the utter blackness of night in the dungeon had been replaced by a sickly grayness in which objects could be seen, though dimly, the only proof that it was day.

To my surprise that morning I received something better than the usual fare of maize bread and water. A little meat, in the form of a stew, flavored very heavily with peppers and spices in the usual manner of the country, supplemented the flat, tasteless bread. I ate hungrily of this, and it seemed delicious after my diet of water and unleavened maize loaves.

Very soon afterward I wished I had not done so, for though I drank my pannikin of water with my meal, I presently began to feel a burning thirst. There was no more water, and for a time I endured the thirst, which grew worse continually, hoping the jailer would come by, and bring more water at request.

But nobody came. Hours passed: the thirst grew almost unendurable. I felt as if my mouth were of leather within, all moisture drawn out of it by the fiery condiments that had entered my blood.

So intolerable was it at last that I called out again and again, at the top of my voice, almost screaming.

That brought the jailer, scowling and threatening.

"What is it that you're yelling about?" he demanded.

"Water—a little water," I begged.

"You've had your day's ration of water, all you're allowed."

"I am terribly athirst."

"You'll be thirstier yet, if we have to put a gag in your mouth to keep you quiet!"

I was struck silent by that, and he went away.

Thereafter I did no more crying out: not so much from dread of the gag, as from a new terrible realization that had come over me.

This thirst was by deliberate design. I had been tricked into eating the food so that I should suffer.

Perhaps this was the first touch of the much greater suffering I was to undergo, the beginning of the process by which the Inquisition broke down its victims: first, the mental tortures of fear, suspense, and bewilderment in the long days of solitary confinement; then a gradual beginning of physical pain, of which this inflicted thirst might be the forerunner.

After that, the Audience of Torment itself, with its grisly implements which I had been shown. And there, under the most devilish cruelties their minds could conceive, they would seek to take from me my will power, my manhood, even my sanity, until I would screech and gibber like an ape, no more than a poor witless beast, and the lie they desired could be extorted from my suffering lips.

If I could be spared that I would almost welcome the public humiliation of the auto-da-fé, with its yellow *sanbenito* and lengthy sermon, and the final purgatory of the stake. For life would be quenched by the searing flames of the stake in a few minutes, while the agony of the Question, which really was an accusation, put to me again and again, would last for hours, perhaps days.

But no, they would not spare me: I had not even this dreadful hope. And somehow I must summon up the courage to endure whatever enormities they inflicted on me, forgo any hope of cessation of the agony which I could gain by babbling all I knew, for the sake of *her*, whose name I must not even breathe to the eager listening ears of the Inquisitors.

It was sheer living hell, this state of my mind, and yet such are the insistent demands of the body that even in my mental anguish I could not forget my thirst that became more and more unbearable, until my tongue began to swell and my lips grew thick and dry, ready to crack.

At last the grayness of day faded and the intense blackness of night set in once again. I sat with my back against the stone wall, moaning feebly.

Hours passed. Then I saw a glimmer of light. It grew brighter. I heard footsteps. Were they coming for me now?

For a moment fear brought me upright, then I sank back prostrate on the stones of the floor.

The light gleamed through my bars, cast by a horn lamp in the hands of one clad in the black and white Dominican robes, who was accompanied by the jailer.

I heard a voice, kindly and soft. "Who is this man?"

The guard's rough voice responded with my name.

"Of what is he accused?" asked the gentle voice.

"Heresy, treason, and blasphemy," said the jailer. It was the first time I had heard my charges formulated into words.

"Oh, surely not. I must speak to him," said the friar in the same sweet kindly manner.

The door was unlocked and he entered, seating himself on a stool that the jailer brought, and placing the horn lantern on the floor. He was a little old man with a natural tonsure—that is, he was entirely bald, save for a ring of silvery hair at his temples and around the back of his head. Since he was almost toothless, his chin jutted out, and upon his face were countless fine lines. His eyes were dark and soft.

"How are you, my poor friend?" he asked me.

In spite of myself I groaned.

"What is the matter with you?" he said.

"Water——" I gasped.

"This poor man is thirsty!" the old voice cried out, as if with indignation. "Bring him water instantly!"

A pannikin was held to my lips, and I gulped the precious, thirst-quenching liquid, feeling the life flowing back into me; and with it an intense sensation of gratitude to the kind old man who had relieved my suffering.

"My son," he said, when he saw I was refreshed, "I am Fray Marcos de la Coruña, chaplain of this prison. I am most sorry to see you here."

"Padre, I am here by misfortune." My tongue still was thick from the long thirst I had endured.

"Look upon me as your friend," said the old friar gently. "Perhaps you would like to speak—to me alone—about your situation here." His voice was mild, and to the jailer he said, "Leave us."

When the man was gone, he turned to me. In his hands was a breviary, and at his waist a rosary of large carved beads with a crucifix of silver. Altogether he looked ancient, benignant, sincerely sorry for me and my sufferings, and anxious to bring whatever comfort he could.

Yet some instinct warned me not to trust him fully.

"I am a faithful Catholic," I said, "and have never in all my life held one heretical view. Of treason it is impossible to charge me, for I have done nothing but good for the Spanish Crown; and furthermore I am not a Spanish subject."

"The blasphemy?" prompted Fray Marcos gently.

"My conscience is clear. I have never spoken impiously or irreverently of God the Father, God the Son, God the Holy Spirit, or Blessed Mary, Mother of Christ."

"My son," he said, "see—I am your friend and I am sorry for you. Relieve your soul of anything that burdens it, else it will be lost. Do not fear to confess all. You acted perhaps in anger, or in excitement. If so, you are at fault, but surely you will be more greatly at fault if you do not confess the truth, perform penance, and receive the consoling comforts of Holy Church for your soul's health."

In so kind and gentle a manner did he speak, his old face seeming so pure and good in the dim light, that for a moment I could have gone down on my knees to him and wept with gratitude for such sympathy and charity.

But then again came that faint inner cautionary voice. Kind as he seemed, this old man was a Dominican, and hence of the Inquisition. So I spoke guardedly in answer to his questions.

At first these were of a general nature, concerning the mode of my life in the past. But receiving nothing from this, he began to press and coax me on matters of the accusations. When I failed to admit any of the charges, I thought he seemed restive, as if impatient. From this he soon recovered, however, and resumed his gentle manner.

"My son," he said, "you are not candid with me. Do you not perceive that I am trying to save you? Come, confess your sins, and I myself will act as a mediator for you with the Grand Inquisitor, and I promise he will grant you grace."

"You promise that?"

"I do."

"How will I know?"

"He himself will so state to you."

"That he will release me?"

"That he will grant you grace," said the old man placidly.

It seemed to be a confirmation, and yet he had not answered my question *exactly*.

All at once I remembered something that had been told me when I first saw Esteban de Pulgar: *Grace can mean many things . . . pardon complete, pardon in part, or most important of all . . . a state of acceptance with God. . . .*

Grace for my soul only—that was what this promise meant! Grace for my soul, but the fire for my body!

I shrank in horror from the thought. No, I did not believe in this promise of grace. Even were the Grand Inquisitor himself to come to my cell and solemnly assure me of full pardon, there would be some means by which these masters of casuistry would avoid carrying out the promise.

Suddenly it was clear as light. The Inquisition held itself aloof from the actual punishment of those it convicted, *except canonically, as by penances*. Physical punishments, such as executions, were performed by the officials of the law, the "secular arm," so-called, to which the prisoner was "abandoned." In a promise of leniency to me only the *canonical* penalties would be implied. The physical penalties, the Inquisition could and would hold, were outside its holy activities and solely the affair of the civil powers.

At the same moment I knew that this seemingly kind old man, with his gentle voice and soft eyes, was in truth a spy, a false friend seeking to win my confidence with the gift of a little water for my thirst, and promises that were no promises at all.

"I am waiting for your answer, my son," said the soothing voice.

"I have no answer," I said hopelessly.

The old face flushed with anger and Fray Marcos arose.

"Since you seem to wish it, I will set it on the record against you that you stubbornly and wickedly refuse to confess your sins and set your soul at peace with God!" he said in a voice suddenly harsh.

"I have confessed all the sins of which I have any knowledge."

He made a gesture as if rejecting my words, then raised his voice to call the guard.

So quickly was the jailer at his side that I knew he had all the time been hovering just out of sight down the corridor, to listen and act as witness of any admission of guilt cajoled out of me. This was the final fullest proof that it had been one of the myriad tricks and duplicities practiced by the Inquisition.

With his stool and lantern the old friar departed. The iron cage door slammed shut and was locked. I was alone again, chained to the stone wall.

5.

I expected them to come for me next day, but they did not come. Nobody came, except the jailer with the pannikin of water and the flap of maize bread which are my daily ration. That day passed, another day succeeded, and still no one came. None has come in the endless procession of days that have followed since . . . how many months since, I have lost count.

And this brings me up to the present moment.

With the lengthening of time, here alone in my cell, my suspense grows until sometimes I can hardly support it. No word, no hint of what will be done to me, nothing. But I have the threats made by the jailer, the chaplain, and the Inquisitors to keep me company, occupy my imagination, multiply in my mind the horrors that, struggle with myself as I may, I cannot prevent myself from picturing.

The days and nights are endless darkness, distinguishable from each other only by degrees of dimness. In my chains I cannot even exercise. My face and body are gaunt, and I am weak from the poor fare I receive. Often I long for death.

In this solitude and misery I have only my thoughts. Considering what is important in life, I have come to know that what men usually regard as important is not important; and that which does not seem important often is really most important. Men live most fully, struggle most bravely, and die most cheerfully, not for gold or power or fame, but for something as intangible as an ideal.

Myself as instance: those years I campaigned under Iberville, whether in peril, whether wounded, whether suffering cold or hunger, whether deprived of everything that seems to make life worth while, were my happiest. And this because I had then an ideal and a dream. They were Iberville's, but I assimilated them and they became my own. The dream was of the greatness of France, and the ideal was the spirit of France as I understood it: the generous, civilizing, artistic, heroic spirit of France. To this dream and this ideal I devoted all the years of my early manhood, and they appear to me now as the worth-while years of my life.

Many things deflect a man from the true purposes of his existence; and in my case the wiles of women have been the greatest enemies to my full realization of myself. I have found the allurements of women irresistible, sought them out, and played with them the endless game for which they live.

Out of this came a cynical view of them. I learned that they exist in a separate world, their thoughts and aims different, their values incurably personal. The great heroic dreams and ambitions are not theirs: rather, those dreams and ambitions, since they represent risks, frighten and repel them. They cling to what they can touch and feel secure upon; and therefore they seek with their great potent lure of sex to bind men to them, keep them from flying to the clouds, throttle the dreams. Also: where man's cunning ends, woman's cunning only begins; and a man who would master woman must first master himself, which I have never been able to do.

Yet who am I to judge them? What do I know of their necessities, imposed on them by their nature, and their viewpoints, which make to them the winning of a battle unimportant compared to a wedding vow uttered at the altar, the death of a dynasty a small thing beside the birth of a baby?

I have known men who were happy and content because of women: though it was contentment that seemed to me to bind them to the earth and to a routine of life without incident. Adventure is like a religion: it requires of the adventurer faith, in it and in himself, and devotion to it above all other considerations. But latterly I have wondered if all life does not have its adventures, even that of the settled existence?

When I think of the three women with whom my latter life has been entangled, this thought develops.

La Demoiselle, ambitious, selfish, vain and vengeful, seeking only to use me for her purpose; Doña Joya, full of whims and vagaries, unfaithful, also vain, and with cruelty like a corrosive beneath her smooth surface, hating me, perhaps betraying me; such women are worse than valueless, creating in a man bitterness and scorn for their sex and all it represents.

But Dolores—when I think of her I know that woman herself can be an ideal and also a dream for which a man may willingly die. And why she, of the three?

I have liked sophistication in women, yet where the others are sophisticated, she is naïve. I have liked experience in life, but where the others are wordly-wise, she is innocent. I have liked subtle women, armed women, women with whom every encounter is like a fencing duel, yet, unlike these, she is trustful and unguarded.

Knowing nothing of men, nothing of life, nothing of evil, she would seem the least likely of all her kind to fasten her imprint strongly on my soul: yet that is what she has done.

Lovely she is, but that is not the answer in her case, for there are others perhaps as beautiful, although not to my eye. She has charm, and wit, and grace, but others had these things also and never won my heart.

I think it is because she is the first I have ever known who believes in me utterly, in everything I do, gives me unfaltering and complete love, joyfully would surrender her fate and future to me without asking any guarantees or assurances, because she expects of me constancy and honor equal to her own. And I? Strange as it might seem to anyone who knew the St. Denis of my past, I find that I, who never had any conscience about women before, have given to this one the complete devotion which she takes for granted in her simple childlike trustfulness.

This has its dreadful side: for I carry always in my fate her fate also, making my situation in the clutches of the Inquisition twice as ominous and dreadful.

But it also has its wondrous side. Crouching here in my cell, a corpse already to every intent and purpose, the thought of her is like a light in this darkness, or a faint sweet music of bells from afar, alone sustaining me in this cramped space, this suspense of waiting for my doom, when from every black corner the demon of insanity seems to leer at me. . . .

6.

This morning no food or water was brought to me.

When I realized that the others in my tier of cells had received their rations while I alone was omitted, it brought me out of the dull lethargy that recently has possessed me, and my mind has become active with fears and speculations.

Already I have supplied the reason: before a prisoner is taken to the torture chamber, in order to avert his vomiting under torment—so that the nice sensibilities of the reverend judges may be spared—the victim is given no food or water for at least eight hours before.

It means that the day has arrived for me to go to the Audience of Torment!

Weakened as I am by my confinement, I find myself cowering at this thought. And I do not take shame from it; for however bravely a man may face death, the body shrinks instinctively from the prospect of long-drawn-out agony.

It is now past noon. I know this, because we in this lowest tier can hear, very faintly, almost inaudibly, a bell struck somewhere above at that hour.

There it is! The sound for which I have been straining my ears. . . .

Again. Distant footfalls, probably on the stone stair.

No question of it now. Several men are approaching this cell.

I must prepare, as best I may, for what is coming.

A light of lanterns glimmers in the passageway.

They are at my cell door. The key grates, the iron gate is thrown open.

He is looking at me: a man dressed in the black uniform of the familiars. He is swarthy of features, with drooping eyelids that give a special grimness to his visage.

I feel myself staring back at him with the close penetrating scrutiny of a trapped and tortured animal now facing its final executioner.

"Bring him out!"

Weakly I rise and watch as my leg shackles are unchained from the wall. Now I am shuffling down the passage, black familiars before and behind me, the clanking of my irons a dreadful accompaniment to my slow steps.

Nobody speaks. As I begin mounting the stone stair, it requires a special effort each time I lift my feet with their heavy shackles.

A body so spent and feeble, how much pain can it withstand?

I *must* withstand . . . whatever is necessary.

It has just come to me with terrible clarity what I must do when the ordeal begins. I shall bite out my own tongue, so that I cannot, even in my babblings during my suffering, utter any word that may betray *her* to them. I must remember. Take the tongue as far back as I can with my teeth, bite through, however it hurts, sever it completely if I can. . . .

We have reached the top of the first flight. Before me yawns the door of the torture chamber. I see within it the lurid glare of the furnace for heating the irons. The two sworn tormentors, in their leather aprons and black masks, stand grimly awaiting me, naked to the waist, muscular arms folded.

As I look at them I am caught by a horrible sort of curiosity: a morbid, shaking curiosity, as to what form of torture they have decided upon for me.

A roaring is in my ears, and I feel faint, so that they half drag me into the room. About me I stare with the wild eyes of one half demented.

There are the judges, expressionless of face, seated at ease, in their white wool habits and black mantles, with the notary ready to take the record.

Dolores . . . Dolores . . .

I pray you are far, far away from this city now. And that you will never know how it will be with me here, in this room.

I will be faithful to you, beloved. . . .

God have mercy . . . Holy Mary have mercy on me in this my hour of extremity . . .

7.

I have just returned to life.

I have been dead. I do not understand it, but I am sure of it.

My heart stopped beating, I was dead. Yet somehow I am now alive, very weak and faint in that thin feeble margin between life and death, but living.

I begin to remember now. The judges were there, sitting, when I was brought into the Audience of Torment.

The usual questions were asked me: Was I ready to confess my heretical thoughts, acts, and words? Was I ready to name other heretics or apostates or atheists of whom I had knowledge? Was I ready to reveal any *fautors* who had conspired to obstruct the Holy Office in the discharge of its duties?

To each I shook my head.

There was a solemn adjuration delivered by Pulgar. I had refused, he said, to make confession to Fray Marcos de la Coruña, and set my soul at peace with God, which was sufficient evidence of heresy to condemn me. There was, therefore, no reason for me to conceal any other matters in my knowledge, since my case was hopeless anyway. By making such revelations I would spare myself the torment to which the holy tribunal would regretfully have to submit me in case I refused.

I still resolutely shook my head.

Suddenly I was seized and bound, a gag of iron called a *bocado*—"bridle bit"—thrust into my mouth.

So quickly did it take place that I did not have time to carry out my attempt to bite off my tongue: evidently it was a trick others had tried before, and they were ready for me.

Pulgar, looking at the familiars, said one word: *"Escalera."*

Instantly I was lifted from my feet, held flat on my back, and laid upon a short narrow engine in the shape of a ladder, which was so inclined that my head was below the level of my feet, for a reason soon apparent.

With amazing speed the two tormentors worked, while the familiars held me. Arms, legs and body were lashed to the sides of the ladder so tightly that any movement by me caused the whipcord to cut into my flesh.

Now my head was fastened by a brutal metal device that held it rigidly in position.

My jaws were pried open, the gag removed, and my mouth held distended by a prong of iron, called a *bostezo*—"yawning."

Pulgar gave a nod.

With that the torture of water, most complex, most cruel, most favored by the Holy Office, became a sea of agony for me.

I could not move, head and body held rigid, mouth gaping with its iron prong. My nostrils were plugged. A long strip of linen, called the *toca*—"hood"—was placed across my jaws.

On this strip the tormentors began to pour water, the weight of the liquid carrying the *toca* down deep into my mouth, clear into my throat. At once I began to feel all the torments of suffocation.

Looking back on it, I think the most pathetic part of it was the manner in which my poor body, independent of my will and driven by its instincts, made continual futile efforts to ease its condition.

Constantly my throat sought to swallow the water, the cloth—*anything*—in the involuntary manner nature provided, as if it hoped thus to clear a little way for air to pass into my bursting lungs. Some of the water filtered through the cloth, and this stimulated the terrible paroxysmic swallowing. A very little air also managed to enter, enough to keep me conscious, but in no way easing the incredible sufferings of asphyxiation.

Pains shot through my fingers, hands and arms, all over my body; but they were nothing compared to that on which my whole attention was concentrated, the agony of strangulation.

A horror took me at this way of dying. The anguish was unbearable.

Then a confused thought went through my mind. I knew they would stop the pouring water and bring up the *toca* before I died, so that they could revive me and invite me, as I lay there gasping, to give the "confessions" they wanted of me.

I began to long for the instant when relief would come: and then, even as I longed for it, I knew that when the respite came I would probably confess—anything they asked—to stop this suffering.

Or if I summoned resolution not to confess the first time, I would do so the second, or the third, or however many more times I was subjected to the torment, until I was utterly broken in will.

Then came that which I do not at this minute understand.

I said to myself that I must die before they could question me under relief from the torture, yet with the knowledge that torture would be applied to me again if I did not moan out what they wished.

I *willed* myself dead.

It seems incomprehensible. At the moment I felt a pounding and smashing of the heart, and a sense of suffocation more complete and agonizing than before. The world reeled, a blurred dizziness went over me, darkness and flashings of lights came before my eyes.

Yet somehow, in the midst of this, I maintained my will and concentrated it on that one object: death of my body.

I even know when my heart stopped beating.

An instant later I knew nothing.

Blackness covered me. All pain was gone. My lungs no longer labored. Death had taken me.

I *know* I died, because of what I have just heard, a few minutes ago. I died as completely as if a sword had been thrust through my heart, or a leaden ball fired through my brain. *I was dead.*

How long this death lasted I do not know, but when I returned from it I was back in my cell, lying on the pallet.

I opened my eyes in the darkness, then closed them. After a time I heard steps, the door of the cell opened, and a lantern flashed light on me, which I could feel through my closed lids.

"I cannot make it out," a voice said. "I tell you he was dead. I myself examined him. On my reputation as a physician, life had departed. Heart action had ceased, breathing ceased, the body was growing cold.

By this time *rigor mortis* should be setting in. Yet you say he is now breathing?"

The jailer's voice assented.

I did not open my eyes, but I knew the strange voice must be that of the physician whom the Inquisition kept in attendance during the Audience of Torment, to check the condition of its victims. He was plainly worried over the fact that his verdict of death in my case was wrong, fearing that the Inquisitors would hold him culpable for allowing the punishment to stop on a false pronouncement.

"It was sorcery—it can be nothing else," he said after a moment. "Yes, I have heard of such a thing before. A Portuguese traveler, having been in the land of India in the Far East, told of certain persons called *yogis*, who must certainly be worshipers of the devil, who were able apparently to die, by an exercise of will, and bring themselves back to life again after greater or lesser periods of time. It is a state called *catalepsis*, or suspended animation."

He paused, as if contemplating my prone body.

Then, as if reassuring himself, he said, "Yes, sorcery. No doubt of it. He obtained the assistance of the Foul Fiend. I shall report it. This alone is assuredly enough to send him to the stake."

Within me was but one grim thought: I have baffled the Inquisition, told them nothing. They can get nothing from me, and they know it.

What if I die? It takes no very long time, and the victory is mine. And when the flames have done their work I will be beyond their power to hurt me again, ever.

They have left me now, the physician and the jailer. My lungs, throat, mouth, limbs and body are sore, in every tissue it seems. Yet I shall sleep calmly for the first time since I have been in this dungeon.

22. *Dolores*

A long tale this, the living over of my life: but the end of it seems as fraught with fate and fear as all the rest.

Months have passed since the moment when I returned to consciousness after the ordeal in the red-lit chamber of the Audience of Torment. And I find myself still wondering at the incredibilities that have taken place since then.

I remember that some days after my torture a change took place in the lower tier of the dungeon. That morning the guard who brought my food and water was new: a man I had never seen before.

I had recovered a little strength, but still was forced to spend my time almost entirely on the pallet. The circumstance of the new guard, however, awakened me to a dulled conjecture.

Prisoners invariably fear a change in prison. A new broom sweeps clean, as the saying goes, and new guards frequently outdo in rigor those whom they supplant.

But in the dungeon of the Inquisition a change in jailers might be even more significant. Before important autos-da-fé, or when some other major act of the Holy Office is scheduled to take place, guards in the prison are frequently replaced, lest those who have been there for some time may have become acquainted with, and perhaps sympathetic toward, prisoners.

In my own recollection was the case of the prisoner in Cell Three on my own floor, who strangled himself to death with a cord on the day I was brought to the dungeon. His guard—who *might* have given him the cord—now was locked in the selfsame cell, condemned to lengthy imprisonment. But that, of course, did not bring back the prisoner for the auto-da-fé, and the stake.

It is for reasons of this nature that the Inquisition, with its farseeing cunning, prevents when possible such vagaries in human emotion as may affect a guard sufficiently to induce him to help a doomed man to die by his own hand before the Holy Office has opportunity to inflict death on him in the way it prefers.

So this change in guards might mean a change in my fate. Perhaps the judges, after my strange death under torture and return to life, and with the physician's assertion that it was an act of sorcery, had decided there was enough on the record against me without forcing any further confession from me. In other words, it was probable that I was to go to the stake at once, avoiding any further risk that I might die prematurely, and permanently, and cheat the auto-da-fé.

And sure enough, the next day the familiars came for me.

I thought they would take me direct to the judgment hall for final pronouncement of my doom. But no, it was the torture chamber again.

I prepared myself as well as a man weak in body and spirit can do. This time, if I could but bring myself once more to death, I prayed it would be final for me.

One of the tormentors said, "Bring him here."

Half supported by the familiars, I staggered to the seat he indicated. I could not bring myself to watch what new monstrous thing they were going to do to me. Instead, I fixed my attention on the tormentor, seeing in a sort of haze the play of muscles on his naked arm as he lifted some implement. Then I heard blows, and ringing sounds.

In my blurred state of consciousness I did not understand that the shackles had been stricken from my legs until they lifted me to my feet, and I glanced down.

But of course! It was a necessary preliminary. I remembered that El Risero wore no shackles on his limbs in his last tragic march to his pyre. To me this was final proof that my execution was at hand.

"Come," said one of the familiars.

Too weakened even to wonder any longer where next they would take me, I leaned on the men who led me as I climbed slowly the upper flight of stone steps. On that floor was the judgment hall of the Inquisition.

But to my dull surprise, I was conducted instead out into an enclosed court, where the sun beamed brightly—blindingly to me.

Presently, shading my eyes and peering through squinting lids, I could barely make out a half-dozen wretches, evidently brought up from the dungeons like myself, who stood huddling and blinking and screwing up their eyelids, trying to adjust their sight to the glare. Alike they were in their wasted bodies; alike in their pallid skin, sometimes infested with prison sores, which showed through their rags; alike in their long tangled hair and beards; alike in their gaunt faces of suffering. Less human they seemed than beasts, and I knew that I was one with these other pitiful creatures.

"Get them into line," came a command.

Guards obeyed, pushing us into some sort of order. I could make out that men were coming along, examining each prisoner in turn. There seemed to be three inspectors. One wore the black mantle of the Dominicans: that much I could distinguish. The others were not of the order. Behind these, two Dominican friars followed, with papers on which seemed to be lists of names.

As they came in turn to each prisoner, his name was asked and there were some low-voiced questions. The inspecting friar gave an order, a notation was made, and that man was led away, to what destination I could not think.

At last they were before me. I kept my eyes covered and turned down to the ground, resigned to whatever fate had in store for me.

"Who is this one?" asked the chief Dominican.

One of the accompanying friars said, "Number Seven, Lower Tier. St. Denis."

Then I heard a cry of surprise, of shocked disbelief. "Luís—you? It can't be! But—but—yes, it is! Oh, my poor friend!"

It was as if the voice came from another life.

"Beltrán!" I croaked, and lost all strength, so that one of the guards seized me to hold me erect.

"This is he whom I seek," I heard Beltrán say. "You have the writ. Release him to me at once."

"He is yours, Excellency," said the Dominican.

I felt my friend's hand on my shoulder, and in my emotion which was beyond words, I seized it, covering it with kisses, while the tears of weakness ran down my cheeks and into my beard.

"Luís—Luís," I heard him say, as if to comfort me. He took the hand away, placing instead his arm about my shoulders. Then, to someone: "The sun blinds him, cannot you see? Bandage his eyes to shield them from this unaccustomed light that tortures him!"

That done, and still not comprehending what was transpiring, I felt myself led back into the building, down steps outside, and there was a little bustle as a coach of some kind was brought up. I was assisted into it, and then we were riding, somehow, somewhere, through the streets.

Bowing my blindfolded head, I sat humped up, steadying myself against the jolting of the coach by clutching a leather strap I found at the side. Beltrán later told me that his eyes were moist with pity as he gazed at the horror of gruesomeness beside him in the coach, and tried to picture in his mind the strong man he had once known as Luís de St. Denis.

For some time I could not summon strength for words, but at length, in a voice as weak as an insect's creaking, I said, "What . . . are they going . . . to do to me . . . now?"

"Nothing—nothing!" His voice shook with emotion. "You are free!"

"Free . . . ?" I could not understand.

Beltrán took my shrunken fingers in his warm clasp.

"There is much to tell," he said, "but it must wait until you are rested and a little stronger. For the present it is enough for you to know that the Holy Office has released you."

Silently I tried to digest this impossibility, and still was seeking to do so when the coach came to a stop.

"Help him," I heard Beltrán say.

Kind hands assisted me. I groped my way, and my foot was guided to the step of the vehicle, then to the ground. It was evident that a little crowd of onlookers was watching in the street, for I heard expressions of horror and pity as I was conducted into the building.

There were more steps: two flights of them, up which I was half carried. Then I found myself seated in a chair and felt the bandage taken from my eyes. I opened them. I was in a semidarkened room and before me stood Beltrán, with two men servants behind him.

"Help him off with those rags," he directed. "We will wash the prison stink from his body first."

As my eyes accustomed themselves to the subdued inner light, I saw that I was in a bathing room. But where? Assuredly it was not in Beltrán's quarters.

Ready for me was a great marble tub, in which already water had been poured and tempered. As the servants removed my garments, old, foul, and dirt-encrusted, I saw opposite me a mirror, almost of full length, and for the first time beheld my own body with a sense of shock at its shrunken ghastliness.

Over the washboard of my ribs the parched yellow skin was drawn tightly. Like huge knots the joints of my wasted limbs stood out, making me appear like a very old and emaciated man. My long matted beard and hair, which always had been of a fleckless black, now were streaked and tinged with gray; and the haggard eyes staring out from this tangle completed the picture of a famine-stricken wretch. Could such a wreck of a healthy, vigorous body ever be the same again?

"Wash him," commanded Beltrán.

Carefully I was helped into the tub. Oh, the luxury of warm cleansing water flowing over my body for the first time in months! I felt the hands of the servants as they gently lathered soap over my poor gaunt ribs and lank limbs.

After the blessed bath I was dried and clothed in clean undergarments, soft slippers, and a robe. Refreshed, though still dazed and weak, I found myself seated once more in a chair.

Now one of the servants, with scissors and razor, approached me.

"When we have trimmed and combed your hair, and shaved away that beard, you will look like a new man," Beltrán said.

But the barber suddenly stepped back with an exclamation.

"What is it?" asked Beltrán impatiently.

The transparent skin of my face, the eyes deep-set with suffering, the long hair and beard, seemed to have struck the man with awe.

"Excellency," he said, "what does this face remind you of?"

Beltrán did not reply.

"The *Doloroso* in the cathedral!" exclaimed the man.

Beltrán gave me a new curious, appraising stare.

"Hum," he said. "Yes, I see what you mean." Then he smiled at me. "Luís—what a thing! That ascetic face of yours—that beard and long hair—the sad expression of those eyes—to this servant of mine make you seem at this minute to be a living picture of the large image of the Crucified One in the cathedral!"

I remembered the figure of which he spoke. It was of wood, life size, carved and painted by some native artist, and imbued with that curious tortured realism these people somehow succeed in imparting to such statues. To myself I thought that if I resembled that, I must be a terrible spectacle indeed.

But the tense moment passed, the barber recovered from his temporary pause. The scissors began to snip; then came lather and the razor, and my face was clean of beard. My hair was combed and tied. At last they held before me a mirror. I saw that I had been converted from the likeness of a suffering image into a man: very thin, pallid and weak, with hollow eyes and sunken cheeks, but at least a man.

"Now food," said Beltrán.

In another room I ate and took a glass of wine. The viands were delicious but I found I had little capacity. It would take time for me to regain a normal healthy appetite.

In the wine was a sleeping potion, and I fell into slumber soon in a great bed with high posts and a canopy, like a child beginning its recovery from a long and wasting illness.

2.

When I awoke it was morning, and beside my bed was Beltrán, with an alert dark little man in brown serge, whom he introduced as Francisco Piña, a physician. At once, when they saw I was awake, the doctor began to examine me, going over my entire body carefully, looking at my tongue, eyes, and throat, feeling my pulse, and listening to my chest.

When he finished, he said to Beltrán, "The ability of the human body to recover is almost incredible. Given food and care—and prevented from exciting himself—this man will return to health. Aside from the inevitable effects of long imprisonment and ill-treatment, such as extreme emaciation, great weakness, and a temporary difficulty in adjusting the eyes to strong light, I find nothing vitally wrong with him. Time will cure these."

Beltrán smiled at me. "You heard? We'll soon see the color back in your face, the strength in your limbs, the old light in your eyes!"

"But—where am I?" I managed to ask.

"You are in the house of the *Corregidor*."

"The *Corregidor*?" I gaped in amazement. "I never saw this room before——"

He gave me his old impish grin. "Of course not, you rascal! It is not a part of the house with which you would in any likelihood be acquainted. You are in the apartment of the old *Corregidor* himself. The

suite of his wife, the charming Doña Joya—with which you may be
somewhat more familiar—is on the other side of the hall."

I was a little startled. "How came you to bring me here?"

"Because I am now the *Corregidor*."

I simply stared at him.

"You are confused, and I do not wonder," he said. "There have been
some mighty changes, but I must not try to explain them all now,
since the doctor orders otherwise. Yet I will say this much: Don Baltasar
de Lanciego, the old *Corregidor*, has been removed from office because
of inefficiency and inattention, due perhaps to age. He was sent back
to Spain. With him, of course, went his wife; and I fear she was none
too happy over it. Yet with her beauty and her—her other traits—Doña
Joya may not find it difficult to make a place for herself in the court
at Madrid, where a woman who is charming, and also accessible, is
never without friends among the pleasure-loving courtiers. Meantime,
I hold the office of *Corregidor*—as I one day told you I would!"

All this was most astonishing; but there was a far, far greater question in my mind. Dolores—what of her? I wanted to ask, but my tongue
clove to the roof of my mouth. At that moment it seemed so momentous
to me that I could not frame the question, for if anything had happened
to her, I knew I could not live.

The physician interposed. "With all respect, Excellency," he said, "no
more questions. I will not be responsible if he is further agitated."

And with that I had to be content. Yet if being stirred up was the
object to be avoided, I was so much so that although I spent my time
in bed I did not sleep during that day. At night, however, Beltrán's
servants brought with my supper a glass of wine, similar to the one
I drank the evening before, containing a drug the doctor had prescribed. Soon after I partook of it, I again fell into heavy slumber,
from which I did not awaken until the following day.

That morning, in spite of depression of spirits, I felt stronger physically, and after I was bathed, shaved, and robed, the physician said I
might sit up in a lounging chair. From there I stared out of a window
upon the Zócalo, now cleared of debris and being converted into the
park it should have been from the beginning. So filled was I with restless and gloomy thoughts and concerns that when, about noon, I heard
footsteps in the next room, and Beltrán entered, I hardly looked up.

"How are we doing?" he asked.

I continued to gaze out of the window.

"What is it, my friend?" he next said.

"Nothing," I answered, "except that I am oppressed. It seems to me that there is little for me to live for."

"*Que hay!* This does not sound like you, Luís!"

I resolved to have it out with him. "There is something—a fear—that gnaws at my heart, Beltrán," I said.

"Fear? What fear?"

"You perhaps do not even remember it—but on the night of my arrest—I was telling you of a girl——"

"I do seem to remember something of the kind," he said musingly. "Her name—let me see—what did you say it was?"

"Her name is Dolores de Ramón."

"Ah yes—that was it. From some remote northern outpost, wasn't she?"

"San Juan Bautista."

"Do you mean to tell me that you still have an interest in this Dolores?" he demanded, as if surprised, or even half indignant.

I gave him a look almost of despair. "Can you give me any news of her, Beltrán? Good friend—I am terrified for her, and have gone almost crazy wondering what has befallen her. If you have any knowledge, however slight, I beg you tell me!"

"Remember what the physician said about agitating yourself," he warned me solemnly. "As for this girl—it is a little difficult to remember anything concerning one girl, where there are so many. I believe you told me she was dark and rather pretty——"

"*Rather* pretty? She is as beautiful as the dawn!"

"A friend of yours, I think?"

"More than a friend—infinitely more, Beltrán. I love this girl. She has not been out of my mind all the months I have been in prison."

"So you ask me—as easy as if it were snapping my fingers—to find again one girl, among one hundred and forty thousand people in this city—supposing she is here, and not gone off to some other place—so you can have the satisfaction of seeing her again?"

"Will you try? It is asking much, but how greatly I wish this thing I cannot even express to you!"

"I suppose," he said, as if pondering the matter, "that as *Corregidor*

I could cause a search for her if she is still in the city. If found, shall I have her brought at once before you?"

"What do you mean?" I cried in agitation. "You would not arrest her? Treat her with all gentleness and courtesy—and conduct her to me, if she will come, as soon as you can find her." Then I paused at another thought. "No! I take back that request. Do not let her see me as I am just now, Beltrán. Not while I look like a skull! I fear that if she beheld me as I am she would shrink from me——"

He grinned. "Perhaps not," he said. "At least she has not seemed to shrink from you in the hours she has sat by your bedside while you slept."

"Dolores—has been *here?*"

"These two nights." He nodded. "She has watched over you like a mother over her child. And nothing could persuade her otherwise. On one thing only she agreed—at the physician's sternest order—that she would leave as soon as you showed signs of waking——"

"Beltrán—friend of my life! You have been joking with me? How can you show such cruelty? Where is she—now, this instant?"

At that he laughed and turned to the open door into the next room.

"Señorita Dolores," he said, "I have this rogue sufficiently committed to suit me. I believe him, and I will be your witness. Now, since it appears that *not* seeing you agitates him more perhaps than seeing you would do, come——"

An instant later she stood framed in the doorway, with a light in her eyes such as no man can describe.

At first I could hardly believe . . . then a great, almost sacred joy swept over me like a tide.

"Dolores . . ." I little more than framed her name with my lips.

For a moment she remained where she was. And then, in a swift little swoop like a bird's she was beside me, kneeling by my chair, sobbing, her face against mine, her arms about my neck.

Neither of us was aware when Beltrán—that understanding friend—slipped out of the room and closed the door behind him.

I sat, and at first a great constraint kept me motionless and tongue-tied. The prize was mine, and the wonder of it made me tremble, and I dared not put out my hand.

What was I—good Lord!—to touch a thing so rare? I could not speak. Only the softness of her cloud of hair, the firm tenderness of her arms, the wetness of her tears on my cheek, assured me this was no dream, no wild delirium.

"Please—do not weep——" I whispered at last.

"Oh, Luís—let me—let me——" she cried. "I have not known the luxury of real tears—since the day—the terrible day—when I learned you were *lost*——"

The little wail with which she ended brought my arms at last about her and my lips softly caressed her hair, so softly that she did not even know. Or did she?

After a time she lifted her face, with wondrous dark lashes wet with tears, and gazed, it seemed, into my soul.

"Dolores," I said.

"Yes, Luís . . . ?"

"How I have longed for you!"

"Oh, my dear one!"

"The dungeon taught me—how greatly I love you—you are my world——"

"Oh, Luís—*beloved!*"

And for the first time I felt on my lips the pure wonder of her kiss.

3.

How can a man tell of his hours of supreme happiness?

I cannot; for me, it is easier to describe my hours of supreme misery. I can only say that the days following were days of joy so mighty that my mind found it impossible to think of the future, being so full of the present.

I am a man, certes, with sufficient experience in vicissitude so that I never should have ceased considering the possibilities of ill or good that lay ahead: for myself, and now even more importantly, for her. But in those days I became like her, having a blind, unreasoning belief that nothing possible of evil could befall us now, in the state of bliss which requited love is.

Yet my body seemed to take thought of the morrow, even if my mind did not. Perhaps from very joy, it recovered amazingly and prodigiously. My appetite returned, my face and figure filled in, and my strength grew, until within a few weeks, had it not been for the whitening hair at my temples, one would hardly have known I had been in prison, much less suffered the ordeal of torture.

This matter of graying temples, I confess, somewhat dispirited me, for I had always been proud of my thick black hair.

One day, as I sat alone with Dolores, caught up as always by her loveliness and youth, I said to her, rather sadly, "Are you sure that you can love a man so much older than you, and with gray hair in the bargain?"

Her smile and kiss were swift. "As for age, love, you are exactly the age a man for my heart should be. And as for a little gray, do you not know that you have gained just enough white along your temples to make you even more distinguished in appearance, and handsomer than before—not only to my eyes, but to all who behold you?"

From then on my gray hair never again concerned me. But she filled me with such longing that I said, "Ah, why must we wait to be married in San Juan Bautista?"

This was her wish: that her grandfather and her two doting grand-aunts might witness the great event.

But at my tone tears stood beautifully in her eyes. "We need not, heart of my heart—if you so desire it otherwise. I will be your wife—tomorrow—or today—or when, now or any time, you want me!"

I did not press her farther on this. After all, since I had lived thus long without her, I could manage it a little longer to make her happy.

Another problem there was, however, which I had never broached to her, since never until now had I been able to discuss intimately with her matters of importance to us. With a sense of anxiety I turned to this topic.

"There is something I have shrunk from saying——" I said to her.

"Shrunk? From saying to *me*?"

"It might be an obstacle——"

"There can be no obstacle to my love!"

Her eyes almost flashed as she dared me to put her to the test.

"Then it is this," I said. "I cannot live here, in this country. At present all appears serene in prospect, but there is no telling when things may change. My life, furthermore, and my career, are bound up in France. Here I have nothing—what few possessions I had were confiscated by the Holy Office, which never returns anything. I am living at this moment on Beltrán's bounty, which pride will not let me do as soon as I am in full health again."

I paused. She sat waiting, her eyes fixed upon me. At last, as if to prompt me, she said, "Well?"

"It seems to me cruel," I went on, "to ask you to go to a foreign land——"

She gave a little laugh. "Is that all? Is this the 'obstacle' that appears so great to you? Do you think that I have not known this in my heart from the first? And long ago promised myself that when or where you go, I will go also?"

"But you will lose your inheritance——"

"I have never had it. I will not miss it."

"You will give up everything dear to you——"

"*You* are everything dear to me!"

And by her kiss, I knew it was true.

4.

Meantime, there were disclosures, some of them most amazing.

When I was able once more to walk about without assistance, and could feel the spring returning to my step, Beltrán one evening gave a little supper at his house for only four: Dolores and me, himself—and Doña Gertrudis de Valverde y Mendoza.

That she should come thus openly and alone to his house surprised me when he told me of it; and I was struck, on seeing her, by the fact that for this evening she was all in black, and looking most lovely in it, too. She came up to me smiling.

"Don Luís," she said, "you have had many kisses this day, I am sure, but you shall have still another!"

And she gave me a pretty salutation on the cheek.

"Dolores does not mind," said she. "We have been dearest friends—since I became a widow."

A widow! The black garb—so she was in her weeds. I observed that she did not seem overly downcast by her state, and remembered there had never been much affection between her and Don Pedro, her late husband, a harsh man and austere.

Not long was I kept wondering. Don Pedro, they told me, while on an inspection tour in Vera Cruz, some months before, had been taken off by the *vomito*—yellow fever—which was epidemic there.

A moment later Beltrán had his arm about her waist.

"Gertrudis is going to make an honest man of me at last," he said.

"An honest man!" I laughed at his droll twist of a phrase usually applied only to women who marry after being somewhat errant.

"We will wed as soon as her mourning period is over," he went on, "and will then go back to Spain together."

"And give up being *Corregidor?* It was your ambition!"

"The ambition has been achieved. Now there is something more important. My father, the old Conde, is failing; and writes beseeching me to return home and take over his duties. Since I am the heir, I owe this to him, so I have asked for a replacement, who will come from Spain as soon as the royal appointment is made. Gertrudis and I will then be free to go."

Dolores, of course, thought this magnificent. I congratulated them heartily, for they had long been lovers in secret, and now could be so openly. Just the same, the departure of my friend so soon for Spain added another reason for my anxiety to be gone from this place.

That was in the future however, and this evening we made a table of happiness, we four, while I asked questions that were uppermost in my mind.

"I can hardly believe it yet, nor do I understand how my release, from the hellhole I was in, came about," I began.

"Because God willed a miracle for you," Dolores said softly.

"The miracle, I think, is this girl who loves you," said Beltrán.

"Say rather this friend of yours—Beltrán," she returned instantly.

"And there is," put in Gertrudis, with a smile, "the small matter of an event of world-shaking importance that might be counted in on this miracle."

"She refers to the death of your French King," said Beltrán.

"*Le Roi Soleil?* Dead?" I was aghast. Louis XIV had been King forever, it seemed to me. He had, in fact, reigned for seventy-two years, the most glorious years of France; and, as to many another Frenchman, he somehow had appeared to me as immortal. For the moment I felt lost.

"His death occurred September 1, 1715—after you were imprisoned," Beltrán went on. "Of course we knew nothing of it here until a ship made the voyage across the sea with the news."

This was of mightiest importance. My mind raced with speculations on what changes must be occurring both in France and her colonies.

"The old King," continued Beltrán, "is succeeded by his great-grand-

son, a boy only four years old, under the title Louis XV. But the real
ruler at present is the Regent, Philippe, Duc d'Orléans. Between Philippe, the French Regent, and Philip, the Spanish King—both of them
Bourbons, and blood cousins—no love is lost. So our monarch, his obliga-
tion to France buried with the old King, has turned his interest and his
policy toward Italy, through the influence of his Queen, Elizabeth of
Parma. And in so doing, he comes closer to the Vatican at Rome, which
long has desired to reform the excessive severities of the Spanish Inquisition, but has lacked power to do so, since the Holy Office has owed
nominal obedience only to the Spanish Crown, and actual obedience
only to its own desires—at times taking advantage of its position, which
is national and political, rather than religious, to flout His Holiness, the
Pope, quite openly."

I listened, astounded at this news.

"The new policy already has wide effects," said Beltrán. "For one
thing, the rule of Linares in New Spain was weak and unlucky. So he
has been supplanted as Viceroy by Don Baltasar de Zúñiga, Marqués de
Valero y Duque de Arion, one of the great grandees of Spain, a man
much younger and more competent——"

"Who at once showed his competence by dismissing the old *Corregidor* and appointing Beltrán to his post," said Dolores.

He laughed. "Sweet Dolores!" Then he went on, "Do you know, Luís,
what this lady of yours has been doing these months you were in
prison?"

I looked at her. Her lashes drooped. "Nothing," she said.

"Ha! Nothing!" he exclaimed. "Hear this, if it be nothing! When you
did not return after that evening you found her at her *fonda*, she waited
a day, then fearing that something was amiss, went with her uncle,
Don Juan, to the viceregal palace and sought me out."

"I remembered his name," said Dolores shyly. "You said he was your
friend——"

"It was I who should have remembered *her* name—and sought her
out!" Beltrán declared. "But my mind was stunned by what had occurred. She was the clear thinker. Her beauty induced men to do her
behests, and Don Juan de Ramón is enough of a soldier to inspire respect. Her name was brought to me."

"And he came at once," she murmured.

He nodded. "I took her aside and told her what had befallen you.

Not a tear, mind you, did she shed. But she placed in my hands her uncle's bill of complaints against Gaspar de Anaya, and said she was here as a personal witness against him. With that I traced down his dossier: it is a full one, I can assure you. The man is a thief and a cur. But Linares was still Viceroy then, and since you had been seized by the Holy Office, it would only further endanger you to stir up matters against Anaya, for as your accuser he would become twice as venomous against you."

"It was Anaya, then?" I said. "For months I wondered who denounced me."

"You forgot the Santa Hermandad and its thoroughness," said Beltrán. "It traced back the soldiers who were killed until it found they were of Anaya's guard. When he learned through this source that you were rescued from the *ladrones,* he at once renewed his charges, knowing that because you are a foreigner the mere accusation of a crime like heresy, before the Holy Office, would be enough to destroy you."

"It seems I owe this man very much!" I exclaimed.

"He has occasion to rue it: for which he can thank Dolores, who has been his nemesis."

"And you have been in this city—all these months?" I asked her, lifting her hand to my lips.

She suffered me to keep the hand. "Could I leave when I did not even know your fate?" she said simply.

"When weeks passed and Don Juan was forced to return to his duty, I urged Dolores to go with him, fearing danger for her in this place," went on Beltrán.

"How great was the danger, none of you know!" I said.

He looked at me, as if to inquire more, but then went on. "In any case she stayed. Don Juan reluctantly departed, taking with him the *mozo,* Íñigo, for though a native cannot be punished by the Holy Office, he can be made to testify as a witness, and even tortured to obtain evidence against a prisoner accused. So Don Juan got Íñigo out of the city, where he might be an unwitting danger. Dolores would have been left alone—except for my sweet Gertrudis, who befriended her."

"She took me in. I have lived with her since," said Dolores, smiling with affection at her friend.

"She is like a sister to me," said Gertrudis with real sincerity.

"To go on with the story," Beltrán continued, "when the new Viceroy came he brought with him a new Inquisitor General and a desire for reform. Pulgar was recalled to Spain. Meantime Dolores was at me—and Gertrudis with her—to gain an audience with the Viceroy. A pair they are, let me tell you! At last the hearing was arranged."

He paused and smiled at Dolores. "I wish you could have seen this lady on that day, Luís. She was magnificent! With beauty, indignation, charm, pleading, sweetness, and the appeal of tears—every one of woman's most devastating weapons—she told her story. The Marqués de Valero was quite unable to resist her. He ordered an immediate investigation of Anaya's record."

"And the words were no more than out of his mouth," said Dolores, "when Beltrán had the dossier in his hands."

"Which was the finish of Gaspar de Anaya," added Gertrudis.

"I give Valero credit for instant action," agreed Beltrán. "Anaya, that fat swine, was kicked out of office as fast as a successor, with an escort of troops, could ride to Parras with the order. He is under arrest, I understand, and is ordered to the capital for trial. I would not care to be in his shoes. The evidence is overwhelming against him—peculations, cruelties, and injustices without number. It might mean the gallows for him. The very least penalty he can incur is absolute ruin—to be fined everything he has amassed, and sent home in disgrace, more penniless even than he came."

"What of his accusation against Don Diego de Ramón?" I asked.

"Dismissed. Don Diego again commands at San Juan Bautista."

"Now praise be to God!"

"But meantime, do not think that Dolores let up on me, nor her ally, Gertrudis, either. They were at me day and night——"

"He needed no prompting," put in Dolores.

"At last Valero, at my urging, ordered the records of all prisons opened," Beltrán said, "and those unjustly accused freed. On the roster of the prison of the Holy Office was your name and against it as accuser the name of Anaya. That was enough for the Viceroy. I got the writ for your release."

So this was the story, in briefest substance: the death of a King, the coming of a new Viceroy, the devotion of a friend, the love of a woman —and behold, a miracle!

5.

But later that night, after we had seen the ladies home, Beltrán had more to tell me.

"It was not quite as simple as I described it at the supper table," he said, when we were alone. "Almost never in history has the Holy Office given up a prisoner once it had its clutches on him. Not even the Viceroy's writ could have saved you, except for some extraordinary circumstances."

"In what regard?" I asked.

"I am going to mention a subject I did not bring up at supper tonight, for it is terrible, and I did not wish to upset the ladies." For a moment he sat stroking his short black beard, then went on. "Luís, know this: I myself saw the file of the Inquisitorial tribunal on you. There were the charges: heresy, treason, blasphemy. There were the proceedings before the judges of the Holy Office. After that there was a notation that you had been *put to the Question*—did—did they actually——"

I nodded.

His face showed horror. "In what manner?"

"The *escalera*. The torment of water."

"*Dios!* I have heard it described—that no human resolution can withstand it!"

"It was . . . bad."

"Bad? Such torture is the most dreadful thing that can happen to a man! My very toenails cringe at the thought. What did you tell them?"

"Nothing."

"You gave them *nothing?* But they must have wrung something from you!"

"Not one word."

He stared at me. "This is without parallel. How could any human flesh undergo an ordeal so terrible, and still——"

"I uttered no confession. Others were involved."

"Who?"

"Yourself, possibly, for you had befriended me. Dolores, certainly. Do you know what a *fautor* is?"

"No."

"It is one who, knowing a man is accused of heresy, protects him. Dolores knew I was so charged and did not denounce me."

"María santísima!"

"I cannot explain how I was able to resist, Beltrán. I do not fully understand it myself."

He was silent for a long moment. Then he said, "I do believe, Luís, that you are the most courageous man I have ever known."

"Say rather that I am a very stubborn man."

"Call it courage, as I do—or stubbornness, if you prefer—they could not break you down! Do you know that in all its tens of thousands of inquiries there is scarcely an instance in which the Holy Office has failed to break down one whom it put to the Question? Such resolution is almost superhuman! It did this for you—it saved your life!"

With that, for the first time, I felt a little satisfaction—a very humble pride—in having done perhaps better than I knew, and in playing at least a part in deciding my own final fate.

Beltrán went on, "For once the Holy Office seems to have been baffled. No finding or judgment of guilt was entered against your name. That—and also the fact that Anaya was your accuser—brought about your release. The last was sufficient for Valero. But the first decided the new Inquisitor General."

Again he paused. "There is still one more matter," he went on. "A mystery I do not understand."

"And what is that?"

"It sums up to this: someone powerful and important enough to reach the King's ear seems to have taken an interest in you. Your name was contained in a royal *cédula* inquiring concerning your case. Such a thing is unheard of. Know you who could have exerted such influence in your behalf?"

I shook my head. "This mystifies me as much as it does you."

"We owe a debt of thanks to him—or perhaps her," he said. "The royal interest spurred Valero's investigation, and it also encouraged the Inquisitor General to co-operate."

That night, in my bed, I wondered about Beltrán's words.

Someone . . . important enough to reach the King's ear . . .

Who with such power in Spain could be interested in me? And for what reason? I finally gave up trying to guess the answer to a question which seemed impossible to answer.

6.

At the end of the fourth month I felt my old self again, and began to lay plans.

For weeks the city had been filled with talk of the first grand project of the new Viceroy: nothing less than the long-delayed *entrada* into the northern wilderness called Texas, to establish missions and presidios and so take actual, rather than theoretical, possession of that territory.

The Franciscans were in charge. One contingent of soldiers already was marshaling at San Juan Bautista, and a second detachment, with at least a dozen priests, was to march soon from the city of Mexico to join it.

On this I pinned a daring hope. If I could gain permission to travel with this unit to San Juan Bautista—on the very good excuse that my bride-to-be wished to be married there—everything else might fall into place, for the horizon northward was the frontier!

I spoke of the request for such permission to Beltrán, and he thought it reasonable that under the circumstances it would be granted.

Then, one day, there came a summons to the Viceroy's presence.

I was jubilant. It could only mean the fruition of my hopes and dreams. Eagerly I looked forward to telling Dolores that we would start soon, have a leisurely journey under the protection of the expedition, and exchange our wedding vows before Padre Ambrosio, with her family present, in the church at San Juan Bautista.

With Beltrán I went at once to the palace, and with little delay we were ushered into the Viceroy's audience room. As soon as I saw him, I was impressed by the vivid contrast this man made with the old Duque de Linares. Where Linares was weak and feeble, Valero was vigorous. He had a sharp, harsh face with lowered eyebrows, a thin mustache, cold eyes, and a mouth that was like a slit cut by a knife. This man was ice. He was perhaps not cruel, so much as cynical, but it came to the same thing in the end.

Yet in his face I read power to rule, the ability to organize and administer affairs of government and command obedience; and perhaps also even a sense of justice, according to the grim Spanish ideas of justice.

He spoke to me politely, when Beltrán introduced me.

"Señor St. Denis," he said, "I have before me the records concerning you. They are most interesting."

In spite of his manner I felt an indefinable uneasiness.

"I trust they do not prejudice Your Excellency against me," I said.

"On the contrary, they arouse my admiration. You came to New Spain on an errand for the Church, and were arrested—unjustly, it appears. You were beset by *ladrones*, and escaped hanging by the Santa Hermandad—which is most free with the rope. You so impressed my predecessor that he gave you an official position, with a salary. You performed, according to this report, prodigies in suppressing the Zócalo revolt. You were imprisoned by the Holy Office—and put to the Question. Out of all this you emerged unscathed, with your reputation as high, your position as good, as before. Such a man is to be reckoned with."

Thus far his remarks had been kind, even complimentary.

"Your Excellency is most gracious," I said. "Would it please you, My Lord, to extend this graciousness by giving me permission to travel north with the Franciscan expedition, to San Juan Bautista, where I desire to take unto myself a wife?"

At my words his eyes became icy. "The expedition will leave very soon. But you will not go with it."

I think I must have given a gasp.

He went on, "As a matter of fact, this record of yours has caused me to arrive at a decision which I fear you will not like. You are *too* much to be reckoned with, Señor St. Denis—too dangerous a man, to put it bluntly. Therefore, I cannot permit you to remain in New Spain."

He paused, and then with positive finality, delivered my sentence.

"You will hold yourself ready to go to Vera Cruz in two weeks, from where you will sail for Guatemala, there to remain for the rest of your natural life." He turned his cold eyes on my friend. "Until that time, Don Beltrán," he said, "you will be responsible for the person of this man."

I left the palace almost staggering. Guatemala! A land of steaming heat, of fever, of jungles, and of slaves! I might as well be dead as go to Guatemala!

23. *The Reckoning*

Outside on the street, I stopped Beltrán, and said to him in deadly seriousness, "Call soldiers at once and have me placed under arrest!"

"For why?" He gazed at me as if he thought me suddenly insane.

"Because you are my friend."

"And a friend should treat you thus?"

"It is a friendship I will not violate. *Por Dios!* I will not willingly rot in Guatemala! If I am not confined in a prison cell, I will escape from this place, if I must crawl on hands and knees! And I want you to know it, for you have been made responsible for my body."

He gave me a smile that I thought rather sad. "Luís, this does not surprise me. A curse on this cold fish Viceroy! I understand how you feel, my friend, and your loyalty to me I will never forget. But what might happen to me need not concern you. It is yourself we must think about."

"You would have to answer to the Viceroy!"

"True—and so let us consider that phase of it. What if you should— let us say—slip through my fingers? There would, perhaps, be squally times, for this Valero has a temper. But after all, what can even a Viceroy do to me, for no greater crime than letting a man, not even a prisoner but condemned to exile, escape from my custody? I am a Córdoba! And a future Conde, who will have a high place at the royal court! He might rave at me. He might, at worst, deprive me of office and send me back to Spain under displeasure. But I have already resigned my office. To Spain is where I will go in any case. His displeasure I care nothing about. Not even the Marqués de Valero would dare go beyond this with me, situated as I am. No, this is not the reason why I implore you to do nothing rash."

"Then what reason?"

"For one, the flight north without escort would be most dangerous. For another, what will you say to Dolores?"

It was the last that concerned me chiefly. I knew I must tell her, and it would be the hardest thing I had ever done. But after a moment I said, "Beltrán, I am determined; and in fairness to her, I must tell her as soon as I can. I will go to her at once."

I left him, going slowly toward his own place, while I set out for the house of Doña Gertrudis, which was on the other side of the palace area.

Dolores was there, and came at once to me, smiling. But the smile faded when she saw my face.

"Something has happened!" she said.

"Dolores—heart of my heart——" I began. And then I blurted it out, "I have come to give you back your promise!"

Her eyes widened. "What—do you mean?" she almost faltered.

In a few words I told her of the Viceroy's order. "I could not take you to Guatemala, to die of some disease, or even to live out your life in misery there," I said. "Whatever happens to me now, I can no longer ask you to share my fortunes——"

"Luís!" She looked at me very closely. "You are going to attempt something desperate!"

I drew a deep breath. "I am going to do what I should have done long ago—make the attempt, however dangerous, to get out of this country."

"And leave me? Luís—you can never!"

"I cannot take you——"

"You must! Oh, believe me, you must! I will die if you don't!"

I gazed at her miserably. "You do not understand what you say. This means hardship and weariness such as you have never known. And great peril. I will probably be pursued. If I am captured, there can be for me but one fate: execution. Besides, there are the murderous *ladrones* and the equally murderous Santa Hermandad—I hardly know in the hands of which it would be worse to fall——"

"Oh, Luís—to me one thing would be worse than death or anything else—to be without you!"

She came into my arms and suddenly began to cry, turning her face into my shoulder, and keeping it there while her sobs shook through her. Holding her, seeking to soothe her tears, a great wave of pity for a thing so frail and yet so loyal went through me.

Tear-stained, her face turned up to mine. "If you leave me—hear me—I will follow! You say there are perils—you will have it to remember that I am alone among them! Luís, your life is my life, and if you die—why—why then I would wish to die too——"

The tears came again, and with my arms about her, I considered the prospect. Alone, riding by day and night, I might give a pursuing body of horsemen a very good race of it: provided, always, that I did not fall into some ambuscade along the road. But with a girl so delicate and tender as this one, it would be different. Our pace must be cut to her strength, growing slower as she wearied. Even if we encountered no mishap on the road, we were almost certain to be overtaken, if pursued, long before we reached the frontier.

And yet I knew she spoke the truth: she would not consent to be left behind. With me, or following, defenseless and alone, she would make that journey north.

Should I remain, bow to the Viceroy's command, and go to Guatemala? But no, she repelled that suggestion fiercely. The die was cast for us, she said. It was the north or nothing.

"Come, dry your tears, *querida*," I said at last. "If, as you say, I am all that is dear to you, so are you to me. I will never leave you."

It was a promise made out of my love for her. But even then I did not fully understand the fullness of peril and pain it would mean for her.

I said to myself that by using great caution and forethought, and perhaps in a crisis a brave flourish of weapons, we might win through. I even half convinced myself into a state of mild optimism over the prospect. But in so doing I blinded myself to the truth, partly because I could not bear her unhappiness, partly because I knew her desperate determination, but mostly because I so wanted her.

When I surrendered she stemmed her tears and brightened with a smile.

"You win your wish after all!" she said.

I looked at her blankly.

"Don't you see, you stupid man?" she cried. "There can be no waiting to be married in San Juan Bautista. When we begin this journey, we must go—as man and wife!"

Again she clung to me with tears of a different kind, while I could only caress her and marvel at her. And fear for her, too.

2.

We were married at the Convent of San Francisco, with Beltrán and Gertrudis as our witnesses, and when I kissed my bride I knew I had a wife only if I could keep her.

For the journey we had two good horses, the gift of Beltrán, and for weapons I carried two flintlock pistols in holsters at the saddlebow, also a present from my friend. Gertrudis had given Dolores a riding dress and cloak, and some women's necessaries—weeping that they were so few, since we must carry everything in our saddlebags.

"I cannot promise how much grace I can give you," Beltrán said gravely after the ceremony. "You are newly married, and how can one say where a new-wed couple will choose to stay on the first night of its bliss, or the next, or the days after? I have this much excuse for not at once 'discovering' you are gone. And there is this in your favor—it will be hard for anyone to believe that such a couple as you would start out alone on the journey you are undertaking. I therefore may be able to suggest a false trail—such as that you may have gone to Cuernavaca, or some such place, for your honeymoon. This much I can do, but no more."

"Ah, Beltrán, what a friend you are!" I exclaimed.

They embraced us with tears when we parted.

"*Vaya con Dios!*" they called to us, watching us out of view, and I think yet that farewell, "Go with God," is the most beautiful and touching in any language.

So we began a "honeymoon," as Beltrán had called it, strange and terrible, compounded of love, fear, weariness, and the near presence of death.

It was already evening when we rode out of the city, and we stopped early at an inn, where we had a good supper and pleasant room, for I was determined that this once at least my love should have comfort.

This was the night of our true espousal. Love was awake and crying between us. I kissed her, and she came to me dearly. Past and future were lost or laid to sleep in the present by the spell of our passion.

But next morning the grim business began. We entered the mountains, and gorges appeared, hewn beneath the mighty ranges, shadow-darkened, their savage lips sheer as the verge of Erebus. There were crisscross trails, where it was hard to remember the true road because low-hung clouds swept curtainwise to take away all sense of direction. Yet, somehow, I made our way.

We spoke to no one, either in the infrequent caravans we met, or in the villages and towns through which we hurried, hoping we would not be closely noticed, in case any following made inquiries. At night we stopped at some hut, off the road, and tried to make friends of the householders with a small coin or two out of the slender store Dolores carried, which was our only wealth.

Those were hard, cruel days, and I learned the courage of which a woman can be capable, and how she will lift her spirits by sheer will, so that she smiles and is a sweet comrade even in weariness. Yet by the time we were beyond Zacatecas my heart grew pitiful within me as I watched my new young wife. She looked like a wraith: though no law lays down that a wraith shall be unlovely. Rather, she seemed more *spirituelle* as her face grew thinner, her eyes larger. Youth saved her from appearing drawn, but weariness and the everlasting strain had begun to undermine youth's powers of resistance.

And the tragedy of it was that in spite of it all, I was beginning to realize how very impossible it was that we should ever win through. At the top of each pass to which our horses toiled, I strained my eyes backward, expecting to see the dust cloud made by riders on our trail. At every bend in the road ahead, or clump of bushes beside it, I glanced forward in apprehension, searching for possible lurking enemies.

Yet for days we were fortunate beyond all expectation, encountering no especial danger on the road. Then the inevitable happened.

The outset of it was startling.

Riding around a corner of the mountain on a trail above a steep and high cliff, Dolores gave a little cry.

Not fifty feet ahead on the road sprawled a black figure on the ground. Above it stooped another, apparently robbing it.

With a shout, I drew a pistol from the saddle holster, and spurred forward.

The stooping scoundrel—a knave in *mozo* costume, barefooted and with huge sombrero—glanced up, saw me, and went up a steep six-foot cut-bank like a tree cat, into the heavy underbrush above it.

I raised my pistol on him and pulled the trigger. The weapon misfired, the flint snapping sparks but without a report.

In an instant he was gone, I supposed to some inaccessible hiding place on the mountainside. Pulling up my horse, I glanced about. Save for Dolores, who had remained where she was, and the prostrate figure on the ground, nobody was in sight. Above the cut-bank, the thick shrubbery, mingled with trees, ran to a low ridge, and behind that the mountain lifted its massive shoulders skyward.

Dismounting, I sought to help the man on the road. He was a priest —a Jesuit—his black cassock all stained and dabbled with blood from a great stab wound in his back. When I turned him over, his head sagged and the mouth fell open to expose uneven yellow teeth. He was dead.

I stood up and looked back at Dolores. "Now here is devil's business!" I said. "This poor soul is sped!"

Her answer was a scream: not of horror, but of warning.

From the bushes at the top of the cut-bank, beside which I was standing, the murderer, whom I had thought far fled, leaped on my shoulders like a mountain panther on an elk, stabbing at me with a great knife.

I felt the sudden weight, which nearly bore me off my feet, and swerved instinctively, so that the slashing knife ripped only my coat. Then, before he could get in a second blow, I blindly clutched above, seized my assailant with both hands, and gave a great forward heave, with all my strength.

It was a wrestler's throw, and caught him by surprise. All too well I hurled him, for he struck on the rim of the cliff, the knife in his hand gleaming; and then, carried by his own momentum, went bodily over into the abyss. I remember yet his look of sudden horror as he clutched vainly with his hand for an instant, trying to save himself, then lost his grip and hurtled down, with a cry as he disappeared, and then a dull crash far below that ended him.

I turned. Dolores was swaying in her saddle, and I ran to support her.

Overtaxed as she was, it was a mercy that she did not faint and fall at the scene of violence and death she had just witnessed. But I held her, she recovered, and presently sat bravely erect, her face white as a shroud beneath the black tide of her hair.

"It was my life or his," I said, seeking to explain to her. "He was a *ladrón*. The man he murdered was a priest—alone and afoot. What sacrilege! The *ladrón* probably wanted our horses. He thought if he could finish me, you would be easy prey——"

She put her hand on my shoulder, and looked down at me with a little smile that told me she understood it all the time.

"I was giddy for a moment only because of my terror for you," she said. "That dreadful knife—how did you escape it?"

I showed her the rent in my coat. "It was nearer than I like."

"What will we do?" she asked, glancing at the dead priest. "We must bury him, I suppose?"

"I would that we could. But we have not the time."

"Why?"

"*Ladrones* run in packs. One of the trade can only mean that others are near. The boldness of—of the one who went over the cliff—proves it. They cannot be far—perhaps just up ahead of us."

"Then we must ride back the direction from which we came?"

"Impossible. Our only hope is to find some place to hide."

I mounted my horse. There was, I remembered, a narrow little *barranca* leading up into the mountain from the trail a short distance back. It offered at least a chance.

Less than a furlong down the road and around the corner, out of sight of the murdered priest, I found it. But it was so narrow, steep and rocky, that to ride up it was impossible. I glanced at the sun. It was near setting: this appeared to be the best prospect that offered.

"We must try to climb it on foot, and lead the horses up," I said.

Obediently as a child, she let me help her dismount, and when I began the ascent, pulling my animal by the bridle reins, she sought to follow.

I found it hard going, steep, rough, and tortuous; and it became worse. My horse stumbled and scrambled, and finally slipped, lost his footing and floundered, and at last struggled to his feet, panting. As he did so, I heard some rocks which his hoofs had dislodged, go bounding and tumbling down the narrow canyon.

With my heart in my throat, I turned. Toiling up after me, with scratched hands and torn dress, Dolores had halted, seemingly in the direct path of the boulders which were leaping down at her.

"Throw yourself flat!" I cried.

Without hesitation, she obeyed. An instant later one of the rocks, which would have dashed out her brains, leaped directly over her body, just missing the shying horse behind her. Others were deflected slightly to the side. By so little, she missed death.

I left my horse where he was, and hurried back down to where she lay gasping. She was not injured, I quickly saw, but her strength was

near its end. It was more by the blind devotion of a woman clinging
to the man she loves that she had followed me, rather than by any
physical force left in her.

I cursed myself for failing to see the danger in which I had placed
her. Then, after finding for her a safer spot, I left her resting, and took
the two horses up myself, one by one. After that I returned and helped
her also.

Fortune was with us. I found a place where I could take the horses
out of the *barranca* into a little cuplike valley behind the low ridge that
overlooked the road. It was surrounded by trees and hidden from pass-
ers below, and we went along it until we found a smooth place to rest.
Thereafter I tethered the horses, and then climbed on hands and knees
to the top of the low rise, to look over. To my surprise, I was gazing
down almost directly on the dead priest, poor soul, and the scene of
my brief struggle with his murderer.

"We must make no noise," I said to Dolores when I descended to
her again. "I snapped my pistol at that wretch who murdered the padre.
I think now it was lucky it misfired. A shot almost surely would have
brought down on us at once the main band."

"When will they come?"

"Perhaps not until morning, now. The sun is setting and they will be
making camp. But if the missing man does not appear during the night
they will come looking for him."

"They will find—*him*—down there——"

"The priest? Yes, that is true. Perhaps I should have rolled him over
the edge also——"

"Oh no! That would have been too horrible!"

I took her hand, and it was cold. "I felt so too," I told her. "So—let
them find him. They will know the handiwork of their fellow *ladrón*.
Very likely it will make them hurry on down the trail looking for him."

I spoke cheerfully, almost lightly, trying to dispel her fears. But she
was no fool, this girl. Though I did not mention my own great concern,
she sensed it at once.

"The *barranca*——" she said. "If they pass that they may find the dislodged stones and hoof marks where we took the horses up——"

I could not answer, for she knew the truth as well as I. If they found
that *barranca*, God protect us.

We lay fireless, our only comfort the nearness of each other. The afterlight of sunset faded, and a silver crescent moon rose, bathing with its pallid light the peaks.

Dolores gave a little shiver.

"What is it?" I whispered.

"Nothing," she said, so that I hardly heard it. "Only it is so terrible —to die. Why, we haven't even begun to live!"

But almost at once her own superb courage came to her rescue, and she calmed herself. After a time she extended her slim body on the ground, and laid her head on the bundle I made with my coat.

I sat motionless beside her. In the intense quiet of night distant sounds came which I could not have heard by day. Small birds stirred in the trees, and insects creaked. Up on the mountainside above, an owl gave a series of deep hoots, repeated again and again. From what seemed an infinite distance came the rushing of clear water in some stream, reminding me that we were thirsty, with no water near. Far across the canyon a coyote yapped thinly.

For fully an hour I made no movement of any kind. Then, very quietly, I leaned forward to see how she slept. And found her eyes wide open.

"You are not sleeping?" I asked.

"I am resting—and thinking of you," she answered.

"But you need——"

"I think this will be our last night on earth. How can I sleep?" And then, like a child, she said, "Hold me——"

At that I took her in my arms . . . so lovely . . . so devoted . . . so without hope . . .

Terrible, terrible is the grief one feels for his loved one in the brooding shadow of death.

3.

At dawn the peaks flamed red above stark blue as they caught the first light. Dolores lay with her eyes closed, and her face, weary as it was, seemed strangely pure and beautiful.

She was not asleep, and presently she opened her eyes; then sat up and, with a woman's inevitable charming gesture, began putting her hair to rights, giving me a little smile.

The smile told me there was no panic or hysteria here. She would face whatever came, with courage and trust in me.

"The *ladrones* will be moving soon," I told her.

Then I examined the priming of my pistols and silently crept to the rim of our little vale, where I could look down upon the road through the bushes which concealed me. The dead priest was still there, his limbs stiff, his cassock awry, where he had lain all night. A moment later I heard a slight stir and Dolores was lying beside me.

For an hour we spoke not a word. Gradually the sun unfolded the mountains before us, until full daylight revealed everything in our view.

All at once she touched my arm. But I had already seen: it was the first of the *ladrones*.

Down the road from the north he slunk, noiseless and questing, a rusty musket in his hands, under his sombrero a kerchief bound about his head, on his feet sandals of rawhide.

Now he saw the body of the priest and shrank back into some bushes at the side of the trail. A moment later he was gone.

Tensely we waited in our hiding place above. He was back, presently, with two others. Wild and ragged and heavily armed, they came forward cautiously, glancing about uneasily. Then all three of them bent over the corpse, searching it for valuables and evidently finding none. One of them hurried back up the trail.

Very soon, like a straggling pack of hyenas, the rest of the *ladrones* appeared. Altogether I counted fifteen grotesque, deadly figures. To a man they were ragged, with brutish faces, and to a man they bore every weapon they could carry: muskets, knives, machetes, even crude Indian spears and bows. Not one of them was mounted.

For a few minutes they huddled about the dead priest. It was evident that from the wound in the back they were attributing the murder to their absent comrade, and asking each other what had become of him. I began to hope they would soon go on, perhaps not noticing or paying attention to our telltale *barranca*.

But first, two of the *ladrones* seized the stiff corpse by the head and the feet, carried it to the edge of the cliff, swung it, and hurled it over.

All immediately rushed to the verge, to look down and see the body when it landed. There was a shout of laughter at the crash below.

Then I heard a cry, and one of the men was pointing. The others craned to see. Yells of consternation and rage arose. They had discovered the body of their fellow, lying where I had hurled him, at the bottom of the cliff.

Within myself I groaned, for that unlucky discovery made certain that these brigands would not soon pass on. Indeed, among them there was immediate activity. Two began clambering down the cliff, perhaps to retrieve what weapons or possessions were on the person of their dead friend below. Others trotted about like hounds, and I could almost imagine them whining eagerly and fiercely, as they circled, seeking some sign of how he came to his death.

A shout. One had found the marks of my horse's hoofs and perhaps other signs of the struggle near the spot where the *ladrón* went over the cliff.

A short cast northward, and these experts in tracking knew the horse had turned back south.

They halted and every one of them looked up at the brushy little ridge where we lay. Two of them even made as if to climb up toward us.

But someone had a new idea. The tracks of the second horse were found, and now the whole pack followed the hoof marks of the two animals. The pair who had begun to climb hesitated, loitered a moment or two, then trotted off to join their fellows.

"They will find . . . the *barranca*," whispered Dolores.

She was sure nothing could save us now, and so was I. The *ladrones* knew that someone on horseback had done for their comrade. Once they discovered the little side canyon they would be on us in a few minutes and there was no way we could escape.

I knew not what to do. Not only death, but unspeakable torture, was the lot of those who were taken by them after killing or injuring one of their number.

And Dolores . . . she must not fall into their hands! The fate of a woman among such beasts would be unimaginable.

I cocked my pistols and prayed God to forgive me for what I was about to do.

From down the trail, out of sight, a yell signalized the discovery of the *barranca* with its signs.

Now it was coming. Now I must be ready.

But at the instant a peculiar sharp whistle came from the north. It was repeated. The shouts down the trail ceased and in a moment the whole pack came rushing back into view.

Speeding from the north we saw a single *ladrón*. They met him, surrounded him, and he was telling them something with excitement, stabbing with a finger toward the direction from which he had come.

Someone ran to the edge of the cliff to recall those who were below with the dead. And then, almost at once, hurrying, almost running, looking back now and then, with haste and fear evident in every face, the whole motley crowd was on the move, disappearing around the bend of the trail toward the south.

"What—happened?" asked Dolores.

"Lie still," I answered. "Something alarmed them. But what?"

Silent as the dead beneath the cliff, we watched the road below.

And all at once a man rode into view from the north, fierce, bearded, murderous-looking, in wide hat, a sword at his hip and a short musketoon held with its butt resting on his thigh.

After a short interval, and before he passed out of our sight, three more followed: each sunburned, bearded, ferocious, yet in no uniform, unless wide hats all alike, and the large-bored musketoons, better than the longer muskets for horsemen, might be called uniform.

I knew, suddenly, what they were!

"Hermandados!" I whispered to Dolores. "These are vedettes of the Santa Hermandad!"

"That is why the *ladrones* fled?" she asked in the same subdued voice.

"Yes, and God guard us if we fall into these hands."

I felt her settle even closer in her hiding place, scarcely breathing.

The vedettes passed below us and were gone. And now the advance guard came, ten chosen men. At their head rode one I knew, Don José Calabanca, with his stark Spanish face, the same who escorted me to the capital.

A little break. Then, as solid in his saddle as a granite block, his face also as stern as if carved from the same impervious stone, Don Miguel Velázquez de Lorea, the merciless Grand Master of the Santa Hermandad! I marked his bushy brows, his fierce mustachios and beard, his ravaged face, his gray eyes, flinty hard.

"Their leader," I whispered. "This is not a man. He is a machine—of death."

She shivered slightly, and I put my arm about her.

But why, I asked myself, this march in force of what was most evidently the whole body of the Santa Hermandad?

Directly behind Lorea rode the main body of the dread brotherhood.

Every man grim and hawk-eyed, musketoons across saddlebows, they streamed steadily past us, not breaking pace, evidently on some errand of great import, neither knowing nor caring about the *ladrones* fleeing before them, or the two dead men who lay out of sight under the cliff below them.

Dolores drew in her breath with a little hiss.

Two figures had appeared whom I recognized: squat, swarthy Verdugo, the hangman of the Hermandad; and with him the priest who served as clerk at the "trials" of this body, and then said the brief last rites for the prisoners who were executed.

But these were not what caused Dolores to catch her breath.

With armed guards behind and before, his wrists lashed to his saddlebow, white as a corpse and staring at nothing like a man damned, rode Gaspar de Anaya!

With amazement we gazed down at him. Gone now were all the pride, arrogance, and brutal domineering manner I had known in him when he was Governor. His garments were stained and wrinkled as if he had many nights slept in them; his mustache, no longer waxed, drooped beside the weak, half-opened mouth; his eyes with great dark circles under them had the look of a lost and beaten dog. Almost I felt sorry for the pudgy, inferior, and contemptible little man, now shorn of his power and in mortal fear. And yet I knew that he deserved any fate, however severe, that awaited him.

So Dolores and I, whom that evil man in the days of his ascendancy had hounded, saw his fall. Hidden above the road down which he was led, we saw it. And when he was lost to view around the bend of the trail, he went forever out of our lives.

After him and his escort came six picked horsemen, riding with gun butts on thighs, keen eyes glancing back as often as forward: the rear guard. They in turn disappeared, and the road below us at last was vacant.

The deathly array of the Santa Hermandad had passed.

4.

It was like a sending of the saints.

And yet it was easy enough to understand, if one but considered the situation. Beltrán had told me that Anaya was ordered to the capital for trial. Because of the military expedition being mounted at San Juan

Bautista, none of the few regular troops in the north could be spared. Furthermore, the Santa Hermandad was known to be incorruptible and impervious to bribery, which some of the soldiers were not. So to Lorea and his grim followers had been given the task of conveying the deposed Governor to his final accounting.

But for Dolores and me the event had a different and great importance.

Marching southward, the Santa Hermandad, whose very name was a terror, swept all bands of *ladrones* before it, as we had witnessed in the particular murderous pack that threatened us. Like jackals the brigands left the roads and took refuge in their most remote fastnesses. Nor would they return until the fear of this visitation had subsided.

So at the last, though he did not know it or intend it, Gaspar de Anaya did us a great service. For when he and his escorting Hermandados were gone, we rode northward without any further molestation.

We had not seen any pursuers, but I continued to take precautions. And the long journey had wearied my companion so that her slim shoulders sagged, and she smiled little and spoke less, saving her slight reserves of strength. So we rode in short stages. And one evening, when at nightfall we came upon a cluster of ten wooden crosses by the trail, I drew rein.

"I know this place," I told her. "There is an Indian village down in this canyon, where we may find shelter."

Vividly I remembered the tiny settlement of natives where I spent a night with Herrera and his men, the iron *grillos* locked on my legs. Dolores assented silently, and guided her mount after me down the narrow slanting path into the depths below.

After a time we came to the spring I had seen before. A small figure was there: a girl, for water. At sight of us she scurried away.

All at once I recognized the little figure. "Isabelita!" I called.

At her name she halted and looked back with startled eyes.

I smiled at her. "Do you not remember me?" I asked. "I gave you a *cuartillo* one day."

Ah yes! She knew me now, and, childlike, was my friend. In a moment she came walking back, her little bare feet winking along the path. Dolores smiled at her, the child responded. I lifted her to the saddle in front of me, and so we came down to the village, giving Isabelita her moment of triumph, riding into it to the admiration of the natives.

Men were in the village this time, for the forced work in which they had been engaged on my former visit was finished. These stood at a distance, suspicious and unfriendly: wide cheekbones, hair like helmets of black, eyes brilliant and watchful, faces somber.

But Isabelita's young mother—pregnant again, I saw, with three children already to care for—welcomed us in her poor Spanish, and then turned to the little knot of men, telling them, both in words and by pantomime which I thought vivid, of the night when the *soldados* committed outrages in this village, and only I was kind.

At this the men relaxed their sullen looks and drew near, signing for us to dismount. My small generosities had borne fruit: we were to be given sanctuary.

That evening, for the first time in weeks fully relaxed, Dolores and I sat together before the *jacal* of our hosts, and watched the sunset fade, the night come down over the mountains like a cave. The huts became shadowy cones, firelight in tiny slivers gleaming through chinks in stick-and-mud walls. Women returned from the spring with ollas gracefully balanced on their heads. From the little dwellings came the soft pat-pat of *tortillas* being made; sleepy children whimpered; low voices of men growled in the center of the village.

At last we went within for a bite of simple fare, and then Dolores took to a pallet with a sigh like a baby's for lost sleep.

Not the next day did we resume our journey, or the next after that. And with rest she began to regain her old gaiety and hopeful outlook.

One thing we did not know. During the days while we rested in the village at the bottom of the canyon, many passed along the road far above: men mounted and afoot, animals carrying riders or baggage, and all heading north. It was the second contingent of the force which was to make the *entrada* into the Texas country; and though it left the city of Mexico after we did, it reached San Juan Bautista before us.

5.

Our journey to Dolores' home was near its end. I remember, when we first saw at a distance the town, how she was like a child returning home, her face all alight with joy as she viewed the *casas*, the church, the presidio, and the beloved white *estancia* on the hilltop.

I took note of something else: a considerable encampment just beyond the fort. This I supposed was occupied by the first contingent of soldiers gathered for the expedition. Had I known the second contingent was there also, I would have been more concerned.

At the moment, however, our hearts were high with anticipation. This was the goal toward which we had struggled, and we looked forward to our welcome, and safety, and pleasant rest.

I observed some little stir in the encampment, and also at the presidio as we rode through the village, but paid no attention to it. As for Dolores, she gazed lovingly on everything about her, greeting persons she knew, exclaiming over small shy tots who sucked their thumbs and stared at us, taking pleasure even in the dusty burros and mongrel dogs, because they were grateful to her eyes after long absence.

Together we rode up the hill. At the gate Don Diego's *mozos* hastened to take our horses and care for our small baggage, and I saw and greeted Íñigo, who was there.

But from long habit, I lifted my pistol holsters from the saddle and carried them with me into the house.

I will pass over the scene of joy that followed: how the two grandaunts came rushing when they learned Dolores was there; how they embraced her, and exclaimed over her, and cried out endearments and blessings to the saints and the Holy Mother; how they almost overwhelmed her with tears of happiness and the peculiar heart-warming affection of a Spanish family.

I laid my holsters on a table and stood aside, watching with half-amused sympathy the reunion, and awaiting my turn to be greeted.

In the midst of this I heard a door open and close, and Don Diego stood looking at us.

Crying out his name Dolores ran to him, all eager love and happiness. But though she wound her arms about him, he did not open his own arms or even look at her, gazing instead at me, dry, stern, unsmiling.

Perplexed and hurt, she stepped back from him.

"Don Diego—dearest Grandfather—what is the matter?" she asked. He did not seem to hear or recognize her. Instead, he spoke to me. "This woman is, I understand, your wife?"

"She is," I said, wondering.

He turned to the door and threw it open. Four soldiers, armed with muskets, stood without.

"Arrest these two," he ordered.

Never in my life have I been so thunderstruck. I could not stir as the soldiers rushed in and grasped me by the arms. Dolores sank into a chair, and behind her stood her two aunts, all three looking as if the earth suddenly had sunk from beneath their feet.

"Don Diego—what does this mean——" began Doña Estrella.

"Peace, woman!" he rasped. She fell silent, awed by his manner.

It was I who next spoke. "Why do you arrest us?"

"Because a message was brought from the city of Mexico, with word that you had absconded from the capital, contrary to the orders of the Viceroy. You are to be returned, as prisoners, to be dealt with at his pleasure."

When I had thought my lone hand had finally won against the world's odds, to have this last disaster fall upon us!

I looked over at Dolores, and never have I seen a face so stricken and forlorn. She had dreamed of this home-coming as a haven and a hope. And these were her people, flesh of her flesh, her family which had reared her, which she loved with all the warmth of her heart. Now in a minute all was destroyed, the love, the hope, the haven.

She did not upbraid her grandfather, or even speak to him. Instead she did what any girl with a broken heart would do: she began to sob, pitifully, uncontrollably. And I could not even go to her to comfort her.

Don Diego stared at her with a face that seemed of flint.

After a moment, he said to the soldiers, "Take them."

But as he spoke, he passed his hand across his eyes, and when he did so, I saw it tremble.

In that instant, looking on almost like a spectator, though I was so mightily involved, I knew there was tragedy—hideous, blinding tragedy —on both sides in that little tableau before me.

My long, lonely vigils in the dungeon had gifted me with a power of perception I had lacked before, and, watching Don Diego, I understood, in that moment, something of what he was, and what he felt. His loyalty to his duty, that was like a kind of madness, compelled him to act thus, as if he were unfeeling. It was the habit of his long soldier's life, unbending as iron; proof against any malice, injustice, or disappointment he might suffer at the hands of others; proof also against any personal consideration, even his love for this girl about whom he had wrapped his heart.

I knew also that a struggle fierce and grim was going on within him, tearing his soul. Not in all his life's experience had he been called upon for a sacrifice so terrible as this. His own life he had always carried lightly: flinging it like a missile in the enemy's face, in the many battles he had fought. But here was no intoxication of martial fury, no ring of glory in the air, no victory to be won. It was not even his own life that he was throwing into the remorseless maw of his Spanish sense of duty. It was a life he loved far more than his own: the life of the child who had brightened and softened his age.

Bitter as was the thing he was doing to me, I could not hate him for it. Instead, I found room in my heart to admire Don Diego Escalante de Ramón, that great soldier of Spain. Selflessness like his is not often encountered in this world.

Then I made a last appeal. "Don Diego, I know you to be a man of justice and honor. Therefore, listen to me. If it is a crime to escape from the capital against the Viceroy's command, I am guilty. Take me. But Dolores—your own granddaughter—what unlawful thing has she done?"

He had regained his rigid inflexibility. "You are man and wife," he said. "She went with you. She shares your culpability."

"What if she were not my wife?"

"But she is."

"If I were dead—what then?"

"If you were dead—why——"

I think he sensed in that moment what I was going to do, but too late. While he was still uttering the words I acted.

With a sweep of my hands I thrust my guards aside, and for the moment stood free.

The next instant, seizing one of the pistols from my holsters on the table, I leaped across the room.

There was no avenue of escape, and I knew it. Instead, I placed my back in a corner where none could come at me from behind.

There was a moment's deathly silence, then all four soldiers swung their muskets on me.

I heard Don Diego's hoarse voice, "Surrender! You cannot get away!"

"Tell your men to shoot!" I cried back at him. "And shoot to kill!"

"Hold your fire!" he commanded them instantly.

There is no way in which I can account for the desperation of what I was doing, except perhaps that it was the long train of misfortunes, culminating in this last disaster, which had so worn me down that I was careless of continuing my existence. I had faced dangers before, diced with death. But in taking risks I, who was fond of life, had always considered and assessed them.

But now, in all reality, I craved death. I felt a curious sort of elation in scorning death—if by death I could buy something I desired more than my life.

"If I were dead—she would be free, wouldn't she?" I cried, almost with a note of triumph. "You know it, Don Diego!"

I raised the pistol and cocked it.

"And I free her now!"

There were cries and exclamations, and a scream from Dolores, for they all now saw what I meant to do.

But none of them could move quickly enough to stay me, as I placed the muzzle of the weapon at my temple.

Before I could pull the trigger, a voice cried out:

"*Texias—nai!*"

6.

I do not think anything could have arrested my finger on the trigger at that moment except the surprise of hearing those words, "Friend—no!" spoken in the tongue of the Neches.

In the tense room every eye turned toward the speaker. Two men had entered, both robed as Franciscans, girdled, tonsured. One, comfortably portly and benignant, was Padre Ambrosio. The other was dark-visaged and intense, his eyes flickering about the room to take in every detail before coming to rest on me.

"Padre Hidalgo!" I cried out.

"What is happening here?" he demanded.

"I have arrested this man to send him and his wife back to the capital," said Don Diego.

"And I will spatter my brains on this wall rather than go!" I answered.

The priest gazed first at the Commandant, then at me, and I noticed how magnificent were the lines and hollows of his dark face, in the story they told of his life of devotion to the cross he preached.

"My son," he said to me, "suicide is a deadly sin."

"I will commit that sin, Padre, rather than see my wife put on trial for what I alone did."

"Trial? What charge?" he asked.

"This man and woman fled clandestinely from the city of Mexico, contrary to the injunctions of the Viceroy," said Don Diego.

Padre Hidalgo raised his hand, and it was almost like a benediction.

"I can solve this matter," he said. "Padre Ambrosio and I learned down at the mission here of the arrival of this couple. And also of the soldiers going to the *estancia*. We came in haste, for we feared some terrible misunderstanding such as this might take place——"

"Misunderstanding?" echoed Don Diego. "How can there be misunderstanding?"

Padre Hidalgo spoke almost soothingly. "I conversed with the Viceroy before I left the capital with the second contingent which has just arrived," he said. "He then had already sent out messengers in all directions to forestall these two. His Excellency related to me the orders he had given: that Señor de St. Denis be banished from New Spain."

He turned his eyes, dark and piercing, on Don Diego. "I showed him, Commandant, how his orders were not contravened if Señor de St. Denis left New Spain—but to another destination than Guatemala, which the Viceroy had nominated. The Confraternity of San Francisco has been to much trouble over this man, Don Diego—not only here, but in Europe also. First, because he performed for the Church a great service. Second, because he is of most important use to us in this grand mission project soon to be launched. Third, because he kept a certain promise in the face of death by torment."

For a moment his eyes rested on me. I knew the promise to which he referred—the compact between himself and me. And suddenly the mystery that had so baffled Beltrán was explained to me.

Someone powerful and important enough to reach the King's ear . . .

Why, that "someone" was no individual at all, as he and I had thought. It was the world-wide order of Franciscans!

And the promise I had kept sent Padre Hidalgo to his superiors—as he told me later—and at last to the *Comisario General* of the order in New Spain, from whom went representations to the supreme *Ministro General* in Spain itself, and so to the King's ear!

But Padre Hidalgo continued, "When I so explained the matter, the

Marqués de Valero struck his hands together and cried out: 'Take him! In the name of God take this troublesome gadfly of a Frenchman! But rid me of him in the dominions of Spain!'"

Don Diego was staring at him with a look of inward dawning hope, strange in a face that so rarely displayed emotion.

Suddenly he seemed to recover himself, and drew himself up as if on the parade ground.

"Señor Padre," he said gruffly, "you are *Custodio* and spiritual commander of the *entrada*. If you command, it is my duty to declare this man free, and place him in your custody."

"I do so command."

Don Diego gave an order, and the soldiers raised the muzzles of their guns which were pointing at my breast.

"Return to your barracks," he barked. "Dismissed!"

Saluting him, they filed out.

In perfect silence I walked across to the table and laid on it my pistol. A moment later Dolores was in my arms, covering my face with tears and kisses.

As for Don Diego, the fierce erectness of the soldier seemed all at once to depart from his figure. Two steps to a chair he took, and sank into it, sitting with shoulders stooped and head bent, for the first time looking to me like an old man.

"Dolores," I whispered, "see your grandfather. He loves you and he is dying within because he thinks he has lost your love!"

She understood, as she always has understood these things. In a moment she was kneeling before him, looking into his face. Then suddenly they embraced in the return of full affection and understanding. And when Don Diego raised his head there were tears in his eyes, I swear the first those eyes had known in half a century at the very least.

7.

The events since that day hardly need relating.

Dolores and I received the blessings of her grandfather and her aunts; and Don Diego paid me the stiff compliment of saying that he thought I was not entirely unworthy of her.

That they were to lose her so soon was a cause of sorrow, but we must go, for we were banished from New Spain, and I was to guide the Franciscan *entrada* to a beautiful place on the San Pedro River, which I had marked on my way south. When we said farewell to them, she had a veritable little pack train of her own: six mules laden with gifts of clothing, silver, and other presents showered upon her.

Our party included twelve friars under Padre Hidalgo, and sixty soldiers, with equipment and commissary, making a not unimpressive spectacle as we made our way north through the thorny wastes. Dolores and I were present at the dedication of the ground on which was to be built the mission called San Antonio de Valero,* in honor of the Viceroy. Some may criticize me for thus acting as a guide for Spaniards, but it was the least I could do to repay the Franciscans for what they did for me. Let us say that though I assisted Spain, with sword and cross to make firm her flimsy claim to the Texas land, it was of at least equal importance that I was able to bear speedy warning of their movement to my countrymen in Louisiana.

Old Bernardino and the Neches watched with admiration the dedication, and an escort of Neches warriors conducted my wife and me north to the Red River, where they parted with us. There I found Marbot and Jaccard, in garrison at the fort, which was much extended and augmented in force. And there also was my old friend, Captain Noirel, commanding and delighted to see me.

From Noirel I learned that the pendulum had swung back in Louisiana. With the death of Louis XIV, Crozat's concession was revoked. Cadillac was gone back to France, and also La Demoiselle and her mother.

Bienville is again Governor, as he should have been from the first, and I see a better day for this colony.

Dolores and I, at this present, are guests at the residency on Dauphin Island in Mobile Bay. I have just finished a conference with Bienville, giving him a complete report on Spanish plans and strength, and we are laying out moves to checkmate them if they approach Louisiana.

Bienville! A strange, but after all, a heart-warming man.

When I appeared here in Mobile, with my young wife, he treated me like a brother lost and found again. And I believe in my soul that were she not already possessed of a husband, he would fall in love with my Dolores.

---

* Later to be known as the Alamo, cradle of Texas liberty in a day far after the time of St. Denis. This was the actual founding of what became the city, San Antonio.

At this moment she and I sit in a room on the upper floor of the residency, looking out upon the Gulf's blue waters, foam-flecked in the fresh breeze. It is a pretty room Bienville has given us for our stay: a room with memories for me, since it was once the boudoir of that strangely beautiful and disturbing creature, La Demoiselle.

But we are not to remain here long. Very soon we return to Natchitoches and take residence there, Noirel happy to be my lieutenant in the great movements ahead to halt the Spaniard.

So there is to be no rest for me: nor do I want it. It appears that I am fated to continue to ride the red earth of the farthest frontiers of France, defending them for my King and country. And I am proud that I am chosen to do it.

I gaze now over at Dolores, more lovely each day it seems to me, knowing that at last I have fairly won her, to have and to hold forever.

I say to her, "And still you do not know what manner of man I am."

She smiles, and comes for my kiss. "I know what manner of man you are—you are my love."

MISSISSIPPI R.

Fort St. Louis

OHIO R.

L O U I S I A N A

MISSISSIPPI R.

RED R.

Santa Fe

NEW MEXICO

Chihuahua

CONCHOS R.

SAN PEDRO R.

RIO GRANDE

San Juan
Bautista

COAHUILA

Parras

Culiacán

Durango

Zacatecas

Compostela

Querétaro

TAMAULIPAS

San Antonio
(de Valero)

T E X A S

New Orleans

Natchez

Fort Condé (Mobile)

Biloxi

LAKE PONTCHARTRAIN

DAUPHIN I.

MOBILE BAY

GULF OF
MEXICO

Toluca

Mexico City

Cuernavaca

Cholula

GUATEMALA

Guatemala

PACIFIC
OCEAN

palacios